IMPRISONED IN THE BLOOD SEA TOWER by a jealous god, Mina's search for an escape leads her to the Hall of Sacrilege and to an unexpected discovery. But it is even more unwelcome to most of the gods of Krynn.

The heroes fighting the spread of the terrifying Beloved gain new allies in a paladin and a wizardess, but the vampiric cult is growing faster than they can move; they must find the root of the evil and stop it there.

The second installment in *The New York Times* bestselling author Margaret Weis's Dark Disciple trilogy continues the story started in *Amber and Ashes*, set in the world of DRAGONLANCE.

> "Weis [uses] conventional fantasy elements on the grand scale to produce excellent reading."
> —Chicago Sun-Times

> "Demonstrate[s] . . . complete mastery of the art of turning classic fantasy elements into equally classic well-told tales."
> —Roland Green, Booklist

the Dark Disciple

AMBER AND ASHES

AMBER AND IRON

AMBER AND BLOOD

AMBER AND IRON

the Dark Disciple

Volume 2

MARGARET WEIS

AMBER & IRON

The Dark Disciple, Volume 2

©2006 Wizards of the Coast, Inc.

Cover art by Matt Stawicki
First Hardcover Printing: February 2006
This Edition First Printing: November 2006

9 8 7 6 5 4 3 2 1

ISBN-10: 0-7869-4086-7
ISBN-13: 978-0-7869-4086-8
620-95623740-001-EN

U.S., CANADA,
ASIA, PACIFIC, & LATIN AMERICA
Wizards of the Coast, Inc.
P.O. Box 707
Renton, WA 98057-0707
+1-800-324-6496

EUROPEAN HEADQUARTERS
Hasbro UK Ltd
Caswell Way
Newport, Gwent NP9 0YH
GREAT BRITAIN
Save this address for your records.

Visit our web site at www.wizards.com

DEDICATION

This book is dedicated with deep appreciation to the members of the Whitestone Council and all those volunteers who have dedicated their time and talents to Dragonlance. These people have been of immense help to me. They are always there to answer my questions. They keep the dragonlance.com site running smoothly. They assist with researching and writing and playtesting the game product. Some of them have been working with Dragonlance for years, ever since the beginning.

Cam Banks
Shivam Bhatt
Ross Bishop
Neil Burton
Richard Connery
Luis Fernando De Pippo
Matt Haag

Andre' La Roche
Sean Macdonald
Joe Mashuga
Tobin Melroy
Ashe Potter
Joshua Stewart
Trampas Whiteman

"Without self-realization, no virtue is genuine."

—Sir Nisargardatta Maharaj

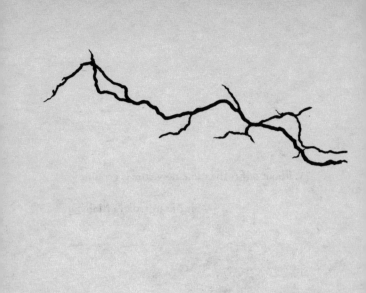

BOOK I

IN THE

NAME

OF

CHEMOSH

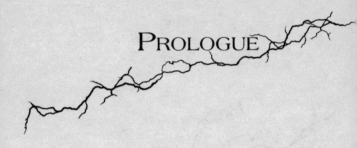

PROLOGUE

*T*imothy Tanner was not a bad man, just a weak one.

He had a wife, Gerta, and a new baby son, who was healthy and cute. He loved both of them dearly and would have given his life for them. He just couldn't manage to stay faithful to them. He felt wretchedly guilty over his "tomcatting" as he called it, and when the new baby arrived he promised himself that he would never so much as look at another woman.

Three months passed, and Timothy kept his promise. He'd actually turned down a couple of his previous lovers, telling them he was a changed man, and it seemed that he was, for he truly adored his son and felt nothing but gratitude and love for his wife.

Then one day Lucy Wheelwright came into his shop.

Though he came from a family of tanners, Timothy had been apprenticed to a cobbler and now made his living making leather shoes and boots.

"I want to know if this shoe can be mended," Lucy said.

She placed her foot on a short-legged stool and hiked up her skirt well past her knees to reveal a very shapely leg and more beyond that.

"Well, Master Cobbler?" she said archly.

Timothy wrenched his gaze from her leg to the shoe. It was brand new. He looked up at her. She smiled at him. Lowering her skirt, she bent over, pretending to lace her shoe, but all the while providing him a view of her full bosom. He noticed an odd mark over her left breast—it looked like a kiss from two lips. He pictured placing his own lips on that spot, and he caught his breath.

Lucy was one of the prettiest girls in Solace and also one of the most unobtainable, though there *were* rumors . . .

She was married, like Timothy. Her husband was a big brute of man and intensely jealous.

She straightened, tugging her chemise back in place, and glanced at the door. "Could you work on the shoe now? I really have a need for it. An aching need . . ."

"Your husband?" Timothy coughed.

"He's away on a hunting trip. Besides, you could bolt the door so that no one interrupts you in your work."

Timothy thought of his wife and his child, but they were not here and Lucy was. He rose from his bench and went over to the door, shutting it and locking it. The hour was almost noon; customers would think he'd gone home for his midday meal.

Just to be safe, he led Lucy to the storeroom. Even as they made their way through the shop, she was kissing him, fondling him, undoing his shirt, her hands fumbling at his breeches. He'd never known a woman so ardent, and he was consumed with passion. They tumbled down on a pile of leather skins. She wriggled out of her chemise, and he kissed the place on her breast over the strange birthmark of two lips.

Lucy put her hand over his mouth. "I want you to do something for me, Timothy," she said, breathing fast.

"Anything!" He pressed his body close to hers.

She held him at bay. "I want you to give yourself to Chemosh."

"Chemosh?" Timothy laughed. This was a most inopportune moment to be discussing religion! "The god of death? What made you think of that?"

"Just a fancy of mine," said Lucy, winding his hair around and around her finger. "I'm one of his followers. He's a god of life, not death. Those horrid clerics of Mishakal say such bad things about him. You mustn't believe them."

"I don't know. . . ." Timothy thought this all very odd.

"You want to please me, don't you?" said Lucy, kissing his ear lobe. "I'm very grateful to men who please me."

She moved her hands down his body. She was skilled, and Timothy groaned with desire.

"Just say the words 'I give myself to Chemosh'," Lucy whispered. "In return, you'll have unending life, unending youth, and *me*. We can make love like this every day if you want."

Timothy wasn't a bad man, just weak. He had never wanted any woman as much as he wanted Lucy at that moment. He wasn't all that religious, and he didn't see the harm in pledging himself to Chemosh if it made her happy.

"I give myself to Chemosh . . . and Lucy," he said teasingly.

Lucy smiled at him and pressed her lips on his left breast over his heart.

Terrible pain shot through Timothy. His heart began to beat wildly and erratically. Pain burned through his arms and down his torso and into his legs. He tried frantically to push Lucy off him, but she had incredible strength and she pinned him down and kept pressing her lips on his chest. His heart lurched. He tried to scream, but he didn't have the breath. His body shuddered, convulsed, and stiffened as the pain, like the hand of an evil god, took him and twisted him, wrung him, shredded him and carried him off into darkness.

Timothy came out of the darkness. He entered a world that seemed all twilight. He saw objects that looked familiar, but he couldn't place them. He knew where he was, but it didn't matter. He didn't care. The woman he'd been with was gone. He tried to think of her name, but he couldn't.

Only one name was in his mind and he whispered that name, "Mina . . ."

He knew her, though he'd never met her. She had beautiful amber eyes.

"Come to me," said Mina. "My lord Chemosh has need of you."

"I will," Timothy promised. "Where do I find you?"

"Follow the road into the sunrise."

"You mean leave my home? No, I can't—"

Pain stabbed Timothy, horrible pain that was like the pain of dying.

"Follow the road into the sunrise," said Mina.

"I will!" he gasped, and the pain eased.

"Bring disciples to me," she told him. "Give others the gift you have been given. You will never die, Timothy. You will never age. You will never know fear. Give others this gift."

An image of his wife came into his mind. Timothy had the vague notion that he didn't want to do this, that he would hurt Gerta terribly if he did this to her. He wouldn't . . .

Pain tore at him, bent and twisted him.

"I will, Mina!" he moaned. "I will!"

Timothy went home to his family. His baby was sleeping in the cradle, taking his afternoon nap. Timothy paid no attention to the child. He didn't recall that it was his child. He cared nothing about it. He saw only his wife and he heard only the voice, Mina's voice, saying, "Bring her. . . ."

"My dear!" Gerta greeted him, pleased but surprised. "What are you doing home? It's the middle of the day?"

"I came home to be with you, my love," said Timothy. He put his arms around her and kissed her. "Come to bed, wife."

"Tim!" Gerta giggled and tried, half-heartedly, to push him away. "It's still daylight!"

"What does that matter?" He was kissing her, touching her, and he felt her melt into his arms.

She made a last faint protest. "The baby—"

"He's asleep. Come on." Timothy pulled his wife down onto their bed. "Let me prove that I love you!"

"I know you love me," said Gerta, and she nestled next to him and began to return his kisses.

She started to unlace his tunic, but he clasped his hands over her hands.

"There's one thing you must do to prove that you love me, wife. I have recently become a follower of the god, Chemosh. I want you to share the joy I have found in following the god."

"Why, of course, husband, if that's what you want," said Gerta. "But I know nothing of the gods. What sort of god is this Chemosh?"

"A god of unending life," said Timothy. "Will you pledge yourself to him?"

"I will do anything for you, husband."

He opened his mouth to say something, then stopped. She sensed some inner struggle within him. His face twisted in pain.

"What's the matter?" she asked, alarmed.

"Nothing!" he gasped. "A cramp in my foot. That's all. Say the words: 'I pledge myself to Chemosh.'"

Gerta repeated the words and added, "I love you."

Then Timothy said something very strange as he bent over and pressed his lips on her left breast above her heart.

"Forgive me. . . ."

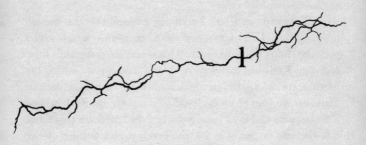

As Ausric Krell, death knight, watched in astonishment, the white kender khas piece went racing across the board, lunged full-tilt at his own dark knight khas piece, and grappled with it. Both pieces fell off the board and began rolling around on the floor.

"Here, now! That's against the rules," was Krell's first outraged thought.

His second, more bemused thought was, "I never saw a khas piece do that before."

His third thought included dawning revelation. "That's no ordinary khas piece."

His fourth thought was deeply suspicious. "Something funny's going on here."

His thoughts after this were muddled, undoubtedly due to the fact that he was engaged in a battle for his undead life against a horrible giant mantis.

Krell had always detested bugs, and this particular mantis was truly terrifying, for it was ten feet tall with bulbous eyes, a green shell, and six huge green legs, two of which held onto Krell while its mandibles clamped onto his cringing spirit and began to chomp into his brain.

Krell figured out after a horrifying moment that this was no ordinary bug. There was a god mixed up in this somewhere, a god who didn't much like him. This wasn't anything out of the ordinary. Krell had managed to offend several gods during his lifetime, including the late and unlamented Takhisis, Queen of Darkness, and her chaotic, vindictive daughter, the Sea Goddess Zeboim, who had been outraged when she found out that Krell was the one responsible for the betrayal and murder of her beloved son, Lord Ariakan.

Zeboim had captured Krell and killed him slowly, taking her time. When there was finally no spark of life left within his mangled body, she had cursed him by changing him into a death knight and imprisoning him on the isolated and accursed isle of Storm's Keep, where he had once served the man he had betrayed, there to live out his eternal existence with the memory of his crime always before him.

Zeboim's punishment had not had quite the impact she had hoped for. Another famous death knight, Lord Soth, had been a tragic figure, consumed by remorse and eventually finding salvation. Krell, on the other hand, rather liked being a death knight. He found in death what he'd always enjoyed in life—the ability to bully and torment those weaker than himself. In life, the spoilsport Ariakan had prevented Krell from indulging in his sadistic pleasures. Now Krell was one of the most powerful beings on Krynn and he took joyful advantage of it.

Just the sight of him in his black armor and helm with the ram's horns, behind which blazed red eyes of undeath, struck terror into the hearts of those foolish or daring enough to venture onto Storm's Keep in search of the treasure the knights had supposedly left behind. Krell enjoyed such company immensely. He forced his victims to play khas with him, livening up the game by torturing them until they eventually succumbed.

Zeboim had been a bother, holding him prisoner on Storm's Keep until he'd attracted the notice of Chemosh, Lord of the Dead. Krell had struck up a deal with Chemosh and gained his freedom from Storm's Keep. With Chemosh protecting him, Krell had even been able to thumb his rotting nose at Zeboim.

Chemosh had in his possession the soul of Lord Ariakan, the beloved son of the sea goddess. The soul was trapped in a khas piece. Chemosh was holding that soul hostage for Zeboim's "good behavior." He had designs upon a certain tower located in the Blood Sea, and he didn't want the sea goddess meddling.

Zeboim, incensed, had sent one of her faithful—some wretched monk—to Storm's Keep to rescue her son. Krell had discovered the monk snooping about and, always happy to have visitors, had "invited" the monk to play khas with him.

To be fair to Krell, he had not known that the monk was sent by the goddess. The thought that the monk might be there to steal the khas piece containing Ariakan's soul never entered Krell's brain—a brain that admittedly was not all that large to begin with and was now further hampered by being encased in a ponderous and fearsome steel helm; a brain on which a giant bug, sent by a god, was now feasting.

The god belonged to this blasted monk, a monk who had not played fair. First, the monk had brought in an unlawful khas piece; second, that khas piece had made an illegal move; and third, the monk—instead of writhing and moaning in agony after Krell had broken several of his fingers—had physically attacked the death knight with a staff that turned out to be a god.

Krell fought the mantis in a blind panic, punching, kicking and flailing at it until, suddenly, it disappeared.

The monk's staff was a staff again, lying on the floor. Krell was prepared to stomp it to splinters when a fifth thought came to him.

Suppose touching the staff would cause it to turn back into a bug?

Keeping a wary eye on the staff, Krell made a wide detour around it as he took stock of the situation. The monk had run off. That was only to be expected. Krell would deal with him later. After all, he wasn't going anywhere, not off this accursed rock. The massive fortress stood atop sheer cliffs raked by the lashing waves of the turbulent sea. Krell righted the board that the monk had overturned. He gathered up the pieces, just to make certain the precious khas piece given to him by Chemosh was safe.

It wasn't.

Feverishly Krell placed all the pieces on the khas board. Two were missing, one of which was the khas piece containing the soul of Ariakan; the khas piece that Chemosh had ordered Krell to guard with his undead life.

The death knight broke into a chill sweat, not an easy thing to do when one has no shivering flesh, palpitating heart, or clenching bowels. Krell fell to his knees. He peered under the table and groped about with his hands. The knight piece was not there; neither was the kender.

"The monk!" Krell snarled.

Spurred on by the vivid image of what Chemosh would do to him if he lost the khas piece containing the soul of Lord Ariakan, Krell set off in pursuit.

He didn't expect this to take long. The monk was broken—both in bones and in spirit. He could barely walk, much less run.

Krell left the tower, where they'd been having such a comfortable, friendly game until the monk ruined it, and entered the keep's central courtyard. He saw immediately that the monk had an ally—Zeboim, the Goddess of the Sea. At the sight of Krell, storm clouds gathered thick in the sky and a sizzling bolt of lightning struck the tower he'd just left.

Krell was not one of the world's great intellectual thinkers, but he did have occasional flashes of desperate brilliance.

"Don't you lay a hand on me, you Sea Bitch, you," Krell bellowed. "Your monk stole the wrong khas piece! Your son is still in my possession. If you do anything to help the thief escape, Chemosh will melt down your pretty pewter boy and hammer his soul into oblivion!"

Krell's ruse worked. Lightning flickered uncertainly from cloud to cloud. The wind died. The sky grew sullen. A few hailstones clunked down on Krell's steel helm. The goddess spat rain at him, and that was all.

She dared do nothing to him. She dared not come to the monk's aid.

As to the monk, he was gamely hobbling over the rocks, vainly trying to escape Krell. The man's shoulders sagged. He sobbed for breath. He was about finished. His goddess had abandoned him. Krell expected the monk to give up, surrender, fall to his knees and plead for his miserable life. That was what Krell himself had done when in a similar situation. It hadn't worked for him, and it wasn't going to work for this monk.

Again, the monk didn't play fair. Instead of surrendering, he hobbled with the last of his strength straight for the cliff's edge.

Mother of the Abyss! Krell realized, shocked. The bastard's going to jump!

If he jumped, he'd take with him the khas piece, and there was no way Krell could recover it. He had no intention of going for a swim in Zeboim-infested waters.

Krell had to catch the monk and stop him from jumping. Unfortunately, that was not proving an easy task to accomplish.

His hulking form encased in the plate and chain mail armor of a death knight, Krell lumbered. He could not run.

Krell's armor clanked and clattered. His ponderous footfalls sent tremors through the ground. He watched, in mounting terror, the monk outdistance him.

Krell found an unexpected ally in Zeboim. She, too, feared for the khas piece the monk was carrying. She tried to stop him. She pummeled the monk with rain and knocked him off his feet with a wind gust. The wretched monk stood up and kept going.

He reached the edge of the cliff. Krell knew what lay below—a seventy-foot fall onto sharp-edged granite boulders.

"Stop him, Zeboim," Krell raged. "If you don't, you'll be sorry!"

The monk held a small leather bag in his hand. He thrust that bag into the bosom of his bloodstained robes.

Krell clambered and stumbled among the rocks, swearing and waving his sword.

The monk climbed onto a promontory that extended out into the sea. He lifted his face to the storm-shrouded heavens lit bright as day by the goddess's fear.

"Zeboim," the monk cried, "we are in your hands."

Krell roared.

The monk jumped.

Krell blundered his way among the rocks, his momentum carrying him along at such a frantic pace that the edge of the cliff was upon him before he realized it, and he very nearly went over into the sea himself.

Krell teetered back and forth for what would have been a heart-stopping moment, if he'd had a heart, before hastily regaining his balance. He stumbled back several paces, then, creeping forward an inch at a time, he peered cautiously over the edge. He expected to see the monk's mangled body lying sprawled on the rocks, with Zeboim lapping up his blood.

Nothing.

"I'm screwed," Krell muttered glumly.

Krell glanced at the sky where the clouds were growing darker and thicker. The wind started to rise. Rain began to pour down on him, along with hailstones and lightning bolts, sleet and snow, and large chunks of a nearby tower.

Krell might have run for protection to Chemosh, but sadly, Chemosh was the god who had given Krell the khas piece for safekeeping—the khas piece that Krell had now lost. The Lord of Death was not known to be either merciful or forgiving.

"Somewhere on this island," Krell reasoned, as he narrowly missed being flattened by a stone gargoyle hurtling past him, "there must be a hole deep enough and dark enough where no god can find me."

Krell turned on his heel and lumbered off through the raging storm.

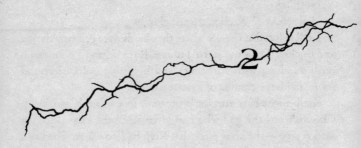

2

Rhys Mason was the monk who had made the desperate decision to leap off the cliffs of Storm's Keep. He was making a gamble, staking his life and that of his friend, the kender, Nightshade, on the fact that Zeboim would not let them die. She could not let them die, for Rhys had in his possession the soul of her son.

At least, this is what Rhys was hoping. The thought was also in his mind that if the goddess abandoned him, he could either die slowly and in torment at the cruel whim of the death knight, or he could die swiftly on the rocks below.

As luck would have it, Rhys jumped into the water in an area around Storm's Keep that was free of rocks. He plunged into the sea, sinking so deep that he left the light of day far above him. He floundered in the bone-chilling darkness, with no way to tell which way was up and which way was down. Not that it mattered anyway. He could never reach the surface. He was drowning, his lungs bursting. When he opened his mouth, he would draw in gurgling, choking death. . . .

The immortal hand of a furious goddess reached into the

depths of her ocean, gripped Rhys Mason by the scruff of his neck, plucked him from the seas, and flung him on shore.

"How dare you endanger my son?" the goddess cried.

She raged on, but Rhy did not hear her. Her fury closed over his head like the dark waters of the sea, and he knew nothing.

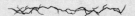

Rhys lay facedown in the warm sand. His monk's robes were soaking wet, as were his shoes. His sodden hair trailed over his face. His lips were rimmed with salt, as was the inside of his mouth and his throat. He gagged, retched and fought to breathe.

Suddenly strong hands began to pummel him on his back, and swung his arms over his head, working his arms up and down in a pumping action to force the water out of his lungs.

Coughing, he spewed seawater out of his mouth.

"About time you came around," Zeboim said, continuing to yank him and pump him.

Groaning, Rhys managed to croak, "Stop! Please!" He gagged up more water.

The goddess let go, allowing his arms to drop limply to the sand.

Rhys's eyes burned from the salt. He could barely open them. He peered through half-shut lids to see the hem of a green gown rippling over the sand near his head. The toe of a bare, shapely foot prodded him.

"Where is he, monk?" Zeboim demanded.

The goddess knelt down beside him. Her blue-green eyes glowed. A restless wind stirred her sea foam hair. She grabbed him by the hair and yanked his head off the ground and glared into his eyes.

"Where is my son?"

Rhys tried to speak. His throat was sore and parched. He

passed his tongue over his salt-coated lips and rasped, "Water!"

"Water!" Zeboim flared. "You swallowed half my ocean as it is! Oh, very well," she added huffily, as Rhys's eyes closed and he fell back limply in the sand. "Here. Don't drink too much. You'll throw up again. Just rinse out your mouth."

Her hand propped him up as she held a cup of cool water to his lips. The goddess's touch could be gentle when she wanted. He sipped the cool liquid gratefully. The goddess brushed moist fingertips across his lips and eyelids, wiping away the salt.

"There," Zeboim said soothingly. "You've had your water." Her voice hardened. "Now stop stalling. I want my son."

As Rhys started to reach into the bosom of his robes where he'd stuffed the leather scrip, pain shot through him and he gasped. He lifted his hands. His fingers were purple and swollen and bent at odd angles. He couldn't move them.

Zeboim regarded him with a sniff.

"I am *not* the goddess of healing, if that's what you're thinking!" she said coldly.

"I did not ask you to heal me, Your Majesty," Rhys returned through clenched teeth.

He slowly thrust his injured hand inside his robes and sighed in relief at the feel of wet leather. He had been afraid that he might have lost the scrip in his dive off the cliff. He fumbled at the bag, but his broken fingers would not work well enough for him to open it.

The goddess seized hold of his fingers and, one by one, yanked the bones back into place. The pain was excruciating. Rhys feared for a moment he was going to pass out. When she was finished, however, his broken bones were mended. The bruising faded. The swelling started to recede. Zeboim had her own healing touch, it seemed.

Rhys lay in the sand, bathed in sweat, waiting for the nausea to pass.

"I warned you," Zeboim said serenely. "I'm not Mishakal."

"No, Your Majesty." Rhys murmured. "Thank you anyway."

His healed hands reached into his robe and drew forth the leather bag. Opening the drawstring, he upended the bag. Two khas pieces fell out onto the sand—a dark knight mounted on a blue dragon and a kender.

Zeboim snatched up the dark knight piece. Holding it in her hand, she lovingly caressed the figure and crooned to it. "My son! My dearest son! Your soul will be freed. We'll go to Chemosh immediately."

There was a pause, as though she were listening, then she said, her voice altering, "Don't argue with me, Ariakan. Mother knows what is best!"

Cradling the khas piece in her hands, Zeboim stood up. Storm clouds darkened the heavens. The wind lifted, blowing stinging sand into Rhys's face.

"Don't leave yet, Your Majesty!" he cried desperately. "Remove the spell from the kender!"

"What kender?" Zeboim asked carelessly. Wisps of cloud coiled around her, ready to carry her off.

Rhys jumped to his feet. He snatched up the kender piece and held it before her.

"The kender risked his life for you," said Rhys, "as did I. Ask yourself this question, Majesty. Why should Chemosh free your son's soul?"

"Why? Because I command it, that's why!" Zeboim returned, though not with her usual spirit. She looked uncertain.

"Chemosh did this for a reason, Majesty," Rhys said. "He did it because he fears you."

"Of course, he does," Zeboim returned, shrugging. "Everyone fears me."

She hesitated, then said, "But I don't mind hearing what you have to say on the subject. Why do *you* think Chemosh fears me?"

"Because you have learned too much about the Beloved, these terrible undead that he has created. You have learned too much about the woman, Mina, who is their leader."

"You're right. That chit, Mina. I had forgotten all about her." Zeboim cast Rhys a glance of grudging acknowledgement. "You are also right in that the Lord of Death will not free my son's soul, not without coercion. I need something to force his hand. I need Mina. You have to find her and bring her to me. A task, I recall, that I gave you in the first place."

Zeboim glowered at him. "So why haven't you done it?"

"I was saving your son, Your Majesty," Rhys said. "I will resume my search, but to find Mina I require the services of the kender—"

"What kender?"

"This kender. Nightshade, Your Majesty," Rhys said, holding up the khas piece that was frantically waving its tiny arms. "The kender nightstalker."

"Oh, very well!" Zeboim flicked sand over the khas piece and Nightshade, all four-and-one half-feet of him, blossomed at Rhys's side.

"Get me back to normal!" the kender was bellowing.

He looked around and blinked. "Oh, you did. Whew! Thanks!"

Nightshade patted himself all over. He lifted his hand to his head to make certain his topknot was there and it was. He looked at his shirt to make certain he still had one and he did. He had his britches, too—his favorite color, purple, or at least, they'd once been purple. They were now a peculiar color of mauve. He wrung the water out of his shirt, pants, and topknot, and felt better.

"I'll never complain about being short again," he confided to Rhys in heartfelt tones.

"If that is all I can do for the two of you," Zeboim said

bitingly, "I have urgent business . . ."

"One more thing, Your Majesty," Rhys said. "Where are we?"

Zeboim cast a vague glance around. "You are on a beach by the sea. How should I know where? It is all the same to me. I pay no attention to these things."

"We need to be back in Solace, Your Majesty," said Rhys, "in order to search for Mina. I know you are in a hurry, but if you could just take us there—"

"And would you like me to fill your pockets with emeralds?" Zeboim asked with a sarcastic curl of her lip. "And give you a castle overlooking the shores of the Sirrion Ocean?"

"Yes!" cried Nightshade eagerly.

"No, Majesty," said Rhys. "Just send us back to—"

He quit speaking because there was no longer any goddess to hear him. There was only Nightshade, several extremely startled looking people, and a mighty vallenwood tree holding a gabled building in its stalwart branches.

A joyful bark split the air. A black and white dog bounded off the landing where she'd been dozing in the sun. The dog came tumbling down the stairs, dodging in and out of people's legs, nearly upending several.

Speeding across the lawn, Atta launched herself at Rhys and jumped into his arms.

He clasped the wriggling, furry body and hugged her close, his head buried in her fur, his eyes wet with softer water than that of the sea.

Brightly colored stained glass windows caught the last rays of the afternoon sun. People wended their way up and down the long staircase that led from the ground to the Inn of the Last Home in the treetop.

"Solace," Nightshade said in satisfaction.

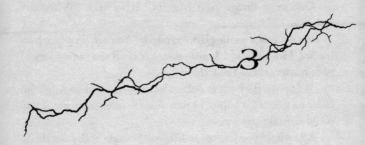

3

ell, I'll be the son of a blue-eyed, elf-loving ogre!" Gerard clapped Rhys on the back, and then shook his hand and then clapped him on the back again, and then stood grinning at him. "I never expected to see you again this side of the Abyss."

Gerard paused, then said half-joking and half-not, "I guess you'll want your kender-herding dog back . . ."

Atta dashed over to give Nightshade a wriggle and a quick lick, then ran back to Rhys. She sat at his feet, gazing up at him, her mouth wide and her tongue hanging out.

"Yes," said Rhys, reaching down to fondle her ears. "I want my dog back."

"I was afraid of that. Solace now has the most well-behaved kender in all of Ansalon. No offense, friend," he added with a glance at Nightshade.

"None taken," said Nightshade cheerfully. He sniffed the air. "What's the special on the Inn's menu tonight?"

"All right, you people, go about your business," Gerard said, waving his hands at the crowd that had gathered. "The show's over." He glanced sidelong at Rhys and said in an undertone, "I

take it the show *is* over, Brother? You're not going to spontane-
ously combust or anything like that?"

"I trust not," answered Rhys cautiously. When Zeboim was
involved, he knew better than to promise.

A few still lingered, hoping for more excitement, but when
the minutes passed and they saw nothing more interesting
than a dripping wet monk and a soaked kender, even the idlers
wandered off.

Gerard turned back to stare at Rhys. "What have you been
doing, Brother? Washing your robes with yourself inside them?
The kender, too." Reaching out his hand, he plucked a bit of
slimy, brownish red plant life from the kender's hair. "Seaweed!
And the nearest ocean is a hundred miles from here."

Gerard eyed them. "But then, why am I surprised? The last I
saw you two, you were both locked inside a jail cell with a crazy
woman. The next thing I know, you've both vanished and I'm
left with a lunatic female who has the power to fling me out of
her cell with a flick of her finger, then she locks me out of my
own jail and won't let me back inside. And then *she* vanishes!"

"I believe I owe you an explanation," said Rhys.

"I believe you do!" Gerard grunted. "Come into the Inn. You
can dry off in the kitchen and Laura will fix you both something
to eat—"

"What's today?" Nightshade interrupted to ask.

"Today? Fourth-day," said Gerard impatiently. "Why?"

"Fourth-day . . . Oh, the menu special will be lamb chops!"
Nightshade said excitedly. "With boiled potatoes and mint
jelly."

"I don't think going to the Inn would be a good idea," said
Rhys. "We need to speak privately."

"Oh, but Rhys," Nightshade wailed, "it's lamb chops!"

"We'll go to my house," said Gerard. "It's not far. I don't have
lamb chops," he added, seeing Nightshade looking glum. "But

no one stews a chicken better, if I do say so myself."

People stared at the monk and kender as they walked along the streets of Solace, obviously wondering how the two had managed to get so wet on a day when the sun was shining and there wasn't a cloud in the sky. They hadn't gone far, however, before Nightshade came to a sudden stop.

"Why are we walking toward the jail?" he asked suspiciously.

"Don't worry," Gerard assured him. "My house is located near the prison. I live close by the jail in case there's trouble. The house comes as part of my pay."

"Oh, well, that's all right then," said Nightshade, relieved.

"We'll have something to eat and drink, and you can retrieve your staff while you're there, Brother," Gerard added as an afterthought. "I've been keeping it for you."

"My staff!" Now it was Rhys who halted. He regarded his friend in astonishment.

"I guess it's yours," said Gerard. "I found it in the prison cell after you'd left. You were in such a hurry," he added wryly, "you forgot it."

"Are you sure the staff is mine?"

"If I wasn't sure, Atta was," said Gerard. "She sleeps beside it every night."

Nightshade was staring at Rhys with wide eyes.

"Rhys——" said the kender.

Rhys shook his head, hoping to ward off the questions he knew was coming.

Nightshade was persistent. "But, Rhys, your staff——"

"——has been in safe hands all this time," said Rhys. "I need not have been worried about it."

Nightshade subsided, though he continued to cast puzzled glances at Rhys as they walked on. Rhys hadn't forgotten his staff. The emmide had been with him when they'd made their unexpected journey to the death knight's castle. The staff had probably saved their lives, undergoing a miraculous transformation, changing from a shabby wooden staff into a gigantic praying mantis that had attacked the death knight. Rhys had thought the staff lost to Storm's Keep and he'd felt a pang of regret, even as he was fleeing for his life, at having to leave it behind. The emmide was sacred to Majere, the god Rhys had abandoned.

The god who apparently refused to abandon Rhys.

Humbled, grateful and confused, Rhys pondered Majere's involvement in his life. Rhys had thought the sacred staff a parting gift from his god, a sign from Majere that he understood and forgave his backsliding follower. When the emmide had transformed itself into the praying mantis to attack Krell, Rhys had taken that to be the god's final blessing. Yet now the emmide was back. It had been given for safekeeping to Gerard, a former Solamnic knight—a sign, perhaps, that this man could be trusted, and also a sign that Majere still took a keen interest in his monk.

"The way to me is through you," Majere taught. "Know yourself and you come to know me."

Rhys had thought he'd known himself, and then had come that terrible day when his wretched brother had murdered their parents and the brethren of Rhys's order. Rhys realized now he'd known only the side of himself that walked in the sunshine along the riverbank. He had not known the side of himself that crawled about in his soul's dark chasm. He had not known that side until it had burst out to shriek its fury and desire for vengeance.

That dark side of himself had prompted Rhys to renounce Majere as a "do-nothing" god in order to join forces with Zeboim. He had left the monastery to go out into the world to find his accursed brother, Lleu, and bring him to justice. He had found his brother, but things hadn't been that simple.

Perhaps Majere and his teachings weren't that simple either. Perhaps the god was a great deal more complicated than Rhys had realized. Certainly life was far more complicated than he'd ever imagined.

A sharp tug on Rhys's sleeve brought him back from his musings. He looked at Nightshade.

"Yes, what is it?"

"Not me," said the kender, pointing. "Him."

Rhys realized Gerard must have been talking to him all this time. "I beg your pardon, Sheriff. I started down a path of thought and could not find my way back. Did you ask me something?"

"I asked if you'd seen anything of that lunatic woman who apparently feels free to let herself in and out of my prison whenever she feels like it."

"Is she there now?" Rhys asked, alarmed.

"I don't know," returned Gerard drily. "I haven't looked in the last five minutes. What do you know about her?"

Rhys made up his mind. Though much was still murky, the god's sign seemed clear. Gerard was a man he could trust. And, the gods knew, Rhys had to trust someone! He could no longer carry this burden by himself.

"I will explain everything to you, Sheriff, at least, as much as can be explained."

"Which isn't much," Nightshade muttered.

"I will be grateful for anything at this point," Gerard stated feelingly.

The explanation was put off for a short while. The salt water crusted on their skin was starting to itch, and so both Rhys and Nightshade decided to bathe in Crystalmir Lake.

The Sea Goddess, having recovered her son, had generously deigned to remove the curse that she'd put on it, and the lake had been restored to its state of crystal purity. The dead fish that had choked the lake had been carted off and dumped into the fields for use in nurturing the crops, but the stench still lingered in the air, and the two washed as swiftly as possible. After he had bathed, Rhys cleansed the blood and salt out of his robes and Nightshade scrubbed his own clothes. Gerard provided clothes for them to wear while their own dried in the sun.

While they bathed, Gerard stewed a chicken in broth flavored with onions, carrots, potatoes, and what he named as his own special secret ingredient—cloves.

Gerard's house was small but comfortable. It was built on ground level, not in the branches of one of Solace's famous vallenwood trees.

"No offense to tree dwellers," Gerard said, ladling out the chicken stew and handing it around. "I like living in a place where if I happen to sleepwalk, I don't break my neck."

He gave Atta a beef bone and she settled down on top of Rhys's feet to gnaw contently. Rhys's staff stood in the corner next to the chimney.

"Is it your—what do you call it?" Gerard asked.

"Emmide." Rhys ran his hand over the wood. He recalled every imperfection, every bump and gnarl, every nick and cut that the emmide had acquired over five hundred years of protecting the innocent.

"The staff is imperfect, yet the god loves it," Rhys said softly. "Majere could have a staff of the same magical metal that forged the dragonlances, yet his staff is wood—plain and simple and flawed. Though flawed, it has never broken."

"If you're saying something important, Brother," said Gerard, "then you need to speak up."

Rhys gave the staff a last, lingering look, then returned to his chair.

"The staff is mine," he said. "Thank you for keeping it for me."

"It's not much to look at," said Gerard. "Still, you seemed to set store by it."

He waited until Rhys had helped himself to food and then said quietly, "Very well, Brother. Let's hear your story."

Nightshade was holding a hunk of bread in one hand and a chicken leg in the other, alternating bites of each and eating very fast, so fast that at one point he nearly choked himself.

"Slow down, kender," Gerard said. "What's the rush?"

"I'm afraid we may not be here very long," Nightshade mumbled as broth dribbled down his chin.

"Why's that?"

"Because you're not going to believe us. I give you about three minutes to toss us out the door."

Gerard frowned and turned back to Rhys. "Well, Brother? Am I going to toss you out?"

Rhys was silent a moment, wondering where to start.

"Do you remember a few days ago I posed a hypothetical question to you. 'What would say if I told you my brother was a murderer?' You remember that?"

"Do I!" Gerard exclaimed. "I almost locked you up for failure to report a murder. Something about your brother, Lleu, killing a girl—Lucy Wheelwright, wasn't it? You sounded like you meant that, Brother. I would have believed you if I hadn't seen Lucy for myself that very morning, alive as you are and a whole lot prettier."

Rhys regarded Gerard intently. "Have you seen Lucy Wheelwright since?"

"No, I haven't. I saw her husband, though." Gerard was grim. "What was left of him. Hacked to pieces with an axe and the remnants tied up in a sack and dumped in the woods."

"Gods save us!" Rhys exclaimed, horrified.

"Maybe he said he didn't want to worship Chemosh," Nightshade said somberly. "Like your monks."

"What monks?" Gerard demanded.

Rhys didn't answer immediately. "You said Lucy has disappeared?"

"Yeah. She told people she and her husband were leaving town to visit a neighboring village, but I checked. Lucy never came back and, of course, we know now what happened to her husband."

"You checked on them?" Rhys asked, startled. "I thought you didn't take me seriously."

"I didn't, at first," Gerard admitted, settling back comfortably in his chair. "But then after we found the body of her husband, I got to thinking. Like I said to you during that same conversation, you're not much of a talker, Brother. There had to be some reason for you to say what you said, and so, the more I thought about it, the less I liked it. I fought in the War of Souls. I battled an army of ghosts. I wouldn't have believed *that* if someone had told me about it. I sent one of my men to the village to see if he could find Lucy."

"I take it he couldn't."

"No one in that village had ever heard of her. As it turned out, she never went near the place, and she's not the only one to disappear. We've had a rash of young people up and vanishing. Leaving their homes, their families, quitting good paying jobs without a word. One young couple, Timothy and Gerta Tanner, abandoned their three-month-old baby—a son they both loved dearly." He cocked an eye at Nightshade. "So you don't have to gobble your food, kender. I'm not going to throw you out."

"That's a relief," said Nightshade, brushing crumbs off his borrowed shirt. He helped himself to an apple.

"Not to mention your own mysterious disappearance from the jail cell," Gerard added. "But let's start with Lucy and your brother, Lleu. You claim he murdered her—"

"He did," said Rhys calmly. He felt suddenly relieved, as though a heavy burden had been lifted from his heart. "He murdered her in the name of Chemosh, Lord of Death."

Gerard sat forward, looking Rhys in the eyes. "She was alive when I saw her, Brother."

"No, she wasn't," Rhys returned, "and neither was my brother. Both of them were . . . are . . . dead."

"Dead as a dormouse," said Nightshade complacently, biting into the apple. He wiped away the juice with the back of his hand. "It's in the eyes."

Gerard shook his head. "You best start from the start, Brother."

"I wish I could," said Rhys softly.

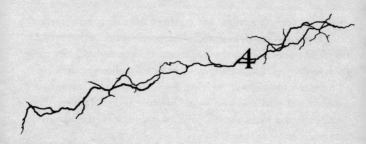

4

*Y*ou see, Sheriff, I don't know where the story starts," Rhys explained. "The story seems to have found me somewhere in the middle. It began when my brother, Lleu, came to visit me in the monastery. Our parents brought him. He had been running wild, carousing, keeping bad company. I saw nothing more in this than the high spirits of youth. As it turned out, I was blind. The Master of our order and Atta both saw clearly what I could not—that there was something terribly wrong with Lleu."

Atta raised her head and looked at Rhys and wagged her tail. He stroked her soft fur. "I should have listened to Atta. She realized immediately that my brother was a threat. She even bit him, something she never does."

Gerard eyed the dog, rubbed his chin. "True enough. Though she's had provocation." He was silent, thoughtful, gazing at the dog. "Now, I wonder . . ."

"Wonder what, Sheriff?"

Gerard waved his hand. "Never mind for now, Brother. Go on."

"That night," Rhys continued, "my brother poisoned my

brethren and our parents. He murdered twenty people in the name of Chemosh."

Gerard sat bolt upright. He regarded Rhys in astonishment.

"He tried to murder me, too. Atta saved my life." Rhys rested his hand gratefully on the dog's head. "That night, I lost my faith in my god. I was angry with Majere for allowing such evil to happen to those who were his loyal and devoted servants. I sought a new god, one who would help me find my brother and avenge the deaths of those I loved. I cried out to the heavens, and a god answered me."

Gerard looked grave. "A god answering you. That's never good."

"The goddess was Zeboim," said Rhys.

"But you didn't take her up on it . . ." Gerard stared. "By heaven, you did! That's why you're not a monk anymore! And that woman . . . That crazy female in my jail . . . And the dead fish . . . Zeboim," he finished, awed.

"She was distraught," Rhys said by way of apology. "Chemosh was holding the soul of her son in thrall."

"She turned me into a khas piece," interjected Nightshade. "Without asking!" Indignantly, he helped himself to more chicken. "Then she whooshed us off to Storm's Keep to face a death knight. A *death* knight! Someone who goes around mangling people! How crazy is that? And then there's her son, Ariakan. Don't get me started on him!"

"*Lord* Ariakan," Gerard said slowly. "The commander of the dark knights during the Chaos War."

"That's the one."

"The one who's been dead fifty or so years?"

"As the tombstones say, 'Dead but not forgotten,' " quoted Nightshade. "That was his whole problem. Lord Ariakan couldn't forget. And do you think he was grateful that Rhys and I were there trying to save him? Not a bit of it. Lord Ariakan flatly refused to go with me. I had to run across the board and knock him to the floor. That part *was* kind of exciting."

Nightshade grinned at the memory, then was suddenly remorseful. "Or it would have been, if Rhys hadn't been bleeding with pieces of bone sticking out of his skin where the death knight broke his fingers."

Gerard glanced at Rhys's hands. His fingers seemed perfectly whole.

"I see," he said. "Broken fingers."

"What happened to us is not important, Sheriff," said Rhys. "What is important is that we must find some way to stop these Beloved of Chemosh, as they call themselves. They are monsters who go about killing young people and turning them into Chemosh's slaves. They appear to be alive but, in fact, they are dead—"

"I can vouch for that," said Nightshade.

"And, what is more, they cannot be destroyed. I know," Rhys added simply. "I tried. I killed my brother. I broke Lleu's neck with the emmide. He shook it off as you would shake off bumping into a door."

"And I tried casting one of my spells on him. I'm a mystic, you know," Nightshade added proudly. Then he sighed. "I don't think Lleu even noticed. I cast one of my more powerful spells on him, too."

"You must appreciate the dire nature of this situation, Sheriff," Rhys continued earnestly. "The Beloved are luring unsuspecting youth to their doom and they cannot be stopped—at least not by any means we have tried. What's more, we cannot warn people about them because no one will believe us. The Beloved look and act in all respects just like anyone else. I could be one of them now, Sheriff, and you would never know."

"He's not, by the way," said Nightshade. "I can tell."

"How can you tell?" Gerard asked.

"My kind can see that they're dead right off," said Nightshade. "There's no warm glow coming from their bodies, like there is from you and Rhys and Atta and anyone else who's alive."

"Your kind," said Gerard. "You mean kender?"

"Not just any old kender. Kender nightstalkers. My dad says there aren't a lot of us around, though."

"What about you, Brother? Can you tell by looking?" Gerard was plainly working hard at not sounding skeptical.

"Not at first glance. But, if I get close enough, as Nightshade says, I can see it in the eyes. There is no light there, no life. The eyes of the Beloved are the dead, blank eyes of a corpse. There are other means by which they can be identified. The Beloved of Chemosh have incredible strength. They cannot be harmed or killed. And I think it likely that they each have a mark upon the left breast, over the heart. The mark of the deadly kiss that has killed them."

Rhys sat in thought, trying to remember all he could about his brother.

"There is something else that is odd about Lleu and might apply to all the Beloved. Over time, my brother—or, rather—the thing that was my brother—appeared to lose his memory. Lleu has no remembrance of me at all now. He has no memory of slaying his parents, or any of the other crimes he has committed. He is apparently unable to remember anything for very long. I have seen him eat a full meal and in the next breath complain that he is starving."

"Yet he remembers he's supposed to kill in the name of Chemosh," said Gerard.

"Yes." Rhys agreed somberly. "That is the one thing they do remember."

"Atta knows the Beloved when she sees one," said Nightshade, with a pat for the dog, who accepted his pat with a good grace, though she was obviously hoping for another bone. "If Atta knows, maybe other dogs know."

"That might explain a little mystery I've been wondering about," said Gerard, regarding Atta with interest. He shook his head. "Though if it does, then it's sorrowful news. You see, I've been keeping her with me when I do my work. She helps with the kender problem and she's useful to me in other ways, too. She's a good companion. I'll miss her, Brother. I don't mind telling you."

"Perhaps, when I return to the monastery, I can train another dog, Sheriff—" Rhys paused, wondering at what he'd just said. *When I return*. He'd never meant to go back there.

"Would you, Brother?" Gerard was pleased. "That would be great! Anyway, back to what I was saying. Every day Atta and I have lunch at the Inn of the Last Home. Everyone there—the usual crowd—has gotten to know Atta. My friends come pet her and talk to her. She is always a lady. Very gracious and polite."

Rhys stroked the dog's silky ears.

"Well, one day—yesterday it was—one of the regulars, a farmer come to sell his wares at the market—took his lunch at the Inn as usual. He bent down to pet Atta like he always does. Only this time she growled at him and snapped. He laughed and backed off, saying he must have got on her bad side. Then he started to sit down next to me. Atta was on her feet in a flash. She moved her body between me and him. Her fur bristled. She bared her teeth, her lip curling back. I couldn't imagine what had gotten into her!"

Gerard looked uncomfortable. "I spoke to her pretty sharply, I'm afraid, Brother. And I marched her off to the stables to tie her up until she learned to behave herself. Now I'm thinking I owe her an apology." Taking a strip of chicken, he handed it to the dog. "I'm sorry, Atta. It seems you knew what you were doing all along."

"What happened to the farmer?"

Gerard shook his head. "I haven't seen him since." He sat back in his chair, frowning.

"What are you thinking, Sheriff?" Rhys asked.

"I'm thinking that if these two can recognize one of these Beloved by sight, that we could set a trap. Catch one in the act."

"I did that," said Rhys grimly. "I stood by helplessly as my brother killed an innocent young girl. I won't be party to the same mistake again."

"That won't happen this time, Brother," Gerard argued. "I have a plan. We'll take guards with us. My best men. We'll ask the Beloved to surrender. If that doesn't work, we'll use more drastic measures. No one will get hurt. I'll see to that."

Rhys remained unconvinced.

"One other question," Gerard said. "What does Zeboim have to do with all this?"

"It seems that there is a war among the gods—"

"Just what we need," Gerard burst out angrily. "We mortals finally achieve peace on Ansalon—relatively speaking—and now the gods start slugging it out again. Some sort of power struggle now that the Queen of Darkness is dead and gone, I'll bet. And we poor mortals are caught in the middle. Why can't the gods just leave us alone, Brother? Let us work out our own problems!"

"We've done so well so far," Rhys said dryly.

"All the trouble that has ever plagued this world has been caused by the gods," Gerard stated heatedly.

"Not by gods," Rhys countered gently. "By mortals in the name of the gods."

Gerard snorted. "I don't say that things were great when the gods were gone, but at least we didn't have dead people walking around committing murder—" He saw that Rhys was looking uncomfortable and stopped his harangue.

"I'm sorry, Brother. Don't mind me. I get riled up over this. Go on with your story. I need to know all I can if I'm going to fight these things."

Rhys hesitated, then said quietly, "When I lost my own faith, I called upon a god—any god—to side with me. Zeboim answered my prayer. One of the few times she has ever answered any of my prayers. The goddess told me that the person behind all of this was someone called Mina—"

"Mina!"

Gerard stood up so fast he upset the bowl of stew, spilling it to the floor, much to Atta's delight. She was too well trained to beg, but, by the Immortal Law of Dogs, if food falls on the floor, it's up for grabs.

Nightshade gave a dismayed cry and dove to save lunch, but Atta was too quick for him. The dog gulped down the rest of the chicken, not even bothering to chew it first.

"What do you know of this Mina?" asked Rhys, startled by Gerard's intense reaction.

"Know of her. Brother, I've met her," said Gerard. He ran his hand through his yellow hair, causing it to stand straight up. "And I tell you, Rhys Mason, it's not something I ever want to do again. She's fey, that one. If she's behind this . . ." He fell silent, brooding.

"Yes," Rhys prompted. "If she's behind this, what?"

"Then I'm thinking I'd better rethink my plan," said Gerard grimly. He headed for the door. "You and the kender sit tight. I have work to do. I'll need you to in Solace a few days, Brother."

Rhys shook his head. "I'm sorry, Sheriff, but I must continue my search for my brother. I've lost precious time as it is—"

Gerard halted in the open doorway, turned around.

"And if you find him, Brother, what then? Will you just keep trailing after him, watching him kill people? Or do you want to stop him for good?"

Rhys made no reply. He gazed at Gerard in silence.

"I could use your help, Brother. Yours and Atta's and, yes, even the kender's," Gerard added grudgingly. "Will all three of you stay, just for a few days?"

"A sheriff asking a kender for help!" Nightshade said, awed. "I'll bet that's never happened in the whole history of the world. Let's stay, Rhys."

Rhys's eyes were drawn to the emmide, standing in the corner. "Very well, Sheriff. We will stay."

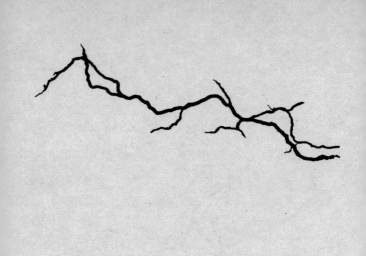

BOOK II

THE

HALL

OF

SACRILEGE

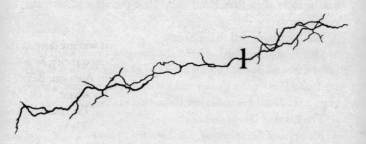

_K_rell!" The voice echoed through the cavernous corridors of Storm's Keep and went on booming even after the echoes had faded, bouncing around the inside of the death knight's empty helm. "Show yourself."

The death knight recognized the voice, and he burrowed deeper into his hole. Even here, far underground, water from the constant storms that lashed his island found its way through cracks and crevices. The rain ran in rivulets down the stone wall. Water seeped into his empty boots and flowed through his shin guards.

"Krell," said the voice grimly, "I know you're down there. Don't make me come after you."

"Yes, m'lord," Krell mumbled. "I'll come out."

Sloshing through the water, the death knight waded along the short corridor that led to an opening sealed off by an iron grate, hinged so that the slaves could open it when they were sent down to clean.

Krell clomped heavily up treacherous stairs carved out of the cliff face. Peering through the eye slits of his helm, Krell saw the black coat and white lace collar of the Lord of Death. He saw no more than that. Krell didn't have the nerve to look the god in the eye.

Krell promptly fell to his knees.

"My lord Chemosh," prayed the cringing death knight. "I know I let you down. I admit I lost the khas piece, but it wasn't my fault. There was a kender and a staff that turned into a giant bug . . . and how I could know the monk was suicidal?"

The Lord of Death said nothing.

Metaphorically speaking, Krell started to sweat.

"My lord Chemosh," he pleaded, "I'll make it up to you. I'll be in your debt forever. I'll do anything you command of me. Anything! Spare me your wrath!"

Chemosh sighed. "You are fortunate that I have need of you, miserable wretch. Stand up! You're dripping on my boots."

Krell rose ponderously to his feet. "You'll save me from her, too?" He jerked his thumb up at the sky to indicate the vengeful goddess. Zeboim's fury was lighting the skies, her thunderous fist pounding the ground.

"I suppose I must," said Chemosh, and he sounded lethargic, too worn-out to care. "As I said, I have need of you."

Krell was uneasy. He didn't like the god's tone. Risking taking a closer look, the death knight was startled by what he saw.

The Lord of Death looked worse than death. One might say he looked alive—alive and suffering. His face was pallid, drawn, and haggard. His hair was ragged, his clothes unkempt. The lace at his sleeve was torn and stained. His collar was undone, his shirt half-open. His eyes were empty, his voice hollow. He moved in a listless manner, as though even lifting his hand cost him great effort. Though he spoke to Krell, he didn't really seem to see him or take much interest in him.

"My lord, what is wrong?" asked Krell. "You don't look well. . . ."

"I am a god," returned Chemosh stonily. "I am always well. More's the pity."

Krell could only imagine there had been some crushing defeat in the war.

"Name your enemy, lord," said Krell, eager to please, "the one who did this to you. I will find him and rip him—"

"Nuitari is my enemy," said Chemosh.

"Nuitari," the death knight repeated uneasily, already regretting his rash promise. "The God of the Dark Moon. Why him, particularly?"

"Mina is dead," said Chemosh.

"Mina dead?" Krell was about to add "Good riddance!" when he remembered just in time that Chemosh had been strangely enamored of the human female.

"I am truly sorry, my lord," Krell amended, trying to sound sympathetic. "How did this . . . um . . . terrible tragedy happen?"

"Nuitari murdered her," said Chemosh viciously. "He will pay! You will make him pay!"

Krell was alarmed. Nuitari, the powerful god of dark magic, was not quite the enemy he'd had in mind.

"I would, my lord, but I am certain you will want to avenge her death on Nuitari yourself. Perhaps I could seek vengeance on Chislev or Hiddukel? They were undoubtedly in on the plot—"

Chemosh flicked a finger, and Krell went flying backward to smash up against the stone wall. He slid down the wall and lay in a heap of jumbled armor at the feet of the Lord of Death.

"You sniveling, craven, squirming toad," Chemosh said coldly. "You will do what I tell you to do, or I will turn you into the spineless jellyfish that you are and hand you over to the Sea Goddess with my compliments. What do you have to say to that?"

Krell mumbled something.

Chemosh bent down. "I couldn't quite hear you."

"As always, my lord," Krell said glumly, "I am yours to command."

"I thought you might be," said Chemosh. "Now come along."

"Not . . . not to visit Nuitari?" Krell quailed.

"To my dwelling, you oaf," said Chemosh. "There is something I need you to do for me first."

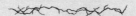

Having determined to take a more active interest in the world of the living with the view to one day ruling over that world, the Lord of Death had left his dark palace on the planes of the Abyss. He had searched for a suitable location for his new dwelling and found it in an abandoned castle overlooking the Blood Sea in the area called the Desolation.

When the Dragon Overlord, Malys, seized control of this part of Ansalon, she ravaged the countryside, laying waste to fields and farmlands, towns and villages and cities. The land was cursed so long as she was in power. Nothing grew. Rivers and streams dried up. Once-fertile fields became windswept desert. Starvation and disease spread. Cities such as Flotsam lost much of their population as people fled the dragon's curse. The entire area became known as the Desolation.

With the death of Malys at the hands of Mina, the dread effects of the dragon's evil magic on the Desolation were reversed. Almost from the moment of Malys's demise, rivers began to flow and lakes to fill. Small shoots of green thrust up out of barren soil, as though life had been there all this time, waiting only for the enchantment that held it in thrall to be removed.

With the return of the gods, this process accelerated, so that already some areas were almost back to normal. People returned and began to rebuild. Flotsam, located about one hundred and fifty miles from Chemosh's castle, was not quite the rollicking, bustling center of commerce—both legal and illegal—that it had once been, but it was no longer a ghost town. Pirates and legitimate sailors of all races roamed the streets of the famous port city. Markets and shops reopened. Flotsam was back and open for business.

Large areas of the Desolation still remained cursed, however. No one could figure out why or how. A druidess devoted to Chislev, goddess of nature, was exploring these areas, when she came across one of Malys's scales. The druidess theorized that the presence of the scale might have something to do with the continuation of the curse. She burned the scale in a sacred ceremony, and it is said that Chislev herself, disturbed by this disruption of nature, blessed the ceremony. The destruction of the scale did nothing to change things, but the story spread and the theory took hold, so these cursed areas became known as "scale-fall."

One of these scale-fall areas Chemosh claimed for his own. His castle stood on a promontory overlooking the Blood Sea on what was known as the Somber Coast.

Chemosh cared nothing about the lingering curse. He had no interest in green and growing things, so it mattered little to him that the hills and valleys around his castle were denuded, barren, empty expanses of ashy soil and charred stone.

The castle he took over was in ruins when he found it, the dragon having slain the inhabitants and razed and burned the castle. He had chosen this location because it was only about fifty miles from the Tower of the Blood Sea. He had intended to use his castle as a base of operation, planning to store here the sacred artifacts he would remove from the wreckage of the

Tower. Here, he had fondly imagined, he would take his time sorting, cataloging and calculating the immense value of the sacred artifacts that dated back to the time of the Kingpriest of Istar.

The castle would not only serve as a depository for the artifacts but as a fortress to guard them. Using rock mined by lost souls in the Abyss, Chemosh rebuilt the castle, making it so strong not even the gods themselves could assail it. The Abyssal rock was blacker than black marble and far harder. Only the hand of Chemosh could shape it into blocks, and the blocks were so heavy only he could lift them into place. The castle was constructed with four watchtowers, one on each corner. Two walls—an inner wall and an outer wall—surrounded it. The most unique feature of this castle was that no gates penetrated the walls. There appeared to be no way in and no way out.

The dead who guarded the castle needed no gates. The wraiths, ghosts and restless spirits Chemosh brought to defend his dwelling could pass through the Abyssal rock as easily as a mortal slips through a leafy green bower. Chemosh needed an entrance for his new disciples, however. The Beloved were dead, but they still retained their corporeal forms. They entered through a magical portal located at a single point in the north wall. The portal could be controlled by Chemosh, the castle's master, and by one other, the person who was to have been the castle's mistress.

Mina.

Chemosh had meant the castle to be a gift to her. He had named it both in her honor and as a tribute to his new disciples. He called it Castle Beloved.

But only Mina's ghost had come to take up residence.

Mina was dead, slain by Nuitari, the God of the Black Moon, the same god who had put an end to Chemosh's ambitious designs. Nuitari had secretly raised up the ruins of the Tower of

High Sorcery of Istar. He had seized the treasure trove of holy artifacts that was to have put Chemosh on the throne as ruler of the heavenly pantheon. Nuitari had captured Mina, taken her prisoner, and in order to flaunt his power over the Lord of Death, Nuitari had slain her.

Chemosh now dwelt alone in Castle Beloved. The place had become loathsome to him, for it was a constant reminder of the ruin of his schemes and plots. Much as he detested the castle, he found he could not leave. For Mina was there. Her spirit came to him there. She hovered near his bed—their bed. Her amber eyes gazed at him but could not see him. Her hand reached out to him but could not find him. Her voice spoke, but she could not talk to him. She listened for his voice, but she could not hear him when he called to her.

The sight of her ghostly form tormented him, and he tried countless times to leave her. He returned to his abandoned dwelling in the Abyss. Her spirit could not follow him there, but the memory of her was there, and her memory left him feeling such bitter pain, he was forced to return to Castle Beloved to find solace in the sight of her wandering ghost.

Chemosh would have his revenge against Nuitari, that much was assured. His plans were vague, however, still in formation. The death knight alone could not dislodge the powerful god from his Tower, though Chemosh did not say that to Krell. He planned to let Krell shake in his boots for a while. Krell owed Chemosh a few uncomfortable hours for losing Ariakan.

Nor did Chemosh tell the death knight that his bungling had worked out for the best. Zeboim was Nuitari's sister, but there was no love lost between the siblings. Chemosh now had a way to acquire Zeboim as a powerful ally.

The Lord of Death, accompanied by a most reluctant Ausric Krell, passed through the inner and outer walls of the castle and entered the main hall, empty, save for a throne that stood upon a dais in the center. There was room on the dais for two thrones, and when he had first built the castle, there had been two thrones. The larger and more magnificent of these thrones belonged to the god. A smaller and more delicate throne was intended for Mina. Chemosh had smashed that throne to pieces.

The wreckage of the throne lay strewn about the hall. Krell, clumping in after him, trod on some of the rubble. Hoping to regain favor in the eyes of the god, Krell began gushing over the castle's architectural design.

Chemosh paid no attention to the death knight's fawnings. He seated himself on his throne and waited, tensely, for Mina's ghost to come to him. The waiting was always agony. Part of him secretly hoped she would not materialize, that he would never see her again. Perhaps, then, he could forget. But if for some reason more time passed than was usual and her ghost did not appear, he felt he would go mad.

Then she was here, and Chemosh gave a sigh that was mingled despair and relief. Her form, wavering and delicate and pale as though she were spun of cobweb, drifted through the hall toward him. She wore some sort of loose-fitting gown made of black silk that seemed stirred by the undercurrents of the deep, for it undulated gently around her ghostly form. She lifted a ghostly hand as she drew near him, and her mouth opened, as though she was saying something. Her words were smothered by death.

"Krell," Chemosh said tersely. "You reside on the plane of death, as does she. Speak to Mina's spirit for me. Ask her what it is she so desperately wants to tell me! It is always the same," he muttered feverishly, plucking the lace on his sleeve. "She comes to me and seems to want to say something to me, and I cannot hear her! Perhaps you will be able to communicate with her."

Krell had hated Mina in life. She had faced him unafraid the first time they'd met, and for that, he'd never forgiven her. He was glad she was dead, and the last thing he wanted to do was act as a go-between for her and her lover.

"My lord," Krell ventured to point out, "you *rule* the plane of Death and Undeath. If you can't communicate—"

Chemosh turned a baleful eye upon the death knight, who bowed and muttered something about being happy to speak to Mina whenever she should decide to put in an appearance.

"She is here now, Krell. Talk to her! What are you waiting for? Ask her what she wants!"

Krell looked about. He saw nothing, but he didn't like to disappoint his lord and so he began talking to a crack in the wall.

"Mina," said Krell in sonorous and mournful tones, "Lord Chemosh would like to know—"

"Not there!" Chemosh said in exasperation. He gestured. "She is here! Next to me!"

Krell stared about the hall, then said as diplomatically as possible, "My lord, the journey from Storm's Keep was a strenuous one. Perhaps you should lie down—"

Chemosh bounded off the throne and strode angrily toward the death knight. "There's not much of you left, Krell, but what there is I'll shred into infinitesimal pieces and scatter to the four corners of the Abyss—"

"I swear to you, my lord!" Krell cried, backing up precipitously, "that I do not know what you're talking about! You say, 'Speak to Mina,' and I would be glad to do your bidding, but there is no Mina for me to speak to!"

Chemosh halted. "You cannot see her?" He pointed to where she was standing. "If I extend my arm, I could touch her." He suited his action to his words and held out his hand to her.

Krell turned his helmed head in the direction indicated and stared with all his might. "Oh, of course. Now that you point her out—"

"Don't lie to me, Krell!" Chemosh cried savagely, clenching his fist.

The death knight recoiled. "My lord. I am truly sorry. I want to see her, but I do not—"

Chemosh shifted his gaze from Krell to the apparition. His eyes narrowed. "You don't see her. Strange. I wonder . . ."

He raised his voice, shouting, so that it echoed through the shadowy realm of death. "To me! Servants, slaves! To me! Now!"

The hall filled with a ghostly throng, constrained to come at their master's bidding. Wraiths and specters gathered around Chemosh and waited in their customary silence for him to command them.

"You see these minions of mine, do you not, Krell?" Chemosh made a sweeping wave of his arm.

Left behind by the river of souls as it flowed through eternity, the undead who had fallen prey to the blandishments of the Lord of Death floated in a stagnant swamp of their own evil.

"Yes, my lord," said Krell. "I see them." They were low creatures, and he cast them a disdainful glance.

"And you don't see Mina standing among them?"

Krell stood dithering in an agony of indecision. "My lord, since my death, my eyesight is not what it used to be—"

"Krell!" Chemosh shouted.

The death knight's shoulders slumped. "No, my lord. I know you don't want to hear this, but she is not among these—"

The Lord of Death flung his arms around Krell, embraced him tightly, crumpling his armor, and staving in his breastplate.

"Krell," cried Chemosh, "you have saved my sanity!"

The death knight's eyes flared in astonishment.

"My lord?"

"What a fool I have been!" Chemosh declared. "But no more. He will pay for this! I swear by the High God who cast me out of heaven and by Chaos who saved me that Nuitari will pay!"

Releasing Krell and dismissing the other undead with an impatient gesture, Chemosh stared at the image of Mina, still floating before him.

"Give me your sword, Krell," Chemosh ordered, holding out his hand.

The death knight drew his sword from its scabbard and handed it to the god.

Gripping the sword, Chemosh stared for another long moment at the ghost of Mina. Then, sword in hand, he raised it and leapt at the illusion.

The image of Mina vanished.

Chemosh stepped back, thinking out loud. "A remarkable illusion. It fooled even me. But it could not fool you, my dear brother, my excellent friend, Lord Krell!"

"I am glad to have pleased you, my lord." Krell was confused—thankful, but confused. "I don't quite follow you, though—"

"An illusion, Krell! Mina's ghost was an illusion! That is why you could not see her. Mina is not in your realm—the realm of death. Mina is alive, Krell. Alive—and a prisoner."

Chemosh grew grim. "Nuitari lied to me. He did not slay her, as he pretended. He has imprisoned her in his Tower beneath the Blood Sea. Why, though? What is his motive? Does he want her for himself? Did he assume I would forget her, once I thought she was dead? Ah, I see his game. He has probably told her I abandoned her. She would not believe him, though. Mina loves me. She will be true to me. I must go to her. . . ."

He paused.

"What if he has succeeded in seducing her? She is mortal, after all," the god continued, his voice hardening, "This Mina once swore to love and follow Queen Takhisis, only to turn from her to me. Perhaps Mina has turned from me to Nuitari. Perhaps they both plot against me. I might be walking into a trap. . . ."

He whipped around. "Krell!"

"My lord!" The death knight was trying desperately to keep up with the peregrinations of the god's thoughts.

"You say that Zeboim recovered the khas piece containing the soul of her son?" Chemosh asked.

"It wasn't my fault!" Krell said hurriedly. "There was a kender and a giant bug—"

"Quit whining! You actually did something right for a change. I am going to send you on an errand."

Krell didn't like the god's sly smile.

"What errand would that be, my lord?" the death knight asked warily. "Where am I going?"

"To Zeboim—"

Krell clunked down onto his knees. "You might as well finish me now, Lord Chemosh, and get it over with."

"Now, now, Krell," said Chemosh soothingly. He was suddenly in an excellent humor. "The Sea Goddess will be glad to see you. You are going to bring her welcome news—provided she allows you to live long enough to tell it. . . ."

The dwarf and half-elf had been gazing into the dragonmetal basin, both of them sniggering at the sight of Chemosh's lamentations over his "dead" mistress and mocking the Lord of Death, making sport of him as they'd done for many days now, when things began to go terribly wrong.

"He's onto us!" said the dwarf, alarmed.

"No, he's not," said the half-elf, sneering.

"I tell you he's figured it out!" cried the dwarf. "Look there! He's got a sword! End the spell, Caele! Quickly!"

"We're in no danger, Basalt, you coward," said Caele, his lip curling. "What do you think? He's going to leap through time and space and cut off our ears?"

"How do you know he can't?" Basalt roared. "He's a god! Just end it!"

Caele took one look at the god's face—livid with rage, his eyes blazing like the eternal fires of the Abyss—and decided his fellow archmage might be right. The half-elf placed both hands on the heavy dragonmetal basin, dug in his feet, and pushed the basin off the pedestal, dumping the contents onto the floor. Blood sloshed over Caele's bare feet and splattered the black robes of the dwarf.

The god and his sword vanished.

Basalt mopped his face with a black sleeve. "That was close!"

"I still don't think he could have done anything to us," Caele muttered.

"We didn't dare risk it."

Caele thought back on the enormous sword the god had been wielding and was forced to agree. He and Basalt stood in silence staring gloomily at the empty dragonmetal basin and the pool of blood. Both of them were thinking of another god who was going to be angry, a god much closer to home.

"It wasn't our fault," Caele muttered, biting his nails. "We have to make that clear."

"It was only a matter of time before Chemosh discovered the deception," Basalt agreed.

"I'm surprised it lasted this long," Caele added. "He's a god, after all. Be certain to remind the Master of that when you tell him what happened—"

"When *I* tell him!" Basalt glowered.

"Yes, of course, you should tell him," stated the half-elf coolly. "You are the Caretaker, after all. You are the one in charge. I am but your underling. You tell the Master."

"I am the Caretaker of the Tower. *You* were the one tasked with casting the illusion spell. For all I know, it was your fault that Chemosh found out! Perhaps you made a mistake—"

Caele quit biting his nails. His long, thin fingers curled to claws. "Perhaps if you hadn't panicked and ordered me to end the spell prematurely—"

"End the spell! What are you talking about?"

The stern voice came from behind them. The two Black Robes exchanged alarmed glances and then, cringing, both turned to face their master, Nuitari, God of the Black Moon.

Both wizards bowed low. They both wore the Black Robes, symbol of their dedication to Nuitari. Beyond that, the likeness between them ended. Caele was tall and gaunt, with straggling, greasy hair that he rarely bothered to wash. He was half-human, half-elven, and united in his hatred of both races. Basalt, the dwarf, was short and stocky. His black robes were neat and clean, his beard combed. He didn't much like anyone of any race.

Straightening, the two tried to appear at ease, as if they were completely unconscious of the fact they were standing on a stone floor awash in dragon's blood, with the overturned basin of dragonmetal wobbling about at their feet.

The tall Caele looked down his long nose at Basalt, who glared up from beneath his heavy black brows at Caele.

"Tell him," Caele mouthed.

"You tell him," Basalt growled.

"Someone had better tell me, and tell me soon," hissed Nuitari.

"Chemosh discovered the illusion," Basalt said, trying to meet the god's dark and unforgiving eye, and finding it difficult.

"He was coming straight at us," Caele whined, "waving a huge sword. I told Basalt the god couldn't harm us, but the dwarf panicked and insisted on ending the spell—"

"I didn't insist that you upend the basin," snapped Basalt.

"You were the one howling like a wounded wyvern—"

"You were just as scared as I was!"

Nuitari made an abrupt gesture with his hands.

Basalt, quailing, asked in a low voice, "Master, will Chemosh come to free her?"

No need to name which "her" he was talking about.

"Perhaps," said Nuitari. "Unless the Lord of Death is more wise than he is obsessed."

Caele looked sidelong at Basalt, who shrugged.

The god's round moon face with its lidless eyes and full-lipped mouth held no expression. The mages could not tell if he was pleased or displeased, surprised, or alarmed, or simply bored with the whole procedure.

"Clean up the mess," was all Nuitari said before he turned on his heel and walked out.

It took both Caele and Basalt to lift the heavy basin, which was in the shape of a serpentine dragon with the coiled tail forming the bowl, back onto the pedestal. Once the basin was in place, they stared down at the pool spreading across the stone tile floor.

"Should we try to salvage some of the blood?" Basalt asked. Dragon's blood, especially that given by a willing dragon, was an extremely rare and valuable commodity.

Caele shook his head. "It's been tainted now. Besides, the blood loses its potency for spellcasting after forty-eight hours. I doubt the Master will be attempting this spell again any time soon."

"Well, then fetch rags and a bucket and we'll—"

"I may be your underling, Basalt, but I am not your lapdog!" Caele returned angrily. "I do not *fetch*! Get your own rags and bucket. I must inspect the basin to see if it was damaged."

Basalt grunted. The basin was made of dragonmetal. He could have dropped it off the top of the Lords of Doom, and it would land at the bottom without suffering a dent. He knew from experience, however, that he could either spend the next half hour in a bitter argument with Caele that the dwarf would never win, or he could go fetch the rags and bucket himself. The pantry where they kept such mundane objects was located some three levels from where they were standing, a long trek up and down the stairs for the dwarf's short legs. Basalt considered magicking away the spilled blood or conjuring up rags. He rejected both, however, for fear Nuitari would find out.

Nuitari had forbidden his mages from using magic for trivial or frivolous tasks. He maintained that for a mage to use magic to wash his supper dishes was an insult to the gods. Basalt and Caele were expected to do their laundry, catch their food (one reason they had devised the contraption in which they had caught Mina), cook and clean—all without the benefit of spellcasting. Other mages who would eventually come to live in the Tower would have to live under the same restriction. They would be required to perform all such menial tasks with labor that was physical, not magical. Basalt stalked off on his errand, returning with aching calf muscles and in a bad mood.

He came back to find Caele amusing himself by drawing stick figures with his toe in the dragon's blood.

"Here," said Basalt, tossing Caele a rag. "Now that you've inspected the basin, you can clean it."

Caele regretted not having taking advantage of the dwarf's departure to leave. The half-elf had continued to hang about the spellcasting chamber in hopes that Nuitari would return and be impressed to find Caele taking such excellent care of the basin that was one of the god's favorite magical artifacts. Since there was still a chance Nuitari might come back, Caele began to wipe away the remnants of dragon's blood.

"So what did the master mean by Chemosh being wiser than he is obsessed?" asked Basalt. The dwarf was down on his hands and knees, scrubbing vigorously at the stained stone with a bristle brush.

"He's obsessed with this Mina, that much is clear. That's how we were able to perpetrate this fraud on him."

"Something that I never understood anyway," Basalt grumbled.

Caele, mindful that the Master might be in earshot, was effusive in his praise.

"Actually, I consider Nuitari's ploy quite brilliant," said the half-elf. "When we first captured Mina, the Master intended to use the threat of her death as a way to keep Chemosh's mouth shut. Chemosh, you see, had threatened to tell Nuitari's two cousins that he had secretly built this Tower and was trying to establish his own power base independent of them. He threatened to tell all the gods that the Master has in his possession a cache of holy artifacts belonging to each and every one of them."

"But the threat of death didn't work," Basalt pointed out. "Chemosh abandoned Mina to her fate."

"This is where the Master's true brilliance shone," said Caele. "Nuitari killed her as Chemosh watched, or rather, the Master *pretended* to kill her."

Caele waited a moment, hoping Nuitari would enter and thank his faithful follower for the compliments. Nuitari did not come, however, and there was no sign he'd overheard the half-elf's flattering remarks. Caele was growing bored with cleaning. He threw down the rag.

"There, I'm finished."

Basalt stood up to inspect the job. "Finished! When did you start? Look at that. There's blood in the scales around the tail, and in the eyes and teeth, and it's seeped in all these little crevices between the scales—"

"That's just the way the way the light hits it," said Caele carelessly. "But if you don't like it, do it yourself. I have to go study my spells."

"This is precisely the reason why I was made Caretaker!" Basalt told Caele's back as the half-elf was walking out the door. "You are a pig! All elves are pigs."

Caele turned, enmity flickering in his slanted eyes. His fists clenched.

"I've killed men for such insults, dwarf."

"You killed a woman for it, at least," Basalt said. "Strangled her and pushed her off a cliff."

"She got what she deserved and so will you, if you keep talking like that!"

"Like what? You have no love for elves yourself. You say worse than that about them all the time." Basalt polished the basin, working the rag deep into the crevices.

"Since the bitch who gave birth to me was an elf, I can say what I like about them," Caele retorted.

"Fine way to talk about your mother."

"She did her part. She brought me into this world, and she had a good time doing it. At least I *had* a mother. I didn't sprout up in a dark cave like some sort of fungus—"

"You go too far!" Basalt howled.

"Just not far enough!" Caele hissed in fury, his long fingers twitching.

The dwarf threw the rag to the floor. The half-elf forgot about studying his spells. The two glared at each other. The air crackled with magic.

Nuitari, watching from the shadows, smiled. He liked his mages to be combative. It kept the sharp edges honed.

Basalt was half mad. Caele was wholly mad. Nuitari knew that long before he'd brought them to his Tower beneath the Blood Sea. He didn't care, not so long as they were good at their jobs, and both were extremely good, for they'd had years to perfect their gifts.

Due to their long life spans, the half-elf and the dwarf were among the few spellcasters remaining on Krynn who had served the God of the Dark Moon prior to his mother's theft of the world. Both had excellent memories and had retained their knowledge of their spellcraft over the intervening years.

These two were among the first to look into the heavens and see the black moon, and they were among the first to fall down on their knees and offer their services to their god. Nuitari transported them to this Tower on one condition—that they not kill each other. Both the dwarf and the half-elf were exceptionally powerful wizards. A battle between would not only end in the loss to him of two valuable servants, it would probably do serious damage to his newly reconstructed Tower.

Caele—half Kagonesti, half-Ergothian—was prone to violent rages. He'd committed murder before and had no compunctions about doing it again. Having renounced both the human and the elven side of himself, he had left civilization, roaming the wilderness like a savage beast until the return of his magic had made life worth living again. As for Basalt, his use of dark magic had gained him numerous enemies, who, when the gods of magic vanished, were elated to find their foe was suddenly powerless. Basalt had been forced to hide deep underground, where he'd lived in despair for years, mourning the loss of his art. Nuitari had given the dwarf back his life.

Nuitari waited patiently to see the outcome. Such flare-ups were frequent between the two. Their dislike and distrust of each other paled in comparison to their fear of him, however, and thus far, nothing had ever come of their altercations. This confrontation was more tense than usual, for both were nervous and on edge after the encounter with Chemosh. Sparks and spells might have flown, but Nuitari gave a loud cough.

Basalt's head jerked around. Caele's eyes flickered in fear. The magical tension whistled out of the room like the air out of an inflated pig bladder.

Basalt thrust his hands into the sleeves of his robes lest he be tempted to use them. Caele swallowed several times, his jaw working, as though he were literally having to masticate his anger before choking it down.

"You want to know why I went to all this trouble to create this illusion of Mina?" Nuitari asked, entering the room.

"Only if you want to tell us, Master," said Basalt humbly.

"I am intrigued by this Mina," said Nuitari. "I find it hard to believe the death of a mere mortal would have such a shattering effect upon a god, yet Chemosh was nearly destroyed by his grief! What kind of power does this Mina hold over him? I wonder, too, about Mina's relationship with Takhisis. There are rumors the Dark Queen was jealous of this girl. My mother! Jealous of a mortal! Impossible. That's why I ordered you to continue using the illusion spell—to stop Chemosh from coming to Mina's rescue so that we could study her."

"Did you learn anything about her, Master?" Caele asked. "I believe you must have found *my* reports particularly enlightening—"

"I read them," said Nuitari. He had found the reports of Mina's behavior in captivity to be extremely enlightening, especially in one regard, but he wasn't about to tell either of them that. "Now that I have satisfied your curiosity, return to your duties."

Caele grabbed up a rag and began polishing the basin. Basalt rinsed out his rag in water that now had a pinkish tinge to it and got back down on his hands and knees.

When Nuitari's footfalls could no longer be heard echoing through the corridors of the halls of magic, Caele flung his rag into the water bucket.

"You finish. I have my spells to study. If the Lord of Death is on his way to tear down our Tower, I am going to need them."

"Go along then," Basalt said grimly. "You're of no use to me anyway. But wash your feet before you leave this chamber. I don't want to see bloody footprints marking up my clean halls!"

Caele, who never wore shoes, thrust his bare feet into the water bucket. Basalt eyed the dried blood spattered on the half-elf's already filthy robes but said nothing, knowing it would be useless. Basalt considered himself fortunate Caele deigned to wear robes at all. He'd spent years running around the forest naked as a wolf and just as savage.

Caele started out the door, then stopped, turning around. "I've been meaning to ask you. When you were alone with Mina, did she talk to you about becoming a disciple of Chemosh?"

"Yes," said Basalt. "I thumbed my nose at her, of course. What about you?"

"I laughed in her face," said Caele.

The two eyed each other suspiciously.

"I'll be taking my leave now," Caele stated.

"Good riddance," Basalt said, but only to his beard.

Shaking his head, he went back to scrubbing and muttering.

"That Caele is a pig. I don't care who hears me say it. That long nose of his is always stuck in the air. Thinks he's Reorx's balls, he does. Lazy bastard, too. And a liar. Leaves me to do the work and he takes the glory."

The dwarf scrubbed vigorously. "Can't let blood soak into the grout. Leaves a permanent stain. The Master would have my beard. I wonder," Basalt added, sitting back on his haunches and staring after the half-elf, "if Caele really laughed at Mina, or if he took her up on her offer to become one of Chemosh's chosen. Perhaps I should make mention of this to the Master. . . ."

Caele shut himself up in his room and took out a spell book. He did not open it, however, but sat staring at it.

"I wonder if Basalt fell for Mina's lies. I wouldn't put it past him. Dwarves are so gullible. I must remember to inform Nuitari that Basalt might be a traitor. . . ."

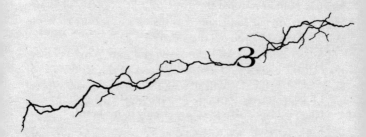

3

The Tower remained standing, undisturbed. Chemosh did not come to tear it down stone by magical stone in order to rescue his beloved mistress.

"Give him time," said Nuitari.

The god had posted himself outside the room in which he kept Mina imprisoned, waiting for the Lord of Death.

More time passed. Mina remained in isolation in her cell, cut off from contact with gods or men, and still her lover did not come to free her.

"I underestimated you, my lord," Nuitari murmured to his unseen foe. "For that, I apologize."

Chemosh would be ecstatic to know the woman he loved was still alive. He would be furious at the deception played upon him. The Lord of Death was not one, apparently, to let either joy or rage rob him of his senses. Chemosh wanted Mina, but he also wanted the powerful holy artifacts Nuitari was keeping under lock and key inside the Tower. The Lord of Death was undoubtedly seeking a way to obtain both.

"What are you doing?" Nuitari asked his fellow god. "Have

you run tattling to the other gods? Are you telling them how big, bad Nuitari restored the Tower of High Sorcery of Istar? How he recovered and claimed as his own a treasure trove of holy artifacts? Did you tell them that?"

Nuitari smiled. "No, I think you did not. Why? Because then all the gods would know the secret of the artifacts and once they all know, they will all want their toys returned. Where would that leave Chemosh? Back in the cold, dark Abyss."

At the end of the Age of Might, the Kingpriest of Istar had decreed that all the holy artifacts of those gods who were not good and righteous gods (as judged by the Kingpriest) were to be confiscated by the Kingpriest's armies of holy warriors. In addition to those that were confiscated, the Kingpriest offered rich rewards for all artifacts deemed to be used for evil purposes. Between the holy warriors, "good" citizens, thieves, and looters, the temples of almost every god on Ansalon was stripped of religious artifacts.

First, people took artifacts that came from the temples of the overtly evil gods—Chemosh and Takhisis, Sargonnas, and Morgion. The temples of the neutral gods were the next to fall victim to the artifact hunters, the claim being made that "any god who is not for us is against us."

Finally, as religious fervor (and greed) spread, holy warriors raided the temples of the Gods of Light, including those of the goddess of healing, Mishakal, for although she was Paladine's consort, Mishakal committed the sin of opening her doors of healing to all mortals, even those who were not deemed worthy of a god's blessing. Her clerics had actually been known to lay healing hands on thieves and prostitutes, kender and dwarves, and even wizards. When the clerics of Majere, god of justice, heard that Mishakal's priests were being beaten and her artifacts stolen, they sought to protest. Their monasteries were then raided. Their artifacts went next.

Soon, the holy artifacts of every god in the pantheon, with the exception of Paladine, were locked up in what had once been the Tower of High Sorcery of Istar but which was now known as *Solio Febalas*, the Hall of Sacrilege. It was whispered that Paladine's priests were starting to grow nervous, and that more than a few had been seen locking up the god's holy relics in their storerooms. But even they were not safe.

When the Cataclysm struck Istar, the Hall of Sacrilege was destroyed in the fire of the gods' wrath. The gods were confident the artifacts had been consumed in the conflagration. They wanted mortals to live on their own for a while.

No one had been more surprised to discover the artifacts intact than Nuitari. His single idea had been to claim the Tower for his own. Finding the artifacts had been a bonus. He knew he could not keep a secret as powerful as this forever. It would be only a matter of time before the other gods discovered the truth and came to him, demanding the artifacts back. The artifacts were in a safe place, guarded both by powerful magical spells and by Midori, an ancient and bad-tempered sea dragon. Such safeguards would keep out mortals; they would not stop a god.

Nuitari didn't have to worry about that.

The gods would stop the gods.

Each god would want his or her own artifacts, of course. Each god would also want to insure that although he got his, no other gods would get theirs.

For example, Mishakal would not want Sargonnas, currently the most powerful God of Darkness, to regain his artifacts. She would seek out allies in her efforts to impede him—unlikely allies, such as Chemosh, who would side with Mishakal in this, for the Lord of Death was locked in a power struggle with Sargonnas and would not want the Horned God growing stronger that he already was. Then there was Gilean, God of the Scales, who might well oppose both the gods of Light and of

Darkness, for fear that the return of these artifacts to any of the gods would upset an already teetering balance.

The sacred fur would really fly when the gods found out Nuitari was in possession of artifacts of Takhisis, the dead Queen of Darkness, and those of the self-exiled god, Paladine. Although their creators were gone, the artifacts remained, as did their holy power, which could be immensely useful to any god or mortal who laid hands on them. The squabbling over these alone might well last for centuries.

Meanwhile, Nuitari's plan was to go about heaven making secret deals, quietly handing over an artifact here and another one there, playing the gods one off the other, all the while strengthening his own position.

Though Nuitari had hated Takhisis and had done his best to oppose her in everything she had ever done, he was like his mother in one regard—he had her dark ambition.

Opposing that ambition were Nuitari's two cousins, Lunitari and Solinari. The gods of White and Red Magic would not give a bent copper for the holy artifacts. The Kingpriest, not trusting wizards or their magic, had not kept any artifacts belonging to wizards. Those magical objects that were found (and there were few, for the wizards had hidden most away) were immediately destroyed. Nuitari's cousins would be furious when they heard he had gone off and built his own Tower. They would be furious—and they would be dismayed, grief-stricken. Since the beginning of time, the gods of the three moons had stood together in unity to guard what was most precious to them—the magic.

The three cousins had no secrets from each other. Until now.

Nuitari felt badly about breaking faith with his cousins, just not badly enough. Ever since his mother, Takhisis, had betrayed him by snatching away the world—his world!—he had determined that from then on he would trust no one. Besides, he had devised the means to appease his cousins. Nothing would be the same between them again, of course. But then, nothing would ever be the same for any of gods. The world—and heaven—had changed forever.

Nuitari wondered what Chemosh was up to, and this brought the god's thoughts back to Mina. Nuitari came here often. Not to question Mina. His Black Robes had been doing that, and they had found out precious little. Nuitari had been content to merely watch her. Now, on impulse (and thinking, too, that Chemosh might yet surprise him), Nuitari decided to interrogate Mina himself.

He had moved her from the crystal cell in which he'd first imprisoned her. The sight of her prowling about had proven to be too distracting for his wizards. He had wrapped her in a magical cocoon of isolation, so she could not communicate with anyone anywhere, and shifted her to a suite of rooms intended as living quarters for the Black Robe archmages who were destined to populate the Tower beneath the Blood Sea.

Mina was lodged in chambers meant for a high-ranking wizard. These consisted of two rooms, a sitting room and study, lined floor to ceiling with bookshelves—and a private bedroom.

She paced her quarters like a caged minotaur, walking the length of the sitting room, going from there into the bedroom, and then retracing her steps into the sitting room. His wizards reported that she sometimes walked like this for hours, walked and walked until she was exhausted. She did nothing else except pace, despite the fact that Nuitari had provided her with books on a variety of subjects, ranging from religious doctrine to poetry, philosophy to mathematics. She never so much as opened a single book, his wizards reported—at least, not that they had observed.

Nuitari had provided other forms of entertainment. A khas board stood on a pedestal in a corner. The pieces were covered with dust. She'd never touched it. She ate little, just enough to keep up her strength for pacing. He was glad he had not gone to the expense of putting down a rug. She would have worn a hole in it.

The God of Dark Magic could have melted through the walls, had he chosen, and taken her by surprise. He decided he would not start off their relationship in such an antagonistic manner and so, removing the powerful wizard lock from the door, he knocked and politely requested permission to enter.

Mina did not pause in her restless pacing. If she glanced at the door, that is as much as she did. Amused, Nuitari opened the door and walked into the room.

Mina did not look up. "Get out and leave me alone. I have answered all your foolish questions I am going to answer, or better yet, tell that Master of yours that I want to see him."

"Your wish is my command, Mina," said Nuitari. "The Master is here."

Mina halted her pacing. She did not cringe or appear the least discomfited. She faced him boldly, defiantly. "Let me go!" she demanded, then she added unexpectedly, her voice low and impassioned, "Or kill me!"

"Kill you?" Nuitari allowed his heavy lidded eyes, which always looked as if they were half-closed, to open. "Has my usage of you been that ill, that you should wish for death?"

"I cannot stand to be confined!" Mina cried, and her gaze roved about the room, as though she would bore through solid rock with her eyes.

She regained mastery of herself in the next moment. Biting her lip and looking as though she regretted her outburst, she added, "You have no right to keep me here."

"No right at all," Nuitari agreed. "But then, I am a god

and I do what I want with mortals, your rights be damned. Though even I don't go about murdering the innocent, as does Chemosh. I have been hearing reports of his Beloved—as he terms them."

"My lord does not murder them. He gives them the gift of life unending," Mina retorted, "lasting youth and beauty. He takes away the fear of death."

"I'll give him credit. He does do that," Nuitari said dryly. "As I understand it, once you're dead, the fear of dying is considerably reduced. At least, that is how you explained it to Basalt and Caele when you tried to seduce them."

Mina kept her gaze level with his, which Nuitari found disconcerting. So few mortals could face him or any god. He wondered, with a flash of irritation, if this chit had been so bold with his mother.

"I told them of Chemosh," Mina said, unapologetic. "That is true."

"Neither Basalt nor Caele took you up on your offer, though, did they?"

"No," Mina admitted. "Their respect and reverence for you is great."

"Let us say they like the power I give them. Most wizards like the power and would be very loath to lose it, even in exchange for 'life unending' which, from what I have observed, is more like death warmed over. I doubt if you'll convert many wizards to the worship of your lord."

"I doubt it myself," said Mina, and she smiled.

Her smile transformed her face, made the amber eyes glow, and Nuitari was drawn to their warm allure. He actually felt himself start to slide into them, felt her warmth congeal around him . . .

He brought himself up with a start and regarded her narrowly. What power did this mortal possess that she could seduce a god with her smile? He'd seen far more attractive mortal females. One of his Black Robes, a wizardess named Ladonna, had been known for her beauty and was far superior in looks to this Mina. Yet there was something about her that, even now, stirred him profoundly.

"Please understand, my lord. I had to try to convert them. It was the only way I could escape."

"Why do you want to leave us, Mina?" Nuitari said, feigning hurt feelings. "Have we mistreated you in any way? Beyond confining you, of course, and that is for your own safety. Basalt and Caele are both, I confess, a little insane. Caele, especially, is not to be trusted, not to mention the fact there are dangerous scrolls and artifacts lying about that could do you harm. I have tried to make your stay as pleasant as possible. You have all these books to read—"

Mina glanced at the shelves and made a dismissive gesture. "I have already read them."

"All of them?" Nuitari regarded her with amusement. "You will forgive me if I don't believe you."

"Choose one," Mina challenged.

Nuitari did so, taking a book off the shelf.

"What is the title?" she asked.

"Draconians: A Study. Can Good Come of Evil?"

"Open to the first page."

Nuitari did so.

Mina began to recite. " 'Scholars have long held that because draconians were created by evil magicks, born of the perverted eggs of good dragons, draconians are evil and will forever remain so, capable of possessing no redeeming qualities. However, a study of a group of draconians who are currently settled in the city of Teyr reveals'—" She stopped. "Do I quote correctly?"

"Word for word," said Nuitari, and he snapped shut the book.

"I read a lot when I was a child at the Citadel," Mina said, and then she frowned, "or I think I must have. I can't really remember reading. All I remember is sunshine, and the waves rushing around my feet, and Goldmoon brushing my hair. . . . Yet I think I must have spent a great deal of time reading, for whenever I pick up a book, I discover I have already read it."

"I'll wager you have not read this one." Nuitari caused a volume to materialize in his hand. "*Spells of Conjuration for the White Robe, Advanced Levels.*"

Mina shrugged. "Why would I want to read it? I have no interest in magic."

"Indulge me," said Nuitari. "Read the first chapter. If you do this for me, I will grant you permission to leave your room for an hour each day. You may walk the halls and corridors of the Tower. Under guard, of course." For your own safety.

Mina eyed him, as though wondering what game he was playing. She reached out her hand.

Nuitari wasn't certain what he expected to gain from this experiment—perhaps nothing more than the pleasure of humbling this young mortal, who was altogether too arrogant and bold for his liking.

"I should warn you," he said, as he handed her the book, "this has a spell on it. . . ."

"What kind of spell?" Mina asked. She took the book from his hands and opened it.

"A spell of warding," said Nuitari, watching in wonder.

He recalled when Caele had picked up this book. The author, a White Robed wizard, had placed a warding enchantment on it, so that only those of the White Robes could use the spells. Caele of the Black Robes had dropped the book with a curse, then spent the next few moments wringing his burned fingers and swearing. He'd sulked for a day and a half over the incident and refused to go back to help Basalt with the unpacking.

A disciple of Chemosh would certainly not be able to handle this book without punishment.

Mina ran her hands over the soft leather binding. She traced with her fingers the title stamped in gold on the cover.

Nuitari wondered if the warding spell had worn off.

Mina opened the book, studied the first page.

"You want me to read this?" she asked, skeptical.

"If you please," said Nuitari.

Shrugging, Mina began to read.

Nuitari was astonished, and he could not remember the last time a mortal had astonished him. She was reading the words of the language of magic, a feat only a trained wizard should be able to do.

Her pronunciation of the words of the spell was flawless. Even after hours of study, White Robed wizards would have stumbled through this spell, and here was Mina, a disciple of Chemosh, with not an ounce of moon-magic in her bones, reading it perfectly the first time. The spidery words should have clogged her mouth, stuck in her throat, burned her tongue. As he listened to her rattle them off in a bored monotone, he regarded her with amazement.

Nuitari might have concluded that Mina was a wizardess in disguise, except for one thing.

She read the spell flawlessly yet without understanding.

So might a human scholar of the elven language read aloud an elven love poem. The human might know and understand and be able to pronounce the words, but only an elf could give the words the delicate shades of meaning the elven author intended. Only a wizard could give these words the life required to cast the spell. Mina knew what she was saying. She just didn't care. Reciting the spell was an exercise to her, nothing more.

Had his mother, Takhisis, taught Mina magic?

Nuitari thought this over and rejected it.

Takhisis detested magic, distrusted it. She would have been well pleased with a world that had no magic in it, for she viewed magic as a threat to her own powers. Takhisis had not taught Mina magic, and she certainly would not have learned to read the language of magic from the mystics of the Citadel of Light. Nor yet from Chemosh.

Strange. Very strange.

Mina halted mid-sentence, looking up at him. "Do you want me to go on? The rest is just more of the same."

"No, that will do," Nuitari said. He took the book from her hands.

"I won the wager. I have an hour of freedom." Mina started toward the door.

"All in good time," Nuitari said, halting her. "I have no one to serve as your escort. Basalt is scrubbing up spilt blood and, as I said, you would find Caele a dangerous companion. I fear you must bear with me a while longer."

Nuitari decided to try another experiment on Mina—an oddity his Black Robes had observed about her. He secretly cast a spell on her. The spell was a simple sleep spell, one of the first learned by the novice mage. Nuitari could have cast it in an eye blink, but he did not want her to have any suspicion that he was working magic on her. Strand by strand, he plied the threads of magic back and forth, back and forth, weaving the spell over her and around her, the magic covering her like a warm blanket. All the while, he kept her engaged in idle conversation, so that she would not notice what he was doing.

"You know nothing of your childhood," he said to her, as he worked his magic. "According to what Basalt wrote, you were found on board an abandoned ship at the age of eight, washed up on the shore of Schallsea Isle near the Citadel of Light. You remember nothing—not your name, not your parents, nor what happened to the ship—"

"That is true," said Mina, frowning. She added impatiently, "I don't see what this has to do with anything."

"Humor me, my dear. You were adopted by Goldmoon, a former follower of Mishakal, who had been the first to bring the worship of the true gods back to the world after the Cataclysm. She was the one who brought the power of the heart into this world during the Fifth Age. Goldmoon was a good woman, a devout woman. She took an interest in you, loved you like a daughter."

He finished his sleep spell and cast it on Mina. Nuitari watched and waited.

Mina tapped her foot on the floor and looked meaningfully at the locked door. "You promised me an hour of freedom," she said.

"All in good time. As a child, you were curious about many things," Nuitari said softly, his wonder and mystification growing. "You were known for asking questions. You were particularly curious about the gods. Why had they left? Where had they gone? Goldmoon mourned the absence of the gods, and because you loved her, you wanted to please her. You told her you would go seeking the gods and bring them back to her— Do you feel at all sleepy?"

She glared at him accusingly. "I cannot sleep, not in this cage. I walk like this half the night trying to wear myself out—"

"You should have told me sooner that you suffered from insomnia," said Nuitari. "I can help."

He reached into the magic, snatching some rose petals from the ethers. As a god, he didn't need spell components to work this magic, but mortals were impressed by them. "I will cast a sleep spell upon you. You should lie down, lest you fall and hurt yourself."

"Don't you dare work your foul magic on me!" Mina cried angrily, striding toward him. "I won't—"

Nuitari tossed the rose petals into the air. They fell down around Mina as he recited the words of the magical sleep spell, the same spell he'd cast on her earlier.

This time, the spell worked. Mina's eyes closed. She swayed where she stood, then collapsed onto the floor. She would have bruised knees and elbows and a bump on her head when she awoke, but then, he'd warned her to lie down.

He knelt beside her, studied her.

She was, to all appearances, fast asleep, wrapped in the spell's enchantment.

He pinched her arm, hard, to see if she was shamming.

She did not awaken.

Nuitari rose to his feet. He cast one more look at Mina, then walked out of the room. He went over again in his mind Basalt's report.

The subject, Mina, is magic-resistant, Basalt had written, *but with this qualification: <u>she is resistant to the magic only if she does not know that magic is being cast upon her!</u>* Basalt had underlined this twice. *If a spell is cast upon her without her knowledge, the magic—even the most powerful—has no effect upon her. However, if she is told in advance a spell is going to be cast upon her, she falls victim to it immediately, without even an attempt to defend herself.*

Basalt concluded by writing, *In several hundred years of practicing magic, I have never before seen a subject behave like this, nor has my fellow wizard.*

Nuitari stood outside Caele's room. Peering through the walls, the god could see Caele lying sprawled on his bed, indulging himself in an afternoon nap. Nuitari knocked on the door and called out the half-elf's name in a peremptory voice. He watched, amused, to see Caele jolt to wakefulness.

Stifling a yawn, Caele opened the door. "Master," he said. "I was just studying my spells—"

"Then you must have them inscribed on the backs of your

eyelids," said Nuitari. "Here, make yourself useful. Take this book back to the library for me."

He tossed the white-bound spellbook of the White Robed wizard at Caele.

Instinctively, Caele caught it.

Blue and yellow sparks leapt off the white binding. Caele yelped and dropped the spell book to the floor. He thrust his burnt fingers into his mouth.

Nuitari grunted. Turning on his heel, he walked off.

This was all very strange.

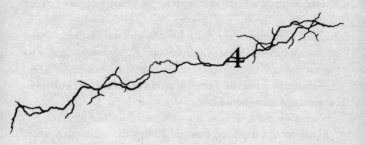

Chemosh stood on the battlements of his cliff-top castle, gazing moodily out at the Blood Sea and thinking of various ways to avenge himself on Nuitari, rescue Mina, steal the Tower, and obtain the valuable artifacts stashed inside. He conceived and then discarded several plans, and after considerable thought, he was forced to admit that the prospect of achieving all of these goals was likely impossible. Nuitari was clever, curse him. In the eternal khas game waged between the gods, Nuitari had anticipated and thwarted Chemosh's every move.

Chemosh watched the waves break on the rock-bound coast. Below those waves Mina languished, trapped inside Nuitari's prison. Chemosh burned with a fierce desire to descend to the ocean floor and march inside and seize her. He avoided the temptation. Chemosh would not give Nuitari the satisfaction of mocking him. He would make Nuitari pay and he would get Mina back. He had yet to figure out how he was going to do this. Nuitari was in complete control of the win.

Almost. There was one piece on the board over which no one had any control. One piece that might give Chemosh the game.

Chemosh was thinking of this plan and that when he noted a wave, larger than the rest, rise up and move rapidly toward shore.

"Krell," he said to the death knight, who was skulking about in obsequious attendance upon his lord, "Zeboim is coming to pay me a visit."

Krell leapt a foot in the air. If steel could have lost color, his helm would have gone white.

Chemosh pointed. "Look at that wave."

Zeboim stood poised gracefully atop the mammoth wave. The water curled underneath her bare feet. Her hair streamed behind her. Sea foam clothed her. She held the wind in her hands and cast it forth as she came. Gusts started to buffet the castle.

"You might try hiding in the wine cellar," suggested Chemosh, "or the treasure vault, or under the bed, if you can fit. I'll keep her occupied. You had best hurry . . ."

Krell needed no urging. He was already running for the stairs, his armor clanking and rattling.

The wave broke over the battlements of Castle Beloved. The torrent of green water, tinged with red, would have drenched the god who stood there, if he had permitted the water to touch him. As it was, the sea swirled about his boots and cascaded down the stairs. He heard a roar and a clatter. Krell had been swept off his feet by the flood.

Zeboim calmly stepped onto the battlements. With a wave of her hand, she banished the sea, sent it back to fling itself in endless fury at the base of the cliff on which he had built his castle.

"To what do I owe the honor of this visit?" Chemosh asked blandly.

"You have my son's soul in your possession!" said Zeboim, her aqua eyes blazing. "Free him—now!"

"I will do so, but I want something in return. Give me Mina," returned Chemosh coolly.

"Do you think I carry your precious mortal around in my pocket?" Zeboim demanded. "I have no idea where your little trollop has gone. Nor do I care."

"You should," Chemosh said. "Your brother is holding Mina against her will. Return Mina to me and I will free your son—if he'll go."

"He will leave," said Zeboim. "He and I had a little talk. He's ready to move on." She thought the deal over. "Give me that wretch Krell"—she ground his name between her teeth—"and we'll call it a bargain."

Chemosh shook his head. "Only if you will give me that annoying monk of Majere. First things first, though. You must restore Mina to me. Your brother has her locked in the Tower of High Sorcery beneath the Blood Sea."

"Rhys Mason is *not* a monk of Majere," cried Zeboim, offended. "He is *my* monk and he is passionately devoted to me. He adores me. He would do anything for me. If it hadn't been for him and his loyal dedication to me, my son would still be a prisoner of that—"

Zeboim paused. Chemosh's last words had just hit her. "What do you mean—Tower of High Sorcery in the *Blood Sea*?" she blazed. "Since when?"

"Since your brother restored the Tower of High Sorcery that was formerly at Istar. His newly built Tower is now at the bottom of the Blood Sea."

Zeboim scoffed. "A Tower in the Blood Sea? *My* sea? Without my permission? You take me for a fool, my lord."

"I'm sorry. I thought you knew." Chemosh feigned surprise. "Brother and sister, so loving and close. He must tell you everything. I assure you, Lady, that your brother, Nuitari, has raised up the Tower that once stood in Istar. He is restoring it to its former glory and he plans to bring Black Robe wizards beneath the ocean to populate it."

Zeboim was struck dumb. Her mouth opened, but no words came out. She glared at Chemosh, convinced he was lying, yet she glanced back uncertainly at the sea that seemed to quiver with her outrage.

"The Tower is not far from here," Chemosh added, gesturing. "A stone's throw. Look to the east. Do you recall where the Maelstrom used to be? About one hundred miles from shore. You can see it from where we stand—"

Zeboim looked beneath the water. Now that it had been pointed out to her, the god was right. She could see a tower.

"How dare he?" Zeboim flared.

Thunder shook the castle walls, causing Krell, cowering at the bottom of a well, to quake in his boots. The impetuous goddess prepared to leap headlong from the battlements.

"We'll see about this!"

"Wait!" Chemosh shouted against the crashing roar of her ire. "What of our bargain?"

"That is true." Zeboim reflected more calmly. "We have business to finish before I shred my brother's eyeballs and feed them to the cat. You will free my son."

"If you free Mina."

"You will give me Krell."

"If you give me the monk."

"And you," said Zeboim haughtily, "you must put an end to these so-called Beloved."

"Am I to be denied disciples?" Chemosh demanded, aggrieved. "I might as well ask you to stop soliciting sailors."

"I do not solicit sailors," Zeboim flared. "They choose to worship me."

The two stood eyeing each other, both of them thinking how to gain what he or she wanted.

Mina will at last be in my grasp, Zeboim reflected. I'll have to turn her over to Chemosh eventually, but for a little while, I can use her to my own advantage.

Should I trust the Sea Witch with Mina? Chemosh asked himself, then thought, reassured, Zeboim does not dare harm her. I will keep her son's soul hostage until we make the trade.

As for Krell, tormenting him has grown to be a bore, Zeboim realized. My monk is far more valuable to me—not to mention entertaining. I will keep him.

Majere is a distinct threat, Chemosh was thinking. Zeboim is a minor irritant. If, as she claims, this meddlesome monk has switched his loyalties from the Mantis God to the Sea Witch, then Rhys Mason no longer poses a threat to me. I know how Zeboim treats her faithful. The poor man will be lucky to survive. And having Krell available to me instead of constantly hiding under the bed will be of considerable advantage.

As for this Tower . . . Zeboim moved on to the next irritant. I'm not surprised at anything that moon-faced little brother of mine would do. He'll pay for his impudence, of course. I'll shake his Tower to ruins! But why is the Lord of Death interested in a Tower of High Sorcery? Why should Chemosh care one way or the other? There's something more here than meets the eye. I must find out what.

So Zeboim didn't know about the Tower. Chemosh considered that interesting. I feared brother and sister were in league. Apparently not. What will she do? What can she do? Nuitari is not someone for even a sister to cross.

The sea rolled, and waves came and went as the two gods viewed this deal from every angle.

Finally, Zeboim said graciously, "I promise Mina will be restored to you. I know how to deal with my brother. Provided, of course, that you free my son's soul in return."

Chemosh was likewise gracious. "I could agree to that. I want

Krell for myself. In return, I give you the monk."

Chemosh is up to something. He is giving in too easily, Zeboim thought, eyeing him.

She is giving in too easily. Zeboim is up to something, Chemosh thought, eyeing her.

Still, thought both, I'm getting the best of this bargain.

Zeboim held out her hand.

Chemosh took her hand and they concluded the deal.

"Bring Mina to me, and I will start your son's soul on its journey to its next bloody conquest," said the Lord of Death.

"I will return with Mina," said Zeboim, "and I will let you know what I find out about this Tower. I'm sure there must be some mistake. My brother would never deceive me."

Liar, thought Chemosh.

"I merely told you as a courtesy," he replied nonchalantly. "What Nuitari does or does not do with his Tower holds no interest for me."

Liar, thought Zeboim.

"Until we meet again, dear friend," she gushed.

"Until we meet again," said Chemosh suavely.

"Ugh, how I hate that wretch!" Zeboim said to herself as she strode across the ocean floor. "I'll make him pay!"

"Conniving witch," Chemosh muttered. "I'll fix her." He raised his voice. "Krell! You can come out now! Mina will soon be restored to us, and when she is, I want to be ready to act."

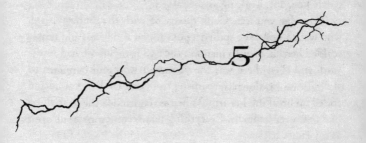

*U*naware his life had been used as a bargaining chip by his goddess, Rhys remained in Solace, as he had promised Gerard. Several days passed after their conversation, during which time Rhys saw very little of the sheriff. Whenever he did run across him, Gerard would always rush past with a wave of his hand and the muttered words, "Can't talk now, but soon. Very soon."

Rhys returned to his work at the inn, where he received a warm welcome from the inn's proprietor.

"I'm glad you're back, Brother," said Laura, wiping her hands on her apron. "We missed you, and not just for cutting up potatoes, either, though no one else around here can cut them into those neat little squares like you do."

"I am pleased to be back," Rhys said.

"You have a way about you, Brother," Laura continued, bustling about the kitchen. She lifted a lid and a gush of spicy steam rolled out of a kettle. She peered into the pot, dipped in a spoon, and shook her head. "Needs more salt. Where was I? Oh, yes. You have a kind of calm that spreads over everyone when you're around, Brother, and evaporates when you're not."

Lifting a ball of bread dough from a crock, she began to deftly knead it, working as she talked.

"The day you left, Cook quarreled with the scullery maid, who was so upset she spilled a pot of ham and beans and nearly scalded herself. Not to mention the two fistfights we had in the yard, and then there was the youngster who took a notion to slide all the way down the banister from tree-level to ground and ended up breaking his arm. When you're here, Brother, nothing like that ever happens. Everything just seems to go as smooth as my lady's backside."

"Oh, dear!" Laura clapped her hand to her mouth and flushed bright red. "I beg your pardon, Brother. I didn't mean to be talking about my lady's backside."

Rhys smiled. "I think you overrate my influence, Mistress Laura. Now, since it is close to supper, I should be starting on those potatoes . . ."

Rhys sliced potatoes and onions, hauled water, and listened sympathetically to Cook's complaints about the scullery maid, then he soothed the scullery maid, who didn't know what she could ever do to please Cook. He enjoyed working in the inn's kitchen. He liked the hectic times, such as dinner and supper, when he was often doing three things at once, working with his sleeves rolled up past the elbow, rushing about with no time to think of anything except worrying that the potatoes were underdone, or that the haunch of meat roasting on a spit over the open fire was cooking unevenly.

When the crowds departed and the doors of the inn closed for the night, Rhys enjoyed the peace and quiet, though there were mountains of crockery to wash, and kettles and pots to scrub, and the floor to sweep, and water to haul, and bread dough to mix so that it could spend the night rising. The simple, homely tasks reminded him of his life at the monastery. His arms elbow-deep in sudsy water, he would wash out ale mugs and reflect on Majere and wonder what the enigmatic god was doing and why he was doing it.

When Rhys ended up breaking a mug, he realized that he was still angry at Majere and that, far from abating, his anger was being fueled by the god's continued stubborn presence in Rhys's life. Like some spoiled and ill-behaved child whose parents persist on coddling him no matter how much he misbehaves, Rhys did not deserve the god's care of him; he felt guilty accepting it when he couldn't return it.

He came to almost resent the emmide. Yesterday he had tried leaving it behind in his room, only to find he felt awkward and uncomfortable without it, almost as if he were walking through Solace naked, and Atta was so bothered by its absence (she kept halting to stare back at him with a puzzled expression), that he eventually gave up and went back to fetch it.

He had other trials of faith. Sometimes Laura would send Rhys to the market to do the daily shopping, if she was too busy to go herself. On his way, he would pass by the street known among the citizens in jest as "God's Row." Here the clerics of the various gods of Krynn were building new temples of worship to welcome back the gods who had long been absent from the world. The temple of Majere was a modest structure located about halfway up the street. Rhys would often see Majere's clerics working in the gardens or walking about the grounds, and he was sorely tempted to enter the temple and thank Majere humbly for his care of his unworthy servant and to ask the god's forgiveness.

Whenever he thought about doing this, whenever his feet started to carry him in that direction, Rhys would see again his brethren lying dead on the floor of the monastery, their bodies twisted in the agonies of their death throes. He would think of his brother and all those his brother had duped and murdered. Even Zeboim—cruel, arrogant, willful, and unreliable as she might be—had done more to help Rhys to find answers to his questions than the good and wise Majere. Rhys would turn away from the temple and return to the business of buying onions.

While Rhys was chopping vegetables and wrestling with his god, Nightshade roamed the streets of Solace, keeping an eye on the Beloved. Atta accompanied the kender, keeping an eye on Nightshade. Atta did not have much work to do to keep the kender honest. Nightshade was particularly inept at the time-honored and much celebrated (among kender, at least) art of "borrowing."

"I'm all thumbs and two left feet," Nightshade would admit quite cheerfully.

He wasn't very good at borrowing because he wasn't all that interested in the things that interested other kender. He wasn't curious enough, he supposed, or rather, he was curious, just not about other people's possessions. He was curious about their souls, especially those souls who had not yet advanced onto the next stage of their life's journey. Nightshade had the ability to communicate with such spirits, be they lost and wandering, angry, unhappy, vengeful, or destructive. He could also, as Rhys had told Gerard, see the Beloved for what they were—walking corpses.

Sometimes, however, the kender's hands would take on a life of their own and start to think for themselves, and then they would find their way into someone's pocket or purse or absent-mindedly stuff a bag of kumquats down the kender's pants' leg or carry off a pie that was reduced to crumbs before Nightshade became conscious of the fact he hadn't paid for it.

Atta had been taught to keep a close watch on the kender, and whenever she saw Nightshade stand too close to anyone or veer off toward the baker's stall, the dog would swiftly interpose her body between that of the kender and the potential victim and herd the kender gently back onto the straight and narrow.

Thus it was that Nightshade was able to steer clear of the sheriff's deputies and concentrate on his search for one of the Beloved in order to set a trap for it.

He was, unfortunately, successful.

Three days after their meeting, at about midafternoon, as Rhys was dicing potatoes, Gerard shoved open the kitchen door and thrust his head inside.

"Brother Rhys?" he called, peering through the steam. "Oh, there you are. If Laura can spare you, I'd be glad of your company."

"Go along, Brother," said Laura. "You've done work enough for six monks this day."

"I will be back in time to help with dinner," Rhys said.

Gerard cleared his throat. "Uh, no, you won't, I'm afraid, Brother."

"We'll make do," Laura said. As Rhys was removing his apron, she frowned at Gerard. "You take care of him, Sheriff."

"Yes, ma'am," said Gerard, fidgeting while Rhys hung up his apron and rolled down his sleeves.

Laura wiped her face with a flour-covered hand. "I've seen you, Sheriff, and my brother, Palin, with your heads together, talking in whispers. You're up to no good, sir, both of you, and I don't want you dragging the Brother here into it."

"No, ma'am," said Gerard. "We'll be careful."

Latching onto Rhys, Gerard hustled him out of the inn.

"Everything's ready," he said, as they hurried down the long flight of stairs. The kender and Atta stood waiting for them at the bottom. "Nightshade's found a candidate. We'll set the trap tonight."

Rhys felt chilled. He would have much preferred being back

at his work in the kitchen. "What does Palin Majere have to do with this?" he asked sharply.

"Well, aside from the fact he's the Lord Mayor of Solace and it was my duty as sheriff to inform him of any danger threatening our city, he is—or was—one of the most powerful sorcerers in Ansalon. Before that he was a White Robe mage. I wanted his advice."

"I've heard he renounced the magic," said Rhys.

"That's true, Brother," Gerard said, adding, with a wink, "but he hasn't renounced those who practice it. Here we are, Nightshade. Where are you taking us?"

"Over to the bridge stairs," said Nightshade. "I'm sorry to tell you this, Sheriff, but he's one of the Vallenwood Guards. You probably know him. His name is Cam."

"Cam! Damnation!" Gerard swore, his brow darkening. "Are you sure?"

Nightshade gave a solemn nod. "I'm sure." He rested his hand on Atta's head. "And so is she."

Gerard swore again. "This is going to be hard!" He frowned at the kender. "I hope to heaven you're wrong."

"I hope so, too, sir," said Nightshade politely, then added in a mutter beneath his breath. "But I know I'm not."

"What is a Vallenwood Guard?" Rhys asked to distract Gerard, who was taking this news very hard.

"They guard the stairs that lead up to the walkways," Gerard explained, pointing overhead to the narrow bridges that ran from tree branch to tree branch. This was a busy time of day and crowds of people were walking the bridges, either going to and from their treetop homes or frequenting the businesses that were built in the trees.

"With the city growing so rapidly, there came to be too many people tromping about on the bridges. They weren't built to carry such a load. Boards came loose and fell down on people's heads. One of the swinging bridges almost collapsed. Several ropes gave way, causing the bridge to sag suddenly. People were hanging on for dear life.

"We decided to limit the number of people who go up there. Either you have to own a house up top, in which case you're given a pass, or you have to prove that you have business up there. The guards man the bottom of the stairs and keep track of who goes up and comes down."

They came within sight of the wooden stairs that led up into the tree branches. Two young men, both wearing green uniforms marked by an embroidered vallenwood leaf on the breast, stood at the base of the stairs, asking people questions, and either allowing them to ascend or sending them on their way.

"That's him," said Nightshade, pointing his finger. "He's one of the Beloved."

"Which one?" Gerard asked, eyeing the kender. "There are two young men standing there. Which one is the Beloved?"

"The one with the red, curly hair and the freckles," Nightshade answered promptly.

"That's Cam, all right," Gerard said with a sigh. "Dammit to the Abyss and back again!"

"I'm sorry," Nightshade said. "He has a really nice smile. He must have been a good guy."

"He is," said Gerard glumly, "or rather, was. What about you, Brother? Can you verify the kender's claim?"

"If Nightshade says he is one of the Beloved, then I take his word for it," Rhys replied.

"What about Atta?" Gerard asked.

They all looked down at the dog. She stood alertly at Rhys's side, and they could all see her gaze was fixed on the red-haired young guard who was chatting and laughing with two girls. A low growl rumbled in her chest. One corner of her lip curled.

"She agrees with Nightshade," said Rhys.

Gerard glowered. "Forgive me, Brother, but you're asking me to trust the word of a kender and the growl of a dog. I'd feel better if I had your opinion. I know young Cam, and I know his parents. They're good people. If I'm going to have to apprehend him, I want to know for sure he's one of these Beloved."

Rhys stood, unmoving. "I am not at all certain I like this, Sheriff. What kind of trap are you proposing we set?"

Gerard didn't answer. Instead he gestured over to where young Cam was talking and laughing with the young women.

"He may be arranging to meet one of those girls this very night, Brother."

Rhys still hesitated, then said, "Take Atta away. If she sees me going near one of the Beloved, she might attack him. I will meet you back at the inn."

When Atta was out of sight, Rhys gripped his staff and walked over to the stairs. He knew what he was going to find. Neither Nightshade nor Atta had ever been wrong before. He walked up to the young man, just as he and the young women burst into laughter.

Seeing Rhys approach, Cam turned from his flirting to attend to his duty.

"Good afternoon, Brother," he said, giving Rhys an engaging smile. "What is your business up top?"

Rhys looked directly into the young man's green eyes.

He saw no light, only shadows—shadows of hope unfulfilled, shadows of a future that would never come to pass.

"Are you unwell, Brother?" asked Cam, placing a solicitous hand on Rhys's arm. "You don't look good. Perhaps you should sit here in the shade and rest. I could bring you some water. . . ."

"Thank you," said Rhys, "but that will not be necessary. I will rest a moment here where it is cool."

Several vendors had put up stalls near the bridge stairs to take advantage of the near-constant traffic. This included an enterprising seller of meat pies, who had set up tables and benches for the convenience of his customers. The two young women with whom Cam was talking were supposed to be selling ribbons from their stall, though at the moment they were doing more giggling than trade.

"Suit yourself, Brother," said Cam, and he turned back to his conversation with the young women.

Ignoring the glares and pointed remarks of the meat pie vendor, who did not like non-paying customers taking up table space, Rhys sat on the bench and listened to the conversation Cam was having with the two girls. He did not need to listen long. One arranged to meet Cam this very night.

Rhys rose to his feet and took his departure, much to the gratification of the meat pie vendor, who bustled over quickly to where the shabby monk had been sitting and dusted off the bench

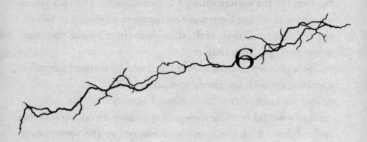

6

Rhys found Gerard and Nightshade standing outside the inn in the company of two people, both of them strangers to Rhys.

"Well, Brother?" Gerard asked.

Rhys had no need to answer. Gerard could tell by the expression on Rhys's face that the news wasn't good. He swore and angrily kicked at a clod of dirt with the toe of his boot.

"The young man arranged to meet one of the young women at a place called Flint's Lookout tonight, an hour after Darkfall," Rhys reported.

"We can discuss business later. You forget that I await the pleasure of an introduction, Sheriff," said one of the two strangers.

"Mistress Jenna, Head of the Conclave of Wizards," said Gerard, "and this gentleman is Dominique Helmsman, Holy Warrior of Kiri-Jolith. Brother Rhys Mason, former monk of Majere."

"*Former* monk?" repeated Mistress Jenna with a quirk of her eyebrow.

A woman in her later years, Mistress Jenna was still alluring, still able to fascinate. Her eyes were large and lustrous; the fine lines around the eyes seemed to fade in the light of their splendor. She was dressed in red velvet robes trimmed with gold and silver. Jewels sparkled on her fingers. The pouches she wore at her waist were made of the finest leather, hand-painted with fanciful flowers and beasts. A very fine emerald hung from a golden chain around her neck. Mistress Jenna was not only one of the most powerful wizards on Ansalon, she was also one of the wealthiest.

"I've never met a 'former' monk of Majere before," she continued archly, "and you must explain why your robes are a rather unusual shade of green."

Rhys bowed but remained silent.

"Brother Mason has found favor in the eyes of Zeboim," said Gerard.

"Not too much favor, I take it," said Mistress Jenna, eyeing Rhys's sea-green robes with amusement.

"You are fortunate in having Zeboim's regard, Brother." Dominique Helmsman stepped forward to hold out his hand. "Far better to have the Sea Witch for you than against you, as my people know well."

Dominique had no need to name his people. His surname, Helmsman, as well as his jet-black skin, proclaimed him an Ergothian, a race of ship-builders and sailors who lived on the island of Ergoth in the western part of Ansalon. Because Ergoth was an island and its people dependent on the sea for their living, the Ergothians built numerous temples to Zeboim and were among the most dedicated of her followers. Thus it was that even an Ergothian Holy Warrior of Kiri-Jolith, god of Light, could proclaim his respect for the dark and capricious goddess of the sea and feel no conflict.

Rhys had heard of these paladins of Kiri-Jolith, god of righteous war, though he had never before met one. Dominique looked to be in his mid-thirties. He was tall and muscular;

his face was handsome, though he seemed somewhat stern and unapproachable, as though he were constantly reflecting on the serious side of life. He wore a brown and white surcoat emblazoned with the head of a bison, the symbol of Kiri-Jolith, over glistening chain mail. His black hair was plaited in a single braid that hung down his back, as was the custom of his people. He carried the longsword that was the sacred weapon of the god buckled around his waist in a scabbard etched with holy symbols. The knight's hand was never far from his sword. By this and other signs (a yelp from Nightshade), Rhys judged the sword to be a holy artifact blessed by the god.

"I am honored to meet you both."

Rhys bowed again to the lady wizardess and then bowed to the holy warrior. Straightening, he stood, staff in hand, looking at them. Atta, well trained, sat quietly at his side. Rhys could see himself in their eyes: a tall, too-thin monk dressed in shabby robes of an unfortunate green color. His only possessions of value: a black and white dog and a plain wooden staff. His only companion: a kender who was sucking dolefully on burned fingers. Nightshade had made the mistake of trying to examine Dominique's holy sword.

Rhys could not blame these two important people for having doubts about him, though they were too polite to show it.

Mistress Jenna broke the silence that was starting to grow uncomfortable.

"This is quite a pretty mystery you have set before us, Brother Rhys Mason. The lord sheriff has told us something about these so-called 'Beloved of Chemosh.' I find his report fascinating, especially the notion they can't be destroyed." She gave a condescending smile. "At least by a monk and a kender mystic."

"I have nothing against mystics," Dominique added in a stern and serious tone, "or against kender. It is just that your powers to deal with the undead are understandably limited."

"He's just mad because I touched his stupid sword," growled Nightshade. He gave the paladin a baleful look. "It's all Atta's fault. She wasn't keeping an eye on me. She was watching them. I don't think she likes either of them, especially the wizardess."

Rhys had noticed that Atta was steering clear of Mistress Jenna. The dog did not growl, as she would have with one of the Beloved, but she pressed close against Rhys's side and kept a suspicious eye on the wizardess.

Mistress Jenna hadn't been meant to overhear, but she proved she had by saying with a shrug, "He's right. She doesn't like me. Dogs take against me, I'm afraid."

"I am sorry, Mistress——" Rhys began.

"Oh, don't apologize!" Jenna smiled. "Most dogs find it difficult to be around wizards. I think it has to do with the spell components we carry: bat guano, newts' eyeballs, dried lizard tails. Dogs don't like the smell. Cats, on the other hand, don't seem to mind. One reason mages tend to use felines as familiars, I suppose."

Gerard cleared his throat. "This is all very interesting, but the two of you have traveled a long distance and there are things we need to discuss——"

"Quite right, Sheriff," said Mistress Jenna briskly. "Let us return to business. We can discuss dogs later. I have a room in the inn. We can talk in far more comfort and privacy there. Brother Mason, if you would lend me your arm to support my feeble steps, I would be grateful."

Mistress Jenna slid her bejeweled hand into the crook of Rhys's elbow. Her steps were no more faltering than Atta's. She was obviously a woman accustomed to being obeyed, however, and Rhys did as she requested.

Mistress Jenna drew Rhys near her and then glanced over her shoulder to see Atta trotting alongside Nightshade.

"Gerard has been touting the praises of this marvelous dog

of yours, Brother. She is trained to herd both sheep and kender, or so I understand."

"Primarily sheep, Mistress," said Rhys with a smile.

"Was she trained to this skill from a puppy?"

"She was born to it, you could say," Rhys replied. "Both her parents were experienced herd dogs."

"The reason I am asking about the dog is not just from idle curiosity. I own a mageware shop in Palanthas and I have such a problem with kender! You can't imagine! I employ a guard, but the expense is considerable and the clever little beasts always seem to outwit him anyway. I was thinking a dog might be far more reliable, and certainly a dog would eat less than this brute I've hired. Would such a thing be possible?"

Jenna seemed serious about her need and truly interested in what Rhys had to say. He guessed this was a woman who could charm the birds out the vallenwoods if she had a mind to do so and not just through the use of her magic. She was also extremely dangerous. As Head of the Conclave of Wizards, Jenna presided over godly magic in Ansalon—magic that had been gone for years with the absence of the gods and had only recently returned. She was a powerful force in this world and he could see that power in her eyes—a flicker of fire smoldering deep beneath a smooth and placid surface, a fire that spoke of deadly battles fought and victories obtained but only at great cost.

Rhys said politely he had no doubt a dog could be trained to handle the job, though—unlike with Gerard—he did not offer to do the training himself. After this subject had been exhausted, while they were ascending the stairs leading to the inn's upper floors, Jenna made her apology.

"I truly did not mean to insult you when I spoke about you and the kender lacking the power to deal with these Beloved, Brother. I fear I offended you."

"Perhaps just a little," he replied.

"I could see that." Jenna patted his arm. "I have a regrettable lack of tact, as I've often been told. Or maybe, like your dog, you don't like the stench of magic."

She cocked an eye at him.

Rhys didn't know what to say. He was confused by the way she seemed to bore into the core of his soul to see what was inside him.

"At any rate," she continued, before he could dredge up some excuse, "I hope you will forgive me. Here is my room. Watch it, Brother!" Jenna said sharply, raising a warding hand. "Don't touch the door handle. You might want to stand back."

Rhys stepped back, narrowly avoiding bumping into Gerard and the paladin, who were coming up the stairs behind him, both so deeply engrossed in their discussion of the notorious outlaw Baron Samuval, who had taken over half of Abanasinia, that neither was paying particular attention to where they were going. Nightshade clumped up after, grumbling about missing his dinner.

They all waited as Jenna spoke some words in the eerie language of magic that Rhys, shut up in his monastery for most of his life, had never before heard. He was reminded of spider's legs, wispy cobwebs and silvery bells. Nightshade stood humming a little tune and looking around in bored fashion. The door glowed briefly a faint blue color then swung open.

"I suppose she thinks that's supposed to impress us," Nightshade said in an aside to Atta. "I could do that—if I wanted to."

The dog, by her look, appeared to share the kender's feelings.

"I always use magic to lock my door," Jenna explained as she ushered them into the room that was the finest the inn had to offer. "Not because I have all that much of value to protect. It's just I'm hopeless about misplacing keys. I am perfectly serious about wanting one of your dogs," she added as Rhys walked past her. "I wasn't just making myself agreeable."

Jenna won Nightshade over by passing around a tray of sweetmeats and offering them their choice of ale or a pale, chilled wine. Once they were settled, with Nightshade penned up in a corner by Atta, everyone turned to Rhys.

"Gerard has told us some of the story, Brother," said the paladin. "But we would like to hear it in your own words."

Rhys told his tale reluctantly. He guessed that neither was going to believe him. He didn't blame them. In their place, he would find his story difficult to swallow. Rhys decided he would not waste time in arguing with them or trying to convince them what he said was the truth. If they scoffed, he'd be on his way. He had to find Lleu. He'd wasted time enough as it was.

Neither Jenna nor Dominique spoke as long as Rhys was talking. Neither interrupted him. Both regarded him with grave attentiveness. At the point when Rhys briefly described the murder of the monks, Dominique murmured a few words, and Rhys realized the paladin was saying a prayer for the souls of Majere's faithful. Dominique frowned when he heard Rhys tell how he had forsaken Majere and shifted his allegiance to Zeboim, but the paladin said no word of reproach.

Rhys deliberately invited Nightshade to offer his own version of events. Rhys had come to value the kender's courage and resolve, and he wanted to make it clear they were friends and partners. Nightshade's tale was lengthy and rambling. He leapfrogged from one thought to another, so that he was occasionally incoherent. Both Jenna and Dominique listened in patience, though sometimes Mistress Jenna was forced to put her hand to her twitching lips to keep from laughing.

When Rhys and Nightshade had no more to tell, the wizardess and the paladin remained silent for a moment. Both looked extremely grave. Gerard said nothing either. He waited for them to speak.

Nightshade fidgeted in his chair, trying to catch Rhys's eye. He jerked his head meaningfully toward the door and mouthed the words, "Let's get out of here!"

Rhys shook his head, and Nightshade heaved a loud sigh and kicked at the rungs of his chair with his heels.

"Well, Brother," said Jenna after a moment, "that is quite a story."

Rhys inclined his head but did not comment.

Nightshade cleared his throat and said loudly, "Say, I smell pork chops. Does anyone else smell pork chops?"

Gerard sat forward. "We believe we have located one of these Beloved. What I propose is that we arrange to set a trap for him—"

"For 'it,'" Dominique corrected. "These Beloved are shells of flesh, nothing more. The soul has managed to escape, or so I devoutly hope and pray."

"*It*, then," Gerard said grimly, remembering that "it" had been a friend. "We will set a trap for it. We must try to take Cam unawares, question him—it."

Jenna was skeptical. "We can *try* to interrogate the Beloved, but I don't think we'll find out anything worthwhile. As the paladin says, the soul has departed. This is nothing more than a mindless slave of Chemosh. If left alive, it will commit more heinous crimes in the name of the Lord of Undeath. I think we should destroy it."

"I agree," said Dominique firmly. "Though from what Brother Rhys has told us, destroying it may not be easy."

Rhys looked from one to the other in astonishment that warmed to a feeling of overwhelming relief. They believed him. He had been fighting this terrible battle with only two friends—a dog and a kender—to aid him. Now he had allies, formidable allies. Now he could share at least part of this unbearably heavy burden.

When Gerard asked for Rhys's opinion, Rhys could not immediately answer. At last he said, his voice husky, "I am afraid I agree with them, Sheriff. I know that this Cam is known to you, but the paladin of Kiri-Jolith is right. This being is not the young man you knew. It is a mindless, soulless monster that will kill again if not stopped."

"That's all very easy for you three to say, but I can't be going about murdering the citizens of Solace!" Gerard exclaimed wrathfully. "The townsfolk would be up in arms if I let a wizard roast poor Cam to cinders or a paladin stick a holy sword through him! People won't see him as a monster. They'll see Cam—the kid who won the sack race at the fair last year! Damn it, I need to be able to talk to him. I need proof he is one of the Beloved. I would think you two would want proof, as well. I mean, we all trust Brother Rhys, but—"

Mistress Jenna raised her hand.

"I understand, Sheriff," she said mildly. "If you need us to capture this thing alive, we will do our best to capture it."

She exchanged glances with Dominique, as much to say they must humor the poor man, then she continued smoothly, "What is your plan for this trap, Sheriff?"

"I was thinking of detaining him on his way home from work, then take him to my office where we could all have a talk."

"That is far too dangerous, Sheriff," protested Dominique. "Not only for yourself, but for innocent bystanders. We have no idea what havoc this thing could wreak if it felt cornered."

Gerard sighed and ran his hand through his yellow hair, causing it to resemble a stand of corn after a high wind. "Well, what do you suggest, sir?" he asked glumly.

"I have an idea," said Rhys. "The Beloved arranged to meet

this girl at a place known locally as 'Flint's Lookout.' This is located outside of Solace, just off the main road leading into town. It's the highest point for miles around with a good view of the city. We could wait for the Beloved there. Few people travel the road after nightfall. It's isolated and a safe distance from town."

Mistress Jenna was nodding her head.

"A good plan," said Dominique.

Gerard glanced around at them. "I want to make one thing clear. You give me a chance to talk to Cam first, alone. Agreed?"

"Agreed," said Mistress Jenna, rather too readily, or so Rhys thought. "I, for one, would be interested to hear what one of these creatures has to say."

Gerard grunted. Though bringing these two to Solace had been his idea, he was clearly not happy with any of this. They arranged a meeting time, then Mistress Jenna, rising, politely indicated it was time to leave.

"I have spells to study," she said, adding, with an apologetic glance at Gerard, "Just in case."

"And I have evening prayers at the temple," said Dominique.

"And I have pork chops in the kitchen!" cried Nightshade happily.

The kender was the first out the door and down the stairs. Atta, after a glance at Rhys, received permission to accompany him. The paladin followed, and Mistress Jenna closed and locked her door, leaving Gerard and Rhys alone together.

"I really hate this!" Gerard muttered. "I know—I brought these two here to help stop these Beloved, but I didn't know it would be Cam! I've watched that kid grow up. When I was posted here before the War of Souls, Cam was always hanging around the barracks. All he could talk about was wanting to be a knight. I taught him how to use a sword. They can say all they want about this monster not being him, but it has his smile, his laugh—"

Gerard stopped his ranting. He looked at Rhys, gave a rueful sigh, and ran his hand through his hair again.

"You are in a difficult position, Sheriff," Rhys said quietly. "I will do what I can to help you."

"Thanks, Brother," Gerard said gratefully. "You know, sometimes I wish I'd been born a kender. No worries. No cares. No responsibilities. Nothing but pork chops. See you tonight, Brother. I'd ask you to say a prayer, but we're up to our eyeballs in gods as it is."

He ran down the stairs, hastening off on his own business. Rhys followed more slowly. He thought regretfully of that feeling of relief he'd experienced.

It hadn't lasted long.

_F_lint's Lookout was located atop a hill overlooking Solace. Gerard and his team assembled near the boulder where, according to local legend, the famed Hero of the Lance, Flint Fireforge, had stopped to rest on the momentous night when a Plainswoman and a blue crystal staff had brought word of the return of the true gods, and the War of the Lance had begun.

The view was spectacular. Smoke from cook fires drifted lazily into the air. The sun's dying rays glinted orange off Crystalmir Lake and sparkled in the diamond-paned windows of the Inn of the Last Home, one of the few buildings visible through the thick foliage of the vallenwood trees.

"It is lovely," said Mistress Jenna, looking about. "So peaceful and quiet. The past seems very close here. One could almost expect the old dwarf to come walking over the hillside, along with his friend the kender. They would have more right to be here than we do."

"We have problems enough with undead without you conjuring up more ghosts, Mistress," said Gerard. He meant it as a jest, but in the tense atmosphere, it fell flat. No one laughed. "We better take our places before night falls."

They left the road and the old dwarf's boulder and entered the outskirts of the forest that blanketed the hillside. They walked among firs and oaks, maples and walnuts, coming to a halt when Gerard deemed they couldn't be seen from the road, yet the road was still in sight.

"We have some time before Cam is due to come," Gerard said.

He had made the walk in grim and somber silence, punctuated occasionally by soft, inward sighs. Rhys's heart ached for his friend, but he knew only too well there was nothing he could say that would bring any comfort.

"I brought a blanket to keep off the damp." Gerard unrolled a blanket and spread it on a bed of dead pine needles. "We might as well be comfortable while we wait."

He gestured to the blanket with bluff gallantry. "Mistress Jenna, please be seated."

"Thank you, Sheriff," Jenna replied with a smile. "But I am not as limber as I was in my twenties. If I sat down on that blanket, it would take three gully dwarves and a gnomish infernal device to hoist me onto my feet again. If no one has any objections, I will commandeer this tree trunk."

Seating herself on the stump of an oak tree, Jenna smoothed out the skirts of her robe and carefully placed a lantern she had brought with her on the ground at her feet. The lantern was small and delicate, made of hand-blown glass set in silver wrought in intricate filigree. Inside, a red candle burned with a blue-white flame.

"I see you admire my lantern, Brother," said Jenna, noting Rhys regarding the lantern with frank curiosity. "You have an eye for beauty. And for value. The lantern is very old. It dates back to the time of the Kingpriests."

"It is lovely," Rhys agreed. "More lovely than useful, it would seem. It gives only a feeble light."

"It is not meant to illuminate the darkness, Brother." Jenna chuckled. "It shields the flame that I use for my magic. The lantern itself is magical, you see. Even this small bit of candle, once placed inside the lantern, will burn for hours on end. The flame cannot be blown out or doused, not even if I was caught in a cyclone or had fallen into the sea. You can take a closer look, Brother. Pick it up, if you want. It won't bite."

Rhys squatted down. Despite what she said, he did not presume to try to touch it. "A relic dating back to the Third Age must be of immense value."

"If I sold it, I could probably buy half of Solace with the proceeds," stated Jenna.

Rhys looked up at her. "Yet you risk such a valuable artifact here this night."

Jenna regarded him intently. He noted how the fine lines around her eyes had a way of intensifying her gaze, concentrating it, like sunlight shining through a prism.

"Either you do not understand the serious nature of this threat, Brother, or you imagine that I do not," she said briskly. "I am not here as Jenna, a long-time friend of Palin Majere. I am here in my capacity as Head of the Conclave of Wizards. I will be making a full report to the Conclave immediately upon my return, for we must determine the best way to deal with this crisis. The same is true of our holy paladin. He will be making reports to the priests and clerics of all the gods of Light, as well as the assembled Council of the Knights of Solamnia. This is not a kender outing for us, Brother. Dominique and I have come armed for battle. We carry with us the best weapons we have at our disposal."

"I am sorry, Mistress," Rhys said quietly. "I meant no disrespect."

He should be grateful. This was what he'd wanted, yet now he was filled with unease. On one hand, he was thankful that at last the world would know of this threat. On the other, fear could lead to inquisitions, torture, persecutions of the innocent. The cure might be far worse than the disease.

"For good or ill, the matter is out of your hands now, Brother," said Mistress Jenna, guessing his thoughts. "Oh, no you don't, sir!"

She plucked away a small hand, belonging to Nightshade, as it was reaching for the lantern. "Look over yonder. I believe I see a poltergeist wandering about the base of that oak tree."

"A poltergeist?" Nightshade said eagerly. "Where?"

"Over there." Jenna pointed. "No, more to the left."

Nightshade hastened off in pursuit, Atta following along dubiously at his heels.

Jenna turned back to Rhys. "You must promise to keep that kender as far from me as humanly possible. By the way, can he really talk to dead people?"

"Yes, Mistress. I have seen him myself."

"Remarkable. You must bring him to Palanthas some time for a visit. There are several dead people I would like to contact. One of them had in his possession a spellbook reputed to have been written by my father, Justarius. I tried to buy it from him, but the old fool said he'd take it to his grave before he sold it to me. Apparently he did, because I searched his house after his death and could not find it."

Jenna glanced into the sky. "Lunitari will be full this night. Excellent for spellcasting." She fixed her prism-eyes upon Rhys. Her expression was serious, her tone grave. "The paladin and I will handle the Beloved, Brother. You watch over our friend the Sheriff."

She glanced at Gerard as she spoke. "He must not be allowed to interfere with our work. If he does, I won't be responsible for the consequences. Now leave me, Brother. I want to go over my spells one final time."

She closed her eyes and clasped her hands in her lap.

"No sign of a poltergeist," said Nightshade, returning, disappointed.

Rhys steered the kender away from both Mistress Jenna and Dominique, not that the paladin would have noticed a hundred kender. Dominique was with them in body, not in spirit. Accoutered in full plate armor, and steel helm, he wore the tabard marked by the symbol of Kiri-Jolith. He knelt on the ground, his sword before him. His eyes shone with holy fervor as he murmured the words of a prayer, asking his god for strength in the hour of trial about to come.

The chill evening wind blew down from the mountains, picking up dry leaves and sending them rustling and skittering along the deserted road. That same chill wind blew through the emptiness of Rhys's soul as he watched the knight pray.

"There was a time when I knew faith like that," he said to himself softly.

A follower of Zeboim, he should be calling upon his goddess for help in his own hour of trial. He did not think the lady would much approve of his companions, however, so he did not bother her. His task, as he saw it, was to make certain everyone came out of this relatively unscathed, including—for Gerard's sake—the wretched thing that had once been a fun-loving, good-hearted young man.

Gerard prowled restlessly beneath the trees, keeping watch down the road. He remained some distance from the rest of the group, making it clear he did not want company. Rhys looked back to see Nightshade creeping up again to stare at the lantern, and he hurriedly suggested that he and Atta and the kender play a game of "Rock, Cloth, Knife."

Nightshade had recently taught Atta how to play this game that required each player to choose in three turns whether he was "rock" (closed fist), "cloth" (open fist) or "knife" (two fingers). The winner was determined by the following: Rock crushed knife. Cloth covered rock. Knife cut cloth.

Atta would place her paw on the kender's knee and Nightshade would interpret this action to be whatever he thought she meant, so that by turns Atta might be "cloth" which covered the rock or "knife" which cut cloth.

"Everyone's so serious," Nightshade remarked. "Atta has knife, Rhys. You have cloth, so you lose. I have rock, Atta. You lose, too. I'm sorry. Maybe you'll win next time." He gave the dog a pat to soothe her wounded feelings. "I've seen livelier gatherings in graveyards. Do you really believe they're going to be able to kill it?"

"Hush, keep your voice down," Rhys cautioned, with a glance at Gerard. "We've both fought the Beloved before. What do you think of their chances?"

Nightshade pondered. "I know the wizardess doesn't put much store in my spellcasting, and that holy warrior looked sideways at your staff. If you want my opinion, I don't think they're going to do much better. Atta! You won! Dishcloth beats both of us!"

The sun had set. The sky was lit with pale yellow that melted into shimmering blue, deepening to starlit black over the mountains. The red moon glimmered orange in the afterglow. The small flame from Jenna's lantern seemed far brighter now that darkness surrounded them.

Jenna sat quite still, her eyes closed, her hands making elaborate motions as she rehearsed her spellcasting. Dominique had finished his prayer. He rose stiffly from his kneeling position and reverently sheathed his sword.

The night's stillness was broken by Gerard.

"Cam's on his way up here! Nightshade! I need you! Come with me. No, the dog stays here."

Nightshade jumped to his feet and went off with Gerard.

Rhys stood up. A word and touch upon her head kept Atta at his side.

Her expression calm, concentrated, Mistress Jenna moved from beneath the tree branches into a patch of red moonlight. She lifted her face to the moon and smiled, as though basking in its blessed rays. Dominique walked over near her and whispered something. Jenna nodded silently in agreement. Reaching into one of her pouches, she drew out an object and clasped it in her hand. Dominique walked off to take up a position some distance from her, yet keeping her within sight.

The two had secretly formed their own strategy, Rhys realized, one they had probably not bothered to discuss with Gerard.

Rhys clasped his emmide tightly.

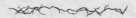

Gerard and Nightshade stood together by the boulder.

"There he is," said Gerard, and he put his hand on Nightshade's shoulder.

A young man was walking energetically up the hill. There was no mistaking him, for he carried a torch to light his way and the firelight shone brightly on his red hair.

"Take a good look at him, Nightshade," said Gerard. "A good look *inside* him."

"I'm sorry, Sheriff," said Nightshade. "I know what you want me to see, but I don't. There's nothing inside him. Not anymore."

Gerard's shoulders slumped. "All right. Go back and stay with Rhys."

"I can help you talk to him," Nightshade offered, feeling sorry for his friend. "I'm good at talking to dead people."

"Just . . . go back," Gerard ordered. A nerve in his jaw twitched.

Nightshade ran off.

"Cam is on his way," he reported, adding sadly, "They don't come much deader."

Jenna and Dominique exchanged glances.

"Nightshade," Rhys said, leaning down to whisper into the kender's ear, "I'm going to join Gerard."

"I'll come with you—"

"No," said Rhys. His gaze went to Jenna and the paladin. "I think you should stay here."

Dominique placed his hand on the hilt of his sword, partially drawing it from its scabbard. The weapon began to shine with an eerie white light.

"You're right. I still have blisters on my fingers." Nightshade peered into the tree branches. "I'll have a great view of the action from up there, and I can still cast my spells, if you need me. Give me a boost, will you?"

Rhys hoisted the kender into the lower branches of the walnut tree. Nightshade scrambled from limb to limb and was soon lost to sight.

Rhys walked softly, moving without sound through the shadows. Atta padded along beside him, her white patches of fur taking on a pinkish color in the red moonlight. Neither Jenna nor Dominique paid any attention to him.

"Here, Brother, take the torch," said Gerard, handing Rhys the flaring light. "Now, back off."

"I think I should stay with you," said Rhys.

"I said back off, Monk!" Gerard flared. "He's my friend. I'll handle this."

Rhys had serious misgivings, but he did as he was ordered, walking back to stand in the shadows.

"Who's there?" Cam called, holding up his torch. "Sheriff? Is that you?"

"It's me, Cam," said Gerard.

"What in the Abyss are you doing here?" Cam demanded.

"Waiting for you."

"Why? I'm off-duty now. I'm free to do what I please," Cam returned, irritated. "If you must know, I'm meeting someone here, a young lady. So I'll just bid you a good-night, Sheriff—"

"Jenny's not coming, Cam," said Gerard quietly. "I told her father and mother about you."

"Told them what?" Cam challenged.

"That you took an oath to Chemosh, the Lord of Death."

"What if I did?" Cam demanded. "Solace is a free city, or so that old fart of a Mayor keeps saying. I can worship any god I choose—"

"Unbutton your shirt for me, son," said Gerard.

"My shirt?" Cam laughed. "What's my shirt go to do with anything?"

"Humor me," said Gerard.

"Humor yourself," said Cam rudely. Turning, the young man started to walk away.

Gerard reached out, seized hold of Cam's shirt and gave it a sharp yank.

Cam whipped around, his freckled face contorted in fury, his fists clenched. His shirt placket gaped open.

"What's that?" Gerard asked, pointing.

Cam glanced down at a burn mark on his left breast. He smiled, then touched it reverently with his fingers. He looked back at Gerard.

"Mina's kiss," Cam said softly.

Gerard started. "Mina! How do you know Mina?"

'I don't, but I see her face all the time. That's what we call the mark of her love for us. Mina's Kiss."

"Cam," said Gerard, his expression grave. "Son, you're in a lot of trouble, more trouble than you can ever imagine. I want to help—"

"No, you don't." Cam snarled. "You want to stop me."

Rhys had heard those words before, or something very like them.

He was going to try to stop me. . . . Lleu's words, spoken as his brother stood over the corpse of the Master. Then there was poor Lucy's husband, hacked to bits. Maybe he had wanted to stop her.

"Now listen to me, Cam—"

"Gerard!" Rhys cried. "Look out!"

His warning came to late. Cam lunged, hands reaching for Gerard's throat.

The attack caught Gerard completely off-guard. He fumbled for his sword, but he did not have time to draw it before the hands of the young man closed with bone-crushing strength around his neck.

Calling upon Kiri-Jolith, Dominique ran to the sheriff's rescue. His sword flared with holy zeal. Rhys was running, too, but the Beloved possessed a grip that was as strong as death and as unrelenting. Gerard would be dead, his windpipe crushed, before either Dominique or Rhys could reach him.

A small black and white furry body dashed past Rhys. Atta launched herself into the air and flung herself at the grappling men. She crashed into them bodily, knocking both Cam and Gerard to the ground, jarring loose Cam's hold on his victim.

Gerard rolled over on his back, gasping for air.

Cam fought with the dog, who was attacking him viciously, her snapping teeth going for his jugular.

"Monk, call off your dog!" Dominique cried.

"Atta!" Rhys yelled. "To me!"

The dog was in a red rage, intent on the kill. The blood of the wolf that had been her distant ancestor pounded in her ears, drowning out her master's command.

Cam seized hold of Atta by the scruff of her neck, wrenched

her off him. He twisted her neck, then flung her limp body away.

Rhys couldn't leave Gerard, who was gasping for breath. Rhys looked back in agony at Atta. He could not see her very well, for she lay outside the light of his torch. She didn't appear to be moving.

There was a rustle of leaves and a crashing sound, and Nightshade tumbled down from his perch amidst the branches.

"She's hurt pretty bad, but I'll take care of her, Rhys!" the kender called with a catch in his voice.

He took Atta into his arms, and with tears running down his cheeks, began to croon to her softly, rocking her back and forth.

Rhys wrenched his gaze from his dog to the confrontation between Dominique and the Beloved. Cam had managed to regain his feet with amazing speed. His throat was slashed half-open, but only a small amount of blood oozed from the wounds.

He grinned at the paladin.

"What are you supposed to be? Huma's ghost?"

Dominique brought forth a holy medallion he wore around his neck. He held it up in front of Cam.

"In the name of Kiri-Jolith, I call upon you to return to the Abyss from whence you came!"

"I don't come from the Abyss," said Cam. "I come from Solace, and get that thing out of my face!"

He knocked aside Dominique's hand, sending the holy medallion flying out of the paladin's grasp.

Coolly and calmly, Dominique plunged his sword in Cam's breastbone.

Cam gave a strangled cry. He stared in disbelief at the sword that was buried in his chest up to the hilt.

Dominique yanked out the blood-smeared blade. Cam's legs

buckled. He fell to his knees, then toppled forward and lay unmoving.

"Blessed be Kiri-Jolith," Dominique said reverently, and started to sheathe his sword.

Cam lifted his head.

"Hey, there, Huma. You missed!"

Dominique staggered backward, nearly dropping his blade in astonishment. Recovering himself, he leaped at the Beloved and brought down his sword in a slashing arc of white fire. The blow severed Cam's head from his neck.

The body lay twitching on the ground. The head rolled a short distance away, ended up facing Gerard.

The Sheriff had managed to regain his breath.

"Cam, I'm sorry—" Gerard began then gasped in horror.

One of the eyes in the severed head winked at him.

The mouth opened and laughed. The headless body rose up on its hands and knees and began to crawl toward the severed head.

Gerard made a gargling sound. "Oh, gods!" he gasped, his throat raw. "Kill it! Kill it!"

Dominique stared at the grotesque corpse wriggling on the ground. He lifted his sword to strike it again.

"Get out of my way!" Jenna cried. "All of you!"

Rhys took hold of Gerard. Dominique joined him, and between them, they half-carried, half-dragged the sheriff deeper into the forest.

Jenna held a glittering orange gemstone in one hand and the burning red candle in the other. She began to chant the words of magic.

As Rhys watched, mesmerized, the candle flame grew larger and larger and brighter and brighter, until it blazed with such fierce intensity that the light made his eyes water.

By the brilliant light, he saw a grotesque sight. The arms of the corpse lifted up the severed head and affixed it back on the neck. Head and body melded together into one. Cam, looking much the same as always, except for a blood-spattered shirt, started walking toward them.

Jenna gave a cry and pointed at the Beloved.

A globe of light leaped from the candle, blazed through the darkness, and smote the Beloved.

Cam cried out and shut his eyes against the glare. He fell once again to his knees and remained crouched there, one hand covering his eyes, the other stretched out as though trying to fend off the spell.

He remained in that attitude, unmoving, his eyes shut against the glare until Jenna gave a gasp and sank, exhausted, to her knees. The bright light vanished, as though an immense breath had blown it out, leaving them in darkness so deep that Rhys was effectively blinded.

From out of the darkness came Cam's voice.

"I guess I'll be going now, Sheriff, unless you've brought along someone else who wants to try to kill me. . . ."

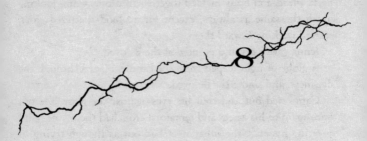

8

Gerard shook off Rhys's attempts to restrain him and staggered to his feet.

"I may not be able to destroy you—or what's left of you," Gerard gasped, barely able to talk. "But I'll set a watch on you day and night. You won't hurt anyone else, at least not in Solace."

Cam shrugged. "Like I said, I'm leaving anyway. Nothing for me around here anymore."

His gaze swept the assembled group. "You have witnessed the power of Chemosh. Take this message back to your wizards and your holy paladins: I *can* be destroyed, but the cost of my destruction will be so great that none of you will have the stomach to pay it."

Cam gave a grin and a cheerful wave, then turned and left them. He did not take the road back into town but headed east.

"Do something, Paladin!" Gerard cried angrily. "Say a prayer! Throw holy water on it. Do something!"

"I have done all I can, sir," Dominique replied. "Hand me the torch."

He held the torch over the area where trampled and bloody grass marked the fight with the Beloved, and began searching. Finding what he sought, he picked up the holy medallion the Beloved had knocked from his grasp.

Dominique regarded it thoughtfully, then shook his head. "I can feel my god's rage. I can also feel his impotence."

Rhys knelt beside Jenna, who was crouched on her knees, staring in disbelief at the place where the Beloved had been standing.

"Are you all right, Mistress?" Rhys asked in concern.

"That spell should have reduced it to ashes," said Jenna, sounding dazed. "Instead . . ."

She held out her hand. A fine sifting of ash, which had once been the orange gemstone, drifted through her fingers and fell to the ground next to a puddle of red wax—all that was left of her candle. A thin trail of smoke spiraled up from the blackened remnants of the wick.

"You've burned your palm," said Rhys.

"It is nothing," Jenna returned, sliding her sleeve hurriedly over her hand. "Give me your aid, Brother. Help me up. Thank you. I am fine. Go see to your poor dog."

Rhys needed no urging. He hastened over to where Nightshade sat beneath the tree, holding fast to Atta. The dog was very still. Her eyes were closed.

Tears trickled down Nightshade's cheeks.

His heart constricting in pain, Rhys knelt down. He reached out his hand to stroke her.

Atta stirred in the kender's arms, lifted her head and opened her eyes. Her tail wagged feebly.

"I brought her back, Rhys!" said Nightshade in a tear-choked voice. "She wasn't breathing, and she'd been so brave, and she tried her best to kill that thing, and I couldn't bear to think of losing her!"

He had to stop a moment to swallow some tears. Rhys's own tears were sliding down his face.

"I thought of all this, and how she and I shared a pork chop tonight, except that I didn't really mean to share. I dropped it and she's quick, when it comes to pork chops. Anyway, all this was in my heart and I said that little spell my parents taught me—the one I used to make you feel better that time we fought your brother. Everything that was in my heart just sort of overflowed and spilled out onto Atta. She gave a snuffle and then a snort. Then she opened her mouth and yawned, and then she licked my face. I think I must have some pork chop grease left on my chin."

Rhys's own heart was so full that he could not speak. He tried, but no words would come.

"I'm so glad she's not dead," continued Nightshade, hugging Atta, who was scrubbing his face. "Who would keep me out of trouble?"

Atta wriggled out of Nightshade's arms. Shaking herself all over, she sat down on Rhys's foot, looking up at him and wagging her tail wildly. The kender stood and brushed himself off, then wiped away tears and dog slobber. He looked up to find Mistress Jenna standing in front of him, regarding him with wonder.

She held out her hand—first removing all her rings.

"I apologize, Nightshade, for casting aspersions on you earlier," Jenna said gravely. "I want to shake your hand. You are the only one whose spell worked this night."

"Thank you, Mistress Jenna, and don't worry about those aspersions you cast," Nightshade assured her. "None of them hit me. I was up in the tree. As for *your* spell, it was a doozy! I still see blue spots dancing around in my eyes."

"Blue spots. That was all it was good for," Jenna said ruefully. "I've used that spell against undead more times than I can count. It has never before failed me."

"At least the Beloved admits that it can be destroyed," Rhys said in thoughtful tones.

"Yeah," Gerard muttered. "At a cost so great none of us will be able to stomach it."

"Of course there is a way to destroy it. Chemosh may promise unending life, but not even he can grant immortality," Dominique stated.

"Why tell us then?" Jenna asked, frustrated. "Why not keep us in the dark?"

"The god hopes to frighten us from pursuing the matter," Dominique surmised.

"He's taunting us," said Gerard, wincing as he massaged his sore neck. "Like a murderer who deliberately leaves a clue near the body."

Mistress Jenna did not appear satisfied with these answers. "What do you think, Brother?"

"The god knows that his secret has been revealed. From now on, every wizard and cleric in Ansalon will be looking for these Beloved. Word will spread. Panic will set in. Neighbor will accuse neighbor. Parents will turn on their children. The only way to prove a person is innocent will be to kill him. If he stays dead, he is not one of the Beloved. The cost of destroying these creatures will be high indeed."

"And Chemosh gains more souls," Nightshade added. "That's pretty smart."

"I think you underestimate us, Brother," said Dominique, frowning. "We will see to it that no innocents suffer."

"Like your god's clerics did in the days of the Kingpriest?" said Mistress Jenna sharply. "I daresay we wizards will be among the first to be accused! We always are."

"Mistress Jenna," said Dominique stiffly, "I assure you that we will be working in close contact with our brethren in the Towers."

Jenna eyed him, then sighed. "Never mind me. I'm just tired, and I have a long night ahead of me." She began sliding her rings back on her fingers. "I must return to the Conclave to make my report. It was good meeting you, Rhys Mason, *former* monk of Majere."

She laid emphasis on that word. Her eyes, shining in Lunatari's red light, seemed to challenge him.

Rhys did not take up her challenge. He did not ask her what she meant. He feared her mocking reply. At least, that's what he told himself.

"You, too, Nightshade. May your pouches always be full and jail cells always be empty. Dominique, my friend, I am sorry I spoke with such ill will. We will be in contact. Sheriff Gerard, thank you for bringing this terrible matter to my attention. Finally, farewell to you, Lady Atta." Jenna reached down to pat the dog, who cringed under her touch but allowed herself to be petted.

"Take good care of your lost master and see to it that he finds his way home. And now, friends and acquaintances, I bid you goodnight!"

Jenna placed her right hand over a ring on her left thumb, spoke a single word, and vanished from their sight.

"Whew!" Nightshade breathed. "I remember when we did that. Do you, Rhys? That time Zeboim magicked us off to the death knight's castle—"

Rhys rested his hand on the kender's shoulder.

Nightshade, taking the hint, fell silent.

Dominique had been listening. He regarded Rhys gravely, not liking the reminder that Rhys followed an evil goddess. He seemed about to say something when Gerard interrupted.

"A fine night's work," Gerard said grimly. "All we have to show for it is crushed grass, a few gouts of blood, and melted candle wax." He sighed. "I'll have to report all this to the mayor.

I'd appreciate it, Sir Dominique, if you'd come with me. Palin's bound to believe you, if he won't me."

"I will be glad to accompany you, Sheriff," said the paladin.

"I don't know what he'll do, of course," Gerard added, as they started off down the hill, "but I'm going to suggest we call a town meeting tomorrow to warn people."

"An excellent idea. You can hold your meeting in our temple. We will end by praying for strength and guidance. We will send out messengers to all our clerics, as well as those of Mishakal and Majere—"

"Speaking of Majere . . ." Gerard halted. "Where's Brother Rhys?"

He turned around to see Rhys, Nightshade and Atta still standing beneath the trees. "Aren't you coming back to Solace with us, Brother?"

"I believe I will remain here for a while," Rhys replied. "Give Atta a chance to rest."

"I'm staying with him," Nightshade added, though no one had asked.

"Suit yourself. See you in the morning, Brother," said Gerard. "Thanks for your help tonight, and thanks to Atta for saving my life. She'll find a big beef bone in her dog dish tomorrow."

He and Dominique continued their walk and their planning and were soon lost to Rhys's sight.

The night had grown very dark. The lights of Solace had gone out. The town had disappeared, swallowed up in sleep. Lunitari appeared to have lost interest in them now that Jenna was gone. The red moon draped herself in a bank of storm clouds and refused to return. A few drops of rain spattered. Thunder rumbled in the distance.

"We're not going back to Solace, are we?" Nightshade heaved a sigh.

"Do you think we should?" Rhys asked quietly.

"Tomorrow's chicken dumpling day," Nightshade said in wistful tones. "And Atta was going to get a beef bone. But I guess you're right. The important people have taken over. We'd only be in the way. Besides," he added, cheering up, "there's bound to be chicken dumplings wherever we end up. Where are we going?"

"East," said Rhys. "After the Beloved."

Monk, dog, and kender set off down the long road just as the storm broke and rain started to fall.

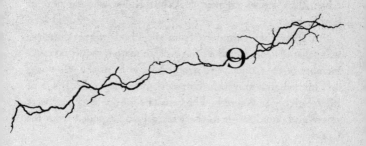

9

*N*uitari arrived late to the Wizards Conclave that had been hastily convened in the Tower of High Sorcery in Wayreth. He found his two cousins, Solinari and Lunitari, already there. The expressions on the faces of the gods were grim, reflecting the grim expressions of the faces of their wizards. Whatever topic was under discussion did not bode well for the Robed mages of Ansalon, apparently.

Nuitari had only to hear the words, "Beloved of Chemosh" to know the reason why. His cousins glanced at him as he entered but said nothing, not wanting to miss any of Jenna's report to her fellows.

This meeting of the wizards that formed the Conclave was not a formal meeting. Formal meetings of the Conclave, held at regularly scheduled intervals, were planned months in advance. They were lavish affairs, conducted by proscribed ritual and ceremony in the Tower's Hall of Mages. This emergency meeting was hastily convened with no time to waste on formal rituals, and it was being held in the Tower's library, where the wizards had ready access to reference books and scrolls dating back to ancient times. The wizards gathered around a large wooden table; Black Robes sat next to White Robes who sat next to Red Robes.

An emergency summons from the Head of the Conclave was generally considered a life-or-death matter, requiring every member of the Conclave to drop whatever he or she was doing and immediately travel the corridors of magic to the Tower of High Sorcery at Wayreth. The penalties for not attending were severe and could result in the wizard being expelled from the Conclave.

An ancient spell, known only to the Head of the Conclave, permitted the mage to issue such an emergency summons. On her return to her home in Palanthas, Jenna had removed a rosewood box from its hiding place within the folds of time. Inside the box was a silver stylus. She dipped it in goat's blood and then wrote the words of the summons upon lamb's skin. She passed her hand over the words left to right, and then right to left, and back again, seven times. The words vanished. The lamb's skin shriveled up and disappeared.

Within instants, the summons would appear to each member of the Conclave as letters of blood and fire. A White Robe, slumbering in her bed, was awakened by the bright light of fiery tracings blazing across the ceiling of her bedchamber. A Black Robe saw the words materialize on the wall of his laboratory. He left immediately, if reluctantly, for he had just finished summoning a fiend from the Abyss, who was undoubtedly smashing up the furniture in his absence. A Red Robe had been battling goblins when he saw the words emblazoned on the forehead of his foe. The Red Robe arrived bruised and out of breath, his hands covered in goblin blood. He'd been forced to leave behind a group of goblin-hunters, who were now looking about in baffled astonishment, wondering what had become of their magic-user.

"There goes my share of the bounty," he muttered as he took his seat.

"Wait until my husband wakes up to find me missing," said the White Robe at his side. "I'll have some explaining to do when I go back home."

"You think you have problems," said the Black Robe, who sighed as he thought of the mess the demon was making in his laboratory. Provided he still had a laboratory.

All personal inconveniences were forgotten, however, as the wizards listened in shock to Jenna's tale. She started at the beginning, telling Rhys's story as he had told it to her. She ended with the ill-fated attack on the Beloved.

"The spell I cast was 'Sunburst,' " she told them. "I assume all of you are familiar with it?"

There was a general nodding of hooded heads.

"As you know, this spell is particularly effective against undead. It should have fried that walking corpse to a crisp. It had no effect on it whatsoever. The Beloved laughed at me."

"Since it is you, Jenna, who cast the spell, I must assume that there is no possibility that you made a mistake. That you mispronounced a word or used an impure spell component."

The speaker was Dalamar the Dark, Head of the Order of Black Robes. Although an elf and one who was relatively young by elven standards, Dalamar appeared older than the eldest human at the table. His black hair was streaked with white. His eyes were set deep within hollow eye sockets. His fine-boned face seemed carved of ivory. Though he seemed frail, he was at the height of his power and well respected among all the Orders.

He should have been head of the Conclave but for a few regrettable mistakes in his past that had led both gods and wizards to oppose him and promote Jenna in his place. The two had been lovers many years ago and were still friends when they weren't rivals.

"Since I am the one who cast the spell," Jenna returned coolly, "I can assure you that there is no possibility that I made a mistake."

Dalamar appeared skeptical.

Jenna raised her hand to heaven. "As Lunitari is my witness," she declared. "Let the god send us a sign if I miscast the spell."

"Jenna made no mistake," said Lunitari with a frowning glance at Nuitari.

"Dalamar didn't say she did," Nuitari returned. "In fact, he said she didn't."

"That wasn't what he meant."

"Stop it, both of you," Solinari intervened. "This is a serious matter, perhaps the most serious we have encountered since our return. Calm your ire, Cousin. Dalamar the Dark acted quite properly in asking for reassurance."

"And he will get it," said Lunitari.

The library was suddenly suffused with warm red light. Jenna smiled with satisfaction. Dalamar cast a glance toward heaven and inclined his hooded head in deference to the god.

"None of us doubts Mistress Jenna's abilities, but even she must admit that there has to be some way to destroy these undead," stated a White Robe. "As the paladin of Kiri-Jolith said, not even Chemosh can make a mortal indestructible."

"There is always a first time for everything," returned Dalamar caustically. "One hundred years ago, I would not have said that a god could steal away the world. Yet it happened."

"Perhaps a sorcerer's spell could destroy it," suggested Coryn the White, the newest member of the Conclave. Although young, she was highly talented and reputed to be a great favorite of the god, Solinari.

Her fellow wizards, even those wearing the White Robes, regarded her with disapproval.

Sorcerers were those who used the wild magic that came from

the world itself, not the godly magic from the heavens. Sorcerers had been practicing magic on Krynn during the gods' absence. Sorcerers were not bound by the laws of High Sorcery but operated independently. In the days prior to the Second Cataclysm, such free agents would have been deemed renegades and hunted down by the members of all three Orders. Many members of this Conclave would have liked to have done that now but did not for several reasons: godly magic had only recently returned to Krynn, the wizards were still finding their way back to the old practices, their numbers were small and they were not yet well organized.

Mistress Jenna, as Head of the Conclave, advocated a policy of "live and let live," and it was being followed for the most part. This did not mean, however, that wizards had friendly feelings for sorcerers. Quite the contrary.

Coryn the White had been a sorcerer who had only recently given up the wild magic for the more disciplined magic of the gods. She knew how the other mages felt regarding sorcerers, and she took a rather mischievous delight in teasing them. She was not teasing this time, however. She was deadly serious.

"Mistress Coryn has a point," stated Jenna grudgingly. All the wizards regarded her in astonishment. A few Black Robes scowled and muttered.

"I have several sorcerers who are customers of mine," Jenna continued. "I will contact them and urge them try their skills against these creatures. I do not hold out much hope that their luck will be any better than ours, however."

"Hope!" a Red Robe repeated angrily. "Let us *hope* that these Beloved stomp the sorcerers into the ground! Do you realize what this would mean for us if a sorcerer could kill these heinous creatures and we could not? We would be the laughing stock of Ansalon! I say we keep knowledge of these Beloved to ourselves. Don't tell the sorcerers."

"Too late," said a Black Robe grimly. "Now that the clerics know about it, they will be holding prayer services with the faithful rolling about on the ground in hysterics and priests flinging holy water on anything that moves. They'll find a way to blame this on wizards. Wait and see if they don't."

"And that is the very reason we must establish guidelines for how we deal with the Beloved and make our position known to the public," said Jenna. "Wizards must be seen to be working with everyone in order to find a solution to this mystery, even if that means joining forces with priests and sorcerers and mystics."

"Thereby admitting that we can't deal with it ourselves," said a White Robe sourly. "What do you say, Mistress Coryn?"

"I agree with Mistress Jenna. We should be open and honest about these Beloved. The problems we wizards have faced in the past came about as a result of cloaking ourselves in mystery and secrecy."

"Oh, I quite agree," said Dalamar. "I say we throw open the doors of the Tower and invite the rabble to come spend the day. We can do demonstrations, set off fireballs and the like, and serve milk punch and cookies on the lawn."

"Be sarcastic all you like, my friend," Jenna returned coolly. "But that won't make this terrible situation go away. Have you anything constructive to suggest, Master of the Black Robes?"

Dalamar was silent a moment, absently tracing a sigil on top of the table with a delicate fingers.

"What I find most intriguing is the involvement of Mina," he said at last.

"Mina!" Jenna returned, astonished. "I don't see why you find her so intriguing. The girl has no mind of her own. She was once a pawn of Takhisis. Now she's a pawn of Chemosh. She's merely traded one master for another."

"I find it intriguing that it is the mark of *her* lips that is burned into the flesh of these wretched creatures," said Dalamar.

"Please don't doodle!" said Jenna, placing her hand over his. "The last time you did that, you burned a hole in the table. As for Mina, she is nothing more than a pretty face Chemosh uses to lure young men to their doom."

Dalamar rubbed out the sigil with the sleeve of his black robe. "Nevertheless, I believe that she is the key that will unlock the door to this mystery."

Nuitari was not surprised that his wizard's thoughts tended in the same direction as his own. The bond between Nuitari and Dalamar was a close one. The two, god and mortal, had endured many trials together. Nuitari planned to eventually establish Dalamar as the Master of the Blood Sea Tower. Not just yet, however. Not until everything was settled with his two cousins.

"I'll wager you wouldn't be so interested in Mina if she were an old hag like myself," said Jenna, giving Dalamar's hand a teasing slap.

Dalamar took her hand and brought it to his lips. "You will never be an old hag, my dear. And you well know it."

Jenna, who did know it, smiled at him and returned to business.

"Do you have anything to add, Mistress Coryn?"

"Judging by the clue the Beloved gave you, the way to destroy these things will not be easily discovered by anyone—cleric, wizard, or sorcerer. I would suggest that those apprentices currently studying in the Tower be instructed to search among the old records for some mention of similar beings, particularly in regard to Chemosh."

"They are already at work," said Jenna. "I have also contacted the Aesthetics and asked them to research the books in the Great Library. I do not believe that they will have much success, however. So far as I know, nothing like these Beloved have been seen upon Ansalon. Is there anything else? Any other questions?"

Jenna cast a glance around the table. The wizards sat in gloomy silence, shaking their hooded heads.

"Very well, then. Let us move on. The Conclave will now consider the guidelines that wizards will be required to follow if they come upon any of these Beloved. First and foremost, we must find some means of detecting them."

"And of protecting the innocent, who are bound to be falsely accused," added a White Robe.

"And of protecting ourselves, who are bound to be falsely accused," said a Black Robe.

"And so it seems to me . . ." said a Red Robe.

Nuitari turned away. Such discussions would likely go on for hours before consensus was reached.

"My cousins," he said. "I would speak with you."

"You have our full attention, Cousin," said Lunitari, and Solinari, coming to stand by her side, nodded his head.

The three gods had been watching the proceedings from their heavenly plane and, despite the fact that no mortal eye could see them, each took on his or her favorite aspect. Lunitari appeared as a vivacious, red-haired woman wearing red robes trimmed in ermine and gold. Solinari took the form of a young and physically powerful man. His robes were white, trimmed in silver. Nuitari took his usual form, that of a man with a moon-round face, heavy-lidded eyes and full lips. His jet-black robes were plain and unadorned.

Lunitari guessed immediately that something was up.

"You have information about these Beloved, Cousin," she said, excited. "Chemosh has said something to you."

Nuitari was scornful. "Chemosh is too busy strutting about being cock of the walk to talk to me. He believes he has done something quite clever. Personally, I am not all that impressed. A way will be found to destroy these shambling corpses, and that will put an end to that."

"Then what do you want to speak to us about?" Solinari asked.

"I have built a Tower of High Sorcery," said Nuitari. "My own tower."

His two cousins stared at him blankly.

"What?" demanded Lunitari, unable to believe she had heard correctly.

"I have built a Tower of High Sorcery," Nuitari repeated. "Or rather, rebuilt an old Tower—the one that used to stand in Istar. I raised up the ruins and added a few of my own touches. The Tower is located beneath the Blood Sea. Two of my Black Robes now inhabit it. I plan to invite more wizards to move in later."

"You did this in secret!" Lunitari gasped. "Behind our backs!"

"Yes," said Nuitari. What else could he say? "I did."

Lunitari was furious. She lunged at him and there is no telling what she might have done, had not her cousin, Solinari, grabbed hold of her and dragged her back.

"Down through the centuries, since the time of our birth, we three have stood shoulder-to-shoulder, side-by-side," said Solinari, keeping fast hold of his raging cousin. "We have been united in the cause of the magic and, because of our unity, magic prospered. When your mother betrayed us, we grieved together and joined forces to try to find the world. When we did find it, we acted in concert to restore magic to it. Only to discover that you have betrayed us."

"Let us ask which of us is the true betrayer," Nuitari said. "My mother, Takhisis, was deposed for her crime, made mortal, and then ignominiously slain by a mortal's hand. Your father, Cousin Solinari, was once a god. He is now a beggar who roams Ansalon living off charity.

Nuitari shook his head. "And what of Nuitari? My mother gone. My father, Sargonnas, the rampaging bull, is intent on his minotaur ruling Ansalon! He has driven the elves from their homeland and is now sending out shiploads of minotaur settlers. He cares nothing for me or what I am about. We all know minotaurs think little of wizards, and that includes my father."

His heavy-lidded eyes shifted to Lunitari. "Whereas *your* father, Gilean, is now the most powerful god in the heavens. Is it any coincidence that his daughter's Red Robes run the Conclave?"

"The balance must be maintained!" Lunitari said, still smoldering. "Let me go, Cousin. I'm not going to harm him. Though I would like to snatch his black moon from the sky and shove it up his—"

"Peace, Cousin," said Solinari soothingly. He turned to Nuitari. "The fact that the Red Robes are quite powerful may well be true, though I'm not saying it is," he added as an aside with a cool glance at Lunitari. "Still, it doesn't excuse what you did."

"No it doesn't," Nuitari admitted. "And I want to make amends. I have a proposition. One I think will be agreeable to you both."

"I'm listening, Cousin," Solinari said. He seemed more grieved than angry.

Lunitari indicated, with an abrupt nod, that she was also interested to hear what he had to say.

"There are now three Towers of High Sorcery on Ansalon," said Nuitari. "The Tower of Wayreth, the Tower of Nightlund, and my Tower in the Blood Sea. I suggest that, as it was in the days of the Kingpriest, each of the Robes be given its own Tower. The Red Robes will take control of the Tower of Wayreth. The White Robes will be ceded control of the Tower in Nightlund. My Black Robes will take over the Tower of the Blood Sea."

The other two gods pondered this suggestion. The Tower of

Wayreth was, to all intents and purposes, under the control of the Red Robes, since Jenna was Head of the Conclave and the Tower was the Conclave's seat of power. The Tower of Nightlund had been closed since Dalamar had been banned from it as punishment. No wizard had been permitted to enter it, precisely for the reason that the gods feared the Tower would become a bone of contention, with both Black Robes and White Robes seeking to lay claim to it.

Nuitari had just provided a solution to the problem. Lunitari reflected on the fact that her cousin's new Tower stood at the bottom of an ocean. It would not be easily accessible and was therefore not likely to pose much of a threat to her own power base. As for the Tower of Nightlund, it was located in the middle of one of the most deadly places on Krynn. If the White Robes did claim it, they would have to first battle their way to its threshold.

Solinari's thoughts on the Blood Sea Tower were much the same as those of his cousin. His thoughts on the Nightlund Tower were also similar, except he was intrigued by the possibility of restoring the accursed land that now lay languishing beneath dark shadows. If his White Robes could remove the curse that lay over Nightlund, people could live there once again and prosper. All Ansalon would be in the debt of his White Robes.

"It's something to consider," said Lunitari grudgingly.

"I would like to think it over. But I am interested," said Solinari.

Nuitari glanced around, as though he feared other immortal ears might be listening, then, with a gesture, he drew his cousins close.

"I had to keep this secret," he said. "Even from you, those whom I most trust."

Lunitari frowned, but she was clearly curious. "Why?"

"The *Solio Febalas*—the Hall of Sacrilege."

"It was destroyed," said Lunitari flatly.

"So it was," said Nuitari. "But the sacred artifacts inside it were not. I have them now under lock and key, guarded by a sea dragon of a particularly nasty disposition."

"The holy artifacts stolen by the Kingpriest," Solinari said, amazed. "You have them?"

"Perhaps I should say now, since we have reached this agreement between us, *we* have them."

"Do any of the other gods know of this?" Lunitari asked.

"Chemosh is the only one and he has kept his mouth shut thus far, though it is only a matter of time before he will spread the word."

"The other gods would give anything to have those artifacts back!" said Lunitari exultantly. "From now on, we wizards, once reviled, will be a power in the world."

"Henceforth, no cleric will dare raise his hand against us," Solinari agreed.

The three fell silent. Nuitari was thinking that this had gone unexpectedly well, when Solinari said quietly, "You know, Cousin, that I can never again trust you in anything."

"Nothing will ever be the same between us again," Lunitari lamented sadly.

Nuitari looked from one to the other. His heavy-lidded eyes were hooded, his full lips compressed.

"Face it, Cousins, a new age has dawned. Observe Mishakal. No longer the gentle goddess of healing, she strides through heaven wielding a sword of blue flame. Kiri-Jolith's priests march to war. Even Majere has left off staring at his navel and involved himself in the world, though I have no idea what he is up to. Trust between us all ceased the moment my mother stole away the world. You are right, Cousin. Nothing will ever be the same. You were fools to think it could."

As he drew his hood up over his moon-face and left them, Nuitari wondered what they would have said if he had told them he had captured Mina. . . .

10

*B*asalt!" Caele accosted the dwarf as he was walking down a hallway. "Is it true the Master has left the Tower?"

"It's true," Basalt replied.

"Where has he gone?"

"How should I know?" Basalt demanded testily. "It's not like he asks my permission."

The dwarf kept walking, his hob-nailed boots ringing on the stone floor as he kicked at the hem of his robe to keep from stepping on it. Caele hastened after him.

"Perhaps the Master has gone to deal with Chemosh," the half-elf said hopefully.

"Or perhaps he's left us to face the Lord of Death on our own," Basalt returned. He was in a grumpy mood.

Caele blanched. "Do you think he has?"

Basalt would have liked to have said yes, just to rattle the half-elf. He needed Caele's help, however, so, reluctantly, he shook his head. "It's something to do with Chemosh, but I don't know what."

Caele was not reassured. He fell in alongside Basalt. "Where are you going?"

"Coming to fetch you. Mina is to be granted freedom to walk up and down the hallway for an hour—under our supervision, of course."

"Under *your* supervision," said Caele. He made an about-face. "I have no intention of playing nursemaid to that scheming bitch."

"Suit yourself," Basalt said complacently. "When the Master returns, where shall I tell him to find you? In your room? Studying your spells?"

Caele halted. Swearing beneath his breath, he turned around. "On second thought, I'll come with you. I would feel badly if some terrible fate were to befall you at the hands of that woman."

"What do you think is likely to befall me?" Basalt demanded, bristling. "There's not one jot or tittle of magic in her."

"Apparently the Master does not share your confidence, since he requested both of us be on hand to guard her—"

"Shut up about her, will you," Basalt growled.

"You are scared of her!" Caele said smugly.

"I am not. It's just . . . well, if you must know, I don't like being around her. There's something uncanny about that female. I haven't had a good night's sleep since the moment we mistook her for a fish and caught her in our net. By the black moon, I wish Chemosh *would* come and take her away, and that would be the end of her."

"Someone could kill her and toss her body to the sharks," Caele suggested.

Standing outside the door to Mina's room, they could hear her inside, pacing.

"We could always tell the Master she tried to escape. . . ."

Basalt snorted. "And how do you plan to murder her? Cast a magic spell on her? That would work, but only if you tell her in advance exactly what you're going to do and how it's going to affect her! Otherwise you might as well be dancing the kender randygazoo."

Caele slid back the sleeve of his robe to reveal a knife strapped to his forearm. "We won't need to tell her in advance how *this* would affect her."

Basalt eyed the knife. The thought was tempting.

"You think Chemosh is mad at us now. . . ."

"Bah! Nuitari will settle his hash." Caele leaned nearer, spoke softer. "Perhaps this is what the Master intends for us to do! Why else would he tell us to remove her from her prison except to trick her into trying to escape. He even gave us orders on what to do if that should happen. 'If she tries to flee, kill her.' That's what he said."

Basalt had been cudgeling his brain, trying to figure out why Nuitari had agreed to release Mina from her safe prison. Much as he hated to admit it, Caele made sense.

"We kill her *only* if she tries to escape," Basalt stated.

"She will," Caele predicted. His eyes glinted with bloodlust. Spittle flecked his lips.

"You're a pig," said Basalt, and he placed his hand on the door and began to chant the spell that would reverse the wizard lock.

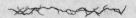

Inside the room, Mina halted her pacing. "The two Black Robes are coming, my lord," she reported to Chemosh. "I can hear them walking down the corridor. Are you certain Nuitari is gone?"

"I would not be talking to you otherwise, my love. Only Nuitari can maintain such a powerful spell around you. Does he frighten you, Mina?"

"Nuitari does not *frighten* me, my lord, but he makes my skin crawl, like touching a snake or having a spider drop down my neck."

"All three cousins are like that. It's the magic. Some of us warned the gods: 'Don't permit your children to wield such power! Keep them subservient to you!' Takhisis would not listen, however, nor would Paladine or Gilean. It was only later, when their own children turned against them, that they began to heed our wisdom. By then, of course, it was too late. Now I have the ability to humble the cousins, take away their power, pull their fangs."

"How do you intend to do that, lord?" Mina asked.

Outside her room, she could hear one of the Black Robes fumbling with the door lock.

"Soon the world will see that wizards are helpless, impotent against my Beloved, and what will the world do? Turn from them in disgust! Even now, the wizards frantically search spell-books and scrolls and artifacts, trying to find some way to stop me. They will fail. Nothing they do will have the slightest effect on the Beloved."

"What of Nuitari?" Mina led the conversation back to where they had started.

"I beg your pardon for straying off the subject, my dear. Nuitari has gone to attend the meeting of his conclave, at which, I'm assuming, he's telling his cousins that he's betrayed them by building a Tower of his own. He won't be back any time soon, and in a few moments, all chaos is going to break loose around here. Be ready."

"I am, my lord," said Mina calmly.

She could hear the dwarf's sonorous voice chanting.

"You understand what you are to do?" Chemosh asked.

"Yes, my lord." Mina resumed her pacing, as though nothing was amiss.

"The Hall of Sacrilege is located at the bottom of the Tower. There is a guardian, and the Hall is probably filled with traps, but I will assist you."

"My lord—" Mina began, then fell silent.

"Speak freely, my love."

"This is so important to you, my lord. Why do you not come yourself? Is this another test? Do you still doubt my love and my loyalty?"

"No, Mina, I do not," Chemosh replied. "As you say, recovering these artifacts is vitally important to me. I know of nothing more important. But I cannot enter the Tower. Not anymore. Nuitari has blocked up the rat hole through which I managed to sneak the last time. He has made this Tower his domain. No other god may enter it."

"Then how will you take control of the Tower, my lord?"

"Many Beloved are here already and more arrive daily. I have placed Krell in command, and he is forming a legion of warriors unlike any ever before seen on Krynn—warriors who can kill yet cannot be killed. You are not to concern yourself with this. Do what I ask of you, then return to me as swiftly as possible. I miss you, Mina."

The Lord of Death was in Castle Beloved on the shores of the Blood Sea and Mina was in a Tower far below the surface of the waves, yet she felt the touch of his hands, his lips brush against her cheek.

"I miss you, my lord," said Mina. Hearing the longing in his distant voice, her own heart ached. The door handle rattled. They had only a few more moments together.

"Ah, Mina, when I believed you were lost to me, I could not bear the thought of going on. I began to regret immortality. Remember, steal one artifact, just one from the *Solio Febalas*. That way I can prove to the other gods I have indeed found the treasure. Then cast upon the door the spell I taught you. After that, Nuitari may rant and rave all he likes, but *I* will be able to enter his tower."

"Yes, my lord."

He was gone.

Mina turned from the god to the two wizards who were by turns clomping and skulking into the room.

The dwarf, Basalt, was a hairy black lump. She had never seen his face. He kept his hood pulled down low whenever he was around her, and between that and his scraggly black beard she'd yet to have a good look at him. She could see the half-elf's face, more was the pity. Caele never wore the filthy cowl that straggled down his back. In truth, the cowl was so coated in grime she doubted the half-elf could peel it off his dirty black robes.

Basalt kept this hood down as usual, but she found Caele staring at her and that made her uneasy.

Before this, the half-elf had never looked at her directly. His gaze sidled about the room until he thought she wasn't looking at him, and then she felt his eyes on her. The expression in his eyes appalled her. His gaze burned with such malevolence that her hand went instinctively to her hip for a weapon.

He looked at her directly, his lips drawn back from his teeth in a wolfish grin. He kept his hands tucked inside the sleeves of his robes, something else that was odd for him. She glanced back at the dwarf. Basalt seemed ill at ease. He had his hood pulled down lower than usual and he kept peering out from under it, first at her, then at the half-elf, then back to her.

They're going to kill me, Mina realized.

She found herself more annoyed than frightened. This could interfere with her lord's plans. She would have to strike first, before they could use their magic on her. She had no weapon and no prospects of gaining one—in this prison cell, at least.

"Why are you vermin here?" she asked coldly.

"You've been granted an hour's freedom to stroll the halls, Mistress," said Basalt gruffly.

He gestured at the open door and then stood to one side, as did the half-elf, to permit her to walk past them.

They were waiting until her back was turned.

She would take on the half-elf first. The dwarf looked less enthusiastic and maybe the sight of his companion writhing on the floor, choking on his own blood, would cause him to have second thoughts.

Mina was almost level with Caele when she saw his hand twitch beneath his sleeve.

He has a knife there. He's going to use that, not his magic. Of course, he takes pleasure in killing with his hands . . .

She tensed, ready to strike, then the Tower shook from bottom to top, knocking her off-balance, so that she lurched into Caele and they both went down onto the floor in a heap.

The compact dwarf was less easy to topple. The shaking of the floor and walls and ceiling sent him staggering, but he maintained his balance.

"What the—" Basalt gasped.

"Nuitari!" A voice yelled, as yet another blow smote the Tower. "Come out of there, do you hear me? Come out and face me!"

"Chemosh!" cried Caele, floundering underneath Mina, who had fallen on top of him.

"No, that's a woman's voice!" Basalt said, his face pale and his eyes wide. "Zeboim! She's found the Tower." He groaned. "What a time for the Master to be gone!"

"You have to talk to her!" Caele gasped, adding with a snarl and a shove, "Get off me, you clumsy bitch!"

Though Mina was slender, she outweighed the scrawny half-elf, and she was impeding his attempts to try to stand. Her legs tangled with his; her feet tripped him. She jabbed him with an elbow and stuck her knee in his gut.

He was just about to throttle her when another blow smote the Tower and this time even the dwarf went down. They could hear the sound of breaking glass. Wooden beams groaned beneath the strain.

Caele realized somewhat belatedly this would be an ideal time to slay Mina, and he reached up his sleeve for his knife.

It wasn't there.

He thought at first he'd dropped it, then, looking up, Caele found it.

Mina stood over him, his knife in her hand.

Leaning down, she pressed the point of the blade against his throat.

"If your lips so much as twitch, I'll slit you from ear to ear," she said. "The same goes for you, dwarf. If you utter a single word of magic, your partner dies."

Seeing by Basalt's irresolute expression that perhaps he might be willing to risk such a tragic loss, Mina called out, "My Lord Chemosh, I pray you, look after these two while I go about your business."

Two stone sarcophagi appeared in the room. On one sarcophagus was a carved figure of Basalt, his eyes closed, his hands folded across his chest. The other sarcophagus bore a similar representation of Caele.

"Get in," said Mina, speaking to Basalt.

He looked at the sarcophagus and shook his hooded head.

Caele twitched just then, and she dug the knifepoint in a little deeper. A sliver of red slid down the half-elf's neck. He held still after that.

"I said, get in," said Mina.

Seeing the dwarf was not moving, she raised her voice, "My lord—"

Basalt hurriedly climbed inside the sarcophagus. A slab of

stone dropped down over the coffin, sealing the dwarf inside.

"You next," she said to Caele. She shifted the blade from his throat to his ribs and walked him over to the other sarcophagus. When he hesitated, she sliced open enough flesh to persuade him to obey.

He hastily climbed inside, and a stone slab dropped down on him.

"Are they dead, my lord?" Mina asked.

"No," Chemosh replied, his voice sounding above the roar of the Sea Goddess's rage. "Not yet. They have air enough to breathe for a short time, *if* they don't panic and use up all their air screaming."

The muffled howls that had been emanating from the half-elf's coffin ceased abruptly.

"Now, be on your way," he told her.

"What about Zeboim?"

"She won't bother you. Strangely enough, she's here to rescue you."

Another quake rocked the Tower, causing Mina to stagger.

"Nuitari?"

"Family issues are going to occupy a considerable amount of time for the Moon-Faced One. He's trying to work things out with his cousins. On his return, he will find that he has considerable explaining to do to his sister. For now, the Tower of the Blood Sea is all yours, Mina. You are alone in it."

"Except for the guardian. I need a weapon, my lord."

"No, you won't, Mina," returned Chemosh. "Only a dragonlance would aid you against this guardian, and unfortunately, I have none of those at my disposal. You have your wits, Mina, and you have my blessing. Use them both."

"Yes, my lord," said Mina, and she was alone.

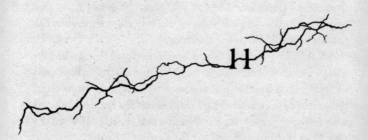

Mina found the long, circular staircase that wound around the Tower's interior and began her descent. The staircase was made of mother-of-pearl and spiraled round and round, reminding her of the interior of a nautilus seashell. She could see here and there cracks in the walls, presumably from the shaking the Tower was enduring at the hands of the outraged goddess, and she worried the next jolt might split the walls. Fortunately the quakes rocking the Tower ceased. Mina could not see outside, but she guessed Nuitari had returned and was now trying to placate his furious sister.

Inside the Tower was silent. The seawater surrounding the structure seemed to suck out the sound, so that every noise made within had a muffled quality to it.

The silence was soothing. Now that she was no longer a prisoner, she felt at home here. She found it comforting, knowing the sea cradled her. Perhaps this stirred some long-buried memory of the shipwreck that had taken her parents from her and left her an orphan, a memory that was always there, lying just beneath the surface. One she could never quite recall.

"Our minds blot out such traumatic events in order to protect us from them," Goldmoon had once told Mina. "You may remember what happened to you some day or you may never remember. Do not fret over it, child. It is quite natural."

Mina had fretted. She felt guilty and ashamed that she had no memory of those parents who had loved her dearly, perhaps even sacrificed their lives for her, and she tried hard to bring to mind their faces or the sound of a mother's voice. She became obsessed with trying to remember, an obsession that ended only when the One God, Takhisis, chided her for wasting her time.

"It does not matter who gave you birth!" Takhisis had said, cold and furious. "I am your mother. I am your father. Look to me for protection and succor and nourishment."

Mina had obeyed the god's command as she obeyed all others given to her by the One God. She had never allowed herself to think about her parents again, not until she had been imprisoned in this Tower below the sea. She had so much time on her hands in the Tower, time to think, time to remember her childhood. The frustration and the shame and the need to know returned. Mina took care to keep her obsession to herself. She did not want to anger Chemosh as she had angered Takhisis.

The spiral stairs were lit by magical globules of light placed at intervals and renewed daily by Basalt. Doors, opening off the stairs, led to the other floors of the Tower. Mina glanced at them curiously. She would have liked to explore, to see how the rooms were constructed and what they looked like, for the Tower intrigued her.

She did not have time, however. "I will postpone that for another day," she said to herself, smiling at the thought, for she knew perfectly well she was never likely to see the inside of this Tower again.

The stairs brought her at last to the Tower's base. She

came up against a door made of steel banded with bronze and inscribed with runes. Runes had also been carved into the stone arch around the door. Mina recognized the runes as being the language of magic, the same as she'd read in the book Nuitari had given her. She knew what the runes said; she just didn't know what they meant.

Giving up on the runes, Mina inspected the door, trying to find some way inside. The door had no handle, no lock. The runes probably provided information on how to open the door. Mina tried reciting them aloud, to no avail. The door didn't budge.

Frustrated, Mina gave the door a kick.

The door revolved smoothly and silently on a center linchpin and swung open.

Mina stepped back, eyeing the door warily.

"This is too easy. This is a trap," she muttered.

She did not enter. Drawing closer to the arched doorway, she examined it carefully.

"What an idiot I am!" she scolded herself. "If this is a trap, it is a magical one and I'll never find it anyway. I might as well chance it."

Mina walked through the door and was pleasantly surprised to find herself emerging safely on the other side. She was less pleasantly surprised to hear the door revolve and slam shut behind her. There were no runes on this side of the door. Apparently, once you got in, you were supposed to know the secret of how to get back out.

Shrugging, Mina turned away. She'd deal with that problem when the time came. Now she had her task before her. An amazing task. She stood before what looked to be an enormous fish bowl.

Mina and the other children in the orphanage had kept fish in glass bowls filled with water. The children were taught to feed the fish and care for them. They observed their habits and marveled at how the creatures breathed water as easily as people breathed air. This globe was similar to those fish bowls, except it was much, much larger—as big in circumference as the Tower itself. The glass walls were covered with runes etched into the glass. Shafts of sunlight illuminated the globe and the creatures swimming inside.

"It is beautiful," Mina said softly, awed. "Beautiful and deadly."

The graceful jellyfish, drifting along at the mercy of the swirling currents, killed their prey by stinging it with a venom that paralyzed the victim and prevented it from escaping. These jellyfish were enormous, several times Mina's size, with tentacles long enough to ensnare a full-grown man.

A gigantic squid, large enough to drag a ship beneath the waves, lay sprawled across the floor, its arms trembling as it slept. Stingrays slithered up the crystal sides of the globe. Monstrous bull sharks swam about, their jaws, filled with the rows of razor-sharp teeth, opening and closing. The floor was covered with fire coral, pretty to look at, burning to the touch.

Inside the center of the globe, surrounded by its lethal guards, was the *Solio Febalas.*

Mina stared, astonished. The Hall was not at all what she expected.

The structure resembled a child's sand castle. It was simple in design with four walls, a tower at each corner, and crenellations on the battlements. There were no windows. She could see, from this angle, what appeared to be a door, but she could not make out any details. What was truly amazing was that the Hall of Sacrilege, supposedly containing any number of sacred artifacts, was only about four feet tall and four feet wide.

"It must be an illusion, a trick of the water," Mina said to herself.

She ran her hand over the rune-etched surface of the crystal wall that blocked her way.

"The question is: how do I reach it? I stand outside an impenetrable wall of crystal encompassing water in which are swimming hundreds of deadly creatures. I have no idea how to get inside the globe, and if I manage that, I cannot breathe water, and even if I could, I would have to battle sharks and men-of-war and—"

She caught her breath. A large coral reef that formed a hillock inside the crystal globe gave a lurch, displacing thousands of fish, which swam away from it in flashing-scaled panic. A head emerged from beneath the coral reef, now revealed to be a huge shell, like that of a tortoise.

Gleaming yellow eyes fixed on Mina. She had found the guardian—a sea dragon.

More to the point, the sea dragon had found Mina.

The guardian of the Hall of Sacrilege was a sea dragon known as Midori. Reclusive, bad-tempered, and irritable, Midori was the oldest dragon on Krynn, which made her the oldest living creature in the world.

She numbered her years not by decades but by centuries. She was not sure exactly how old she was. She'd lost count around the ten-century mark. The passage of time meant little to her. Midori marked her life by momentous events and then only those events that had affected her directly.

One of these was the Cataclysm, for it had been a distinct annoyance. The fiery mountain that had struck the world, killing thousands and destroying a city, had also collapsed a wall of her sea cave, rudely waking her from a fifty-year nap. Rocks tumbled down, half-burying her and wholly burying her treasure hoard. She managed to dig out most of her treasure, but some valuable objects were irretrievably lost. Furious, Midori left her ruined lair and swam into the open sea to find out what all the commotion was about.

A confirmed recluse, a dragon who made no secret of the fact that she loathed and despised every other being on the planet, Midori was forced to seek out others of her kind and actually have conversations with them. This did not improve her humor.

She heard the tale of the Cataclysm from an excited young sea dragon, who told her the history of the human Kingpriests and their transgressions and subsequent punishment by the gods. Midori listened in growing ire. Humans were like fish. Here one minute, gone the next, and always plenty more where the others came from. She saw no reason why the gods should have destroyed a perfectly good lair over such a paltry matter. Seething, Midori moved what remained of her treasure into another lair and went back to sleep.

She slept through the War of the Lance, the Summer of Flame, the Chaos War, the Theft of the World, and the arrival of the Dragon Overlords, who never suspected her existence. She would have continued deep in slumber, but for a horrific scream that jolted Midori out of her sleep and caused her to open her eyes for the first time in several centuries.

The scream was the death cry of Takhisis

Midori had never thought much of the Dark Queen. Some sea dragons had taken part in Takhisis's wars. Midori had not been one of them. Her life was precious to her, and she saw no need to risk it for another's cause. If Takhisis ruled the world or if she didn't, it was all the same to Midori. But now, like the child who long ago left home, yet likes to know that her Mama is still there in case she's needed, Midori felt bereft and even a little fearful.

If such a terrible fate could befall a god, no one—not even a dragon—was safe.

For the second time in her life, Midori left her lair and went out to discover the truth. She swam slowly and ponderously through the water, not burdened by years so much as by as the weight of the enormous shell on her back. Whereas land dragons have spiny protrusions on their backs and wings that enable them to fly, sea dragons have an enormous shell, like that of a tortoise, and flippers instead of clawed feet. The shell was designed for defense. Midori could withdraw her head and feet into it for safety, and that was where she slept. Over the centuries, as she slept, her shell had been overgrown by coral and barnacles, so that swimming with it was tantamount to picking up and moving a coral reef.

Thinking that this latest calamity might have something to do with Istar and that other Cataclysm, Midori returned to the Blood Sea and there came across Nuitari, busily raising up the ruins of some rotting old tower. The god was startled and not particularly pleased to see a sea dragon, for he had no idea one was in the vicinity and he feared she might cause trouble.

Nuitari was respectful to Midori, however, and told her the whole story—all about the Irda, Chaos, world-snatching, alien dragons, skull totems, a time-traveling kender, a girl named Mina, the War of Souls, the death of one god and the voluntary exile of another.

As Midori listened, her fears grew. A world where even gods could die was obviously a much more dangerous place than she'd realized. She was thinking of this and wondering how she would ever have a good epoch's sleep again, when, unexpectedly, Nuitari made her an offer. He needed a guardian for some relics he'd picked up off the sea floor. The job was hers, if she wanted it.

Midori didn't like Nuitari. She considered him a whining,

ungrateful child, not worthy of the mother who had given birth to him. She didn't particularly relish working for him, but she didn't like the thought of returning to her lonely lair, either. She needed to keep an eye on things. Besides, if she grew bored or if he annoyed her too much, she could always leave. Midori agreed to move into Nuitari's newly restored Tower, there to guard his store of valuable religious artifacts.

Nuitari assured her that, since his Tower was located far beneath the Blood Sea, there was little likelihood of any mortals annoying her. The only one who did come was Caele, a mongrel half-elf who was forced to visit her every so often to beg her to give him a drop or two of her blood.

Midori would have refused, but Caele groveled so well and flattered her so lavishly, and he was obviously so frightened of her, that she found she actually enjoyed his visits. She would emerge from her lair and toy with him for a time, long enough for him to utterly debase himself, and then she would snarlingly grant his request, snapping at him as he collected her blood just for the pleasure of seeing him leap about in panic.

No one else came to disturb the dragon's rest and ruminations. Nuitari built a lair specially designed for her—a large crystal-walled globe flooded with seawater located at the base of the Tower. Inside the enormous globe, the dragon could swim at her ease, coming and going as she desired by swimming through a magical portal placed in the crystal wall.

In the center of the globe was the Hall of Sacrilege—not really a hall, but more of a small castle, where the artifacts were stored. Any mortal trying to gain access to the artifacts would not only have to be able to swim, they would have to find a way to avoid the sea dragon, and the other denizens of the deep. The dragon couldn't abide commotion, so she admitted into her globe only those creatures who were quiet and kept to themselves, such as jellyfish and stingrays. Sharks were stupid and uncouth, but they made a tasty snack, and they entertained her by fighting her giant squids. Sea urchins, with their constant chatter, were banned.

All in all, a pleasant way to pass one's twilight years.

Midori was dozing, her head half-in and half-out of her shell, lulled into a tranquil state by the undulating motions of the jellyfish, when she heard the door leading to the underwater chamber open. A person entered.

Thinking it was the half-elf after more blood, Midori decided she didn't want to be bothered with him now. She was about to tell him to go drain his own blood or she would do it for him, when she realized, suddenly, that this was not the half-elf. This was an intruder.

Midori withdrew into her shell and held very still. She was, to all appearances, a vast coral formation. Fish swam, undisturbed, around her. Sea plants, growing on her back, swayed back and forth with the currents that swirled around the globe. Only an acute observer, looking very closely, would have seen the dragon's yellow eyes gleaming from out of the shadowy depths of her shell.

What Midori saw amazed her more than anything else had amazed her in several millennia.

She came out to investigate further.

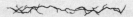

Mina watched the dragon in a terror that seemed to paralyze her. The dragon's jaws gaped. Fangs glistened in the eerie green sunlight, as the dragon sucked in a breath that sent hundreds of helpless fish disappearing into the beast's gullet.

The dragon's jaws snapped shut. Two huge flipper-like legs thrust the ponderous shell up from the seaweed-covered floor. The dragon's tail lashed the water, stirring up clouds of silt. The flipper legs propelled the beast through the water. Head and neck outthrust, the dragon lunged straight at Mina.

Mina feared the dragon meant to crash through the crystal wall. She ran back to the door and pushed on it frantically.

The door would not open. Mina looked over her shoulder. The dragon was almost on her. The eyes were enormous—slits of black surrounded by green-gold flame. It seemed the eyes alone could swallow her. The dragon's jaws opened.

Mina pressed her back against the door, a prayer to Chemosh on her lips.

The dragon reached the crystal wall, made a sudden turn, following the curve of the globe, and hung there, floating. The dragon spoke, words and fish gushing from her mouth.

"Where did *you* come from?"

Mina had expected violent death, not an inane question. She couldn't find breath enough to answer.

"Well?" the dragon demanded impatiently.

"I came from . . . the Tower. . . ." Mina indicated with a feeble gesture the door behind her.

"I don't mean that," snapped the dragon, irate. "I mean where did you come from? Where have you been?"

Mina had heard that some dragons liked to play games with their victims, asking them riddles and toying with them before the kill. This dragon didn't sound as if she were playing, however. This dragon appeared to be quite serious.

I am obviously not a wizard, yet I am here in this Tower. The guardian must think I am here at Nuitari's invitation. That is why she hasn't killed me. This may work to my advantage.

"I am a friend of the god's," Mina replied. This, at least, was true. She just didn't mention which god had befriended her. "When those tremors shook the Tower, he sent me to see that the artifacts are safe."

The dragon's slit eyes narrowed. She was displeased. "Do

you refuse to answer my questions?"

Mina was perplexed. "It's just . . . I didn't think you'd be interested. I have no objection to answering. As to who I am, my name is Mina. As to where I came from, I do not know. I am an orphan with no memory of my childhood. As to where I have been, I have been in almost every part of Ansalon. To tell you my tale would take too long. I am supposed to check the artifacts—"

"You waste my time. Come inside and check the artifacts then. No one's stopping you," the dragon snarled irascibly.

Mina realized that the dragon must think Nuitari had revealed the secret of how to enter the globe.

What a fool I was to mention that, Mina thought in irritation. Now what do I say? That I forgot what the god told me? Not even a gully dwarf would believe that!

The dragon glared at her. "Well, what are you waiting for? As for that rigmarole you told me about being an orphan—"

The dragon paused. Her eyes flared open. Her head thrust forward and banged against the crystal.

"By my teeth and tonsils," exclaimed the dragon. "By my lungs and liver. By my heart and stomach, tooth and toenail! *You don't know!*"

Mina couldn't understand what this was all about. "What don't I know?" she asked the dragon.

But the creature was muttering to herself and no longer paying attention.

Mina caught a few words of the dragon's ranting: ". . . bastard . . . liar . . . we'll see about *that!*"

Mina could make no sense of any of it.

"What is it I don't know?" Mina asked again. Something twisted inside her. She had the feeling that this was desperately important.

"You don't know"—the dragon paused—"how to get inside. Do you?"

That hadn't been what the dragon meant. The dragon was now teasing, taunting. Her slit eyes glinted. Her green lip curled. "There's no trick to it, really. Just walk right through the crystal wall. As to breathing under water, you won't have any trouble. It's all part of the magic, isn't it?"

The beast is trying to lure me inside, Mina reasoned. I could stay here and remain safe from the dragon, but that would mean failing my lord.

"Chemosh, be with me!" Mina prayed and walked up to the crystal wall.

She placed both her hands on the glass. Her fingers traced the sharp edges of the runes engraved on the surface. She focused on her destination—the sand castle in the center of the globe and, keeping her gaze fixed on that and away from the dragon, Mina drew in a deep breath, shut her eyes, and walked forward.

The crystal melted like ice at her touch and she found herself inside the globe.

Mina experienced a strange sensation. She was not floundering, drowning, gasping for breath. It was as though her body had lost its solidity. She did not breathe the water so much as she was one with the water. She was water, no longer flesh. The sensation was marvelous, liberating, and frightening all at once. She could not take time to try to understand what had happened. Tensing, Mina turned to face the dragon, certain that now the creature must attack.

The dragon's lips drew back from the yellowed fangs in a grin. To Mina's astonishment, the dragon flipped herself around ponderously in the water and swam down to the floor of the globe, where she settled herself on the bottom.

"You will excuse me," said the dragon. "I am old and all this excitement has worn me out. Please don't let me deter you from your task."

Sharks circled Mina. Jellyfish floated uncomfortably close.

The squid's eyes opened. The sea creatures watched her. None of them came near her.

Mina began to swim through the water, heading toward the sand castle, keeping her enemies in sight.

Moving in lazy circles, the sharks accompanied her. The squid propelled itself through the water, but kept its distance.

Puzzled beyond measure, Mina continued to swim. The sea creatures followed her, watching her. The dragon watched her, gold-green eyes gleaming with what might have been amusement.

Of course, there will be traps.

Arriving at the structure, Mina swam around to the front and floated there, swaying gently with the currents, to gaze at it in perplexity. The water had not been playing tricks on her eyes. The *Solio Febalas* was a child's play castle made of sand, which looked as though it would crumble at a touch.

She would have to get down on her hands and knees to crawl through the doorway, and even with her slender build, it would be a tight fit.

There are no artifacts! This is a hoax perpetrated by Nuitari, but why? Why go to all this trouble? Certainly, Mina reflected, the ways of the gods are beyond man's comprehension. My lord will be exceedingly disappointed.

Mina glanced back at the dragon, who appeared to be enjoying her discomfiture. Mina wondered if she should continue to investigate or give up and swim back.

At least, I should look inside, she determined. My lord will be outraged enough as it is. I should be able to provide him with all the details.

Mina approached the sand castle with caution, mindful of traps and half-afraid she would bring down the entire structure if she bumped into it. The top of the walls came to her shoulders.

Mina reached out her hand to gingerly touch the wall. The structure was made of sand that had been fused together and was hard as marble. Nothing happened when she touched the wall. She glanced back again at the dragon and then outside the crystal globe, fearing Nuitari must come at any moment.

No one was there and the dragon hadn't stirred.

Mina swam around to the front of the sand castle and found the entrance—a door, about three feet in height, made of thousands of pearls that shimmered with a pinkish-purple luster. A single rune carved out of a large emerald was embedded in the center. Mina brushed the tips of her fingers across the emerald.

The rune flashed a blinding green. The pearl door flew open with explosive force. Too late, Mina understood the trap. The building was air tight, sealed against the water. When the door opened, the seal broke. The water rushed inside, carrying Mina with it.The rush of the water ceased. The door shut and sealed, leaving the castle once again airtight.

Leaving Mina, once again, a prisoner.

Small wonder the dragon had looked amused.

The force of the water had swept Mina off her feet and tumbled her about. She lay on her stomach in water that was up to her chin. The water level was sinking fast, however. There must be a drain in the floor. She could hear the water gurgle as it swirled away.

Mina could not see a thing in the pitch darkness. She raised herself up slowly off the floor, fearful of hitting her head against the low ceiling. She felt nothing. She reached up her hand, still felt nothing. She tried straightening to her full height.

She did not hit her head. She stood perfectly still, afraid to move when she could not see. Gradually, her eyes became accustomed to the gloom. The room was not as dark as she'd first thought. There were no lights, but some objects around the room gave off a soft glow, so she was able to make out her surroundings.

Mina looked about her. She looked up, and she looked down. Her breath caught in her throat. Tears burned her eyes, causing the lights to blur together.

She was in an immense chamber. One hundred paces would not have carried her halfway across it. The ceiling on which she was afraid she might hit her head was so far above her that she could barely see it.

And, all around her, were the gods.

Each god had an alcove carved out of the wall, and in each alcove was an altar. Artifacts, sacred to each god, stood on the altar or on the floor before the altar.

Some of the artifacts shone with a radiant light. Some flickered, some glimmered. Some of the artifacts were dark, and some seemed to suck the light from the others.

Mina fell, trembling, to her knees.

The holy power of the gods seemed to crush her.

"Gods forgive me!" she whispered. "What have I done? What have I done?"

12

Nuitari arrived back at his Tower to find it under siege. His sister, Zeboim, goddess of the Deep, was apparently intent upon shaking it to bits.

Although they were siblings, born to Takhisis and her consort, the god of Vengeance, Sargonnas, Nuitari and Zeboim were as different as foaming waves and black moonlight. Zeboim had inherited her mother's volatile nature and fierce ambition but lacked her mother's discipline. Nuitari, by contrast, was born with his mother's cold and calculating cunning, tempered by his passion for magic. Zeboim was close to their father, Sargonnas, and often worked with him to further the cause of his beloved minotaurs, who were among the sea goddess's chief worshippers. Nuitari despised their father and made no secret of it. He didn't think much of minotaurs either, one reason there were few minotaur mages.

Nuitari had known his sister was going to be upset over the fact he'd raised up the old Tower of High Sorcery in her sea without first seeking her permission. Knowing her, he knew she was capable of refusing him out of sheer caprice. Also fearing this would put ideas into her head, Nuitari had felt it was wiser to build his Tower first and ask his sister's pardon later.

He was attempting to do just that, but Zeboim refused to listen.

"I swear to you, Brother," Zeboim fumed, "not one of your Black Robes will dare set foot on water or face my wrath! If a wizard should try to take a hot bath, I will push him under! Any ship that transports a wizard will capsize. Rafts carrying wizards across rivers will sink. If a wizard puts his toe in a stream, I will swell it to a raging river. A wizard who so much as drinks a glass of water will choke on it——"

She continued like this, ranting and raging and stamping her feet. With every stamp, the ocean floor trembled. Her fury rocked the Tower on its foundations. Nuitari could only guess at the havoc the tremors were wreaking inside. He'd lost contact with his two wizards, and that worried him.

"I am sorry, dear sister, if I have upset you," he said contritely. "Truly, it was unintentional."

"Raising up this Tower without my knowledge was unintentional?" Zeboim howled.

"I thought you knew!" Nuitari protested, all innocence. "I thought you knew everything that went on in your ocean! If you didn't, if this comes as such a surprise to you, is it my fault?"

Seething, Zeboim glared at him. She flopped and floundered but could see no way out of the net that had so neatly trapped her. If she claimed she had known he was building the Tower, then why hadn't she stopped him if it so offended her? To admit she hadn't known was to admit she didn't know what was happening in her own realm.

"I have been preoccupied with other, more important matters," she said loftily. "But now that I know, you must make reparations."

"What do you want?" Nuitari asked smoothly. "I will be only

too happy to accede to your demands, dear sister. Provided they are reasonable, of course."

He assumed that she'd found out not only about the Tower but also about the Hall of Sacrilege. He figured she would ask for her holy artifacts to be returned to her in exchange for her permission to keep his Tower. Nuitari was prepared to hand over one artifact or maybe even two, if she persisted in her threats against his wizards. Her response was completely unexpected.

"I want Mina," declared Zeboim.

"Mina?" Nuitari repeated, amazed. First Takhisis. Then Chemosh. Now Zeboim. Did every god in the universe want this girl?

"You are holding her prisoner. You will bring her to me. In return, you may keep your Tower," Zeboim offered magnanimously. "I won't make you tear it down."

"How kind of you, sister," Nuitari said in honeyed, poisonous tones. "What do you want with this human female, if you don't mind my asking?"

Zeboim looked up at the sunlit surface of the ocean.

"Just how many of your Black Robes do you think are currently sailing the high seas, Brother?" she asked. "I know of six right now."

She lifted her hands and the seawater began to bubble and boil around her. The sunlight vanished, overrun by storm clouds. Nuitari had visions of his wizards pitching off rolling decks.

"Very well! You will have her!" he said angrily. "Though I don't know why you want her. She belongs to Chemosh, body and soul."

Zeboim smiled a knowing smile, and Nuitari guessed immediately that she and Chemosh had made some sort of bargain.

"That's why the god did not come to claim his trollop,"

Nuitari muttered. "He has made a deal with Zeboim. I wonder what for. Not my Tower, I trust."

He eyed his sister. She eyed him back.

"I'll go fetch her," said Nuitari.

"You do that," said Zeboim. "And don't be long about it. I grow bored so easily."

She gave his Tower a little shake for good measure.

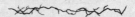

Upon entering the Blood Sea Tower, Nuitari summoned his wizards.

They did not respond.

He thought this ominous. Caele was usually always on hand, falling over himself to be the first to gush over the return of the Master, and Basalt, solid and reliable, would be waiting to launch into grievances against Caele.

Neither appeared in response to their master's summons.

Nuitari called again, his tone dire.

No answer.

Nuitari went to the laboratory, thinking they might be there. He found it an ungodly mess—the floor awash in spilled potions and broken glass, a small fire burning in a corner, several escaped imps wandering about freely. Nuitari put out the fire with an irritated breath, trapped the imps and locked them back inside their cages, then continued his search for the missing wizards. He had a feeling he knew where to look.

Arriving at Mina's chambers, he found the door standing wide open. Nuitari entered.

Two stone coffins and no sign of Mina.

Nuitari pried the stone slabs off the sarcophagi. Caele, gasping for air, clutched at the sides of the coffin and pulled himself up. The half-elf looked half-dead. He tried to stand, but his legs were too wobbly. He sat in the coffin and shivered. Dwarves being accustomed to living in dark places, Basalt had taken his confinement in stride. He was far more worried about facing his irate god, and he kept his head down, his hood lowered, trying desperately to avoid Nuitari's baleful gaze.

"Uh, if you'll pardon me, Master, I will just go attend to the cleaning up. . . ." Basalt tried to sidle out of the room.

"Where is Mina?" Nuitari demanded.

Basalt glanced about furtively, as if hoping he she might be hiding under the couch. Not finding her, he looked back at the Master and almost immediately looked away again.

"It was Caele's fault," Basalt said, mumbling into his beard. "He tried to kill her, but he bungled it as usual, and she took his knife—"

"You snake!" Caele hissed. Crawling weakly out of the coffin, he raised a feeble hand against the dwarf.

"Stop it, both of you!" Nuitari commanded. "Where is Mina?"

"Everything happened at once, Master." Caele whined. "Zeboim started shaking the Tower, and the next thing I knew Mina had my knife and was threatening to kill me—"

"That is true, Master," said Basalt. "Mina threatened to kill poor Caele if I tried to stop her, and of course, I feared for his life, and then Chemosh came and forced us inside these coffins—"

"You lie," Nuitari said calmly. "The Lord of Death may not enter my Tower. Not anymore."

"I heard his voice, Master," gasped Basalt, flinching. "His voice was everywhere. He spoke to Mina. He said the Tower was hers. Except for the guardian . . ."

"The guardian," repeated Nuitari, and he knew where Mina had gone—the Hall of Sacrilege. He relaxed. "Midori will deal with her, which means there won't be much left. I must come up with something to placate my sister. I will put Mina's remains in a pretty box. Zeboim can trade that to Chemosh for whatever it is he has promised her—a promise he probably doesn't mean to keep anyway."

He looked back at his two wizards, who stood cringing before him. "Start cleaning up this mess." He glanced at the coffins. "Don't get rid of those. They might come in useful in the future if you dare disobey me again."

"No, Master," Basalt mumbled.

"Yes, Master," Caele gulped.

Satisfied, Nuitari departed to retrieve Mina's corpse.

Nuitari expected to find the sea globe in an uproar—blood in the water, the dragon looking satiated, sharks fighting over the scraps. Instead, jellyfish undulated about the globe in maddening calm and the dragon was asleep on the sandy bottom.

Apparently he'd been worried over nothing. Mina had not come here after all. Nuitari sent an urgent message to his wizards to search the Tower for her and was starting to leave to assist them when the dragon spoke.

"If you're looking for the human, she's inside your sand castle."

Nuitari stood aghast for a moment, then surged through the crystal wall to confront the dragon.

Midori watched him from deep within the black depths of her shell.

"You allowed her to enter?" Nuitari raged. "What kind of guardian are you?"

"She told me you had sent her," replied the dragon. The shell shifted slightly. "She said you wanted her to make certain the holy artifacts had not been damaged by the quakes."

"And you believed her lies?" Nuitari was aghast.

"No," said Midori, green-gold eyes glittering. "Not any more than I believe your lies."

"My lies?" Nuitari could not make sense of this. He'd never lied to the dragon, not about anything important. "What—Never mind that! Why did you let her pass?"

"Next time, do your own dirty work," Midori snarled, drawing her head back into her shell. She closed her eyes and feigned sleep.

Nuitari didn't have time to puzzle out what was bothering the dragon. He had to stop Mina from walking off with his artifacts. Unseen and unheard, the god materialized inside the *Solio Febalas*.

There was Mina. She was not ransacking the place, as he expected. She was on her knees, her head bowed, her hands clasped.

"Gods of Darkness and Gods of Light and those Gods who love the twilight in between, forgive my desecration of this holy place," Mina was praying softly. "Forgive the ignorance of mortals, forgive the arrogance and fear that led them to commit this crime against you. Though the souls of those who stole these sacred objects are long since passed, the weakness in men remains. Few bow down before you. Few honor you. Many deny your existence or claim man has outgrown his need of you. If they could but see this blessed sight as I see it and feel your presence as I feel it, all mankind would fall to your feet and worship."

Nuitari had intended to grab her by the scruff of her neck and twist her body in his bare hands until her bones cracked and her blood ran red. Like his wizards, he did not believe in using magic for frivolous purposes.

But he did not kill her. Looking around the chamber, he saw what she saw—not artifacts to be bartered like pigs on market day. He saw the sacred altars. He saw the divine light. He saw the awful power of the gods. He felt what she felt—a holy presence. Nuitari drew back his hand.

"You are the most irritating human," he said, exasperated. "I do not understand you!"

Mina lifted her head and turned to look at him. Her face was stained with tears. She reminded him of a lost child.

"I do not understand myself, Lord," she said. She bowed her head. "Take my life as punishment for my transgression into this holy place. I deserve to die."

"You do deserve to die," Nuitari told her grimly. "But today you are lucky. I have promised you to my sister who has, in turn, promised you to Chemosh."

He might have been talking of someone else. Mina remained where she was, crouched on the floor, crushed, ground down by the weight of heaven.

"Didn't you hear me? You are free to go," he said. "Though I must warn you that if you have, by some mischance, tucked a blessed ring or a vial of life-restoring potion up your sleeve, you should divest yourself of it before you depart. Otherwise, you will find your luck has run out."

"I have touched nothing, Lord," she said.

Rising to her feet, she walked toward the door. She moved slowly, as though reluctant to leave. Her eyes lingered on the holy relics of the gods.

"I don't suppose it would do me any good to ask how you managed to circumvent my magical safeguards?" Nuitari asked. "How you broke into a door that was magically sealed and trapped, and then made your way through rune-encrusted crystal walls, and how you came to breathe seawater as easily as air. I suppose Chemosh aided you in all this."

"I prayed to my lord, yes," Mina replied absently.

Nuitari waited for details, but she did not elaborate.

"I would like to know, though," Nuitari continued, "how you managed to slip past the dragon. She said you told her some far-fetched story that I had sent you. I think, in truth, she must have been asleep and is afraid to admit it to me."

Mina smiled a half-smile at this. "I believe I did say something of the sort, Lord. The dragon was wide awake. She saw me, spoke to me, and posed riddles for me to answer. After that, the dragon permitted me to enter the globe."

"Riddles?" Nuitari was skeptical. "What riddles?"

Mina thought back. "There were two: 'Where did you come from?' the dragon asked me, and 'Where have you been?'"

"Not much in the way of riddles," Nuitari stated dryly.

Mina nodded. "I agree, Lord. However, the dragon grew angry when she thought I was evading the questions. That is what made me think they were riddles meant to trick me."

The sea floor heaved and lurched. The Tower shook on its foundations, and a voice called out in warning, "Make haste, Brother! I grow weary of waiting!"

Nuitari removed the seal from the door and gestured to Mina.

"I will spare your life this time," he said. "I will not be so generous the next, so let there be no next time."

He ushered her through the door, which was the last trap. It would not be tripped by the thief, but by the artifact the thief was trying to carry out of the Hall. Mina had said she did not have anything in her possession and Nuitari believed her. He was not surprised to see her pass through the door without harm. He sealed the door swiftly, making a mental note to strengthen the spells he'd cast upon it. He'd had no idea that Chemosh—even at a distance—would prove so adept at breaking through magical barriers.

A whisk of his hand and Mina was gone, transported through water, crystal globe, and Tower walls to the sea beyond, where Zeboim was waiting for her.

Not exactly trusting his sister, Nuitari kept an eye on her, wanting to make certain his sister would keep her word and cease her attacks on the Tower. The moment she had Mina, Zeboim clasped the young woman in a fond embrace and the two disappeared.

Nuitari returned to the globe to question the dragon, only to find Midori gone.

Such absences were not unusual. The dragon occasionally went on hunting trips. He had the feeling, though, that this time she'd left without any plans to come back. She'd been exceedingly angry with him.

Nuitari stood inside the sea globe, staring at the *Solio Febalas*. He thought back over everything that had anything to do with Mina.

She was, he decided, nothing but trouble.

"Good riddance," he muttered. He went off, with a grim sigh, to see if he could find and placate the dragon.

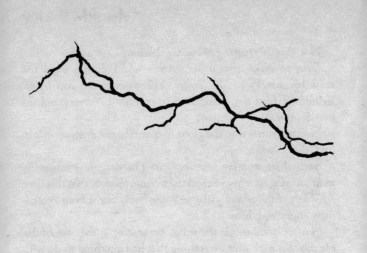

BOOK III

MINA'S
KISS

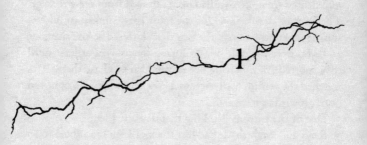

*T*he tavern, if one could dignify it by that term, existed inside an overturned boat that had been blown ashore during a storm. The tavern's name was the Dinghy, though local wit called it the Dingy.

The Dingy lived up to its name. It had no tables, no chairs, no windows. Its patrons either stood grouped around the bar that had been cobbled together out of rotting wooden beams, or they squatted on overturned vegetable crates. Cracks in the hull provided what light managed to struggle in, along with a modicum of fresh air that fought a losing battle against the stench of dwarf spirits, urine, and vomit. Those who frequented the Dingy came here mainly because they'd been thrown out of every other place.

Rhys and Nightshade sat on crates as near one of the cracks as possible, and even then Nightshade found that the smell almost ruined his appetite. Atta's nose twitched constantly, and she sneezed and snuffled.

In addition to no tables and no windows, there was no laughter, no merriment. The bartender dispensed a dubious liquor he claimed was dwarf spirits, but that probably wasn't, pouring it into dented tin mugs that had been salvaged from the wreckage. The patrons drank alone for the most part, sunken in misery, staring in stupefaction at the rats that skittered across the floor and who were the only ones enjoying themselves, at least until they spotted Atta. Having been forbidden to chase them, Atta watched the vermin with narrowed eyes and, when one came too near, growled at it.

One of the patrons drinking that day was Lleu.

Rhys and Nightshade had lost track of Lleu for a short time, then, quite by accident, they picked up his trail, heading south from Solace, not east. They traced him to the city of New Port located on New Bay in the southern portion of New Sea. Rhys wondered why his brother was traveling south, when the other Beloved were being drawn to the east. He had his answer when he reached New Port. Lleu had booked passage on a ship sailing to Flotsam, due to leave in a few days' time.

Finding Lleu had not been difficult. Rhys had simply gone from disreputable bar to disreputable bar, giving Lleu's description to the barkeeps. In New Port, they located him on the third try.

The barkeepers always remembered Lleu, for he stood out from the other customers, who were generally a slovenly lot, slaves to the dwarf spirits that ruled their lives. Those "caught by the dwarf," as the saying went, were generally gaunt and pale—for the liquor became bread and meat to them; their eyes were dull, their cheeks hollow. Lleu, by contrast, was hale and hearty, handsome and charming. He had long since abandoned the robes of a cleric of Kiri-Jolith and was now wearing the shirt and doublet, leather boots and woolen stockings of a young man of genteel birth.

Somehow or other he'd come by money, for his clothes were well-to-do and he had managed to pay the steep price for his voyage. Perhaps one of his victims had been wealthy. Either that, or he'd taken to thieving, which wouldn't be surprising. After all, Lleu had nothing to fear from the law, who would be in for a severe shock if they tried to hang him.

When Rhys entered the Dingy, Lleu looked at him, then looked away. There was no recognition in the dead eyes. Lleu had no memory of Rhys or of anything. Lleu knew his name, and that was all he knew. Chemosh told him who he was, presumably. What he had been was forever lost.

The other patrons in the tavern were absorbed in drinking and wanted nothing to do with a stranger, so Lleu kept up a cheerful conversation with himself. He bragged about his carousing and the women who threw themselves at him. He laughed at his own jokes and sang bawdy songs, and Rhys's heart ached. Lleu drank until he ran out of coins to pay for his spirits, then he tried to drink on credit. The barkeep was having none of that, however, yet Lleu continued to sit there, his mug in his hand.

This went on throughout the afternoon. Lleu would forget from one moment to the next he had nothing to drink and would lift the mug to his lips. Finding it empty, he would bang the mug on the crate and demand more in a loud voice. The barkeep, knowing he couldn't pay, simply ignored him. Lleu would continue to bang the mug on the crate until he forgot why he was doing this, and then he would set it down. After a few moments, he'd pick it up and shout for more drink.

Rhys sat watching the thing that had once been his brother and making an occasional show of drinking the liquor he'd been forced to purchase in order to placate the barkeep. Nightshade had been bored, at first, then he fell to trying to hit the rats with dried beans he'd found in some old sacking stuffed inside the crate on which he was seated. The kender had come by (Rhys did not like to ask how) a slingshot, and though he was clumsy in its use at first, he had since acquired a certain amount of skill. He could hit a rat with a bean at twenty paces and send it somersaulting head over tail across the dirt floor. He was growing tired of the sport, however. The intelligent rats now kept to their holes and, besides, he'd run out of beans.

"Rhys," said Nightshade, wrapping up the slingshot and shoving it in his belt. "It's time for supper."

"I thought you'd lost your appetite," said Rhys, smiling.

"My nose lost it. My stomach didn't," Nightshade returned. "Atta thinks it's suppertime, too, don't you, girl?" He patted the dog on the head.

Atta looked up and wagged her tail, hoping they were going to leave.

"We can't go yet," Rhys began, then, seeing Nightshade's face fall and Atta's ears droop, he added, "but you could both go for a walk. I have this leftover from lunch."

He and Nightshade had helped a farmer put a wheel back on a wagon that morning on their way into town and, although Rhys had refused to accept payment, the man had shared his food with them. Rhys handed over a packet of dried meat to the kender.

"I'll take it outside to eat it," Nightshade said. "That way my nose can feel hungry along with my stomach."

He stood up and stretched out the kinks. Atta shook herself all over, starting with her nose and ending with her tail, and looked eagerly at the door.

"What about you?" Nightshade asked, seeing that Rhys remained seated. "Aren't you hungry?"

Rhys shook his head. "I will stay here and keep watch on Lleu. He said something about meeting a young woman later this evening."

Nightshade took the food, but he didn't immediately go off with it. He stood looking at Rhys and seemed to be trying to make up his mind whether to say something or not.

"Yes, my friend," said Rhys mildly. "What is it?"

"He's leaving on a ship in two days," Nightshade said.

Rhys nodded.

"What are we going to do then? Swim across New Sea after him?"

"I'm talking to the captain. I have offered to work on board the ship in return for passage."

"Then what?"

Leaning near, Nightshade looked his friend straight in the eye. "Rhys, face it! We could still be chasing your brother when you're ninety and using that stick of yours as a cane! Lleu will be as young as ever, going from tavern to tavern, slinging down dwarf spirits like there's no tomorrow. Because, you know what, Rhys, for him *there is no tomorrow!*"

Nightshade sighed and shook his head. "It's not much of a life you have. That's all I'm saying."

Rhys didn't defend himself because he couldn't. The kender was right. It wasn't much of a life, but what else could he do? Until someone wise found a way to stop the Beloved, he could at least try to prevent Lleu from claiming any more victims, and the only way he could do that was to track his brother like a hunter tracks the marauding wolf.

Nightshade saw his friend's face darken, and he felt immediately remorseful.

"Rhys, I'm sorry." Nightshade patted his hand. "I didn't mean to hurt your feelings. It's just that you're a good man, and it seems to me you should be going around doing good things instead of spending your time stopping your brother from doing bad ones."

"I am not hurt," said Rhys, touching Nightshade gently on the shoulder. "Has anyone told you that you are wise, my friend?"

"Not recently," said Nightshade with a grin.

"Well, you are. I will consider what you have said. Go along and eat your supper."

Nightshade nodded and squeezed Rhys's hand. He and Atta turned and were heading outside, when suddenly the door burst open with a slamming bang that jolted the drunks out of their stupor and caused several to drop their mugs. A gust of wind, smelling strongly of the sea, swirled about the interior of the tavern, kicking up the dust and spinning it into miniature cyclones that ushered in Zeboim.

The goddess casually knocked aside the kender, who was in her way, and stared about the shadowy room for Rhys.

"Monk, I know you're here," she called in a wave-crashing voice that rattled the timbers and set the rats fleeing. "Where are you?"

Her sea green dress frothed around her ankles, her sea foam hair tangled in the wind that whistled through the cracks in the hull. The barkeep gaped. The drunks stared. Lleu, sighting a beautiful woman, leaped up and made a gallant bow.

Rhys, startled beyond measure, rose to meet the goddess.

"I am here, Majesty," he called out.

Atta ducked between his legs and hunkered there, growling. Nightshade picked himself off the floor. He'd managed, by some nifty acrobatics, to save his lunch, and he stuffed the meat into his pocket.

"I'm here too, Goddess," he sang out cheerfully.

"Shut up, kender," said Zeboim, "and you—" She raised a warding hand, pointed at Lleu. "You shut up as well, you disgusting piece of carrion."

Zeboim focused on Rhys, smiling sweetly. "I have someone I want you to meet, Monk."

The goddess gestured and, after a moment's hesitation, another woman entered the tavern.

"Rhys, this is Mina," said Zeboim casually. "Mina, Rhys Mason—my monk." ·

Rhys was so amazed he fell backward, tripping over his staff and stepping on Atta, who yelped in protest. He could say nothing; his brain was in such turmoil it could make little sense of what he was seeing. He had a fleeting impression of a young woman who was not so much beautiful as she was arresting, with hair like flame and eyes like none he'd ever before seen.

The eyes were an amber color and he had the eerie impression that, like amber, they held imprisoned everyone she had ever met. The amber gaze fixed on him, and Rhys felt himself drawn to her like all the others, hundreds of thousands of people caught and held like insects in resin.

The amber seeped around him, warm and sweet.

Rhys cried out and flung up his arm to block her gaze, as he might have flung up his arm to block a blow.

The amber cracked. The eyes continued to confine their poor prisoners, but now he could see flaws, tiny cracks and striations, branching out from the dark pupils.

"Rhys Mason," said Mina, holding out her hand to him. "You know the answer to the riddle!"

"Him?" Zeboim scoffed. "He knows nothing, Child. Now we really *must* be leaving. This was a fleeting visit, Rhys, my love. Sorry we can't stay. I just wanted the two of you to meet. It seemed the least I could do, since I'm the one who commanded you to search the world for her. So farewell—"

Lleu gave a hollow cry, an unearthly wail, and flung himself at Mina. He tried to seize hold of her, but she stepped back out of his way.

"Wretch," she said coldly. "What do you think you are doing?"

Lleu fell to his knees. He held out his hands to her, pleading.

"Mina," Lleu cried in wrenching tones, "don't turn away from me! You know me!"

Rhys stared and Nightshade gaped, his mouth hanging open. Lleu, who did not remember Rhys, remembered Mina.

As to her, she regarded him as she might have regarded one of the rats. "You are mistaken——"

"You kissed me!" Lleu tore open his shirt to reveal the mark of her lips, burned into his flesh. "Look!"

"Ah, you are one of the Beloved," Mina said, and she shrugged. "You have my lord's blessing——"

"I don't want it!" he cried vehemently. "Take it away!"

Mina stared at him, puzzled.

"Take it away!" Lleu shrieked. His hands clawed at her, clawed at the air when he could not reach her. "Take it away! Free me!"

"I don't understand," Mina said, and she seemed truly bewildered by his request. "I gave you what you wanted, what all mortals want—endless life, endless youth, endless beauty . . ."

"Endless misery," he wailed. "I can't stand your voice constantly dinning in my ears. I can't stand the pain that drives me out into the night, the pain that nothing can drown, not the strongest liquor. . . ."

Lleu clasped his hands together. "Take the 'blessing' away, Mina. Let me go."

She drew back, haughty and aloof. The amber hardened, the cracks sealed. "You gave yourself to my lord. You are his. I can do nothing."

Lleu lurched forward, still on his knees. "I beg you!"

Zeboim cast the Beloved a look of disgust and drew Mina away.

"Come, Child. Speaking of Chemosh, he will be growing impatient. As for you, Monk"—Zeboim glanced back at Rhys over her shoulder and her look was not friendly—"I will talk to you later."

Storm winds blew into the tavern, caught up Rhys, and flung him back against the wall. Sand stung his face. He could not see for the sand and the lashing rain, but he could hear people cursing, crates being tossed about the room. The storm raged for an instant and then subsided. Rhys found Atta cowering under a crate. Lleu was still on his knees. Hoping against hope his brother's memory had returned, Rhys hastened over to him.

"Lleu, it's me, Rhys. . . ."

Lleu shoved him aside. "I don't give a damn who you are. Get out of my way. Barkeep, more spirits!"

The barkeep appeared, rising up from behind the bar. He stared around at the overturned crates and upended drunks, and then he scowled at Lleu.

"Fine friends you have. Look at this mess! Who's going to pay for it? Not you, I suppose. Get out," he shouted, shaking a clenched fist. "And don't come back!"

Muttering that he had better things to do and better places to go, Lleu stalked out of the tavern, slamming the door behind him.

"I will pay for the damage," said Rhys, handing over his last coin. Whistling to Atta, he started after Lleu, saying to Nightshade in passing, "Hurry! We have to follow him!"

A whimper from Atta caused Rhys to stop and look back.

Nightshade was staring at the place where Mina had been standing. His eyes were round and wide, and Rhys saw in astonishment, tears were rolling down the kender's cheeks.

"Oh, Rhys," Nightshade gulped. "It's so sad. So very sad!"

He buried his face in his hands and wept as though his heart would break.

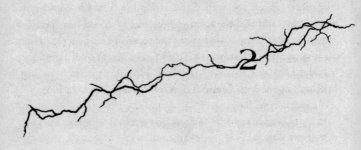

Rhys hastened back to his friend.

"Nightshade," he said in concern. "I'm sorry for being so thoughtless. That was a bad fall you took. Where does it hurt?"

But all Nightshade could say was, "It's so sad! I can't bear it!"

Rhys put his arm around the kender and led him from the tavern. Atta trotted after them, looking anxiously at her friend, and every now and then giving his hand a sympathetic lick.

Torn between his worry for his friend and his concern that he might lose track of his brother, Rhys did his best to soothe Nightshade, all the while keeping Lleu in sight.

His brother strolled along the docks, hands in his pockets, whistling an off-key tune, not a care in the world. He greeted strangers as though they were old friends and was soon in conversation with a group of sailors. Rhys thought back to only moments before, when his wretched brother had been begging for death, and he assumed he knew why the kender was sobbing.

Rhys patted Nightshade consolingly on the shoulder, thinking he'd soon regain his composure, but the kender was completely undone. Nightshade could only repeat, gulping and blubbering, that it was all so sad, and he cried even harder. Rhys was worried that he was going to have to leave his friend in this state, but then he saw his brother enter a bar in company with the sailors.

Certain Lleu would be there for some time, especially if the sailors were buying, Rhys steered Nightshade into a quiet alley. The kender plunked down on the ground and sobbed dismally.

"Nightshade," said Rhys, "I know you're sorry for Lleu, but this won't help—"

Nightshade looked up. "Lleu? I'm not sorry for him! It's her!"

"Her? Do you mean Mina?" Rhys asked, astonished. "She's the one you're crying over?"

Nightshade nodded, prompting more tears.

"What about her?" Rhys had a sudden thought. "Is she one of the Beloved? Is she dead?"

"Oh, no!" Nightshade gulped. Then he hesitated. Then repeated, "No . . ." only this time more slowly.

"Are you crying for the terrible evil she has done?" Rhys's voice hardened. His hand clenched around the staff. "If she lives, that is good. She can be killed."

Nightshade lifted a tear-stained face and stared at him in amazement. "Did you really just say that? You want to kill her? You—the monk who lifted a fly out of puddle of beer so that it wouldn't drown?"

Rhys recalled his brother's despairing plea and Mina's callous and uncaring reply. He thought of young Cam in Solace, all the young people, slaves of Chemosh, driven to murder, the imprint of her lips over their hearts.

"I wish I'd killed her as she'd stood there before me," he said.

Rhys reached over and shook the kender, pinching his shoulder hard. "Answer me! What is so sad about her?"

Nightshade shrank away from him.

"I really don't know," the kender said in a small voice. "Honest! The feeling just came over me somehow. Don't be mad, Rhys. I'll try to stop crying now."

He gave a hiccup, but more tears slid down his cheeks, and he hid his face in Atta's fur. She nuzzled his neck and licked away his tears. Her brown eyes, fixed on Rhys, seemed to reproach him.

The kender rubbed his shoulder where Rhys had gripped him, and the monk felt like a monster. "I'll go fetch some water."

He gave the kender an apologetic pat that only made Nightshade cry harder. Leaving him in Atta's care, Rhys walked to a nearby public well. He was drawing up the bucket when he felt a divine presence breathing down his neck.

"What secret have you been keeping from me, Monk?" Zeboim demanded.

"I have no secrets, Majesty," Rhys said, sighing.

"What riddle is that girl talking about then? What is the answer?"

"I do not know what Mina meant by that question, Majesty," Rhys said. "Why don't you ask her?"

"Because she is a little liar. You, for all your faults, are not, so tell me the riddle and tell me the answer."

"I have told you, Majesty, that I don't know what she was talking about. Since I am not a liar, I assume you must believe me." Rhys filled his water skin and started to walk back to the alley.

Zeboim fumed along beside him. "You must know! Put your mind to it!"

Rhys heard his brother's voice, his despairing plea for death. He felt Nightshade's tears on his skin. Losing patience, Rhys rounded angrily on the goddess.

"All I know, Majesty, is you had in your possession the person you commanded me to find. You have no business asking me anything!"

Zeboim halted, momentarily taken aback by his anger. Rhys walked on, and Zeboim hastened to catch up. She slid her arm through his arm and held on tightly when he tried to shake her off.

"I like it when you're forceful, but don't ever do it again." She gave his hand a playful slap that numbed his arm to the elbow. "As for Mina, I introduced you to her, didn't I? You know what she looks like now. I let her go, that is true, but I didn't have any choice in the matter. You recall my son? His soul trapped in a khas piece?"

Rhys sighed. He did, indeed.

"You'll be glad to know he's been freed," Zeboim said.

Rhys found his elation at this news easy to contain.

The goddess was silent a moment, watching Rhys through narrowed eyes, trying to see into his heart.

He opened his soul to her. He had nothing to hide, and eventually she gave up.

"You are telling the truth. Perhaps you *don't* know the answer to this riddle," Zeboim said in a hissing whisper. "If I were you, I would find out. Mina was troubled by you. I could see that. Don't worry that you can't find her, Brother Rhys. Mina will be the one to find you!"

With that and a flurry of rain, she disappeared.

Nightshade and Atta were both fast asleep. The kender had his arms around Atta's neck. She had one paw laid protectively over his chest. Rhys looked at them, sprawled on the cobblestones of a squalid, refuse-laden alley. Atta's fur was matted, and her once glossy coat had lost its luster. The pads of her paws were rough and cracked. Whenever they passed rolling meadows and green hills, Atta would gaze longingly out over the grasslands, and Rhys knew that she wanted to run and run across the green sward and never stop until she came trotting back to him, exhausted and happy.

As for the kender, Nightshade was eating meals on a regular basis, which was more than he'd been doing before Rhys had found him. His clothes were ragged, his boots so worn that his toes poked through. Worse, the kender's cheerful, lively spirit was being ground out of him by the road they trudged, day after day, following a dead man.

Kender should never cry, Rhys thought remorsefully. They are not meant for tears.

Rhys slumped down on a barrel. He lowered his head into his hands and pressed his palms into his eyes. He tried, for comfort's sake, to bring to mind the green pastures and white sheep and the black and white dog racing over the hillside. But it was all gone. He could see nothing except the road—a road of bleakness, degradation, emptiness, death, and despair.

Shame filled him, and self-loathing.

"I was so smug, so arrogant," he said, as bitter tears burned his eyelids. "I thought I could flirt with evil and yet go my own way. I could make a show of serving Zeboim, yet she would never lay claim to me. I could walk a path of darkness without losing sight of the sunlight. But now the sunlight has vanished and I am lost. I have no lantern, no compass to guide me. I stumble along a path so choked and overrun with weeds that I cannot see where to put my feet. And there is no end to it."

The staff of Majere, which he had looked upon as a blessing, now seemed a reproach.

Think on what you might have been, Majere seemed to say to him. *Think on what you have thrown away. Keep this staff always, that it may remind you and be a torment to you.*

Rhys heard off-key humming in a voice he had come to recognize. Wearily, he raised his head and saw Lleu sauntering past the entrance to the alley that was already growing dark with the coming of night.

Lleu—going to keep a tryst with some luckless young woman.

Rhys had no choice. He reached down and shook Nightshade awake. Atta, startled, jumped to her feet. Catching a whiff of Lleu, she growled.

"We have to go," said Rhys.

Nightshade nodded, and rubbed his eyes that were gummed with tears. Rhys helped the kender to stand.

"Nightshade," Rhys said remorsefully, "I'm sorry. I didn't mean to yell at you. And, the gods know, I never meant to hurt you."

"It's all right," Nightshade replied with a wan smile. "It's probably just because you're hungry. Here." He dug into a pocket and produced the maltreated meat. He plucked off bits of pocket fuzz and removed a bent nail. "I'll share."

Rhys wasn't hungry, but he accepted a portion of the meal. He tried to eat it, but his stomach heaved at the smell, and he fed his half to Atta when Nightshade wasn't looking.

The three of them set off down the road and into the night, following the Beloved.

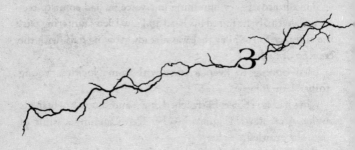

They tracked Lleu to a wharf where he had arranged to meet a young woman. She did not appear, however, and after waiting for over an hour, Lleu cursed her roundly and left, turning into the first tavern he came upon. Rhys knew from experience his brother would remain there all night, and he'd find him either here or near about the tavern the next day. He and a yawning Nightshade and a drooping Atta found a sheltered doorway and, huddling together for warmth, they prepared to get what sleep they could.

Nightshade was snoring softly and Rhys was drifting off when he heard Atta growl. A man dressed in white robes that gleamed in the light of his lantern stood over them, gazed down on them. His face was smiling and concerned, and Rhys soothed Atta's worries.

"It's all right, girl," he said. "He's a cleric of Mishakal."

"Huh?" Nightshade woke with a start, blinking at the lantern light.

"Pardon me for disturbing you, friends," said the white-robed man. "But this a dangerous place to spend the night. I can offer you shelter, a warm bed, and a hot meal in the morning."

Moving closer still, he held the lantern high. "Bless my soul! A monk! Brother, please accept my hospitality. I am Revered Son Patrick."

"Hot meal . . ." Nightshade repeated. He looked hopefully at Rhys.

"We accept your invitation, Revered Sir," Rhys said gratefully. "I am Rhys Mason. This is Nightshade and Atta."

The cleric gave them all polite greeting, even Atta, and though Patrick glanced curiously at Rhys's aqua-green robes he politely refrained from comment. He lit their way through the city streets.

"A long walk, I'm afraid," he said in apology. "But you will find peace and rest at the end of it. Rather like life itself," he added with a smile for Rhys.

As they walked, he told them that this part of New Port was known as Old Port, so-called because it was the oldest part of the new city. New Port had not existed until the Cataclysm had sundered the continent of Ansalon, elevating parts of the continent and sinking others, causing some parts to split wide open and other parts to break off. One of these massive splits allowed the creation of a vast body of water known as New Sea.

The first settlers to arrive at this location—refugees fleeing the destruction up north—were visionaries, who saw immediately the advantage of building here. The land configuration formed a natural harbor. Ships that would soon be plying the waters of New Sea could dock here, take on goods, refit and overhaul, whatever was needed.

The city began modestly, with a stockade overlooking the harbor. New Port's rapid growth soon overflowed the stockade and expanded along the waterfront and inland.

"Like an ungrateful child who discovers wealth and success, and then refuses to acknowledge the humble parents who brought him into the world, the wealthy parts of the city are now far removed from the lowly docks that were its cause for success," Patrick explained, sadly shaking his head.

"The flourishing merchants who fund the ships and own the warehouses live far from the stench of fish heads and tar. Brothels and gambling dens and taverns like the Dinghy have shouldered out more reputable establishments on the waterfront. Housing is cheap down by the docks, for no one of means wants to live there."

They passed row after row of ramshackle dwellings made of wood taken from abandoned warehouses, and walked dismal streets paved with mud. Drunken sailors and slovenly women lurched past them. Even though the hour was past midnight, several children ran up to them to beg for coins or rooted through heaps of refuse in hopes of finding food. Whenever they came upon such children, Patrick stopped to speak to them, before continuing on his way.

"My wife and I have started a school down here among the docks," he explained. "We teach the children to read and write, and send them home with at least one good meal in their bellies. Hopefully we can help some of them find better lives outside this wretched place."

"The gods bless the gift and the giver," said Rhys quietly.

"We do what we can, Brother," said Patrick, with a smile and a sigh. "We do what we can. Here we are. Come inside. Yes, Atta, you can come, too."

The Temple of Mishakal was not a grand edifice, but a very modest building that had evidently undergone recent repairs, for it smelled strongly of whitewash. The only sign that it was a temple was the holy symbol of Mishakal newly painted on one of the walls.

Rhys was about to enter when he saw in the lantern light something that stopped him in his tracks so that Nightshade bumped into him.

Posted on the outside of the little temple, nailed to the wall, was a missive bearing the words, written in bold letters in red ink: *Beware the Beloved of Chemosh!*

Below was a paragraph of text, describing the Beloved, urging people to look for the mark of "Mina's Kiss" and warning people to refrain from taking any vow to serve the Lord of Death.

"Ah," said Patrick, seeing Rhys frown, "do you know about these Beloved of Chemosh?"

"To my sorrow, yes," Rhys replied.

"Do you think your warning will help stop the Beloved?" Nightshade asked the cleric.

"No, not really," Patrick replied sadly. "Few of the people around here can even read, but we talk to all who enter our temple, urging them to be careful."

"What has been the reaction?" Rhys asked.

"As you might expect. Some now fear that everyone they meet is out to slay them. Others think it's a plot to try to coerce people into joining the church." Patrick smiled wryly and shrugged. "The majority scoff at the entire notion. But we can discuss this further in the morning. Now, come to your beds."

He hustled them inside and led them to a room where a row of cots had been set up. He gave them blankets and wished them a good night.

"May the blessing of Mishakal guard your rest this night, my friends," he said as he left.

Rhys lay down on the cot, and perhaps Mishakal did touch him gently because, for the first night in many long, weary nights, he did not dream of his wretched brother.

Rhys did not dream of anything.

Rhys was up with first light to find Nightshade happily devouring a bowl of bread and milk in company with a pleasant looking woman who introduced herself as Revered Sister Galena. She invited Rhys to sit down and break his fast. He gladly did so, for he discovered he was unusually hungry.

"Only if I may be allowed to do some work for you in payment," he added with a smile.

"It's not necessary, Brother," said Galena. "But I know you won't take 'no' for an answer, so I accept your offer with grateful thanks. Mishakal knows we can use all the help we can get."

"The kender and I must take care of some business first," Rhys said, washing up his dishes, "but we will return in the afternoon."

"Can I stay here, Rhys?" Nightshade asked eagerly. "You don't really need my help, and the Revered Sister said she'd teach me how to paint walls!"

Rhys looked uncertainly at Galena.

She smiled broadly. "Of course he can stay."

"Very well," said Rhys. He drew Nightshade off to one side. "I have to go find Lleu. I'll meet you back here. Don't say anything about knowing one of the Beloved," he added in an undertone. "Don't say anything about Zeboim or about Mina or about being able to talk to dead people or that you're a nightstalker—"

"Don't say anything about anything," Nightshade said with a wise nod.

"Right," said Rhys. He knew his advice would be useless, but he felt bound to try. "And keep your hands to yourself. I have to go now. Atta, watch!"

He pointed at the kender. Nightshade had gone over to help Galena wash up, and of course, the first words out of his mouth were, "Say, Revered Sister, do you have anyone in your family who is recently deceased? Because, if you do—"

Rhys smiled and shook his head and went in search of Lleu.

He found his brother strolling the docks in company with a young woman who had a baby in her arms and a little boy of about four walking beside her, holding onto her long skirts. Lleu was at his most charming. The young woman was looking at him with adoring eyes, hanging on his every word.

She was pretty, though she was far too thin and her face, in repose, looked haggard. Her smile seemed forced. Her laughter was shrill, too loud. She appeared determined to like Lleu and even more determined that he should like her.

"You broke our date last night," Lleu was saying.

"I'm sorry," the young woman replied, worried. "You're not mad at me, are you? The old crone who was supposed to come watch the children didn't turn up."

Lleu shrugged. "I'm not mad. I can always find pleasant company . . ."

The young woman grew even more worried. "I have an idea. You can come to my place tonight, after I put the children to bed."

"Very well," said Lleu. "Tell me where you live."

She gave him directions. He kissed her on the cheek, patted her little boy on the head, and chucked the baby under the chin.

Rhys's gorge rose at the sight of the Beloved caressing the children and it was all he could do to keep silent. Lleu at last took himself off, heading, undoubtedly, for yet another bar. Rhys followed the young woman. She entered one of the hovels near the docks. He waited a moment, pondering his course of action, then made up his mind. Crossing the street, he knocked on her door.

The door opened a crack. The young woman peered out.

She seemed startled to see a monk and opened the door a little wider. "Well, Brother. What can I do for you?"

"My name is Rhys Mason. I want to speak to you about Lleu. May I come inside?" Rhys asked.

The young woman was suddenly cold. "No, you may not. As for Lleu, I know what I'm about. I don't need you to lecture me on my sins, so go on about your business, Brother, and let me go about mine."

She started to shut the door. Rhys interposed his staff between the door and the frame, holding it open.

"What I have to say is important, Mistress. Your life is in danger."

Rhys could see, over her shoulder, the baby lying on a blanket on a straw pallet in the corner of the small room. The little boy stood behind her, watching Rhys with wide eyes. The woman, following the movement of his eyes, threw the door wide open.

"My life!" She gave a bitter laugh. "Here is my life! Filth and squalor. Look for yourself, Brother. I am a young widow left destitute, with two small children and barely enough to hold body and soul together. I cannot go out to work, because I am afraid to leave the children, so I take in sewing. That barely pays the rent on this dreadful place."

"What is your name, Mistress?" Rhys asked gently.

"Camille," she returned sullenly.

"Do you think Lleu will help you, Camille?"

"I need a husband," she said in hard tones. "My children need a father."

"What about your parents?" Rhys asked.

Camille shook her head. "I am alone in the world, Brother, but not for long. Lleu has promised to marry me. I will do anything I must to hold onto him. As for my life being in danger"—she scoffed—"he may be a little too fond of his drink, but he is harmless."

Behind her, the baby started to wail.

"Now, I must go tend to my child—" She tried again to close the door.

"Lleu is *not* harmless," said Rhys earnestly. "Have you heard of Chemosh, the god of death?"

"I know nothing of gods, Brother, nor do I care! Now will you leave or must I summon the city guard?"

"Lleu will not marry you, Camille. He has booked passage on board a ship to Flotsam. He leaves New Port tomorrow."

The young woman stared at him. Her face paled, her lips quivered. "I don't believe you. He promised! Now go! Just go!"

The baby had worked himself into a frenzy. The little boy was doing his best to soothe him, but the baby was having none of it.

"Think about what I have said, Mistress Camille," Rhys pleaded. "You are not alone. The Temple of Mishakal is not far from here. You passed it on your way. Go to the clerics of Mishakal. They will assist you and your children."

She pushed at him, kicked at his staff.

"Lleu has a mark on his breast," Rhys continued. "The mark of a woman's lips burned into his flesh. He will try to make you give your soul to Chemosh. Do not do it, Mistress! If you do, you are lost! Look into his eyes!" he pleaded. "Look into his eyes!"

The door slammed shut. Rhys stood on the street outside, listening to the baby's screams and the mother's voice trying to soothe it. He wondered what to do. If this young woman fell victim to Lleu, she would abandon her children to walk with the Lord of Death.

Then Rhys remembered the missive posted on the temple wall, and his heart eased. He was not alone in his battle against the Beloved. Not anymore. He could seek out help.

Rhys returned to the clerics of Mishakal and their humble temple to find Nightshade happily whitewashing the walls and Atta lying under a table contently gnawing on a bone. She wagged her tail when she saw Rhys but was not about to relinquish her bone long enough to go greet him.

"Look, Rhys, I'm working!" Nightshade called proudly, waving his paintbrush and splattering himself and the floor with white paint. "I've already paid for supper."

"I told him we feed everyone in need," said Patrick. "But he insisted. He's a most unusual kender."

"Yes, he is," said Rhys. He paused then said quietly, "Revered Son, I must speak to you on a matter of importance."

"I thought you might," Patrick replied. "Your friend has been telling us some very interesting stories. Please, Brother, seat yourself."

Galena brought Rhys a bowl of stew. Patrick sat beside him as he ate, keeping him company. He refused to let Rhys talk business until he had finished his meal, explaining it was bad for the digestion.

Thinking what he had to say, Rhys agreed. Instead, he urged Patrick to tell his story.

"My wife and I were both mystics in the Citadel of Light. When the gods returned, the leaders of the Citadel agreed all mystics would be given a choice—we could serve the gods or we could remain mystics. Our founder, Goldmoon, was both, and the leaders believed this is what she would have wanted. My wife and I prayed for guidance and the White Lady came to each of us in a dream, asking us to follow her, so we did.

"We are originally from New Port. We knew there was great need here, and we decided to return to do what we could to help. We're starting with the school for the children and a house of healing. A humble beginning, but at least it's a beginning. None of the other gods have a presence in this city—except Zeboim, of course," Patrick added with a sigh and a sidelong glance at Rhys.

He said nothing but continued eating.

"Zeboim's temple was the last the people left after the gods vanished, and the first they came back to. In fact, there were some who didn't leave at all. They kept bringing their gifts, year after year. 'You never know with the Sea Witch', they say in these parts. 'She might be playing one of her little games. We don't dare take a chance.' "

Rhys looked at Nightshade, happily sloshing paint around. A good deal of it was actually hitting the wall. Rhys reached down, stroked Atta's head.

"Forgive me for asking, Brother," Patrick said after a moment, "you are obviously a monk, but I am not familiar with your order—"

"I was a monk of Majere," Rhys replied. "I am not anymore. That was excellent," he told Galena, as she removed the bowl. "Thank you."

Patrick seemed about to say something else, then changed his mind. Galena carried the dishes to the kitchen before returning to sit with her husband.

"What is it you need to discuss with us, Brother?" Patrick asked.

"The Beloved," said Rhys.

Patrick's expression darkened. "Nightshade told us that you have been tracking one of them and that it is here, in our city. This is bad news, Brother."

"It gets worse. The Beloved has taken up with a young woman. I fear he means her harm. I tried to warn her, but she is a widow with two children and in desperate need. She thinks he will marry her and she refused to listen to my warnings. He is meeting her tonight. We must stop him."

"Judging by the information on the Beloved we received from the Citadel, stopping him will not be easy," said Galena, troubled.

"Yet we must do something," Patrick said. "Do you have any ideas, Brother?"

"We could try to apprehend him. Lock him up in a prison cell. He will undoubtedly escape from jail," Rhys admitted. "Locks and iron bars will not be much of a hindrance to him, but at least this young woman and her children will be safe. You can take them into your care, keep her away from him until he has left this city."

"When will that be?"

"Lleu has booked passage on a ship out of New Port. He intends to leave tomorrow."

"Then he will attack someone else." Patrick frowned. "I don't like letting him go."

"I am trying to acquire passage on the same ship. I will continue to do what I can to prevent Lleu from harming anyone."

"I still don't like it," said Patrick.

Galena rested her hand on his arm. "I know how you feel, but, husband, think of this poor young mother! We need to save her and her children."

"Of course," said Patrick immediately. "Our first care must be for her. Then we will decide what to do with the Beloved. Where is he now?"

"I left him in a bar. He will spend the day there, come out at night."

"Wouldn't it be better for us to apprehend him there?"

"I thought of that," said Rhys. "But this young woman is the type of vulnerable person Chemosh seeks out. We can stop this Beloved, but what of the next one who finds her? She must be made to see the danger for herself."

"Are there truly that many of these monsters around?" Galena asked, shocked.

"We have no way of knowing," said Rhys. "But it is certain their numbers grow daily."

Nightshade came over to join them, trailing paint spatters all along the floor.

"I saw ten yesterday," he reported. "Down by the docks and up in the city."

"Ten!" Galena was horrified. "This is appalling."

"Lleu is supposed to meet this young woman tonight at her house. We can capture him when he arrives."

"Are you certain he is one of the Beloved?" Patrick asked, regarding Rhys intently. "Forgive me for questioning you, Brother, but our fear is the innocent may suffer along with the guilty."

"Lleu is—or was—my brother," Rhys replied. "He murdered our parents and the brethren of my Order. He tried to murder me."

Patrick's expression softened. He looked at Rhys as if much made sense to him now. "I am truly sorry, Brother. Where does this young woman live?"

"Not far," said Rhys. He shook his head. "I can't describe to you the exact location. Her dwelling is one of many on the street, and they all look alike. It will be easier for me to take you there. You should summon the city guard."

"We will be ready, Brother."

"I will return at nightfall," said Rhys. Taking hold of his staff, he rose to his feet. "Thank you for the meal."

"There is no need to leave, Brother. You should stay and rest. You look worn out."

"I wish I could," said Rhys, and he was in earnest. The peace of this quiet place was soothing balm to his tormented soul. "But I have to meet again with the ship's captain, try once more to persuade him to take us on as passengers."

"He thinks kender are unlucky," said Nightshade cheerfully. "I told him I could make the voyage really interesting. I saw the souls of quite a few dead sailors roaming about the ship, and I told him they all wanted to talk to him. He didn't seem to like to hear that, though. He got really mad, especially when I mentioned the mutiny and the fact he'd had them all strung up from the yard-arms. I think they still have hard feelings."

Rhys looked at Patrick and coughed. "I don't suppose you could continue to keep the kender—"

"Of course. He's been quite a help today."

"He can whitewash the floor as well as the walls," added Galena, with a glance at the trail of white spatters.

Rhys whistled to Atta, who left her bone with regret.

"I'll keep it for her," Galena offered. She picked up the bone and placed it on a shelf. Atta kept her jealous gaze on it every inch of the way.

"Brother," said Patrick, accompanying Rhys to the door, "you might think about enlisting the aid of Zeboim's cleric. He's a powerful force with these ships' captains. They'd be willing to listen to him, and he'd be more than willing to listen to you."

"A good idea, Revered Son," Rhys said quietly. "Thank you."

"We will keep you in our prayers, Brother," Patrick added as Rhys and Atta took their leave.

"Pray for that young woman," Rhys said. "Your prayers will be better spent."

Patrick stood in the doorway watching Rhys walk off down the street. The monk's staff thumped the cobblestones. The black and white dog padded along at his side.

Thoughtful, Patrick turned away.

"Where are you going, my dear?" Galena asked.

"To have a word with Mishakal," he replied.

"About that young woman?"

"You and I can take care of her." Patrick glanced back out the window to see Rhys and Atta vanish around the corner. "This problem is one only the goddess can handle."

"And what is that?" asked his wife.

"A lost soul," said Patrick.

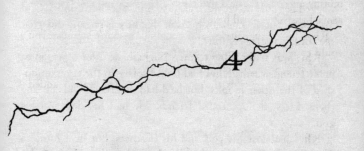

*R*hys seriously considered Patrick's advice regarding Zeboim's priest. He chose, finally, to go to the ship's captain alone. Rhys did not like the idea of being any more beholden to the goddess than he already was—or rather, than she thought he was. Truth be told, he'd done far more for her than she'd done for him.

He was kept waiting for hours, for the captain with a vessel making ready to sail is a busy man and has no time to talk to potential passengers, especially those who can't pay their way. Noontime came and went and finally, late in the day, the captain told Rhys he could spare him a few moments.

Rhys eventually persuaded the man to agree to let him and Atta on board the vessel. The captain was adamant about Nightshade, however. A kender on board ship was bad luck. Everyone knew that.

Rhys suspected this was a superstition the captain had just conveniently made up, but all his arguments fell on deaf ears. Rhys finally and reluctantly agreed to leave the kender behind.

"We'll miss Nightshade, won't we, Atta?" Rhys said to the dog as they walked back toward the temple.

Atta looked up at him with her soft brown eyes and gently wagged her tail and crowded close to him. She didn't understand his words, but she knew by his tone that he was sad and did what she could to offer comfort.

Rhys was truly going to miss Nightshade. Not a person to make friends easily, Rhys had found solace in the companionship of the other monks, but he'd had no true friends among them. He had not needed friends. He had his dog and his god.

Rhys had lost his god and his brothers, but he'd found a friend in the kender. Looking back on these last bleak weeks, Rhys knew with certainty he could not have gone on if it hadn't been for Nightshade, whose cheerful outlook on life and unfailing optimism had kept Rhys afloat when the dark waters seemed about to close over him. The kender's courage and—odd as it might sound when speaking of a kender—common sense had kept them both alive.

"The clerics of Mishakal will take him in," Rhys said to Atta. "The goddess has always had a soft spot in her heart for kender." He sighed deeply and shook his head. "The hard part will be convincing him to stay behind. We'll have to sneak out while he's asleep, slip away before he knows we're gone. Fortunately, the ship sails with high tide and that is at dawn——"

Thinking about Nightshade, Rhys was not paying particular attention to where he was going and suddenly discovered he'd taken a wrong turn. He was in a part of town completely unfamiliar to him. He was annoyed by this mistake, and his annoyance grew to worry when he noted the hour was far later than he'd thought. The sky was a pinkish red color; the sun was sinking behind the buildings. People around him were hurrying home to their suppers.

Fearing he would be late for his meeting with the clerics and the city guard, Rhys hurriedly retraced his steps, and after stopping several people to ask directions, he and Atta once more found themselves on the street that led to the temple.

He was walking as fast as he could, with Atta trotting behind, and not watching where he was going. His first notion that anything was amiss was Atta trying to nudge him out of the way by pressing her body against his leg. The dog had often done this, for Rhys would sometimes become so absorbed in his meditations that he would walk headlong into trees or tumble into brooks if the dog wasn't there to watch out for him.

Feeling her weight against him, he lifted his head and looked right into the bright light of a lantern. The light blinded him, so he could not make out any details about those he'd nearly run down, except there was a group of perhaps six men.

He nimbly side-stepped to avoid a collision with the leader, adding contritely, "I am so sorry, sir. I am in a hurry, and I wasn't watching—"

His voice died. His breath caught in his throat. His eyes had grown accustomed to the light, and he could now see quite clearly the burnt-orange color of priestly robes and the rose-symbol of Majere.

The priest lifted his lantern so that the light shone on Rhys, who could not believe his bad fortune. He had taken such care to avoid Majere's priests. Now he had literally run right into six of them. What was worse, the lead priest, the one with the lantern, was, by his garb, a High Abbot.

The abbot was staring at Rhys in astonishment, his startled gaze taking in the monk who was wearing the robes of Majere, but in the aqua green colors of Zeboim. Astonishment darkened to disapproval and what was worse, recognition. The abbot swung the lantern close to Rhys's face, so that he was forced to avert his eyes from the flaring light.

"Rhys Mason," said the abbot sternly. "We have been searching for you."

Rhys didn't have time for this. He had to reach the temple of Mishakal. He was the only one who knew where to find Lleu, who was probably already on his way to the young woman's house.

"Excuse me, Your Holiness, but I am late for an urgent appointment." Rhys bowed and started to leave.

The abbot grabbed hold of Rhys's arm, detaining him.

"Forgive me, Holiness," said Rhys politely but firmly. "I am late."

He made a swift, deft move to break the abbot's grip. Unfortunately, the Abbot was also trained in the art of "merciful discipline," and he executed a skillful countermove that kept Rhys in his grasp. Atta, at Rhys's feet, growled threateningly.

The abbot fixed the dog with a look and raised his hand in a commanding gesture. Atta flopped down on her belly and laid her head between her paws. Her growl subsided. She feebly wagged her tail.

The abbot turned back to Rhys.

"Do you run from me, Brother?" the abbot asked in a tone that was more sorrowful than censorious.

"Forgive me, Your Holiness," said Rhys again. "I am in haste. A matter of life and death. Please, release me."

"The immortal soul is more important than the body, Brother Rhys. This life is fleeting, the soul eternal. I have received reports that your soul is in peril." The abbot held Rhys firmly. "Return with us to our temple. We would talk with you and find a way to bring the lost sheep back to the flock."

"I would like nothing better, Holiness," Rhys replied earnestly, "and I promise I will come to your temple later this night. Now, as I told you, I am urgently needed elsewhere. The life that is in peril is not my own—"

"Forgive me if I do not entirely trust you, Brother Rhys," said the abbot.

The priests of Majere, crowding around him, nodded their cowled heads.

"Members of our Order have been searching Ansalon for you, and now that we have found you we intend to keep you. Come, walk with us, Brother."

"I cannot, Holiness!" Rhys was starting to grow angry. "Walk with me, if you do not believe me! I go to the Temple of Mishakal. Her clerics and I are on the track of one of the Beloved who intends to take the life of a young mother."

"Are you the sheriff of this city, Brother?" asked the abbot. "Is it your responsibility to apprehend criminals?"

"In this case, yes!" Rhys retorted.

The sky was dark now, the stars were out. The young woman would have put her little ones to bed and would be watching, waiting for Lleu. "The Beloved is—or was—my wretched brother. I am the only one who can recognize him."

"Nightshade knows him," said the abbot imperturbably. "The kender can point him out to the guards."

Rhys was taken aback. The abbot seemed to know everything about him.

"The kender knows Lleu, but he does not know where this young woman lives. I didn't tell him or the clerics of Mishakal."

"Why not?" asked the abbot. "You could have given the clerics the location of the young woman's house."

Rhys fumbled for an answer. "All the dwellings look alike. It would have been difficult—"

"Lie to others if you must, Brother Rhys. Never lie to yourself. You want to be there. You want to destroy the monster that was once your brother with your own hands. You have made this a personal vendetta, Rhys Mason. You are consumed with hatred and the desire for revenge, yet," the priest added, his voice softening, "Majere still loves you."

He reverently touched the staff that Rhys held in his hand.

As though a lightning blast lit up the darkness, turning night to terrible day, Rhys saw himself in stark clarity. The abbot spoke the truth. Rhys could have given Patrick the location of the young woman's house. He had deliberately withheld it. He wanted to be there. He wanted to confront his brother, and he had been willing to sacrifice the young woman's life for his own hateful need.

Rhys longed to fall to the ground at the abbot's feet. He longed to spew out the poison that was eating him up inside. He longed to beg for mercy, for forgiveness.

The Abbot had hold of his forearm. Dropping his staff, Rhys took hold of the Abbot's arm with his free hand, and giving a yank, he jerked the abbot off his feet and flung him to the ground.

"Atta, watch him!" Rhys ordered.

The dog leaped to her feet. She did not attack the abbot. She stood over him, her teeth bared, growling a warning. The abbot said something to her, but Atta had direct orders from her master now and wasn't about to disobey him.

"Brother Rhys—" the abbot began.

"She won't hurt you if you don't move, Holiness," said Rhys coldly. He was watching the other priests, who were now circling him.

Rhys lifted up his staff with his foot and flipped it into his hands. He wondered uneasily if the staff would continue to fight for him. After all, he was opposing Majere's servants. He held the staff out in front of him, half-expecting it to splinter and crack. The staff remained firm and felt warm and comforting in his grasp.

"I don't want to hurt any of you," Rhys said to the priests. "Let me pass."

"We don't want to hurt you either, Brother," said one of the priests, "but we have no intention of letting you go."

They meant to try to subdue him, render him helpless. Rhys carried the image of the young woman and the terrible fate that awaited her in his mind. The five priests came at him in a rush, intent on dragging him to the ground.

Rhys lashed out with the staff. He clouted one of the priests on the side of the head, knocking him down. He thrust the end of the staff into another priest's midriff, doubling him over, and struck a third on the back of the head—all in a flurry of moves that took only seconds.

He saw at once the priests were not as well trained in the art of merciful discipline as their abbot, for the two remaining on their feet fell back, watching him warily. The abbot must have tried to rise, for Rhys heard Atta bark and snap. He glanced back to see the abbot wringing a bleeding hand.

Wishing desperately he'd never walked this street, never set foot in this city, Rhys planted the butt end of the staff firmly in the cobblestones, and gripping it with both hands, used it to launch himself into the air. He vaulted over the heads of the startled priests and landed on the pavement behind them. Whistling to Atta, Rhys dashed off down the street.

He risked a glance backward, thinking they might be pursuing him, but he saw only Atta tearing along after him. Two of the priests were tending to the fallen. The abbot nursed his bleeding hand and gazed after Rhys with a sorrowful expression.

Rhys put all thoughts of the sins he'd committed out of his mind as he ran.

He reached the temple of Mishakal and found Patrick, his wife and Nightshade, along with the city guard, gathered in front of the building. Nightshade was pacing back and forth, peering up and down the street.

"Brother, you're late!" Patrick cried.

"Where have you been?" Nightshade wailed, clutching at him. "It's way after dark!"

"Come with me!" Rhys gasped. He shook off the kender and kept running.

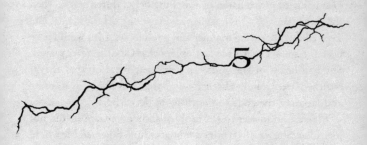

_T_he young mother's name was Camille.

The only child of a wealthy merchant widower, she had been raised with every indulgence and was headstrong and spoiled. When, at sixteen, she had fallen in love with a sailor, she had willfully ignored her father's command and run off to marry the sailor. Two children came along shortly thereafter.

Her father had refused to have anything to do with her and even went so far as to change his will to leave his money to his business partners. Time might have softened the old man, who truly loved his daughter, but he died within a week of making the change. Shortly after her father's death, Camille's husband fell from the rigging of his ship and broke his neck.

She was now a widow, destitute, with two small children to support. Her duenna had taught her to do fancy sewing, and Camille, swallowing her pride, was forced to go to the homes of the wealthy young women who had once been her peers to beg for work.

This did not bring in much money. She was twenty-one, lonely, half-starved, and in despair. The only other thing she had to sell was her body, and she was facing the horrible choice of turning to prostitution or watching her children starve when she met Lleu.

With his charming manner and good looks, Lleu would have been the answer to her prayers, except that Camille never prayed. She had heard of the gods—some vague mention that they'd returned after a long absence—but that was about it. Remote and far away, the gods had nothing to do with her.

He *was* the answer to her problems, though. Camille did not love Lleu. She was determined to marry him, however. He would support her and her children, and in return, she would be a good wife to him. The notion that he might be playing her false had never entered her mind. Though she'd known him only a couple of days, he had seemed to dote on her and her children. When she heard from the monk that Lleu had booked passage on a ship, Camille felt the blow in the pit of her stomach and found it easy to convince herself the monk had been lying.

She fed her children the meager amount of food that there was in the house, going without a meal herself. She put the baby to bed, then spent some time talking to her little son, a child of four, promising him he would soon have a new daddy, who would love him dearly, and that there would be lots to eat and warm clothes to wear and a fine new house where they would all live together.

The little boy fell asleep in her arms, and she carried him to the straw pallet in the corner of the one room dwelling and laid him down. She tucked a blanket around him, then did what she could to make herself pretty. She sat in the lone rickety chair to wait for Lleu.

He arrived later than she'd expected. He reeked of dwarf spirits but did not appear to be drunk. He greeted her with his usual charming smile and kissed her on the cheek. She shut the door behind him and bolted it.

Lleu stood in the center of the room with his arms held out. "Come to me, my sweet," he said gaily.

She gave herself to his embrace. His kisses were ardent and impassioned. When his hot hands began to explore her body, however, Camille drew away from him.

"Lleu, we need to talk. You promised to marry me. I love you so, I don't want to wait. Promise me you will marry me tomorrow."

"I will marry you, but you must promise me something in return," Lleu said, laughing.

"You will marry me?" Camille cried, ecstatic. "Tomorrow?"

"Tomorrow, the day after, whenever," Lleu said carelessly.

"What is it you want of me?" Camille asked, drawing near to him.

She thought she knew the answer and was prepared to give her body to the man who was going to be her husband. Lleu's reply caught her by surprise.

"I am a follower of Chemosh," he said. "I want you to join me in his worship. That is all I ask. Do that, and you will be my wife."

"Chemosh?" Camille repeated. She drew back, startled and uneasy. "You never said anything before about a god called Chemosh. Who is he?"

"The Lord of Life Unending," Lleu replied. "You have but to swear to him that you will serve him, and in return, he will grant you endless youth, endless beauty, endless life."

His words sounded glib, a speech he had memorized and was speaking by rote, like a bad actor in a bad play. The monk's warning came back to Camille.

"Come now, Lleu. Intelligent people don't believe in the gods," she said, forcing a laugh. "Worshipping gods is for the weak-minded, the superstitious."

"My wife must believe in my god, Camille," said Lleu and

his charming smile was gone. "If I am to marry you, you must swear to follow Chemosh. He will reward you with endless youth, endless—"

"Yes, you said all that," Camille snapped. She temporized. "After I am your wife, I will gladly learn about Chemosh. You will teach me."

"I will teach you now," said Lleu, and he bent over her and nuzzled her neck, kissing her.

His kisses were sweet, and he had promised to marry her. What would it hurt to give in to his silly demand? Swear to Chemosh. She was saying only words anyway. She slid her hands inside his open collar and saw, beneath her fingers, the mark of a woman's lips burned into his flesh.

Camille pushed him away.

She looked at him, looked into his eyes.

There was nothing there. No love. No desire. No life. Fear wrung her, twisted inside her.

"Get out!" Camille ordered shakily. "Go away! Whatever you are! Leave my house!"

"I can't," Lleu returned, his voice harsh. "Mina won't let me. The pain is too much to bear. You must swear to Chemosh. He will give you endless youth, endless beauty—"

Camille was trapped. He was between her and the door, and even if she could escape, she would not leave him alone with her children.

"Lleu, just go, please go," she begged.

"Endless life," said Lleu. "Endless youth—"

If she could reach the door, she could open it and shout for help.

Camille tried to dart around him. He was too quick for her. He seized hold of her wrists and dragged her close.

"Swear to Chemosh!" he ordered her.

He squeezed her wrists, so that the joints cracked and she

cried out in pain. He threw her to the floor and flung himself on top of her, pinning her with his knees. He ripped off her blouse, exposing her breasts, and bent over her to kiss her. She writhed beneath him, trying to push him off her, but he was incredibly strong.

"Mommy?" Her little boy's quavering voice came from somewhere behind her.

"Jeremy!" she gasped. "Please, Lleu, no. Don't hurt me . . . not while my child is watching . . . "

"Swear to Chemosh!" he said again, his breath hot on her face. He squeezed her arms with crushing force. "Or I'll kill your brat."

"I'll swear!" Camille moaned. "Don't hurt my child."

"Say it!"

Pain and her fear were too much for Camille to bear.

"I swear my soul—"

A blow struck the door. A dog barked ferociously.

A voice shouted, "Mistress, it is Brother Rhys Mason. Are you all right?"

"Help, Brother!" Camille screamed, hope giving her renewed strength. "Help me!"

"Break it down!" the monk ordered, and there was a rush of feet and a crashing thud. The wooden door shivered.

Lleu still straddled her, still hurt her. He seemed unaware of the commotion.

"Swear!" He slavered at the mouth. His saliva dripped on her.

"Once more should do it!" the monk said.

Again the thud, and this time the door burst asunder.

The monk and a kender came tumbling inside. The monk sprang at Lleu, but her little boy, Jeremy, reached him first.

"Stop hurting my mam!" cried the child, and he struck Lleu with his small fist.

Lleu gave a hideous shriek. His flesh blackened and withered. His eyeballs dried up and fell from the sockets. His lips pulled back from his teeth in a rictus grin. The hands holding Camille were the rotting hands of a corpse. The sickening stench of death filled the small room, but Lleu would not die. His corpse kept hold of her. His skull leered at her. His mouth kept moving.

"Swear to Chemosh!"

Camille went mad with terror. She shrieked hysterically and flailed about in panic, trying to fling the corpse off her.

The little boy, after one paralyzed moment of shock, grabbed hold of the corpse intending to tear it off his mother. At his touch, Lleu burst into flames. The fire consumed his body in an instant. Greasy soot and ash drifted horribly about the room, falling on the little boy, coating his hair and his skin.

The child made no sound. He began to shake and then his eyes rolled back in his head. His body went stiff.

"Jeremy!" Camille wept and tried to crawl to her son, but everything went dark, and she fainted.

Rhys witnessed the dreadful end of the Beloved, his mind and soul consumed in horror, as his brother's body was consumed in the unnatural fire. He heard Patrick, standing in the door behind him, suck in a breath, heard one of the guardsmen retching. Nightshade stared, dumbfounded. The little boy stood stock-still. The young woman lay in a pile of black ash. Nothing seemed to move except the soot floating about the room.

Then the little boy collapsed. He fell to the floor, his limbs writhing and jerking, his tongue protruding from his mouth.

"He's having some sort of fit! Rhys, what do I do?" Nightshade cried, hovering over him.

"Get out of my way," Patrick ordered, elbowing Nightshade aside. "I will take care of him."

Patrick took hold of the child, prized open his mouth, and stuffed a wadded handkerchief inside to keep him from biting his tongue. Gathering the twitching little body in his arms, he spoke soft words, praying to Mishakal.

Seeing the child in good hands, Rhys went to the aid of the unconscious mother while Galena ran to pick up the baby.

"We must get them out of this accursed place!" Patrick said urgently, and Rhys whole-heartedly agreed.

Handing his staff to Nightshade, Rhys lifted up the young woman in his arms and carried her out the door. Patrick followed with the little boy, and Galena came after them with the baby. Rhys gave the young mother into the care of the clerics and then forced himself to go back into the shack.

The Sheriff of New Port, a grizzled veteran of the last war, accompanied him. They both stood in the center of the room looking about the place with its gruesome coating of black, greasy ash.

"I've never seen the like," the sheriff said in awe. "What did you use to destroy that monster, Brother? Is that staff of yours magical, or have you got a holy touch . . . or what?"

"It wasn't me," said Rhys.

He was just now coming to grips with what he'd seen, with what he'd found out, and the knowledge sickened him. He remembered Cam's words, about how the price they would have to pay to destroy one of the Beloved would be more than they could stomach.

He glanced back over his shoulder at the little boy who lay on the street, twitching spasmodically, while Patrick prayed over him.

"It was the child."

"What do you mean—it was the kid? You're saying a kid did

this?" The sheriff pointed to a few charred bones mingled with ash. "A kid caused that thing to burst into flames?

"The touch of innocence. The Beloved can be destroyed . . . but only by the hand of a child."

"Gods save us!" muttered the sheriff. "If what you say is true . . . Gods save us." He squatted down on his haunches to stare at the blackened mess on the floor.

Rhys walked back outside, into the fresh air. The young mother woke with a scream and stared about wildly, fighting Galena when she sought to comfort her. When she realized she was safe and her children were still alive, she clutched her baby to her chest and began to sob uncontrollably.

"How is he?" Rhys asked, squatting down beside Patrick and the little boy.

"His body is healed," the cleric said softly, stroking the ash-filled hair. "Mishakal did that, but his mind . . . He has witnessed such horrors that he may never recover."

Galena looked at Rhys, her eyes pleading. "I heard what you said to the sheriff, Brother. I can't believe it. Surely you are mistaken. You think that only children can kill these Beloved. That's too awful."

"I know what I saw," said Rhys. "The moment the child struck him, the Beloved 'died.'"

"I saw it, too," said Nightshade.

The kender looked very pale under the black streaks of ash. He stood with one arm around Atta's neck, his other hand scrubbing at his cheeks.

"The little boy hit Lleu on the leg and—*whoosh*! Lleu rotted away on the spot and then went up in flames. It was pretty awful." Nightshade's voice quivered. "I wish I hadn't seen it, and I hang around dead people all the time."

"Innocence destroys, and in turn, innocence is destroyed," Rhys said.

The sheriff left the shack, wiping his hands on his trousers. "The only way to test this theory is to try it again."

Galena rounded on him angrily. "How could you even suggest that, sir? Would you put your own child through what this one has gone through tonight?"

"Begging your pardon, Ma'am," said the sheriff, "but that thing meant to murder this young woman and maybe her children into the bargain. The gods know how many people the Beloved in there has murdered up to this point. Now we've found a way to stop it."

Rhys thought back to Mistress Jenna. She might feel sorrow over forcing a child to slay one of the Beloved, but she would probably not hesitate to do so.

"We can't keep such vital information to ourselves," the sheriff was saying. "Patrick here tells me the kender saw ten of these Beloved today alone. Now, granting that the kender is probably exaggerating—"

"I am not!" Nightshade cried indignantly.

"—that's still at least two or three walking around my city and murdering innocent people like this young woman here. If there's a way to stop them, I have a right to try, and so do the officers of the law in other cities and towns."

"I think we are all of us too shaken to make any decision right now," said Patrick. "Let us meet in the morning, after the horror of this terrible scene has faded, then we can discuss it. In the meanwhile, we will shelter the mother and her children. You are welcome to return with us, as well, Brother Rhys. And you, too, Nightshade."

"I thank you, but I must leave this night," Rhys said. "My ship sails—"

"No, it doesn't," said Nightshade.

Rhys looked at the kender. He had no idea what he was talking about.

"Your ship doesn't sail," Nightshade repeated. "Well, yes, it probably does, but you don't need to be on it. Lleu is gone, Rhys. You don't have to chase after him anymore. That's all over now."

Nightshade took hold of Rhys's hand and said quietly, "We can go home. You and me and Atta. We can go home."

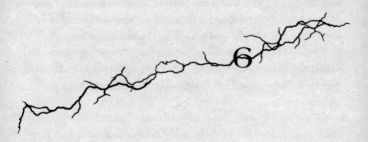

6

*R*hys stood in the darkness, staring at Nightshade. He could feel the touch of the kender's hand. He could hear the kender's words, and to some part of him the words made sense. Another part kept thinking he had to go to that ship. He had to keep following his brother. He had to stop him from killing anyone else. He had to . . . He had to . . .

"It's over," he said. "Lleu is gone."

Rhys felt no sadness over his brother's death. His brother had died long ago. This thing had not been Lleu, though he still called it that.

"Yes, Rhys," said Nightshade. He didn't like the way his friend looked—sort of lost and dazed—and the kender held onto his friend's hand tightly.

Rhys stared up the street and down, and he realized, suddenly, this street and all streets were no longer highways to bleak despair. They all led one place. As Nightshade said, they led home. Rhys's grip on his staff strengthened. He longed to go back home, but he wasn't ready to be received there. He could not show up on the doorstop in filthy, discolored robes, stained with the blood of innocents and the black ashes of death. He had to discard the world, cleanse his body, cleanse his soul. Naked as a babe, chastened and humbled, he would stand before his god and beg his forgiveness. Then he would go home.

"Thank you, Nightshade," Rhys said. Bending down, he kissed the kender on the forehead. "You are a true friend."

Nightshade swiped his hand across his eyes and hid a sniffle in his sleeve.

Gripping his staff tightly, Rhys looked searchingly around the street. A crowd had gathered. The story of what had gone on was being eagerly bandied about, and the tale was growing wilder with each telling. The sheriff ordered people repeatedly to go home, but no one listened, and the crowd grew larger and more unruly. Several young rascals decided they wanted to see the gruesome sight for themselves and tried to rush the dwelling, precipitating a fight with the guardsmen.

The sheriff, envisioning even more crowds once the sun rose, determined that the best way to end this would be to tear down the hovel and leave the curious nothing but a pile of lumber to stare at. He sent men racing off for tools. Some of the guardsmen couldn't wait, but were already ripping down the shack, using their bare hands. Others were holding the crowd at bay. Patrick and Galena were nowhere to be found.

"I told them to take that poor woman and her children back to the temple," the sheriff told Rhys. "They've been through enough without this." He glowered around at the people standing in the street, craning their necks and pushing and shoving to get a better view.

"Thanks for your help in this, Brother," the sheriff added. "Too bad we didn't get here a little sooner, but what's done is done and we're rid of one of these monsters at least." He turned back to the task at hand.

Rhys was quiet and thoughtful on his way back to the temple.

Nightshade was quiet, too, and he glanced at Rhys every so often and then gave a deep sigh. Atta trotted after, looking from one to the other, not understanding.

They entered the temple that smelled strongly of fresh paint. The interior was quiet, after the hubbub of the street.

"How is the young woman?" Rhys asked,

"Galena has taken her to the kitchen and is urging her to eat something. On top of everything else, the poor woman is half-starved. She'll feel better once she has some nourishment."

"And the little boy?"

Patrick shook his head. "We will pray to Mishakal and leave the child in the blessed hands of the goddess. What will you do, Brother, now that your dark quest is ended?"

"I have some explaining to do," Rhys said ruefully, "and many prayers of contrition to make and sins to repent. Can you tell me where to find the Temple of Majere?"

"You mean the one in Solace?" Patrick asked.

"No, Revered Son. The temple here in New Port."

"There is no temple to Majere in New Port," Patrick said. "Don't you recall our conversation yesterday, Brother? There are only two temples to the gods in New Port—our temple and that of Zeboim's."

"You must be mistaken, Revered Son," Rhys said earnestly. "Just this evening, I met a group of Majere's priests, one of whom was an abbot. He spoke of a temple here . . ."

"You can ask the sheriff if you want, Brother, but as far as I know, the closest temple to Majere is the one in Solace. I have not heard of any priests of Majere hereabouts. If there were, they would have undoubtedly sought us out. You say you met these priests last night?"

"Yes," Rhys replied. "Our meeting was not particularly cordial. That is what delayed me. The abbot recognized me, knew my name."

He lapsed into silence, his feeling of peace and ease suddenly draining from him.

Patrick regarded him strangely. "Did you know this abbot?"

"No," said Rhys. "I had never seen him before. I did not think about it at the time—I was too upset—but now that I look back on our meeting, I find it very odd he would have known me. How could he?"

Nightshade tugged on his sleeve.

"Rhys," said the kender, and then he stopped.

"What is it?" Rhys asked somewhat impatiently.

"It's just that . . . if you hadn't been late, we would have reached the shack on time to stop Lleu before he could hurt the mother, then the little boy wouldn't have had to hit the Beloved, and he wouldn't have gone up in flames."

Rhys stood in silence, gripping his staff.

"The priests kept you away just long enough, Rhys," Nightshade persisted. "Just long enough for you to be late, but not long enough for you to be too late. Now Revered Patrick here tells us that there aren't any priests of Majere for maybe a hundred miles in any direction and . . . well . . . I can't help but wondering . . ."

Nightshade quit talking. He didn't like the way Rhys looked.

"Wondering what?" Rhys asked harshly.

Nightshade didn't know whether he should go on or not. "I think maybe this should wait until morning."

"Tell me," Rhys said.

"Maybe these priests weren't real," Nightshade suggested meekly.

"Do you think I am lying about this?" Rhys demanded.

"No, no, no, not that, Rhys." Nightshade stumbled over his tongue in his haste. "I think you *think* the priests were real. It's just—"

He didn't know how to explain himself, and he looked to Patrick for help.

"He is saying that the priests were real, Brother—as real as Majere made them," Patrick said.

Rhys stood in the peace of Mishakal's temple, thinking back on the horrific events of that night. He was suddenly deeply and intensely angry.

"What do the gods want of me?" he cried out.

Patrick looked grave. Atta cringed at his tone, and Nightshade took a step backward.

"They play games with my life," Rhys continued in a rage, "and with the lives of others. That poor child and his mother. Was it necessary to make them suffer like that? They will be cursed with the terrible memory of this night for the rest of their lives. If Majere wanted me to know how to destroy these Beloved, why didn't he just come to me himself and tell me? Why does Zeboim bring Mina to me and then snatch her away?"

"Brother Rhys," said Patrick, resting his hand on the monk's arm. "The ways of the gods are not for mortals to understand. . . ."

Rhys looked at him coldly. "Spare me the sermon, Revered Son. I've heard it all before."

He turned so suddenly he stepped on Atta, who yelped in pain. She gave her hurt paw a quick lick and then ran forgivingly after her master. Nightshade hesitated. He flashed Patrick an agonized glance.

"I think he's really mad at me," said the kender.

"No," said Patrick. "He's mad at the heavens. It happens to all of us at one time or another." He gave a wan smile. "I have to admit I'm not overly pleased with the gods myself at this moment, but they understand. Go after him. He needs a friend."

Rhys must have been walking very fast, for Nightshade saw no sign of him or Atta in the street. He called out Rhys's name, but there was no answer. The kender called out Atta's name, and he heard her bark.

Following the sound, he found Rhys's staff lying on the pavement. Rhys was dragging the aqua-green robes over his head.

"Rhys," said Nightshade, frightened. "What are you doing?"

"I quit," Rhys said.

He flung the robes in a heap by the staff and walked off, clad only in his breeches and boots, his chest and shoulders bare. He looked back over his shoulder to see Nightshade standing rooted to the spot and Atta nosing the robes.

"You coming or not?" Rhys asked coldly.

"Uh, sure, Rhys," said Nightshade.

"Atta!" Rhys called.

The dog looked at him and then lowered her head to pick up the staff.

"Leave it!" Rhys ordered savagely.

Atta jumped back. Startled by his tone, she stared at him.

"Atta, come!"

She assumed she was at fault, though she had no idea what she'd done wrong. Head down and tail drooping, the dog slunk toward him. Rhys waited for her, but he did not apologize for his bad temper, either to her or to the kender. He stalked off down the street.

Rhys had no idea where he was going. He needed to walk off his fury and let the sea breeze cool his fevered skin. He heard Nightshade panting behind him and Atta's nails clicking on the pavement, so he knew they were following him. He didn't look back. He just kept walking.

"Rhys," said Nightshade after a few moments, "I don't think you can quit a god."

Rhys heard the kender's voice and the dog's barking, but it

was muffled and disembodied, as if wrapped in a thick fog.

"Rhys," Nightshade persisted.

"Please, just . . . be quiet!" Rhys said through clenched teeth. "Keep Atta quiet, too."

"All right, but before we're both quiet I think you might want to know that someone's following us."

Rhys halted. He had broken the first rule of the Master. He had given in to his emotions. He had allowed rage to overcome him, completely forgetting in his blind fury that he and the kender were alone in the middle of a dark night in the very worst part of the city. He started to turn around to confront the threat behind and realized there was also a threat in front.

A large minotaur stepped out from an alley.

Rhys had never seen one of these man-beasts before and he was taken aback by the sheer size and brute strength of the beast. Rhys was tall for a human male, yet he came only to the minotaur's chest. Clad in a leather vest and loose-fitting pants, the minotaur was a daunting sight. His feet were bare and covered with fur. A golden ring encircled the top of one of his sharp horns, and gold glinted in one ear. Dark eyes, set close together above a fur-covered snout, gazed coolly down on Rhys.

"Those are my lads coming up behind you," the minotaur remarked. He glared down at Atta, who was in a frenzy of barking. The minotaur laid a gigantic hand on the hilt of a huge dagger he wore in a broad sash at his waist. "Silence the mutt or I'll silence her for you."

"Atta, quiet," Rhys said. Atta's barks subsided to growls interspersed with pants. He could feel her body quivering against his leg.

"We have no money," Rhys said as calmly as he could. "It would be useless to rob us."

"Money?" The minotaur snorted and then laughed so that

the gold on his horn flashed red in the light of several flaring torches now surrounding Rhys and Nightshade. "We're not after money. We got money!"

The beast thrust his muzzle into Rhys's face. "What we need are hands and legs and strong backs."

He straightened and gestured. "Take him, mates."

"Aye, Capt'n," called out several guttural voices.

Two burly minotaurs approached Rhys, who realized now what kind of trouble had found them. They'd run afoul of a press gang, minotaur pirates, seeking slaves for their ships.

7

*T*his un's a kender, Capt'n," stated one of the minotaurs in disgust. He held his torch so close to Nightshade's head that the smell of singed hair wafted on the air. "You want him, too?"

"Sure, I like kender," said the captain with a chortle. "Baked, with an apple in his mouth. And grab the dog. I like dogs, too."

"I would not grab me, if I were you!" Nightshade said in his deepest voice, which sounded rather like he was suffering from a cold in the head. He held up his left hand and pointed his finger at the minotaur. "Any who dare touch me will find himself feeble as a newborn babe. Er, make that calf."

All the minotaurs laughed uproariously at this. One of them started toward Nightshade.

"Whoa, I'd be careful if I were you, Tosh," said the captain, winking. "They're ferocious, these kender. Why, he might step on your little toe!"

The minotaurs grinned at their captain's humor. One offered to write to Tosh's widow if he didn't come back alive, and that drew more laughter. Rhys had no idea what Nightshade was up to, but he had confidence in his friend. He quietly watched and waited.

"I warned you," said Nightshade, and he began to waggle his finger at Tosh who was closing on him. Then the kender started to sing a little song, " 'By the bones of Krynn beneath my feet, I smite you on the beak and leave you weak.' "

The minotaurs roared. Their mirth increased when Tosh suddenly collapsed and went down heavily on his knees.

"C'mon, Tosh," said the captain, when he could talk for laughing. "Quit your fooling now and get up."

"I can't, Capt'n!" Tosh howled. "He's done somethin' to me. I can't stand up nor walk nor nothin'."

The captain ceased his laughter. He stared at his man, as did the other minotaurs in silence. None of them said a word and then, suddenly, they all started laughing harder than before. The captain doubled over and wiped his streaming eyes.

Tosh howled again, this time in rage.

The captain straightened and, still chuckling, reached out his huge hand to seize the kender. Rhys leaped into the air, lashed out with his foot, and struck the minotaur in the midriff.

The blow would have crippled a human, knocked the breath from his body, sent him flying backward. The minotaur captain gasped, coughed once, and looked down at his gut in astonishment. He lifted his horned head to glare at Rhys.

"You hit me with your foot!" The captain was indignant. "That's no way for a man to fight! It's . . . not honorable."

He clenched fists that were the size of war hammers.

Rhys's foot ached. His leg tingled as though he'd kicked a stone wall. Hearing the other minotaur come up behind him, he tried to stand balanced, ready to fight. Atta crouched on her belly, growling and baring her teeth. Nightshade stood his ground, his spellcasting finger shifting threateningly from one minotaur to the next.

The captain eyed the three of them, and suddenly he relaxed his fists. With the flat of his hand, he clouted Rhys a blow on the shoulder that sent him staggering.

"You're not afraid of me. That is good. I like you, human. I like the kender, too. A kender with horns, by Sargas! Look at old Tosh there, flopping about like a fish on a hook!"

Reaching down with his enormous hand, the captain grabbed hold of Nightshade's collar, plucked the kender off his feet, and held him, kicking and flailing, high in the air.

"Bag him, lads."

One of the minotaurs produced a gunny sack. The captain dropped Nightshade into the sack, then reached down and grabbed hold of Atta by the scruff of her neck and flung her inside the bag along with the kender. Nightshade gave a cry that was extinguished by the sack closing over his head. The minotaur pulled the drawstring, hefted the sack, and slung it over his shoulder.

"Take them to the ship," the captain ordered.

"Aye, sir. What about Tosh?" the minotaur asked, as they were about to dash off.

Tosh was rolling about helplessly on the pavement, looking up at them with pleading eyes.

"Leave him for the city guard," the captain growled. "Serves the lubber right. Maybe I'll make the kender First Mate in his place."

"No, Capt'n, please!" Tosh groaned and struggled and succeeded only in making himself look even more pathetic.

"The rest of you get back to the ship afore the guard finds us. Leave me one of those torches."

The other minotaur ran off, carrying Nightshade and Atta with them. The captain turned to Rhys.

"What about you, human?" the minotaur asked, amusement glinting in his black eyes. "Are you going to kick me again?"

"I will come with you," Rhys said, "if you promise not to hurt my friend or the dog."

"Oh, you'll come with me, all right."

The captain laid a hand on Rhys's shoulder. Huge fingers bit deeply and painfully into Rhys's shoulder muscles, nearly paralyzing his arm. The captain propelled Rhys along, giving him a shove and another pinch when it seemed Rhys might be slowing down.

The captain glanced up ahead, to make certain his men were out of earshot, then said softly, "Could you teach me to fight like that? With my feet?" He massaged his belly and grimaced. "It is not honorable, but it would certainly take an opponent by surprise. I can still feel that blow, human."

Rhys tried to envision himself teaching the art of merciful discipline to a minotaur and gave up. The captain kept his grip tight on Rhys's arm and steered him along.

A short distance down the street, they came to the place where Rhys had flung away his staff and divested himself of his robes.

The captain saw Rhys's gaze go the staff and halted.

"I saw you toss that away. Why would you do that?" The practical minotaur shook his head. "The staff looks good and solid. The robe is serviceable and it is the color of our sea goddess's eyes."

He picked up the robes and smoothed them reverently, then tossed them at Rhys. "Nights at sea grow cold. You'll need clothes for warmth. Do you want your staff?"

From what Rhys had heard, slaves on board a minotaur ship measured their lifespan by days. If he had been carrying the blessed staff, he, Nightshade, and Atta might not now be in such dire peril. He looked at the staff, remorse filling his heart. To take it now would be wrong, like a small child who kicks his father in the shins, then runs sniveling back to his parent the moment he is in trouble.

Rhys shook his head.

"I'll take it then," said the captain. "I need something to pick my teeth."

Chuckling at his own jest, the captain reached down to pick up the staff. Rhys thrust his arms into the sleeves and was pulling the robes over his head when he heard a roar. He looked up to see the captain sucking his fingers and glaring at the staff.

Roses sprouted from the wood. Thorns as long as a man's thumb glistened in the torchlight.

"You pick it up," the captain ordered. He clamped his teeth over a thorn stuck in his palm, yanked it out, and spat it onto the street.

Rhys could barely see the staff for the tears in his eyes. He clasped his hand around it, expecting the thorns to prick his flesh, too, for he deserved the punishment far more than the minotaur. The wood was smooth to the touch. The staff did not harm him

The captain gave the staff a wary glance. "I see now why you threw it away. The thing is god-cursed. Put it down. Leave it for some other fool to find."

"The curse is mine," said Rhys quietly. "I must bear it."

"Not aboard my ship," the captain snarled. He spat out another thorn. His eyes began to gleam. "Or maybe we should see how you handle that staff in a fight. We're alone now. Just the two of us. If you beat me, I'll give you your freedom." The minotaur reached for the hilt of the enormous sword he wore thrust into a sash around his broad waist. "Come, monk. Let's see how you handle the god-cursed staff!"

"You hold my friend and my dog hostage," Rhys pointed out. "I gave you my word I would come with you, and I will."

The captain's snout twitched. He rubbed it, eyed Rhys. "So your word means something, does it, monk?"

"It does," Rhys replied.

"What god put the curse on you?"

"Majere."

"Humpf. A stern god, that one. Not a god to cross. What did you do to anger him?"

"I betrayed someone who had put his faith and trust in me," Rhys answered steadily. "Someone who was good to me."

Minotaurs have a reputation for being savage and brutal killers. Their god, Sargonnas, was a cruel god, intent on conquest. The minotaur race knew something of honor, however, or so Rhys had heard.

The captain again rubbed his muzzle. "You deserve the curse, then."

"Yes," said Rhys. "The staff is my constant reminder."

"It will not harm me or my crew?"

"Not unless you try to touch it."

"No one will do that," said the captain, giving the staff a baleful glance. He yanked out another thorn, then, raising his head, he sniffed the air. "The tide is shifting." He nodded in satisfaction and spat out the thorn. "Make haste, monk."

Rhys fell into step beside the minotaur. He had to take two strides to every one of the beast-man's to keep up.

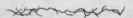

The minotaur's ship was anchored far out at sea, a long distance from the docks. A boat manned by stout minotaur crewmen was on hand to ferry them to the ship. Another boat, bearing Nightshade and Atta, had already set off and was crawling across the water.

Rhys sat across from the captain, who was handling the tiller. The boat jounced over the waves. Rhys watched the shoreline with its sparkling lights slip away from him. He did not curse his fate. He had brought this on himself. He hoped, somehow, to be able to bargain for the kender's life and for Atta's. It was not right they should suffer because of him.

The minotaur ship, silhouetted against the starlit sea, was a lovely thing to look at. Three-masted, it boasted a prow carved in the shape of a dragon's head. Its single bank of oars were drawn up out of the water. He watched the minotaur crew rowing the shore boat and saw the muscles ripple across their broad backs. Slaves aboard a minotaur ship manned the oars, and Rhys wondered how long he would be able to keep going in their place, chained to the bench, plying the oars in time to the rhythmic beat of the drum.

Rhys was strong, or he had been strong, before this heart-breaking journey had taken its toll. Poor food, lack of food, tramping the road, and sitting in taverns had taken its toll on both body and spirit.

As if to prove him right, weariness overcame him. His head dropped to his chest, and the next thing he knew he was being pummeled to wakefulness by one of the crew, who was pointing to a rope ladder hanging from the side of the vessel.

The small boat bobbed up and down and back and forth. The ladder was also bobbing, only neither the ladder nor the boat were doing it together. At times, they were close, and at other times an enormous chasm opened between the boat and the ship—a chasm filled with inky black seawater.

The captain had already gone aboard, ascending the rope ladder with ease. The minotaur crewmen were glaring at Rhys and pointing emphatically at the ladder. One of the minotaurs indicated with hand gestures that if Rhys didn't jump on his own, the minotaur would heave him.

Rhys lifted the staff. "I cannot jump with the staff," he said, hoping his gesture would be understood if his words were not.

The minotaur shrugged his shoulders and made a throwing motion. Rhys had the feeling the minotaur meant he should toss the staff into the sea. He considered it likely that was probably where they would both end up. He eyed the ship's rail, which seemed far, far above him, then, hefting the staff like a spear, he aimed and threw.

The staff sailed in a graceful arc up over the ship's rail and landed on the deck. Now it was Rhys's turn.

He stood on the bench, trying to time his leap with the wildly plunging boat. The rope ladder swung near him. Rhys lunged at it in desperation. He snagged it with one hand, missed with the other, and scrabbled for purchase. He very nearly lost his grip and plunged into the sea, but the minotaur boosted him from below and Rhys was able to clamber up the ladder. Two more minotaurs grabbed him as he reached the rail and hauled him over the side and dumped him on the deck.

All seemed confusion on board, with the captain bellowing orders and sailors running every which way in response, racing across the deck and climbing into the rigging. Canvas sails unfurled, and the anchor was cranked aboard. Rhys was in everyone's way, and he was bumped, shoved, trampled, and cursed. Finally a minotaur, on orders from the captain, picked Rhys up bodily and hauled him over to where crates containing cargo were being lashed to the deck.

The minotaur grunted something Rhys did not understand. He gathered from the jabbing finger that he was to stay here, out of the way.

Holding fast to the staff, Rhys watched the organized frenzy in a kind of daze until a familiar voice roused him.

"There you are! I was wondering where you'd got to."

"Nightshade?" he called, looking around and not seeing him.

"Down here," said the kender.

Rhys looked down, and there was the kender locked inside a crate. Atta, woebegone, was inside another crate. Rhys squatted down, squeezed his hand through the slats, and managed to stroke the dog on the nose.

"I'm sorry, Nightshade," he said ruefully. "I'll try to get us out of this."

"That's not going to be easy," said Nightshade morosely, peering out at Rhys from behind the slats.

The kender and Atta had been put with the rest of the livestock. A crate containing a slumbering hog was stacked next to his.

"There's something fishy about this, Rhys, and I don't mean the smell. Don't you think it's strange?"

"Yes," Rhys said grimly. "But then, I know so little about minotaurs . . ."

"I don't mean that. For one thing," Nightshade explained, "do you see any other prisoners? What sort of press gang goes out and only brings back two people, one of whom is a kender—though I *am* a kender with horns," he added with considerable pride.

"For another, the sight of a minotaur pirate ship anchored off a city like New Port should have the people up in arms. There ought to be bells ringing the alarm, and women screaming, and soldiers soldiering, and catapults flinging stones. Instead, the minotaurs were walking the streets as if they were at home."

"You're right," Rhys said, thoughtful.

"It's as if," Nightshade said in a hushed tone, "*no one ever saw them*. Except us."

He sat back on his heels in the crate and gazed at Rhys.

The ship was underway now, sailing over the ocean in a stiffening breeze. Catching the wind, the ship sliced through the water. Black waves curled back from the sides. Foam spattered Rhys's face.

With the strong wind to propel them, the oars were pulled inside. The drums were silent.

The ship's speed increased. Sails bellied out, the strain drawing them taut. The wind blew harder and harder. Rhys was nearly blown off his feet, and he clung to the rail to keep himself upright. The deck heaved, nearly plunging into the waves at one point, rising up over the tops the next. Salt water washed over the deck.

Certain they were bound to sink, Rhys looked back at the minotaurs, to see how they were reacting to this fearful journey.

The captain stood at the helm, his chest puffed out like the sails. He faced into the teeth of the wind, sucking it gratefully into his lungs. The crewmen, like Rhys, were in good spirits, drinking in the wild wind.

An enormous wave reared up beneath them. The ship slid up the surface of the wave, rising higher and higher and it kept going, taking flight.

The wave broke with a thunderous crash, far below the ship's keel. The minotaur vessel left the sea to sail the waves of night.

Atta howled in terror. Nightshade beat on the slats of the crate.

"Rhys! What's happening? I can't see! No, wait! If it's horrible, don't tell me. I don't want to know."

Nightshade waited. Rhys remained silent.

"It's horrible, isn't it," the kender said miserably, and he slumped over in his crate.

Rhys gripped the railing. The wind whipped around him. The ocean dropped away. The sea boiled and frothed far beneath the ship. Wisps of clouds fluttered like tattered sails from the mast.

"I told you so, Rhys," Nightshade shouted. "You can't quit a god!"

Rhys slid his hand over the staff. He knew every knothole and whorl, every imperfection. He could feel the grain of the wood, the stripes that marked the lifespan of the tree and told the story of its growth—the summers that were hot and dry, the gentle rains of spring, fall's glorious and defiant colors, and the silent, waiting winter. He could feel, within the staff, the breath of the god, and not just because this staff had been blessed by the god. The breath of the god was present in all living things.

The breath of god was hope.

Rhys had lost hope, or rather, he'd thrown hope away. It kept coming back to him, though. Stubborn, persistent.

He stood braced on the lurching deck, the wind of a dark and evil night lashing him, the ghostly ship bearing him to some unknown destination. He rested his head on his staff and closed his eyes and looked within.

The kender was wise, as kender often are to those with the wisdom to understand.

You can't quit a god.

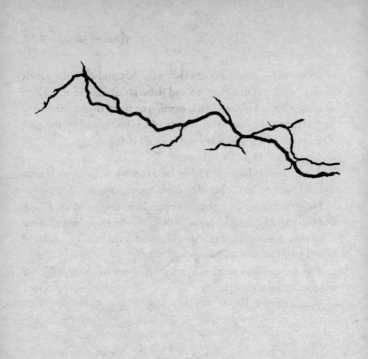

BOOK IV

THE TOWER

OF THE

BLOOD SEA

*C*hemosh stood on the ramparts of his fortress castle, watching the travesty that was taking place on a patch of scorched ground in front of him. The handsome brow of the Lord of Death was furrowed. He stood with his arms crossed over his chest. Occasionally he would grow so frustrated he had to quit watching and take to pacing the ramparts. He would then halt, looking back in hopes that things would have taken a turn for the better. Instead, it seemed they were going from bad to worse.

"Here you are, my lord," said Mina, emerging from a door set in one of the corner towers. "I have been searching for you everywhere."

She went to him and put her arms around him.

He pushed her away, repulsed by her touch. "I am not in a good humor," he told her. "You would do well to leave me."

Mina followed his irate gaze to where the death knight, Ausric Krell, was attempting to train the Beloved of Chemosh into a fighting force.

"What is wrong, my lord?" Mina asked.

"See for yourself!" Chemosh gestured. "That undisciplined

mob is my army. The army that is going to march below the sea to conquer Nuitari's tower. Bah!" He turned away in disgust. "That army could not raid a kender picnic!"

Krell was attempting to form the Beloved into ranks. Many of the undead simply ignored him. Those who did obey his commands would take their places in line only to forget why they were there a few moments later and wander off. Krell tried to bully and threaten those who refused to obey, but they were immune to his terrifying presence. He could break all the bones in their bodies and they would shrug it off and take another drink from their hip flasks.

Krell went to round up those who had wandered away and order them back in line. While he was gone, more deserted, forcing Krell to go thudding in pursuit. Some of the Beloved simply stood where they'd been told to stand, taking no interest in anything, staring up at the sky or down at the grass or across at each other.

"This is what I do to recruits who don't obey my commands!" Krell howled in a rage. "Let this be a lesson to you!"

Drawing his sword, he began slashing at the Beloved, hacking off arms and hands and heads. The Beloved dropped down dead on the ground, where they began to wriggle themselves horribly back together in a few moments.

"There! Did the rest of you see that?" Krell turned around, only to discover the rest of the company had departed, heading in the direction of the nearest town, driven by their desperate need to kill.

"I have created the perfect soldier," Chemosh fumed. "Impervious to pain. Ten times stronger than the strongest mortal. Unaffected by magic of any type. They know no fear. They can't be slain. They would kill their own mothers. There's just one problem." He drew in a seething breath. "They are all *idiots!*"

Mina remembered that she had once envisioned an army of dead men—corpses marching to battle. Like the Lord of Death, she had imagined this would be the perfect army. Like him, she now began to realize the very traits that could make a man weak were those that also made him a good soldier.

"Nothing is going right for me!" Chemosh left off watching the ridiculous scene on the parade ground and stalked over to the door that led back inside his castle. "Everyone has failed me. Even you, who profess to love me."

"Do not say I have failed you, my lord," Mina pleaded.

She caught up with him and twined her hands around his arm.

"Haven't you?" He glared at her and flung her away. "Where are my holy artifacts? You were inside the *Solio Febalas*. You had my artifacts in your grasp, and you came back with nothing. Nothing! And you refuse to go back there."

Mina lowered her eyes before his rage. She looked down at his hands, at the lace falling over the slender fingers. His hands had not caressed her for many nights now, and she longed for his touch.

"Do not be angry with me, my dearest lord. I have tried to explain. The *Solio Febalas* is . . . holy. Sanctified. The power and majesty of the gods—all the gods—are in the chamber. I could not touch anything. I did not dare! I could do nothing but fall to my knees in worship. . . ."

"Spare me this drivel!" Chemosh snarled. "Perhaps you fooled Takhisis with your show of piety. You do not fool me!"

He walked off, leaving Mina standing in hurt silence. Reaching the door, he paused, then turned around and stalked back.

"Do you know what I think, Mistress?" he said coldly. "I think you took some of those artifacts and you are keeping them for yourself."

"I would not do such a thing, my lord!" Mina gasped, shocked.

"Or maybe you gave them to Zeboim. You two are such friends—"

"No, my lord!" Mina cried.

He seized hold of her, gripped her tight. Mina flinched in pain.

"Then go back to the Blood Sea Tower! Prove your love for me. Nuitari's magic cannot stop you. The dragon will let you pass—"

"I cannot go back there, my lord," Mina said, her voice low and trembling. She shrank in his grasp. "I love you. I would do anything for you. Just . . . I can't do that."

He hurled her from him, flung her back against the stone wall.

"As I thought. You have the artifacts and you want their power for yourself." Chemosh pointed a finger at her. "I will find them, Mistress! You cannot hide them from me, and when I do . . ."

He did not finish his threat, but glared at her, his gaze dark and menacing. Then, turning on his heel, he stalked off. He threw open the door with a bang, entered, and slammed it shut behind him.

Mina slid down the wall, too weak to stand. She was drained, bewildered, and confused. Chemosh had been pleased at her description of the wonders she had discovered in the Hall of Sacrilege. His pleasure had quickly waned when she spoke of her reverence and her awe.

"Never mind that. What wonders of mine did you bring out with you?" he had demanded.

"Nothing, my lord," Mina had faltered. "How could I dare touch anything?"

He had risen from their bed and stalked out and he had not come back.

Now he believed that she was lying to him, hiding things

from him. Worse, he was jealous of Zeboim, who had done all she could to foster his jealousy, though Mina was not aware of that.

"Forgive me for not bringing this charming young human back to you immediately," Zeboim had said to Chemosh, upon their return. "We took a little side trip. I wanted her to meet my monk. You remember him—Rhys Mason? You traded him to me for Krell. It proved a most interesting experience."

Chemosh would have thrown himself into the arms of Chaos before he would have given Zeboim the satisfaction of asking her what had occurred. He had asked Mina about the monk, but she had been vague and evasive, arousing his suspicions further.

Mina had not wanted to talk about that fleeting and disturbing visit. She could not get the monk's face out of her mind. Even now, bitterly unhappy and grieving, Mina could see the man's eyes. She did not love the monk. She did not think of him in that way at all. She had looked into his eyes and she had seen that he knew her. Just as the dragon knew her.

I am keeping secrets from my lord, Mina admitted to herself, consumed with guilt. Not the secrets of which he accuses me. Still, does it matter? Perhaps I should tell him the truth, tell him why I cannot go back to the Tower. Tell him it is the dragon who frightens me. The dragon and her terrible riddles.

Terrible—because Mina could not answer them.

But the monk could.

Chemosh would not understand. He would mock her or, worse, he would not believe her. Mina, who had slain the powerful Dragon Overlord, Malys, afraid of an elderly, practically toothless sea dragon? Yet Mina *was* afraid. Her stomach shriveled whenever she heard that reptile voice ask, "Who are you? Where did you come from?"

Chemosh emerged into the great hall to find Krell just entering. Several of the Beloved milled about aimlessly, some calling for ale, others demanding food. A few glanced up at the Lord of Death, but they looked away without interest. They paid no attention at all to Krell, who cursed them and shook his mailed fist at them. They paid no attention to each other, and that was strangest of all.

"You might as well field a regiment of gully dwarves, my lord," Krell growled. "These numbskulls you have created—"

"Shut up," Chemosh ordered, for, at the moment, Mina was walking down the stairs. She was very pale and had obviously been crying, for her eyes were red and there were traces of tears on her cheeks. Chemosh felt a stab of remorse. He knew he was being unfair to her. He didn't truly believe she had stolen artifacts and was keeping them from him. He'd said that to hurt her. He needed to lash out, hurt someone.

Nothing was going right for him. None of his grand schemes were turning out as he'd expected. Nuitari laughed at him. Zeboim mocked him. Sargonnas, who was currently the most powerful god in the Dark Pantheon, lorded it over him. The White Lady, Mishakal, had recently come at him in a blaze of blue-white fury, demanding that he destroy his Beloved or face the consequences. He'd spurned her, of course. She'd left him with a warning that her clerics were declaring open war on his followers and it was her intent to wipe all his disciples off the face of Krynn.

She could not easily destroy his Beloved; he'd seen to that, but Chemosh did not have all that many living followers, and he was starting to realize their value.

He was brooding on this and his other troubles, when Krell suddenly nudged him.

"My lord," the death knight said softly. "Look at that!"

The Beloved had, only moments before, been roaming aimlessly about the hall. Some had even bumped into the Lord of

Death and never noticed. Now, however, the Beloved were still. They were silent. Their attention was fixed.

"Mina!"

Some spoke her name in reverence.

"Mina!"

Others cried it in agony.

"Mina . . ."

No matter whether spoken in admiration or in supplication or in dread, her name was on the dead lips of all the Beloved.

Her name. Not the name of their god, their lord. Not the name of Chemosh.

Mina stared in astonishment at the throng of Beloved that pressed around the staircase and lifted their hands to her and called out her name.

"No," Mina said to them in confusion. "Do not come to me. I am not your lord. . . ."

She felt Chemosh's presence, felt it pierce her like a thrown spear. She raised her head, stricken, to meet his gaze.

Hot blood flooded her face. The hot blood of guilt.

"Mina, Mina . . ." The Beloved began chanting her name. "Kiss me again!" cried some, and "Destroy me!" wailed others.

Chemosh stood there, watching, amazed.

"My lord!" Mina's despairing voice rose over the growing tumult. She ran down the stairs, tried to approach him, but the Beloved surged around her, desperate to touch her, plead with her, curse her.

Chemosh recalled a conversation he had overheard between Mina and the minotaur, Galdar, who had been her loyal friend.

"I raised an army of the dead," said Mina. "I fought and killed two mighty dragons. I conquered the elves and brought them under the heel of my boot. I conquered the Solamnics and saw them run from me like whipped dogs. I made the Dark Knights a power to be feared and respected."

"All in the name of Takhisis," said Galdar.

"I wanted it to be in my name. . . ."

I wanted it to be in my name.

"Silence!" Mina's voice rang through the hall. "Stand aside. Do not touch me."

At her order, the Beloved fell back.

"Chemosh is your lord," Mina continued, and her guilt-ridden gaze went to him, standing at the opposite end of the hall. "He is the one who gave you the gift of unending life. I am but the bearer of his gift. Never forget that."

None of the Beloved said a word. They stood aside, allowing her to pass.

Krell snorted. "She thinks she's so smart. Let *her* command your sorry excuse for an army, my lord."

The death knight had no idea how close he came to being snapped in twain and tossed into oblivion. Chemosh contained his fury, however.

Mina walked swiftly through the throng of the Beloved. She crossed the hall, her pace increasing. Reaching him, she fell to her knees before him.

"My lord, please do not be angry with me! They don't know what they are saying——"

"I am not angry, Mina." Chemosh took hold of her hands and raised her to her feet. "In truth, I am the one who should be asking for your forgiveness, my love."

He kissed her hands then kissed her lips. "I am in an ill humor these days. I took out my frustration and anger on you. I am sorry."

Mina's amber eyes shone with pleasure and, he noted, relief.

"My lord, I love you dearly," she said softly. "Believe that if you believe nothing else."

"I do," he assured her, stroking her auburn hair. "Now, go to our chamber and make yourself lovely for me. I will join you shortly."

"Come to me soon, my lord," she said and, giving him a lingering kiss, she left him.

Chemosh looked with annoyance at the Beloved who, now that Mina was gone, were once more milling about. Scowling, he made a peremptory gesture to Krell.

The death knight scented blood, and he came forward with alacrity. "What is your command, my lord?"

"She is up to something, and I need to know what. You will watch her, Krell," said Chemosh. "Day and night. I want to know her every movement. I want to hear her every word."

"You will have the information, my lord."

"She must not suspect she is being spied upon," Chemosh cautioned. "You cannot go bumbling about, rattling and clanking like a steam-powered golem created by some mad gnome. Can manage that, Krell?"

"Yes, my lord," Ausric Krell assured him.

Chemosh saw the fiery glow of hatred burning in the empty eye sockets, and his doubts were satisfied. Krell had not forgotten that Mina had bested him in his own tower, taken him by surprise, nearly destroyed him. Nor would he forget that the Beloved had meekly obeyed her commands, while they'd scoffed at his.

"You can rely on me, my lord."

"Good," said Chemosh.

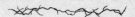

Mina sat before a mirror in her bedchamber, brushing her long auburn hair. She wore a gown of finest silk that her lord had given her. Mina's heart beat fast in the anticipation of his touch and with the joyful knowledge that Chemosh loved her still.

She wanted to make herself pretty for him, and it was then she saw a string of black pearls lying on the nightstand.

Thinking of her lord, Mina lifted the pearls. She heard instead the voice of Zeboim, found the goddess standing behind her.

"The necklace is enchanted," the sea goddess said. "It will bring you your heart's desire."

Mina was troubled. "Majesty, thank you, but I have all that I desire. There is nothing I want . . ."

She stopped in midsentence. She had just remembered there was something she wanted. Wanted very much.

"The pearls will lead you to a grotto. Inside you will find what you long for. No need for thanks, child," the sea goddess said. "I delight in making mortals happy."

Zeboim fussed with the pearls, arranged them to best advantage on Mina's slender neck.

"Remember who did this for you, child," Zeboim told her as she vanished, leaving behind the lingering odor of bracing sea air.

Chemosh entered the room to find Mina brushing her hair.

"What——" He stared. "Where did you get that necklace?"

"Zeboim gave it to me, my lord," said Mina. She kept her gaze on her reflection as she continued to brush her hair. "I have never seen black pearls before. They shine with a lovely, strange radiance, don't they? Like a dark rainbow. I think they are very beautiful."

"I think they look like rabbit turds on a string," Chemosh said coldly. "Take them off."

"I believe you are jealous, lord," said Mina.

"I said take them off!" Chemosh commanded.

Mina sighed, reluctantly raising her hands to the clasp. She fumbled at it, unable to release it. "My lord, if you could help me——"

Chemosh was prepared to rip the pearls from her throat . . . Then he paused.

Since when does the Sea Witch bestow gifts on mortals? he asked himself. Since when does that selfish bitch give gifts to anyone, for that matter? Why should Zeboim bring Mina pearls? There is more to this than meets the eye. They plot against me. I do wrong to object. I must appear to be as stupid as they obviously think I am.

Chemosh lifted Mina's luxuriant hair and put it aside. The tips of his fingers brushed the pearls.

"There is magic here," he said accusingly. "Godly magic."

Mina's reflection looked out at him. Her amber eyes shimmered with unshed tears. "The pearls *are* enchanted, my lord. Zeboim told me that they would bring me my heart's desire."

Mina took his hand, pressed her lips upon it. "I know that I have lost your regard. I would do anything to raise myself again in your esteem. Anything to recover the happiness we once shared. *You* are my heart's desire, my lord. The pearls are meant to please you, to bring you back to me!"

She was so lovely, so contrite. He could almost believe she was telling the truth.

Almost.

"Keep the pearls," Chemosh said magnanimously. He took the brush from her and set it aside. He gathered her into his embrace. "The necklace is beautiful, but not so beautiful as you, my dear one."

He kissed her, and she yielded to his touch, and he gave himself to pleasure.

He could afford to enjoy her.

Ausric Krell was watching from the shadows.

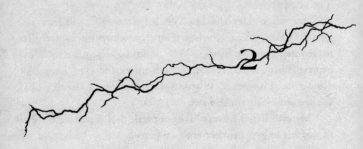

2

Mina slept fitfully, drifting in and out of dreams. She woke to find herself alone in the bed. Chemosh had left sometime during the night; she was not certain when.

Unable to go back to sleep, Mina watched the pale, gray shadow of morning steal through her window and thought of Zeboim and the goddess's gift. Her heart's desire.

She had not lied to the god. Chemosh was her heart's desire, but there was another, something else she wanted just as much as she wanted his love. Something she needed, perhaps more than his love.

She threw off the blankets and rose from her bed. She cast off the silken gown and dressed in a plain linen shift she had found in the abandoned servants' quarters and a pair of soft leather shoes. She hoped to be able to slip out of the castle without attracting Chemosh's attention. If she did run into him, she had her excuse prepared. She did not like lying to her lord, however, and hoped she could avoid him and also avoid the Beloved who, if they saw her, would start their clamorous pleading and moaning.

She wrapped herself in a thick, warm shawl and drew it over her head. Leaving her bedchamber, Mina padded softly through hallways that were still dark.

She pondered her lies to her lord. She had told Chemosh the truth when she said that she loved him and would do anything to regain his favor. She did love him, more than her life. Why lie to him about this? Why not tell him the truth?

Because a god would not understand.

Mina was not sure she herself understood entirely. Goldmoon had told her time and again it did not matter who Mina's parents had been. The past was past. It was the here and now of her life that mattered. If her father had been a fishmonger, and her mother a fishmonger's wife, would that make a difference?

"But what if," the small Mina had argued, "my father was a king and my mother a queen? What if I am a princess? Wouldn't that make a difference?"

Goldmoon had smiled and said, "I was a princess, Mina, and I *thought* that made a difference. I found out, when I opened my heart to Mishakal, that such titles are meaningless. It is what we are in the sight of the gods that truly matters. Or rather, what we are in our hearts," Goldmoon had added with a sigh, for the gods had been gone a long time by then.

Mina had tried to understand and tried to put all thoughts of her parents from her mind, and for a time, she had succeeded. She had, of course, asked the One God, but Takhisis had given Mina much the same answer as Goldmoon, only not as gently. The One God had considered this longing of Mina's a weakness, a cancer that would eat away at her unless it was swiftly and brutally cut out.

Perhaps it was the terrible memory of Takhisis's punishment that made Mina reluctant to speak of this to Chemosh. He was a god. He could not possibly understand. Her secret was only a little one. It was harmless. She would tell him everything once she knew the truth. Then, together, they could both laugh over the fact that she was a fishmonger's daughter.

Keeping to back stairs and ruined passages, Mina made her way to what had once been the kitchen and from there to a buttery, where the castle's former owners had stored barrels of ale, casks of wine, baskets of apples and potatoes, smoked meats, bags of onions. The ghosts of good smells still lingered, but there were so many ghosts flitting about the palace of the Lord of Death that Mina paid scant attention. She hungered, but not for food.

Mina had no idea where Chemosh was. Perhaps he was recruiting disciples or judging souls or playing khas with Krell, or doing all three at once. She would have given odds that she knew where he wasn't—in the storeroom. His sudden appearance, therefore, standing right in front of her, came as a considerable shock.

She expected recriminations, accusations, a tirade. He regarded her with mild interest, as though they'd met over breakfast, and asked, "You are up early, my dear. Going out?"

"I thought I would go for a swim in the sea, my lord," Mina replied faintly, giving the excuse she had prepared.

She could not know, of course, that this was the one excuse that Chemosh would find most suspicious.

"Isn't it a bit cold for sea-bathing?" he asked archly, a peculiar smile on his lips.

"Though the air is cold, the water is warm and will seem that much warmer," Mina faltered, her cheeks burning.

"You still wear the pearls, I see. They hardly go with such a plain gown. Aren't you afraid you will lose them?"

"The clasp is strong, my lord," Mina said. Her hand went involuntarily to the necklace. "I don't think—"

"Why are you in the storeroom?" he asked, glancing around.

"This way is closer to the shore, my lord," Mina returned. She had overcome her shock and was now starting to feel irritated. "My lord, am I your prisoner, that you feel the need to question my comings and goings?"

"I lost you once, Mina," Chemosh said quietly. "I don't want to lose you again."

Mina was suddenly overwhelmed with guilt. "I am yours, my lord, always and forever, until—"

"Until you die. For you will die someday, Mina."

"That is true, my lord," she replied. She looked at him uneasily, wondering if this was a threat.

He was opaque, unreadable.

"Have a good swim, my dear," he said, kissing her on the cheek.

Mina remained for long moments after he left, her hand clutching the pearls. Her heart failed her. Her conscience rebuked her. She almost turned to run back to her room.

To do what? To pace away the hours, as she had done in the Tower of High Sorcery? To be a pawn of first one god, then another, then another, and another after that. Takhisis, Chemosh, Zeboim, Nuitari . . . "What is it they want of me?" Mina demanded in frustration.

She stood alone in the cold and empty storeroom, staring, unseeing, into the darkness. "I don't understand! I give and I give to them, and they give me nothing in return. Oh, they say they do. Chemosh claims he gave me power over the Beloved, yet when he sees that I wield power over them, he is clearly jealous. Zeboim gives me pearls that promise me my heart's desire and they bring me nothing but trouble. I cannot please these gods. Any of them!

"I must do something for me. For Mina. I must know who I am."

Resolute, she continued on her way.

～⌁⌇⌁～

Chemosh had given her the secret to the magical portals that allowed entrance and exit from the castle. Mina feared he might have negated the magic, and she was relieved when the portal worked and she was able to leave. The storeroom opened into a yard filled with tumbledown outbuildings. Beyond this, a gate in the wall opened onto a path leading to the shore. The gate itself was gone. Rusting iron bands and blackened timbers were all that was left.

Once outside the castle wall, Mina stopped to look around. She had no clear idea where to go to find this grotto. Zeboim had said only that the pearls would guide her. Mina touched the pearls, thinking she might feel some sensation or an image would leap into her head.

The early morning sun shone on the water. The castle was built on a rock-bound promontory. Here, where Mina stood, the shoreline swept back from the promontory to form an inlet that had been carved out of the rock and was fronted by a crescent-shaped sandy beach that extended for about a half-mile, ending at a rock groin jutting out into the water. The groin on one side and the cliffs on the other broke the force of the waves, so that by the time they came to shore on the beach, they rolled meekly over the sand, leaving behind bits of foam and seaweed.

The sand was wet, and so were the rock walls behind it. Mina—child of the sea—realized that when the tide was in, the beach would be under water. Only when the tide was out could someone walk or play on the shore.

Mina scanned the cliff face and saw no grotto. She felt a bleak sense of disappointment. Her fingers ran over the pearls, one by one.

They felt bumpy—like pearls.

Movement out to sea caught her eye. A ship—a minotaur vessel to judge by the garishly painted sail—plied the ocean. She watched curiously, thinking it might be sailing in her direction, then realized it was moving rapidly away from her. She watched the ship until it vanished over the horizon line and disappeared from sight.

Mina sighed and looked around again and wondered what to do. She decided to go for a swim.

Her story concocted, she had better keep to it. Chemosh might be watching. That thought in mind, she glanced back at the castle ramparts. He was not there, or if he was, he was taking care not to be seen.

She stepped onto the path leading down to the beach. The moment her foot touched it, Mina knew exactly where to go. Though she had never set foot upon this path, she felt she knew it as well as if she had walked it every day for the past year.

Whispering an apology to Zeboim for having doubted her, Mina hastened toward the beach. She did not know where she was going, yet she knew where she was and she knew that every footfall brought her closer. The sensation was most disconcerting.

Mina kept on, running across the wet sand that was firm underfoot. She eyed the waves, trying to determine if the tide was coming in or going out. Judging by the wetness of the rocks, the tide was coming in. When the tide was in, the water level would be at least up to her shoulders, maybe higher, depending on the cycle of the moons.

Mina reached the rock groin with still no sign of a grotto. She clambered over jagged-edged boulders of granite, cursing the fact that her soft leather shoes had not been made for rock climbing.

On the far side of the groin, the shoreline curved sharply.

Mina, looking back over her shoulder, could not see the castle, and anyone walking the castle walls could not see her.

Sand dunes extended beyond the rock groin. At the top, the land flattened out. There was likely a road up there, a road that led to the castle. Mina took a step forward, heading into the dunes, and knew immediately this was the wrong way. She was lost, with no idea where she was or where she was going.

Mina shifted direction, walking back toward the cliffs, and the sensation of being somewhere familiar returned. She continued on, leaving the sand dunes behind and climbing over rock-strewn ground, pausing every so often to look at the cliffs, trying to spot an opening.

She saw nothing but trusted now that she was heading in the right direction, and she kept going. She was further convinced by signs on the ground that someone else had recently come this way before her. She saw the print of a boot in a sandy patch—an extremely large boot.

Mina began to think she should have brought a weapon. She kept on walking, moving more cautiously, keeping her ears and eyes open.

The grotto turned out to be so well concealed she passed it without knowing. Only when the next step gave her the sinking sensation of being lost did she realize she'd missed the mark. She turned around and stared at the cliff face, and still she could not find it.

At length, she ventured around a large heap of rock and there was the opening to the grotto, half-buried by a rockslide. At one time the grotto must have been wholly buried, she realized, venturing near it. She could see where debris had been cleared, piled up on either side. The work had been done recently, by the looks of it. The ground beneath the slide was still moist.

Mina stood outside the grotto. Now that she'd reached it, she was hesitant to go inside. This was an ideal place for an ambush, out of sight of the castle walls. No one could see or hear her if she needed help. She remembered the large boot print. It had been three times the size of her own foot.

Putting her hand to the pearls, Mina felt their reassuring warmth. She had come all this way, risked her lord's ire. She could not go back now.

The opening was large enough for two broad-shouldered men to pass through it, but the ceiling was low. She had to stoop her head and shoulders to make her way inside. She was bending down when, from somewhere inside, she heard a dog bark.

Mina's heartbeat quickened in excitement. Fear vanished. The monk had been in her mind's eye ever since their encounter. His visage was clear; she could have painted his portrait. She could see his face—chiseled, gaunt. Eyes—large and calm as dark water. Orange robes—the color sacred to Majere, decorated with the god's rose motif, hung from his thin, muscular shoulders; the robes were belted around a lean waist. His every move, his every word—controlled and disciplined.

And the dog, black and white, looking to the monk as master.

"Thank you, Majesty," Mina said softly, and she raised the pearls to her lips and kissed them.

Then she entered the grotto.

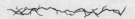

Ausric Krell, moving silently and stealthily, followed Mina at a discreet distance. Surprisingly, Krell could move silently and stealthily when he wanted to. The death knight didn't like sneaking around like some slimy gutter-living thief. Krell enjoyed clanking about in his armor. Rattling steel meant death, struck terror into those who heard him coming. But he could manage stealth when required. Like his life, his armor was the stuff of accursed magic, and though he was bound to his armor forever, he could clang and clatter or not, as he chose.

Krell would have sacrificed far more in order to be able to knock Mina off that high perch on which she stood, sneering down at him.

Mina had never made any secret of the fact that she despised him for his betrayal of Lord Ariakan. Not only that, she had bested him in combat, and she had humiliated him in front of the Lord of Death. The Beloved had no respect for Krell, not even when he was hacking them to bits, but Mina had only to quirk her little finger and they fawned over her and cried out her name.

Krell could have killed her outright, but he knew he would never get away with it. Chemosh might glower at her and curse her, but he still jumped into her bed every night. Then there was Zeboim, his archenemy, lavishing gifts on her. Zeboim might take offense if Krell murdered her darling and thus the death knight had to restrain himself, act subtly. A difficult task, but hatred can move mountains.

Now all Krell had to do was catch Mina in an act of betrayal. He knew from sad experience what happened when you angered a god, and Krell entertained himself, as he sneaked after her, by picturing in vivid detail the torment Mina was going endure. It is amazing how long someone can live after being disemboweled.

As Krell watched Mina enter the grotto, he leaped to the conclusion that she was going to meet a lover. Slipping close, Krell was immensely pleased to hear a man's deep voice. He was somewhat disconcerted to hear what sounded suspiciously like the shrill voice of a kender as well, but Krell was open-minded. *Whatever takes your fancy* had always been his motto.

Rubbing his gloved hands in glee, he sidled near the entrance, hoping to hear more clearly. He found, to his disappointment, that the sounds emanating from the grotto were muffled and indistinct. Krell was not worried. It didn't matter what was truly going on in there. He could always make something up. The jealous Chemosh would be quick to believe the worst. Krell hunkered down outside the grotto and waited for Mina to emerge.

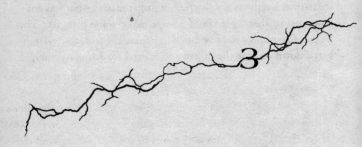

3

*R*hys lost all sense of time aboard the minotaur ship. The journey through the lashing waves of night, tossed on the storms of magic, seemed endless. Winds wailed in the rigging, sails billowed. The ship heeled precariously. The captain roared, and the crew cheered and shouted defiance into the wind.

As for him, he spent the dark night in prayer. Rhys had quit the god, but his god had refused to quit him. He knelt on the deck, his head bowed in shame and contrition, his cheeks wet with tears, as he asked humbly for the god's forgiveness. Though the night and the ghostly voyage were terrible, he was at peace.

Day dawned. The ship sailed out of the sea of magic and settled down on calm water. The minotaur captain hauled the quivering kender and the limp dog out of their crates and handed them over to his crew. He looked down at Rhys, who still knelt on the deck.

"You've been praying, I suppose," said the captain with an approving nod. "Well, Brother, your prayers are answered. You made it safely through the night."

"I did indeed, sir," said Rhys quietly, and he rose to his feet.

The minotaurs manhandled them into the shore boat, then rowed them onto an unknown landing. Rhys stared down into seawater that was the color of blood. He looked into a sun rising up out of the sea, and realization smote him. During the tumultuous night, their ship had sailed through time and space. They were now on the other side of the continent.

Rhys saw a fortress castle silhouetted against the fading stars, but that was all he saw before the minotaurs lifted him from the boat and dragged him over a wet beach and across sand dunes to the side of a cliff.

Arriving at the site of a rockslide, the minotaurs dumped Rhys and the kender and the dog onto the ground and began to lift up gigantic boulders and hurl them aside. He did not understand their language, but he heard the words "grotto" and "Zeboim" and he had the impression, from their hushed and reverent attitude, that behind the rockslide was some sort of shrine to the sea goddess.

At last, the minotaurs cleared the slide and entered the grotto, leaving Rhys outside with a guard. He heard banging and hammering and the clanking of iron. The minotaurs returned and picked up Rhys and hauled him inside, along with Atta and Nightshade.

Chains dangled from iron rings that had been newly driven into the stone walls. Working by the dim light that managed to straggle inside, the minotaurs chained Rhys and Nightshade to the iron rings, tossed down a small sack of food and a bucket of water, then departed without a word, refusing to answer any of Rhys's questions.

The chains were attached to heavy manacles at the ankles and wrists and were long enough to allow Rhys and Nightshade limited movement. Each of them could lie down on the stone floor or stand up and walk about five paces.

Traumatized by the events aboard ship, Atta was too shaken to stand. She rolled over onto her side and lay panting on the cavern floor. Rhys, exhausted, took the terrified dog in his arms and did his best to try to soothe her. Nightshade's clothes were soaked, and the grotto was cold. He sat huddled in a miserable heap, trying to warm himself by slapping himself on the arms.

"Those minotaurs weren't ghosts, Rhys," Nightshade said. "I thought at first they might be, but they weren't. They were extremely real. Too real, if you ask me." He rubbed his shoulder where one of the minotaurs had pinched him. "I'll be black and blue for a month."

There was no answer, and Nightshade saw that Rhys had fallen asleep sitting up, with his back against the rock wall.

"I guess there's nothing else to do except sleep," Nightshade said to himself. He closed his eyes and hoped that when he woke up, this would prove a dream, and he would find himself in the Inn of the Last Home on chicken dumpling day. . . .

Rhys woke suddenly, jolted out of sleep by a bright shaft of sunlight falling on his face. The light illuminated the grotto, and he could see, at the far end, a few feet from him, an altar carved out of stone. The altar was covered with dust and had seemingly been long abandoned. Frescoes adorned the cavern walls. They were so faded he could not make out what they had been. A large conch shell adorned the altar.

Nightshade lay on the floor beside him. Atta was curled around his legs. And there was his staff propped up against a wall some distance away. On orders of their captain, the minotaurs had brought the staff wrapped up in a large piece of leather. They had left it for him, though out of his reach.

The grotto in which they were imprisoned was circular in

shape, about twenty paces across in any direction. The ceiling was high enough that the minotaurs had been able to stand without stooping, though Rhys remembered the large beasts had experienced considerable difficulty making their way inside and down the narrow corridor that opened into this chamber.

Fresh air flowed into the grotto from the shaft. Rhys did not remember seeing any other passages, but he was the first to admit he'd been too drained and exhausted to pay much attention.

Atta woke refreshed from her nap. Jumping to her feet, she regarded Rhys expectantly, tail wagging, ready for him to say they were going to leave this place and head out for the road. Rhys rose stiffly to his feet, chains clanking. The sound frightened Atta. She jumped back away from him, as the chains dragged across the stone floor. Then, warily, she crept forward to give the chains a sniff and watched in puzzled wonderment as Rhys, grimacing from the stiffness in his back and neck, hobbled across the floor to the water bucket.

The minotaurs had left a tin cup for dipping and drinking. Rhys gave Atta water and then drank himself. The water was brackish but slaked his thirst. He glanced at the food sack, but the smell was rank and he decided he wasn't that hungry. He hobbled back to his place against the wall and sat down.

Atta stood over him, staring at him. She nudged him with her nose.

"Sorry, girl," Rhys said, reaching out to fondle her ears. He showed her his manacled wrists, though he knew she couldn't understand. "I'm afraid—"

Nightshade woke with a terrified yelp. He sat bolt upright, staring around wildly. "We're sinking!" he cried. "We're all going to drown!"

"Nightshade," said Rhys firmly. "You're safe. We're not on the ship anymore."

It took Nightshade a while for this to penetrate. He peered about the grotto in perplexity, then looked down at his hands. He felt the weight of the manacles and heard the clank of the chains, and he let out a glad sigh.

"Whew! Prison! That's a relief!"

Rhys could not help but smile. "Why is prison a relief?"

"It's secure and it's on solid ground," said Nightshade, and he gave the stone floor a grateful pat. "Where are we?"

Rhys paused a moment, wondering how to put this, then decided the best way was just to be blunt. "I think we're on the coast of the Blood Sea."

Nightshade gaped at him. "The Blood Sea."

"I think so," said Rhys. "I can't be sure, of course."

"*The* Blood Sea," repeated the kender. "The one on the *other side* of the continent?" He laid emphasis on this.

"Are there two Blood Seas?" Rhys asked.

"There might be," said Nightshade. "You never know. Red water, the color of blood, and—"

"—the sun rising up out of it," Rhys concluded. "All of which leads me to believe we are on the eastern coastline of Ansalon."

"Well, I'll be a dirty yellow dog," breathed Nightshade. "No offense," he added, patting Atta. He spent a few moments letting this sink in, then, sniffing the air, he saw the sack and brightened. "At least, they're not going to starve us. Let's see what's for breakfast."

He stood up, and very quickly and inadvertently sat back down. "Heavy!" he grumbled, meaning the manacles.

He tried again, standing up carefully and then sliding his feet forward, jerking at his arms to drag the iron chains along with him. He managed to reach the sack, but the effort cost him, and he had to stop to rest once he got there. Opening the sack, he peered inside.

"Salt pork." He grimaced, adding sadly, "I hope that's not

my neighbor—the pig in the next crate. She and Atta and I got kind of friendly." He started to reach in his hand. "Still, bacon is a pig's destiny, I guess. Are you hungry, Rhys?"

Before he could respond, Atta began to bark.

"Someone's out there," warned Rhys. "Perhaps you should sit back down."

"But they left us food to eat," Nightshade argued. "They might be hurt if we didn't."

"Nightshade, please . . ."

"Oh, all right." The kender shuffled his way back to his place by the wall and squatted down.

"Atta, quiet!" Rhys ordered. "To me!"

The dog swallowed her barks and came back to lie down beside him. She remained alert, her ears pricked, her body tensed to spring.

Mina entered the cave.

Rhys didn't know what he had expected—Zeboim, the minotaur captain, one of the Beloved. Anything but this. He stared at her in astonishment.

She, in turn, stared at him. The light inside the small chamber had grown increasingly brighter with the rising of the sun, but still it took a while for her eyes to adjust to the grotto's shadowy interior.

After a few moments, Mina walked over and stood gazing down at Rhys. Amber eyes regarded him intently, and she frowned.

"You are different," she said accusingly.

Rhys shook his head. His brain was numb with exhaustion, his thought process as stumbling as the chained-up kender.

"I am afraid I do not know what you mean, Mistress—"

"Yes, you do!" Mina was angry. "Your robes are different! You were wearing orange robes decorated with roses when I saw you at that tavern, and now your robes are a dirty green. And your eyes are different."

"My eyes are my eyes, Mistress," said Rhys, baffled. He wondered where she'd dredged up that image of him as he had been, not as he was. "I cannot very well change them. And my robes are the robes I was wearing when we met—"

"Don't lie to me!" Mina slapped him across the face.

"Atta, no!" Rhys seized hold of the furious dog by the ruff and dragged her bodily back from the attack.

"Do something with that mutt," said Mina coldly, "or I'll break its neck."

Rhys's cheek stung. His cheekbone ached. He held fast to the outraged dog. "Atta, go to Nightshade."

Atta looked at him to make certain he meant it, then, her head down and her tail drooping, she slunk off to lie down beside the kender.

"I am telling you the truth, Mistress," Rhys said quietly. "I do not lie."

"Of course you lie," Mina said scornfully. "Everyone lies. Gods lie. Men lie. We lie to ourselves, if there is no one else to lie to. The last time I saw you, you were wearing orange robes and you recognized me. You looked at me and I could see in your eyes that you knew all about me."

"Mistress," said Rhys helplessly, "that was the first time I ever saw you in my life."

"That look isn't in your eyes now, but it was there when we met before." Mina's fist clenched, her nails dug into her palms. "Tell me what you know about me!"

"All I know is you took my brother's life and made him one of your slaves—"

"Not *my* slave!" Mina cried with unexpected vehemence. She glanced around guiltily, as though fearing someone might be listening. "He is *not* my slave. None of them are my slaves. They are followers of my lord Chemosh. Stop that blubbering, kender! What's wrong with you? You were sniveling like that the last time I saw you!"

She rounded on Nightshade, who crouched on the floor, his eyes brimming with tears that trickled down his cheeks. He was trying to be quiet. His lips were clamped shut, but every so often a whimper would escape him.

"I can't help it, ma'am." Nightshade wiped his sleeve across his nose. "It's so sad."

"What's so sad? If you don't quit that, I will give you something to cry about."

"You already have," said Nightshade. "It's you. You're so sad."

Mina laughed. "Don't be ridiculous! I am not sad. I have everything I want. I have my lord's love and trust, and I have power . . ."

She fell silent. Her laughter died away, and she clutched the shawl more closely around her. The air in the grotto was chill, after being out in the warmth of the sunshine. "I am not sad."

"I don't mean *you* are sad," Nightshade faltered. He glanced at Rhys, seeking his help.

Rhys had none to give. He had no idea what the kender was talking about.

"When I look at you, I feel sad."

"You should," Mina said ominously. She turned back to Rhys. "Tell me, monk. Tell me the answer to the riddle."

"What is the riddle, Mistress?" Rhys asked wearily.

Mina thought back. "The dragon seemed surprised to see me. She was not angry or furious. She was surprised. She said, 'Who are you? Where did you come from?' "

Mina knelt down in front of Rhys to meet him at eye level. "That is the riddle. I cannot answer it, but you can. You know who I am."

Rhys tried his best to explain. "Mistress, the dragon asked

you the eternal riddle—the riddle all mankind asks and which none can answer. 'Who *am* I? Where do I come from?' We strive throughout our lives to understand—"

Mina's gaze grew abstracted. She stared at him, but she did not see him. She was seeing the dragon.

"No," she said softly. "That is not right. That is not how she said it. The inflection is wrong."

"Inflection?" Rhys shook his head. "I don't know what you mean, Mistress."

"The dragon did not say, 'Who *are* you?' The dragon said, 'Who are *you*? Where did *you* come from?' "

Mina's amber eyes focused again on him. "Do you hear the difference?"

Rhys shrugged. "I don't know the answer. It is the dragon to whom you should be talking, not to me."

"The dragon grew angry. She thought I mocked her, and she would have nothing more to do with me. I truly do not know what she meant, but you do, and you will tell me."

Mina caught hold of his chin and slammed his head against the jagged stone wall. The blow sent splinters of fiery pain through his skull. His vision blurred, and for a moment, he was afraid he would pass out. He tasted blood in his mouth from biting the inside of his cheek. His head throbbed.

"I cannot tell you what I do not know," Rhys said, spitting out blood.

"*Will* not tell me, you mean."

Mina glared at him. "I have heard you monks are trained to withstand pain, but that's only when you are alive."

She leaned over him, put her hands on the stone floor on either side of him. Her amber eyes, up close, seemed to swallow him. "One of the Beloved would tell me whatever I wanted him to tell me. The Beloved would not lie to me. You could taste Mina's kiss, monk."

Her lips brushed his cheek.

Rhys's stomach clenched. His heart shriveled. He thought of Lleu, a monster burning with pain who could find ease only in murder.

Rhys drew in a breath and said, as calmly as he could manage, "I must swear an oath to Chemosh, and that I will never do."

Mina smiled in disdain. "Do not pretend to be so righteous, monk. You are sworn to Zeboim. She told me as much. If I ask her, she will sell your soul to Chemosh—"

"I am sworn to Majere," said Rhys quietly.

Mina sat back on her heels. Her lip curled. "Liar! You abandoned Majere. Zeboim told me as much."

"Thanks to a kender's wisdom and my god's refusal to abandon me, I have learned my lesson," Rhys said. "I asked Majere's forgiveness and he granted me his blessing."

Mina laughed again and gestured to Rhys. "Here you are, chained to a wall in a grotto far from anywhere. You are completely at my mercy. This is a strange way for a god to show his love."

"As you say, Mistress, I am chained to a wall. I have no doubt but that you mean to kill me, and, yes, my god loves me. For at last I have the answer to *my* riddle. *I* know who I am."

Rhys looked up at her. "I am sorry, Mistress, but I do not know you."

Mina stared at him seething silence. The amber eyes burned.

"You are wrong, monk," she said at last, when she could speak. "I will not kill you. I will kill them." She pointed at Nightshade and Atta. "You have all day to reflect on my riddle, monk—a day in which you can imagine their agony. They will die in excruciating pain. The dog first, and then the kender. I will return with the setting sun."

She left them, stalking angrily out of the grotto.

Lurking about outside the rock walls, Krell heard Mina announce her departure, and he had just time enough to remove himself from sight before she emerged. Her face was pale, her amber eyes glinted, her lips compressed. Her expression was not the expression of a woman in love. She looked angry clear through, angry and thwarted. Krell was not worried by such details, however. He knew what his master wanted to hear, and he was prepared to tell him.

Now all Krell needed was a name.

He had tried his best to eavesdrop on the conversation, but it had been muffled and indistinct. He understood very little of what was said, but it occurred to him, after several moments, that the man's voice sounded familiar to him.

Krell was positive he'd heard that voice somewhere before. He could not recall where. He'd heard so many voices lately that all of them rattled around in confusion inside his empty helm. What he did know was that the sound of the man's calm voice dredged up some very violent feelings. Krell had a grudge against that voice. If only he could remember what.

The death knight followed Mina until he saw she was headed back to the castle, and then he turned back to the grotto. He was intending to enter, to see this man for himself, and discover just where and when they'd met . . .

A blast of wind and rain, sea foam and fury spewed out of the cave.

"What do you mean you are sworn to Majere?" The goddess shrieked and howled. "You are mine! You gave yourself to me!"

Krell knew that voice if he knew no other. Zeboim. And she was in a tempest.

Krell had no idea why his nemesis was in there; nor did he

care, for it had just occurred to him that Chemosh would be impatient for his report.

"I must not keep my master waiting," Krell said to himself and turned and fled.

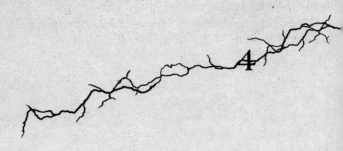

4

What do you mean you are sworn to Majere?" Zeboim cried tempestuously. "You are mine, monk! You gave yourself to me!"

The goddess had materialized in the grotto in a gust of wind and drenching rain. Her green dress foamed around her. Her long hair, whipped by the wind, lashed Rhys's face, drawing blood. Her gray-green eyes scorched him. Gnashing her teeth, she struck at Rhys, nails curled to claws.

"You ungrateful wretch! After everything I've done for you! I could scratch your eyes out! Eyes be damned, I could rip out your liver!"

Nightshade cowered against the wall. Atta whined. Rhys said a silent prayer to Majere and waited.

Zeboim straightened, her hands twitching. She drew in a breath, then drew in another. Slowly she mastered her fury. She even managed a tight-lipped smile.

Zeboim knelt beside Rhys, slid her hand seductively up his arm, and said softly, "I will give you another chance to come back to me, monk. I will save you from Mina. I will save you from Chemosh. I ask only one little favor in return."

"Majesty, I—"

Zeboim put her fingers over his mouth. "No, no. Wait until you have heard what I want. It is small, smaller than small. Infinitesimal. A mere nothing. Just . . . tell me the answer."

Rhys was puzzled.

"The answer to the riddle," Zeboim clarified. "Who *is* Mina? Where *does* she come from?"

Rhys sighed and closed his eyes. "In truth, I do not know, Majesty. How could I? Why does it matter?"

Zeboim rose to her feet. Clasping her arms together, her fingers drumming, she began to pace the cavern, her green dress roiling around her ankles.

"Why does it matter? I ask myself the same thing. Why does it matter who brought this irritating human into the world? It doesn't matter to me. It matters to my brother for some bizarre reason. Nuitari even went so far as to visit Sargonnas to ask him what he knew about Mina. Apparently she had a friend who was a minotaur or some such thing. This Galdar was found, but he was of no help."

Zeboim gave an exasperated sigh. "The long and short of it is—now all of the gods are exercised over this stupid question. The dragon who started it has vanished without a trace, as though the seas swallowed her up, which they didn't. I can vouch for this much at least. That leaves you."

"Majesty," Rhys said. "I do not know—"

Zeboim halted in her pacing and turned to face him. "She claims you do."

"She also claims I was wearing the orange robes of Majere when we met. You were there, Majesty. You know I was dressed in the green robes you gave me."

Zeboim looked at him. She looked at his robes. She looked back to him. She ceased to see him. Her gaze grew abstracted.

"I wonder . . ." she said softly.

Her eyes narrowed, her focus coming back to him. She crouched in front of him, lithe, graceful and deadly. "Give yourself to me, monk, and I will set you free. This minute. I will even free the kender and the mutt. Pledge your faith to me, and I will summon the minotaur ship, and they will carry you wherever it is in this wide world that you want to go."

"I cannot pledge to you what I no longer have to give, Lady," Rhys replied gently. "My faith, my soul are in the hands of Majere."

"Mina is as good as her word," Zeboim returned angrily. She pointed at Nightshade. "She will kill both your dog and the wretch of a kender. They will die slowly and in agony, all because of you."

"Majere watches over his own," Rhys said. He looked at the staff, propped up against the wall.

"You will let those who trust you die in torment just so you can find salvation! A fine friend you are, Brother!"

"Rhys is not letting us die in torment!" Nightshade cried stoutly. "We *want* to die in torment, don't we, Atta! Oops," he added in a low voice. "That didn't come out quite right."

Zeboim rose, majestic and cold. "So be it, monk. I would slay you myself right now, but I would not deprive Mina of the pleasure. Rest assured, I will be watching and savoring every drop of blood! Oh, and just in case you were thinking that this might help you—"

She pointed a finger at the staff, and it exploded in a blast of ugly green flame. Splinters of wood flew about the cavern. One of the splinters sliced the flesh on Rhys's hand. He covered the wound swiftly, so that Zeboim would not see.

The goddess vanished with a clap of thunder, a gust of rain-laden wind, and a sneer.

Rhys looked down at his hand, at the long, jagged tear made by the splinter. Blood welled from the wound. He pressed the hem of his sleeve over it. All that remained of the staff—the splinter that had cut him—lay on the floor at his side. He picked up the splinter and closed his hand over it.

He had Majere's answer, and he was content.

"Don't look sad, Rhys," Nightshade was saying cheerfully. "I don't mind dying. Neither does Atta. It might be kind of fun to be a ghost—I could slide through walls and go bump in the night. Atta and I will come visit you in our ghostly forms. Not that I've seen many dog ghosts, mind you. I wonder why? Maybe because the souls of dogs have already completed their journeys, and they are free to run off to play forever in grassy fields. Maybe they chase the souls of rabbits. That is, if rabbits have souls—don't get me started on rabbits. . . ."

Rhys waited patiently for the kender to finish his metaphysical ramblings. When Nightshade had talked himself out and was settling down to play rock, cloth, and knife with Atta, Rhys said, "You can squeeze your hands through the manacles, can't you?"

Nightshade pretended not to hear. "Cloth covers rock. You lose again, Atta."

"Nightshade . . ." Rhys persisted.

"Don't interrupt us, Rhys," Nightshade said, interrupting. "This is a very serious game."

Rhys tried again. "Nightshade, I know—"

"No, you don't!" cried Nightshade, glaring at Rhys. Going back to the game, the kender slapped Atta lightly on the paw. "That's cheating. You can't change your mind in the middle! You said 'rock' the first time. . . ."

Rhys kept quiet.

Nightshade kept glancing at him out of the corner of his eye, squirming uncomfortably. He continued to play, but he forgot what he'd said he was—rock, cloth, or knife—and that confused the game.

Suddenly he cried, "All right already! The manacles on my wrists might be a little loose."

He looked down at his feet and brightened. "But I could never squeeze my feet through the manacles on my ankles!"

"You could," Rhys said, "if you smeared some of the grease from the salt pork on them."

The kender thrust out his lower lip. "It'll ruin my boots."

Rhys glanced at the boots. Two of the kender's pink toes could be seen poking out through holes in the soles.

"When it grows dark," Rhys said, "you will squeeze loose and take Atta and leave."

Nightshade shook his head. "Not without you. We'll use the grease to free your hands—"

"The manacles are tight on my wrists and tighter still around my ankles. I cannot escape. You and Atta can."

"Don't make me go!" Nightshade pleaded.

Rhys put his arm around the kender's shoulders. "You are a good and loyal friend, Nightshade, the best friend I have ever known. Your wisdom brought me back to my god. Look at me."

Nightshade shook his head and stared stubbornly at the floor.

"Look at me," Rhys said gently.

Nightshade lifted his head. Tears stained his cheeks.

"I can bear the pain," Rhys said. "I am not afraid of death. Majere waits to receive me. What I could not bear is to see the two of you suffer. My death will be so much easier if I know you and Atta are both safe. Will you make this last sacrifice for me, Nightshade?"

Nightshade had to swallow a few times, and then he said miserably, "Yes, Rhys."

Atta gazed at her master. It was a good thing she could not understand what he was saying. She would have most decidedly refused.

"That is well," said Rhys. "Now I think we should have something to eat and drink, and then get some rest."

"I'm not hungry," Nightshade mumbled.

"I am," Rhys stated. "I know Atta is."

At the mention of food, the dog licked her chops and stood up, wagging her tail.

"I think maybe you are, too," Rhys added, smiling.

"Well, just a little," said Nightshade and, with a mournful sigh, he slipped his hands out of the manacles and clanked over to the sack of salt pork.

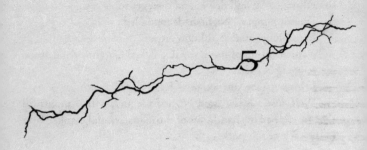

5

The ocean boiled as Zeboim stalked into the water, and she was wreathed in steam when she boarded the minotaur vessel. The captain bowed low to her, and the crew knuckled their shaggy foreheads. "Where are you bound, Most Glorious One?" the captain asked humbly.

"The Temple of Majere," said the goddess.

The captain rubbed his snout and regarded her with an apologetic air. "I fear I do not know—"

Zeboim waved her hand. "It is on some mountain somewhere. I forget the name. I will guide you. Make haste."

"Yes, Most Glorious One." The captain bowed again and then began to bellow orders. The crew raced into the rigging.

Zeboim lifted her hands and summoned the wind, and the sails billowed.

"North," she said, and the waves curled and foamed beneath the prow as the wind bore the ship over the waves and up into the clouds.

The winds of the goddess's will drove her ship through the ethers foaming beneath the keel and carried her to a remote realm that appeared on no maps of Krynn, for few mortals had ever seen it or were aware it existed. Those who did know of it had no need to map it, for they knew where they were.

It was a land of tall mountains and deep valleys. Nothing grew on the towering mountains. The valleys were gashes cut into the stone with smatterings of grassy hillocks and the occasional scraggly pine or wind-bent spruce. The nomads who dwelt in this desolate region roamed the mountains with their herds of goats, eking out a harsh existence. These humans lived now as they had lived centuries ago, knowing nothing of the world beyond and asking nothing from that world except to be left alone.

As the goddess neared her destination, she shrouded the ship in clouds, for fear Majere, who was a solitary, reclusive god, would know of her coming and depart before she could speak to him.

"Gracious Lady, this is madness," said the minotaur captain. He cast a haggard look over the prow. Whenever the clouds parted, he could see his ship sailing perilously close to jagged, snow-capped peaks. "We will smash headlong into a mountain and that will be the end of us!"

"Anchor here," Zeboim ordered. "We are close to my destination. I will make the rest of the journey on my own."

The captain was only too happy to obey. He heaved the ship to, and they drifted on the clouds.

Wrapping herself in a gray mist that she wound around her like a silken scarf, Zeboim descended down the side of the mountain, searching for Majere's dwelling. She had not been here in eons and had forgotten precisely where it lay. Emerging onto a plateau that spanned the distance between two peaks, she thought this place looked familiar, and she lifted the veil of mist with her hands and peered out. She smiled in satisfaction.

A simple house, built of time, with spare, elegant lines, stood on the plateau. In addition to the house was a paved yard and a garden, all surrounded by a wall that had been constructed stone by stone by the hands of the owner. Those same hands had built the house and they also tended the garden.

"Ye gods, I'd go crazy as a blowfish, stuck here all alone," Zeboim muttered. "No one to listen when you speak. No one to obey your commands. No mortal lives to tangle and twist. Except . . . that's not quite true, is it, my friend?" Zeboim smiled a cruel, sardonic smile. Then she shuddered.

"Listen to me. I've been here only a few moments and already I'm talking to myself! Next thing you know I'll be chanting and prancing around, waving my hands and ringing little bells. Ah, there you are."

She found her prey alone in the courtyard, performing what appeared to be some sort of exercise or perhaps a slow and sinuous dance. Despite the bone-chilling cold that set the Sea Goddess's teeth to chattering, Majere was bare-chested and bare-footed, wearing only loose-flowing pants bound around his waist with a cloth belt. His iron-gray hair was tied in a braid that fell to his waist. His gaze was turned inward, body and mind one as he moved to the music of the spheres.

Zeboim swooped down on him like a diving cormorant and landed in the courtyard right in front of him.

He was aware of her. She knew by the slight flicker of the eyes. Perhaps he'd been aware of her for a long time. It was hard to tell, because he didn't acknowledge her presence, not even when she spoke his name.

"Majere," she said sternly, "we need to talk."

The gods have no corporeal forms, nor do they need them. They can communicate with each other mind-to-mind, their thoughts roving the universe, knowing no bounds. Like mortals, however, the gods have secrets—thoughts they do not want to share, plans and schemes they do not want to reveal—so they find it preferable to use their avatars not only when they need to communicate with mortals but also with each other. The god permits only a portion of himself or herself to enter into the avatar, thus keeping the mind of the god hidden.

Majere's avatar continued with the exercise—hands moving gracefully through the thin, crisp air; bare feet gliding over the flagstone. Zeboim was forced to do her own dance—dodging out of his way, leaping to one side—as she sought to keep up with him and keep his face in view.

"I don't suppose you could stand still for a moment," she said, finally irritated. She had just tripped over the hem of her gown.

Majere continued to perform his daily ritual. His gaze looked to the mountains, not to her.

"We both know why I'm here. That monk of yours—the monk Mina is about to disembowel, or flay, or whatever bit of fun she plans to have with him."

Majere turned away from her, his movements slow and proscribed, but not before she had seen a flicker in his gray eyes.

"Ah ha!" cried Zeboim, darting around to confront him. "Mina. That name is familiar to you, isn't it? Why? That's the question. I think you know something about her. I think you know a lot about her."

The hand of the god moved in a graceful arc through the air. Zeboim reached out and caught hold of his wrist. Majere was forced to look at her.

"I think you made a mistake," she said.

Majere remained standing perfectly still, calm and composed. He had every appearance of continuing to stand like that for the next century, and the impatient Zeboim released her grasp. Majere continued with his exercise as though nothing had happened to interrupt him.

"Here's my theory," said Zeboim. She was worn out from

trying to keep up with the god and seated herself on the stone wall as she expounded her views. "You either knew or realized something about Mina. Whatever this is or was, you decided to have your monks deal with it, and thus Mina's first disciple—the monk's wretched brother—arrived at your monastery. What was supposed to happen? Were the monks meant to pray him back to life? Remove the curse from him?"

She paused to allow Majere to provide her with answers, but the god did not respond.

"Anyway," Zeboim continued, "whatever was supposed to happen didn't, and what did happen was disastrous. Perhaps Chemosh found out and acted to thwart your plans. His disciple murdered the monks. All except one—Rhys Mason. He was to have been your champion, but oops! You lost him. He was, understandably, furious at you. Where were you when your monks were being slaughtered? Off doing your little dance?

"It all has to do with this business of free will." The goddess rubbed her arms, trying to keep warm. "You gods of Light are always promoting free will, and here we have a prime example of why such a notion is so utterly ridiculous. Here you are, in desperate need of your disciple, and what does he do? He exerts his free will. He abandons you and turns to me for help.

"You refuse to abandon him, however. Very forgiving and understanding of you, I have to admit," Zeboim added with a shrug. "Had one of my disciples done that, I would have drowned him in his own blood. But not you. Patiently you walk alongside him. Patiently you try to guide him, but somewhere, again, something goes wrong. I'm not sure what, but something."

Majere continued his exercise. He did not speak. He did not look at her. He was listening to her, though. She was certain of that.

"I sprang Mina on you, or rather, on Rhys. I didn't really mean to. We were in a hurry. I had to return her to Chemosh as part of a bargain we made. I thought I should introduce the two, however, since *I* was the one insisting that Rhys find her. I wanted him to know what she looked like. Well, sir! Imagine my shock when Mina claims he knows her! He claims he doesn't, and it's perfectly obvious to me he is telling the truth. The poor sod doesn't know how to lie. I believe him, but Mina doesn't.

"I do. I decide to bring these two together again. As an added bonus, by doing so, I make Chemosh's life miserable, but that's neither here nor there. Mina meets Rhys, and now he doesn't know her and she knows he doesn't know her. She's confused, poor darling. I can't say that I blame her. She says something very interesting to him, however. She says that the first time she saw him he was wearing orange robes. Rhys was wearing no such thing. He was wearing quite charming green robes, which I had given to him, so either Mina is color-blind, or she is daft."

Zeboim paused for breath. Simply watching Majere seemed to wear her out. She no longer expected him to speak.

"I don't believe Mina is either color-blind or crazy. I believe she saw what she saw. I believe she saw Rhys Mason at a time in his life when he *is* wearing orange robes and when he *does* know who she is. Not now, because he doesn't. Not in the past, because he didn't. Which leaves—*a time when he will.*"

Zeboim paused for effect, then said, "Mina saw your monk in the future, a future in which he has returned to you, a future in which he knows something about Mina. He *knows* something, because you've told him."

Zeboim shrugged. "The problem you have, Majere, is that now this future will never come to pass, because Mina plans to torture your poor monk to death.

"Then there's the matter of the kender bursting into sloppy, wet blubbers whenever *he* sees Mina, but I won't bore you with that. He's a kender, after all. You can't expect anything sensible from them."

Zeboim eyed Majere.

"Go ahead. Do your little dance. Pretend you are above all this. The truth is—you're in a pickle. I'm not alone in wondering what is going on with this Mina mortal. My brother, Nuitari, may be a pain in the backside, but he's not stupid. He and the weird cousins are asking questions. Sargonnas does not like the fact these Beloved are congregating in east Ansalon, so near his empire. Nuitari does not like them so near his precious Tower. Mishakal is furious that the hand of a child must be used to destroy them—a marvelous touch of Chemosh's, I must admit. I am quite amused by the thought of sweet little tykes forced to become bloodthirsty murderers.

"Why am I here, Majere? I can see you asking yourself that question. I came to warn you. I am the first god to visit you, but I won't be the last. All the signposts point to you. The rest will find their way to your mountain fastness, and some—I'm thinking specifically of my father—will not be as sweet and charming as I have been. You had best do something before you lose control of the situation completely. If you haven't already, that is."

"Perhaps you'd like to unburden yourself? Tell me the truth? I would be glad to help Rhys Mason—for a price. I'll placate my father and brother, keep them from disturbing you. Tell me what you know about Mina. It will be our secret—I swear it!"

Zeboim waited, rubbing her arms and stamping her feet.

Majere kept moving, gliding over the chill stone. His face was devoid of expression. His eyes fathomless, inscrutable.

"Keep your secret then!" Zeboim cried in nasty tones. "You will have no trouble doing so. Your poor monk will die before he reveals it. Ah, I forgot!" She clapped her hands. "He can't reveal it because he doesn't know it! He will be tortured for information he doesn't have and so can never tell. What a marvelous joke on the poor fellow. That will teach him to put his faith in a god such as you!"

Zeboim left in huff, trailing fog and mist behind her. Returning to her ship, she ordered the minotaurs to up anchor and make haste to find warmer climes.

In the courtyard, Majere tried to continue his ritual, but he found he could not. The mind has to be quiet and still for meditation, and his mind was in turmoil.

"Paladine," he said softly, "Your mortal body cannot hear me, but perhaps your soul can. I have failed you. I ask your forgiveness. I will try to make amends.

"Though I fear it is already too late."

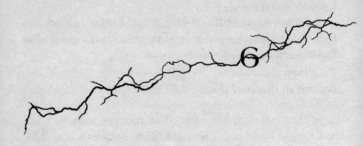

6

Chemosh stood on the battlements of Castle Beloved (he was seriously considering changing the name) watching Mina running along the beach. The waves lapped at her feet, washing away her footprints. He watched until Mina had returned to the castle and he could no longer see her.

Turning, he almost stepped on Ausric Krell.

Chemosh cursed, falling back.

"What do you mean? Sneaking up on me like that!"

"You were the one who ordered me to be discreet," Krell returned sullenly.

"Around Mina, you walking soup kettle! When you are around me, you may clank and rattle as much as you like. Well?" he added, after a pause. "What news?"

"You were right, Lord," said Krell, exultant. "She went to meet Zeboim!"

"Not a lover?" Chemosh repeated, astonished.

Krell saw that he'd made a mistake. "That, too," he said hastily. "Mina went to meet the Sea Witch *and* a lover." He shrugged. "Probably some priest of Zeboim's."

"Probably?" Chemosh repeated, frowning. "You do not know? You did not see him?"

Krell was flustered. "I . . . uh . . . could hardly do that, my lord. Zeboim was there and . . . and you would not want her to know that we were spying—"

"What you mean is you did not want her to know that beneath all that steel plating hides a craven coward." Chemosh began to walk toward the stair tower. "Come along. You will show me where to find this lover. I would like to meet him."

Krell was in a quandary. His story was believable—as far as it went. He'd left out the kender and the dog, which, the more he thought about it, didn't add anything to his tale of lovers and secret assignations. Then there was the liberty he'd taken in the timing of events—Zeboim had arrived, but only *after* Mina had left, something that was odd for two who were supposed to be in a conspiracy.

"Wait, my lord!" Krell cried urgently.

"For what?" Chemosh looked back impatiently.

"For . . . nightfall," said Krell, saved by inspiration. "I heard Mina tell this man she would return to him in the night. You could catch them in the act," he added, certain this would please his master.

Chemosh went exceedingly pale. His hands, beneath the ragged lace, clenched and unclenched. His unkempt hair ruffled in the wind.

"You are right," said Chemosh in a toneless voice. "That is what I will do."

Krell gave a great, though inward, sigh of relief. He saluted his lord, turned on his heel. He would go back to the cave, ensure that when Chemosh arrived he would find what Krell had told him to expect.

"Krell," said Chemosh abruptly. "I am bored. Come play khas with me. Take my mind off things."

Krell's shoulders slumped. He hated playing khas with Chemosh. For starters, the god always won. Not difficult when you can see at a glance all possible moves, all possible outcomes. For finishers, Krell had urgent business in that cave. He had a kender and a dog to dispatch.

"I would be only too happy to give you a game, my lord, but I have the Beloved to train. Why don't you have a romp with Mina? You may as well get your money's worth—"

Krell realized as he was speaking that he'd made a mistake. He would have swallowed his words, if he could, and himself as well, but it was too late for that. The dark eyes of Chemosh had a look in them that made the death knight wish he could crawl inside his armor and never come out.

There was a moment's horrible silence, then Chemosh said coldly, "From now on, Mina will train the Beloved. You will play khas."

"Yes, lord," mumbled Krell.

The death knight clumped after Chemosh, following him down the stairs and into the hall. Krell might be in disgrace, but he had one consoling thought: he would not be in Mina's boots right now for anything heaven or the Abyss had to offer.

Mina took a swim in the ocean, though it was not precisely intentional. The waves kicked up by Zeboim's ire flooded the narrow strip of beach that ran from the rock groin to the cliff on which stood the castle. The water was not deep, and the force of the waves was broken by the rocks. Mina was a good swimmer, and she enjoyed the exercise that warmed her muscles and freed her mind, forced her to acknowledge an unpleasant truth.

She believed the monk. He was not lying. She knew men, and he was the sort who was incapable of lying. He reminded her, in an odd way, of Galdar, her officer and loyal friend. Galdar, too, had been incapable of telling a lie, even when he knew she would have preferred a lie to the truth. Mina wondered, with a pang, where Galdar was. She hoped he was doing well. She wished suddenly she could see him. She wished, for one moment, he was there to put his arm around her—the arm she had miraculously restored—and tell her all would be all right.

Emerging from the sea, Mina wrung the water from her hair and from her sodden gown and gave up wishing for what could never be. She had to decide what to do with the monk. He didn't know her now, but he had known her when she had first met him. There had been recognition, knowledge in his eyes. He'd forgotten, or something had happened to cause him to forget.

One way to restore memory was through pain. Mina had ordered torture used on her prisoners. The dark knights had been experts at it. She had watched men suffer and sometimes die, confident she was doing right, serving a laudable cause—the cause of the One God.

Now she was unsure, uncertain. She was starting to doubt. This morning she had been angry enough that she could have flayed the skin from the monk's bones and never felt a qualm. On reflection she wondered: *Can I torture a man in cold blood? If I did, can I trust information gained by duress?*

Galdar had always been dubious about torture as a means to elicit information.

"Men will say anything to stop the pain," he had once warned her.

Mina knew the truth of that. She was the one in torment, and she would do anything to stop her pain.

There was another way. The dead have no secrets. Not from the Lord of Death.

Putting her hand to the necklace of black pearls, Mina made up her mind. She would tell Chemosh everything. Lay her soul bare to him. He would help her drag the truth out of the monk.

Mina grasped the necklace and tore it from around her neck and tossed it into the sea. Her heart eased, she returned to the castle, dressed herself in something pretty, and went to seek out Chemosh.

She found the Lord of Death in his study, playing khas with Krell.

Mina and the death knight exchanged looks that acknowledged their mutual loathing, then Krell went back to studying the board. Mina observed him more closely. He looked the same cruel, boorish brute he always looked, yet there was a sleek smugness about him that she found new and troubling. She also found it troubling that he and her lord seemed quite cozy together. Chemosh was actually laughing at something Krell had been saying as she entered the study.

Mina started to speak, but Chemosh forestalled her. He cast her a negligent glance.

"Did you enjoy your swim, Mistress?"

Her heart trembled. His tone was chill, his words an insult. Mistress! He might have been speaking to a stranger.

"Yes," Mina replied, and went on quickly before she lost her nerve. "My lord, I must talk with you." She flicked a glance at Krell. "In private."

"I am in the middle of a game," Chemosh returned languidly. "It appears as though Krell might beat me. What do you think, Krell?"

"I have you on the run, my lord," said the death knight without enthusiasm.

Mina swallowed. "After your game, then, my lord?"

"I am afraid not," said Chemosh. He reached out and moved a knight, sliding it across the board and using it to knock one of Krell's pawns to the floor. "I know all about your lover, Mina, so there is no need for you to keep lying to me."

"Lover?" Mina repeated, astonished. "I do not know what you are talking about, my lord. I have no lover."

"What about the man you have hidden away in the grotto?" Chemosh asked, and he twisted around in the chair to look her full in face.

Mina trembled. She could think of ten things to say in her defense, but none of them sounded plausible. She opened her mouth, but no words came out. The hot blood rushed to her cheeks, and she knew in an instant that her flush and her silence had just proclaimed her guilt. "My lord," she said desperately, finding her voice. "I can explain—"

"I am not interested in explanations," Chemosh said coolly, and turned back to his game. "I would slay you for your betrayal, Mistress, but I would then be plagued for eternity by your pitiful ghost. Besides, your death would be a waste of a valuable commodity."

He did not look at her as he continued to speak, but pondered his next move on the board.

"You are to take command of the Beloved, Mistress. They listen to you, obey you. You have battlefield experience. You are the right commander, therefore, to mold them into an army and ready them to march on Nuitari's Tower. You will organize the Beloved and take them off to a camp I have established at a remote place far from here."

The room went dark. The floor tilted, the walls moved. Mina had to grasp hold of a table in order to remain standing.

"Are you banishing me from your presence, my lord?" she asked faintly, barely able to find breath enough to speak the question.

He did not deign to reply.

"I could train them here," she said.

"That would not be to my liking. I find that I grow weary of the sight of them. And you."

Mina moved numbly across a floor that lurched and shook beneath her feet. Coming to Chemosh, she sank to her knees at his side and caught hold of his arm.

"My lord, let me explain! I beg you!"

"I told you, Mina, I am in the middle of a game—"

"I threw away the pearls!" she cried. "I know I have displeased you. I need to tell you—"

Chemosh removed his arm from her grasp and rearranged the lace she had disturbed. "You will leave tomorrow. This day, you will remain locked in your chamber under guard. I plan to visit your lover this evening, and I do not want you to sneak off to try to warn him."

Mina was near collapse. Her legs trembled; her hands shook. She was covered in chill sweat. Then Krell made a noise. He chuckled, low and deep. She looked into the fiery, piggy eyes of the death knight, and she saw triumph. She knew then who had spied on her.

Her hatred of Krell gave her the strength to rise to her feet, burned away her tears, and lent her the courage to say, "As you will, my lord."

Chemosh moved another piece. "You have leave to go."

Mina walked out of that room; she had no idea how. She could not see anything. She could not feel anything. She had lost all sensation. She staggered on as far as she could and managed to reach her bedchamber before darkness overcame her and she sank to the floor and lay there like a dead thing.

After she had gone, Krell looked down at the board and realized, to his astonishment, he had won.

The death knight moved a pawn, snatched up the black queen, and carried her off.

"Your king is trapped, my lord," Krell stated exultantly. "Nowhere to go. The game is mine."

Chemosh looked at him.

Krell gulped. "Or maybe not. That last move . . . I made a mistake. That was an illegal move." He quickly slid the queen back onto her hex. "I apologize, my lord. I have no idea what I was thinking—"

Chemosh picked up the khas board and flung it in Krell's face.

"Should you need me, I will be in the Hall of the Souls Passing. Do not let Mina out of your sight! And pick up the pieces," Chemosh added, as he walked away.

"Yes, my lord," muttered Ausric Krell.

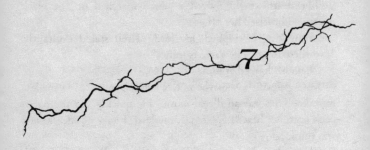

7

The cold of the stone floor roused Mina from her swoon. She was shivering so she could barely stand. Dragging herself to her feet, she wrapped herself in the blanket from her bed and went to stand by the window.

The breeze was moderate. The Blood Sea was quiet. Rolling swells washed over the rocks with barely a splash. Pelicans, flying in formation like a wing of blue dragons, searched for fish. A dolphin's glistening body broke the surface and glided back down.

She had to talk to Chemosh. She had to make him listen to her. This was a mistake or rather, mischief.

Mina walked to the door of her chamber and found it was not bolted as she had feared it might be. She flung it open.

Ausric Krell stood in front of her.

Mina cast him a scathing glance and started to walk around him.

Krell moved to block her.

Mina was forced to confront him. "Get out of my way."

"I have my orders," Krell said, gloating. "You are to remain in your chamber. If you need to occupy your time, I suggest you start packing for your journey. You might want to pack everything you own. You won't be coming back."

Mina regarded him with cold fury.

"You know that the man in the cave is not my lover."

"I know no such thing," Krell returned.

"A maiden does not usually chain her lover to a wall and threaten him with death," Mina said caustically. "What of the kender? Is he my lover, too?"

"People have their little quirks," Krell stated magnanimously. "When I was alive, I liked my women to put up a struggle, squeal a bit. I am not one to sit in judgment."

"My lord is no fool. When he goes to that cave this night and finds an emaciated monk and a sniveling little kender chained to a wall, he will know you lied to him."

"Maybe," said Krell stolidly. "Maybe not."

Mina clenched her fists in frustration. "Are you as stupid as you look, Krell? When Chemosh finds out you lied to him about me, he will be furious with you. He might well hand you over to Zeboim. But you can still save yourself. Go to Chemosh and tell him that you have thought this over and you were mistaken. . . ."

Krell was not stupid. He *had* thought it over. He knew just what he had to do to protect himself.

"My lord Chemosh has given orders he is not to be disturbed," said Krell, and he gave Mina a shove that propelled her backward into the room.

He slammed the door shut, bolted it from the outside, and resumed his stance before it.

Mina went back to the window. She knew what Krell plotted. All he had to do was go to the cave, dispose of the kender and the dog, kill the monk and remove his chains, and leave the body for Chemosh to find, along with evidence to prove the grotto had been her love nest.

Perhaps Krell had already done this. That would certainly account for his smugness. Mina didn't know how long she had been unconscious. Hours, at least. The castle faced east and its shadow lay dark on the blood-red waves. The sun was already sinking toward the end of day.

Mina stood at the window. I have to win back my lord's trust and affection. There must be a way to prove my love. If I could give him a gift. Something he yearns to possess.

But what is there a god cannot have if he wants it?

One thing. One thing Chemosh wanted and he could not get. Nuitari's Tower.

"If I could give him that, I would do it," Mina said softly, "though it cost me my life. . . ."

She closed her eyes, and she found herself beneath the sea. The Tower of High Sorcery stood before her. Its crystalline walls reflected the clear blue water, the red coral, and the green sea plants and multi-colored sea creatures—a constant panorama of sea life glided across its faceted surface.

She was inside the Tower, in her prison, talking with Nuitari. She was in the water of the globe, speaking with the dragon. She was in the *Solio Febalas*, overcome by awe and wonder, surrounded by the sublime miracle that was the gods.

Mina held out her hands. Her longing intensified, welled up inside her. Her heart pounded, her muscles stiffened. She sank to her knees with a moan, and still she held out her hands to the Tower that was everywhere inside her.

The longing took control of her and swept her up. She could not stop. She did not want to stop. She gave herself to the longing, and it seemed her heart would tear itself apart. She gasped for breath. She tasted blood in her mouth. She shuddered and moaned again, and suddenly something snapped within her.

The longing, the desire, flowed out of her outstretched hands and she was calm and at peace. . . .

Krell had figured a way out of his predicament, though not the way Mina had guessed. Her plan required that he leave the castle and he was terrified to do so, for fear Chemosh would return at any moment. Krell might have the brains of a rodent, but he had twice the low cunning to make up for it. *His* plan was simple, and it was direct.

He didn't have to kill the kender, the monk, or the dog. All he had to do was kill Mina.

Once Mina was dead, end of story. Chemosh would have no reason to go to the cave to confront her lover, and Krell's problem would be solved.

Krell detested Mina, and he would have murdered her long ago, but he feared that Chemosh would have murdered him— not an easy thing to do, since Krell was already dead, but Krell was fairly certain the Lord of Death would find a way and it would not be pleasant.

Krell deemed it safe to kill Mina now. Chemosh despised her. He loathed her. He couldn't stand the sight of her.

"She tried to escape, my lord," Krell said, rehearsing his speech. "I didn't mean to kill her. I just don't know my own strength."

Having made up his mind to slay Mina, Krell had only to decide when. In this regard, he dithered. Chemosh had said he was going to the Hall of Souls Passing, but did he mean it? Had the god departed, or was he still lurking about the castle?

Every time Krell started to put his hand on the handle of the door, he had a vision of Chemosh entering the room in time to witness the death knight slitting his mistress's throat. Chemosh might well despise her, but such a gruesome sight could still come as a shock.

Krell dared not leave his post in order to go find out. At last, he snagged a passing spectral minion and ordered it to make inquiries. The minion was gone for some time, during which Krell paced the corridor and pictured his revenge on Mina, growing more and more excited at the thought.

The minion brought welcome news. Chemosh was in the Hall of the Souls Passing and apparently in no hurry to return.

Perfect. Chemosh would be there to witness Mina's soul arrive. He would have no reason to go to the cave. No reason at all.

Krell started to reach for the door handle then stopped. Amber light began to glow around the door frame. As he watched, frowning, the glowing light grew stronger and stronger.

Then Krell smiled. This was better than he'd hoped for. Mina had apparently set the place on fire.

He struck the door with his fist, drew his sword, and strode inside.

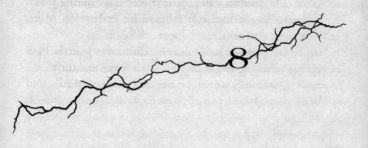

The grotto was redolent with the smell of salt pork. Atta licked her chops and stared longingly at Nightshade, who was dutifully, if dolefully, scrubbing the insides of his boots with a hunk of greasy meat. Rhys had reasoned it would be easier for the kender to slide his feet out of the boots rather than try to slide the boots out of the manacles.

"There, I've finished!" Nightshade announced. He fed what was left of the mangled pork to Atta, who swallowed it in a gulp and then began to sniff hungrily at his boots.

"Atta, leave it," Rhys ordered, and the dog obediently trotted over to lie down at his side.

Nightshade gave his right foot a wriggle and a grunt. "Nope," he said, after a moment's exertion. "It won't budge. I'm sorry, Rhys. It was worth a try—"

"You have to actually move your foot, Nightshade," Rhys said with a smile.

"I did move it," Nightshade protested. "The boots are on there good and tight. They were always a little small for me. That's why my toes broke out there at the tip. Now let's talk about how we're *both* going to escape."

"We'll talk about that *after* you're free," Rhys countered.

"Promise?" Nightshade eyed Rhys suspiciously.

"Promise," said Rhys.

Nightshade grabbed hold of the iron band that was clamped around his ankle and began to push on the band and the boot.

"Bend your foot," said Rhys patiently.

"What do you think I am?" Nightshade demanded. "One of those circus guys who can tie both his legs in a knot behind his neck and walk on his hands? I know I can't do that, because I tried it once. My father had to unknot me—"

"Nightshade," said Rhys, "we're running out of time."

The daylight outside was fading. The grotto was growing darker.

Nightshade heaved a deep sigh. Squinching up his face, he pushed and pulled. His right foot slipped neatly out of the boot. The left foot followed. He removed his boots from the manacles and eyed them ruefully.

"Every dog from six shires will be chasing after me," the kender said grumpily. He pulled on his greasy boots and, grabbing another hunk of salt pork, bent down next to Rhys. "Your turn."

"Nightshade, look." Rhys pointed to the manacles that fit close around his bony ankles. He held up the manacles that were clamped tightly over his wrists, so tightly they had rubbed the skin raw.

Nightshade looked. His lower lip quivered. "It's my fault."

"No, of course, it isn't your fault, Nightshade," said Rhys, shocked. "What makes you think that?"

"If I were a proper kender, you wouldn't be stuck here to die!" Nightshade cried. "I would have lock-pick tools, you see, and I could pick these locks like that." He snapped his fingers, or tried to. Due to the grease, the snap didn't come off very well. "My father gave me my set of lock-pick tools when I was twelve, and he tried to teach me how to use them. I wasn't very good. Once I dropped the pick and it went 'bang!' and woke up the whole house. Another time the pick went right through the lock—I'm still not sure how—and ended up on the wrong side of the door, and I lost that one. . . ."

Nightshade crossed his arms over his chest. "I won't go! You can't make me!"

"Nightshade," said Rhys firmly. "You have to."

"No, I don't."

"It's the only way to save me," Rhys said in solemn tones.

Nightshade looked up.

"I've been thinking," Rhys continued. "We're on the Blood Sea. We must be somewhere close to Flotsam. There is a temple of Majere in Flotsam—"

"There is? That's wonderful!" Nightshade cried, excited. "I can run to Flotsam and find the temple, round up the monks, bring them back, and they'll kick butt and we'll all rescue you!"

"That's an excellent plan," said Rhys.

Nightshade scrambled to his feet. "I'll leave right now!"

"You must take Atta with you," Rhys said. "For protection. Flotsam is a lawless town, or so I've heard."

"Right! C'mon, Atta!" Nightshade whistled.

Atta rose to her feet but didn't follow. She looked at Rhys. She sensed something wasn't right.

"Atta, guard," he said and pointed at the kender.

He often had her "guard" something, which meant she was to watch over an object, not let anyone near it. He'd left her to guard sick sheep while he went to go seek help. He'd often told her to guard Nightshade.

In this case, however, Rhys wasn't leaving. He was staying, and the object she was supposed to guard was leaving. He didn't know if she would understand and obey. She was accustomed to watching over the kender, however, and Rhys hoped she would go along with this now as she had done in the past. He had thought of trying to form a leash for her, but she had never known what it was to be tied up. He guessed that she would fight a leash and he didn't have time for that. Night was coming very fast.

"Atta, here."

The dog came to him. He put his hands over her head and looked into her brown eyes.

"Go with Nightshade," he said. "Watch him. Guard him."

Rhys drew her near and kissed her gently on the forehead. Then he let her go.

"Call her again."

"Atta, come," said Nightshade.

Atta looked at Rhys. He gestured toward the kender.

"Walk away now," Rhys ordered Nightshade. "Quickly."

Nightshade obeyed, walking toward the grotto's entrance. Atta cast one more look at Rhys, then she obediently followed the kender. Rhys breathed a soft sigh.

Nightshade paused. "We'll be back soon, Rhys. Don't—don't go anywhere."

"Be safe, my friend," Rhys replied. "You and Atta take care of each other."

"We will." Nightshade hesitated, then turned and bolted out of the cave. Atta dashed after the kender, just as she'd done many times before.

Rhys sank back against the rock wall. Tears came to his eyes, but he smiled through them.

"Forgive me the lie, Master," he said quietly.

In all the long history of the monks of Majere, they had never built a temple in Flotsam.

Chemosh was always in the Hall of the Souls Passing and he went there very little—a contradiction that can be explained by the fact that one of the aspects of the Lord of Death was always present in the Hall, seated on his dark throne, reviewing all those souls who had left their mortal flesh behind and were about to embark on the next stage of the eternal journey.

Chemosh rarely returned to this aspect of himself. This place was too isolated, too far removed from the world of gods and men. The other gods were prohibited from coming to the Hall, lest they exert undue interference on the souls undergoing judgment.

The Lord of Death was permitted his final chance to try to sway souls to his evil cause, to prevent them from traveling on, to seize them and keep them. Souls who had learned life's lessons were easily able to avoid his snares, as were innocent souls, such as those of infants.

One of the gods of Light or Neutrality could intercede on behalf of a soul, but only by casting a blessing on that soul before it entered the Hall. One such soul was standing before the onyx and silver throne now—a soul that was blackened yet shot through with blue light. The man had committed foul deeds, yet he had sacrificed his life to save children trapped in a fire. His soul's journey would not be easy, for he still had much to learn, but Mishakal blessed him, and he managed to escape the bony, grasping hand of the Lord of Death. When Chemosh snagged a soul, he would seize it and fling it into the Abyss or send it back to inhabit the dead body that would now become its dreadful prison.

The gods of Dark might claim souls as well. Souls already promised to Morgion or cursed by Zeboim would enter the Hall bound in chains to be handed over by the Lord of Death to those gods they had sworn to serve.

Chemosh in his "mortal" aspect came to the Hall only during those times when he was deeply troubled. He enjoyed being reminded of his power. No matter what god a mortal worshipped in life, when that life ended, every soul stood before him. Even those who denied the existence of the gods found themselves here—a bit of a shock for most. They were judged on how they had lived their lives, not by whether or not they had professed a belief in a god during that life. A sorceress who had helped people throughout her life was sent on her way, while the grasping, covetous soul who had regularly cheated customers, yet never missed a prayer service, fell victim to the blandishments of the Lord of Death and ended up in the Abyss.

Some souls could have departed but chose not to. A mother was reluctant to leave her little children; a husband did not want to leave his wife. These remained bound to those they loved until they could be persuaded that it was right for them to continue on, that the living had to go on with their lives and the dead should move forward as well.

Chemosh stood in the Hall watching the line of souls form, a line that was meant to be eternal, and he recalled the terrible time when the line had come to an abrupt and unexpected end. The time when the last soul had appeared before him, and he had looked about in an astonishment that knew no bounds. The Lord of Death had risen from his throne for the first time since he'd taken his place there at the start of creation, and he had stormed out of the Hall in a rage only to find that Takhisis had stolen away the world and taken the souls with her.

Chemosh had then learned the truth of a mortal adage: One never appreciated what one had until it was lost.

One also vowed that one would never lose it again.

Chemosh watched the souls come before him, and he listened to their stories, and wheeled and dealed and passed his judgment, and seized a few and let go a few, and waited to feel the warm glow of satisfaction.

It did not come this day. He felt distinctly dissatisfied. What was supposed to go right was going all wrong. He'd lost control, and he had no idea how it had slipped away. It was as if he were cursed. . . .

With that word, he realized suddenly why he had been drawn here, realized what it was he sought.

He stood in the Hall of Souls Passing, and he saw again the first soul that had come before him when the world was returned—the mortal soul of Takhisis. All the gods had been present at her passing. He heard again her words—part desperate plea and part defiant snarl.

"You are making a mistake!" Takhisis had said to them. "What I have done cannot be undone. The curse is among you. Destroy me, and you destroy yourselves."

Chemosh could not judge her. None of the gods could do that. She had been one of them, after all. The High God had come to claim the soul of his lost child, and the reign of Takhisis, Queen of Darkness, was ended, and time and the universe continued on.

Chemosh had thought nothing of her prediction then. Rants, ravings, threats—Takhisis had spewed such venom for eons. He could not help but think of it now, think of it and wonder uneasily just what the late and unlamented Queen had meant.

There was one person who might know, one person who'd been closer to the Takhisis than anyone else in history. The one person he'd banished from his sight.

Mina.

9

Nightshade left the grotto with a heavy heart—a heart that was too heavy to stay properly in his chest but sank down to his stomach, where it took offense to the salt pork and gave him a bellyache. From there, his heart sank still further, adding its weight to his feet so they moved slower and slower, until it was an effort to make them move at all. His heart grew heavier the farther he went.

Nightshade's brain kept telling him he was on an Urgent Mission to save Rhys. The problem was his heart didn't believe it, so that not only was his heart down around his shoes, flummoxing his feet, his heart was in an argument with his head, not to mention the salt pork.

Nightshade ignored his heart and obeyed his head. The head was Logic, and humans were impressed with Logic and were always stressing how important it was to behave logically. Logic dictated Nightshade would stand a better chance of rescuing Rhys if he brought back help in the form of monks of Majere than if he—a mere kender—stayed with Rhys in the grotto. It was the Logic of Rhys's argument that had persuaded Nightshade to leave, and this same Logic kept him moving ahead when his heart urged him to turn around and run back.

Atta stayed close at his heels, as she'd been commanded. Her heart must have bothered her as well, for she kept stopping, drawing severe scoldings from the kender.

"Atta! Here, girl! You've got to keep up with me!" Nightshade admonished. "We don't have time for lollygagging about."

Atta would trot after him because that was what she'd been told to do, but she was not happy, and neither was Nightshade.

The walking itself was another problem. Solinari and Lunitari were both in the sky this night. Solinari was half-full and Lunitari completely full, so that it seemed the moons were winking at Nightshade like mismatched eyes. He could see the ridgeline up above where he walked and he calculated—logically—that on top of this ridge he would find a road, and that road would lead to Flotsam. The ridge didn't look to be that far away—just a hop, skip, and a jump over some sand dunes, followed by a scramble among some boulders.

The sand dunes proved difficult to navigate, however. Hop, skip, and jump failed utterly. The sand was loose and squishy and slid out from underneath his boots that were already slick from the salt pork. He envied Atta, who pattered along on top of the sand, and wished he had four feet. Nightshade floundered through the sand for what seemed forever, spending more time on his hands and knees than he did on his feet. He grew hot and worn out, and whenever he looked he found the ridge appeared to be moving farther away.

All things do come to an end, however, even sand dunes. This left the boulders. Nightshade figured boulders had to be better than dunes, and he started climbing the ridge with relief.

Relief that soon evaporated.

He didn't know boulders came in such immense sizes or that they would be this sharp, or that climbing them would be this difficult, or that the rats living among the boulders would be this big and nasty. Fortunately, he had Atta with him, or the rats might have carried him off, for they weren't in the least afraid of a kender. They did not like the dog, however. Atta barked at the rats. They glared at her with red eyes, chittered at her, then slunk away.

After only a short sojourn among the boulders, Nightshade's hands were cut and bleeding. His ankle hurt from where he'd slipped and wedged it in a crack. He had to stop once to throw up, but that at least took care of the salt pork problem.

Then, just when it seemed like these boulders must go on forever, he reached the top of the ridge.

Nightshade stepped out on the road that would take him to Flotsam and the monks, and he looked up the road and he looked down the road. His first thought was that the word "road" was paying this strip of rocky wagon ruts a compliment it did not deserve. His second though was more somber. The so-called road stretched on and on, as far as he could see in both directions.

There was no city at the end of either direction.

Flotsam was immense. He'd heard stories about Flotsam all his life. Flotsam was a city that never slept. It was a city of torchlight, tavern lights, bonfires on the beaches, and home fires shining in the windows of the houses. Nightshade had assumed that when he reached the road, he'd be able to see Flotsam's lights.

The only lights he could see were the cold, pale stars and the maddening winking eyes of the two moons.

"So where is it?" Nightshade turned one way, and then the other. "Which way do I go?"

Truth sank home. Truth sank his heart. Truth sank logic.

"It doesn't matter which way Flotsam is," said Nightshade in sudden, awful realization. "Because no matter which way Flotsam is, it's too far. Rhys knew it! He knew we'd never make it to Flotsam and back in time. He sent us away because he knew he was going to die!"

The kender sat down in the dirt and, wrapping his arms around the dog's neck, he hugged her close. "What are we going to do, Atta?"

In answer, she pulled away from him and ran back to the boulders. Halting, she looked at him eagerly and wagged her tail.

"It won't do any good to go back, Atta," said Nightshade miserably. "Even if I could climb down those stupid rocks again without breaking my neck, which I don't think I can, it wouldn't matter."

He wiped the sweat from his face.

"We can't save Rhys, not by ourselves. I'm a kender and you're a dog. We need help."

He sat in the road, mired in despair, his head in his hands. Atta licked his cheek and nudged him with her nose under his armpit, trying to prod him into action.

Nightshade lifted his head. A thought had occurred to him, a thought that made him burning mad.

"Here we are, Atta, half-killing ourselves to help Rhys, and what is his god doing all this time? Nothing, that's what! Gods can do anything! Majere could have put Flotsam where we could find it. Majere could have made that squishy sand hard and those sharp boulders soft. Majere could make Rhys's chains fall off! Majere could send me six monks right now, walking along the road to save Rhys. Do you hear that, Majere?" Nightshade hollered up to heaven.

He waited a few moments, giving the god a chance, but six monks did not appear.

"Now you've done it," said the kender ominously, and he stood up on his two feet, and he gazed up into the heavens, put his hands on his hips and gave the god a talking-to.

"I don't know if you're listening to me or not, Majere," Nightshade said in stern tones. "Probably not, since I'm a kender and no one listens to us, and also I'm a mystic, which means I don't worship you. Still, you know, that shouldn't make any difference. You're a god of good, according to what Rhys says, and that means you should listen to people—all people, including kender and mystics—whether we worship you or not.

"Now I can understand where you might not consider it quite fair of me to be asking you for help, since I've never done anything for you, but you're a lot bigger than me and a lot more powerful, so I think you could afford to be magenta or magnesium, or whatever that word is which means being kind and generous to people even if they don't deserve it.

"And maybe I don't deserve your help, but Rhys does. Yes, he did leave off worshipping you to worship Zeboim, but you must know he did that only because you let him down. Oh, I've heard all that talk about how we're not supposed to understand the minds of the gods, but you gods *are* supposed to understand the hearts of men, so you should understand that Rhys left because he was angry and hurt. Now you've taken him back and that's really good of you, but after all, it's no more than what you should have done in the first place, because you're a god of good, so you're not getting much credit from me for that."

Nightshade paused to draw a breath and to try to sort out his thoughts, which had gotten rather muddled. This done, he continued his argument, growing more heated as he went. "Rhys proved his loyalty to you by turning down Zeboim when she would have rescued him and us, too, and he's proving his loyalty by sitting in that cave waiting to die when Mina comes back to torture him. What are you doing in return? You're leaving him chained up in that grotto!"

Nightshade raised his arms and his voice and shouted. "Does this make any kind of sense to you, Majere?"

He fell silent, giving the god time to respond.

Nightshade heard sea gulls squabbling over a dead fish, waves crashing on the shore, and the wind making the dead grass crackle. None of this sounded to him like the voice of a god.

Nightshade heaved a sigh. "I guess I could offer you something to make this worth your while. I could offer to become one of your faithful, but—to be honest—that would be a lie. I like being a nightstalker. I like helping dead souls find their way off this world if that's what they want, and I like keeping them company if they'd rather stay. I like the feeling I get when I cast one of my mystical spells and the spirit of the earth creeps into me and wells up inside my heart and spills out into my fingertips, and my hands go all tingly and I—me, a kender—can make big, huge minotaur keel over.

"So I guess I can't bargain with you, and you know what, Majere, I don't think people should have to bargain with gods. Why? Because you *are* a god and because you're great, wonderful and powerful, and because I'm just a kender, and Atta's just a dog, and Rhys is just a man, and we need you. So send me those six monks and be snappy about it."

Nightshade lowered his arms, heaved a tremulous sigh and waited expectantly.

The gulls' quarrel ended when one of them flew off with the fish. The waves continued to crash, but they'd been doing that forever. The wind had died away, so the grass was silent. So was the god.

"Maybe not six monks," Nightshade temporized. "How about two monks and a knight? Or one monk and a wizard?"

Atta whined and pawed at his leg. Nightshade reached down to pet her head, but she slid her head out from under his hand. She looked at him and her eyes narrowed. She was not urging him. She was telling him.

Enough of this nonsense. We're going back.

Her intense gaze made him go all squirmy inside.

"Now I know what it feels like to be a sheep," he muttered, trying to avoid her piercing gaze. "Let's wait just one more minute, Atta. Give the god a chance. It's those boulders, you see. I don't have any skin left on my palms— What's that?"

Nightshade caught sight of movement. He whipped around and stared down the road and saw, in the winking moonlight, two people walking his direction.

"Thank you, Majere!" Nightshade cried and he began running down the road, waving his arms and calling, "Help! Help!"

Atta dashed after him, barking madly. The kender was so excited and relieved he paid no attention to the tone of her bark. He kept running, and he kept yelling, "Boy, am I glad to see you!" and it was only when he was much closer to the two people and took a good look at them that he realized he wasn't.

Glad to see them.

They were the Beloved.

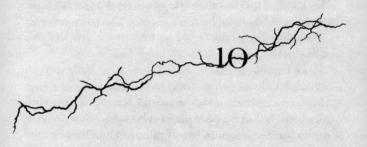

10

Mina stared out the window at the Blood Sea that was calm in the moonlit darkness. The red light of Lunitari glimmered on the rolling waves, forming a moon glade, a red path across the red water that was stained purple from the night. Mina's longing carried her out of her prison to the endless eternal sea. The waves lapped at her feet and she strode into the water . . .

Behind her, the door creaked open.

"Chemosh!" Mina said with heartfelt joy. "He has come to me!"

She was back in the room, back in the prison in an instant. Arms outstretched, she turned to welcome her lover, ready to fling herself at his feet and beg his forgiveness.

"My lord—" she cried.

The words died on her lips. Joy died in her heart.

"Krell," she said, and she made no effort to hide her loathing. "What do you want?"

The death knight clanked ponderously into the room. The helmed head, adorned with the curling rams horns, leered at her. Piggy fire-eyes flared.

"To kill you."

Krell kicked the door shut. He drew his sword from its scabbard and walked toward her.

Mina drew herself up, faced him with scorn. "My lord will not let you touch me!"

"Your lord doesn't give a rat's ass about you," Krell sneered. "Go ahead. Call out to him. See if he answers."

Mina remembered the look of hatred Chemosh had given her, remembered he had banished her from his sight, refused to even listen to her. She imagined herself calling to him for help, and she heard in her heart the echoing silence of his refusal.

She could not bear that.

Krell had threatened her before now, but his threats had been all bluster and bravado. He had not dared harm her while Chemosh protected her. This was Krell's chance. She was alone and helpless. She had no weapons. Not even prayer, for Chemosh had turned his back on her.

Mina searched the room for something, anything, she could use in her defense. Not that it would make a difference. The sharpest sword ever crafted could not so much as dent the death knight's armor.

She did not mean to die without a fight, however. Her soul would go proudly to the Hall of Souls Passing. Chemosh would not be ashamed of her.

Krell was looking about the room as well, though not for the same reason.

"Where is that strange light coming from?" he demanded. "Have you set something on fire?"

A candlestick stood on a table. The candlestick was made of twisted iron, with a clawed foot and three claw-like hands that held the candles. It was big and it was heavy. The trouble was, it was several paces from her.

"Yes," said Mina. "I summoned a fire wight."

She pointed to a part of the room opposite the candlestick.

"A fire wight!" Only Krell would have fallen for that one. His head pivoted.

Mina sprang at the table and lunged for the candlestick. She clasped her hands around the base and grabbed it up and, swinging as she turned, she struck with all her strength at Krell's helm.

The last time she had fought Krell in Storm's Keep, she had swept his head from his shoulders. That time, Chemosh had been with her.

No god sided with her this time. No god fought for her.

The iron candlestick crashed against Krell's helm, but the blow did nothing to him. He might not have even felt it. The shock of the blow and the fell touch of the death knight jarred Mina's arms from wrist to shoulder, momentarily paralyzing her. The candlestick slipped from her hands that had gone suddenly numb.

Krell turned back to her. He seized her arm, twisted it, and flung her against the wall. She gasped with the pain but did not cry out. He penned her in with his arms, so she could not escape. He shoved his helmed head close to her. She could see the emptiness within and smell the foul stench of corruption and death.

"I wish I were a living man," he said, gloating over her. "I would have some fun with you before I killed you, just like the old days. I liked seeing the fear in their eyes. They knew what I was going to do to them, and they'd squeal and beg and plead for their miserable lives, and I'd tell them if they were good little girls and let me have my fun with them I'd let them live. I lied, of course. When I was done, I'd wrap my hands around their necks—soft, slender necks, like yours—and choke the life out of them."

He began to fondle her neck with bruising force.

"I guess I'll just have to settle for choking you."

His fingers clasped around her neck and started to squeeze.

Rage—hot and molten and bitter tasting—boiled deep within Mina. Amber light blazed in her eyes. Amber light shot from her fingertips. She grasped Krell's wrists, yanked his hands from her neck, and flung him off her.

"Living man!" she cried, and her fury shook the castle walls. "You want to be a living man! I grant your wish!"

She pointed at Krell, and amber light suffused him. He screamed and began to writhe inside his armor, and suddenly the armor burst asunder and vanished.

Ausric Krell stood before her, his naked flesh quivering, his naked body shivering. His small piggy eyes were blood-shot, white-rimmed, and staring at her in horrified astonishment.

"Kneel to me!" Mina commanded.

Krell collapsed in a groveling, flabby heap at her feet.

"From now on, you serve me!" Mina told him.

Krell blubbered something unintelligible.

Mina kicked him and he cried out in pain.

"Yes, yes! I serve you!" he whimpered.

Mina walked past the cringing Krell and strode to the door. She touched it, and it burst into amber flame. She walked through the rain of cinders and into the dark hallway. She looked at a stone wall and it melted; stone stairs appeared. She walked the stairs that spiraled round and round, leading upward to the ramparts.

"Tell my lord Chemosh, when he returns"—Mina's voice rang in Krell's ears—"that I have gone to obtain his heart's desire."

Krell remained in a sodden mass on the floor. He was terrified to open his eyes for fear he might see Mina. At length, however, the stone floor began to hurt his bony knees. The cold raised goosebumps on the flesh of his naked arms and shriveled his private parts. Krell pinched his arm and gave a yelp, then he groaned and cursed.

There was no doubting it. Middle-aged, gray-haired, balding, with sallow skin and sagging gut, he had his wish.

Krell was, once more, a living man.

While Ausric Krell was having a very bad time inside Castle Beloved, Nightshade was having a worse time outside it.

He should have recognized Chemosh's undead disciples at once. If he'd been paying attention, he would have noted that the two men—those he had hoped had been set by the god to save Rhys—coming down the road weren't men at all. There was no comforting glow about them, no life light burning inside them. They were nothing but lumps in the night. Atta knew. Her bark had been a warning, not a welcome. Now she stood quivering by his side, growling, her teeth barred.

The two Beloved halted. They stared at Nightshade with their empty eyes, and he began to feel uneasy. He didn't know quite why, though he did sort of remember hearing something from Gerard about someone's husband being hacked to bits. But he'd been thinking of what was for dinner at the time and hadn't been paying attention.

The Beloved he'd met previously had all been pretty docile, so long as they weren't trying to seduce a person, and thus far no human—Beloved or not—had ever tried to seduce Nightshade (not counting that floozy in an alley in Palanthas, and she'd been extremely drunk at the time).

Still, Nightshade didn't like the way these two were looking at him. Most of the Beloved didn't bother to stare at him. Most simply ignored him, and he'd come to prefer it that way.

"Sorry, fellows," said Nightshade, giving them a wave. "My mistake. I thought you were someone else. Someone alive," he muttered beneath his breath.

He didn't know what to do. Should he saunter jauntily past them with a merry "heigh-ho," or should he turn and run? Instinct voted for turning and running. He was about to obey, when he saw one of the men draw a knife.

"What are you doing?" asked his companion. "It's a kender."

"Yes," said Nightshade, backing up. "I'm a kender."

"I don't care," the man said in a nasty voice. "I'm going to send him to Chemosh."

"He's a *kender*," his companion reiterated in disgust. "Chemosh doesn't want kender."

"He's right, you know," Nightshade assured the knife-wielder. "Like they say in the inns, 'We don't serve kender. No kender in the Abyss.' I've seen the signs. They're posted all over."

He looked around uneasily, but no help was in sight, nothing but empty road. He continued to edge backward.

"Chemosh doesn't care," the Beloved returned. "Dead's dead to him, and killing makes the pain go away."

He advanced on Nightshade, brandishing the knife. Nightshade could see dark stains on the blade.

"I murdered a woman last night," the Beloved continued in a conversational tone. "Gutted the bitch. She wouldn't swear to Chemosh, but my pain eased. Try it yourself. Help me kill this runt."

Shrugging, the other Beloved picked up a piece of driftwood to use as a club, and both of them walked toward Nightshade.

The Beloved weren't killing to gain converts to Chemosh anymore, Nightshade realized in dismay. They were just killing!

He was in the act of pointing his finger at the Beloved, ready to drop them like he'd dropped that minotaur, when he remembered suddenly his magic wouldn't work against them. His heart, which had been in his shoes, now scrambled up his innards to seize him by the throat and shake him.

Nightshade had lost precious fleeing time with his almost spell-casting. He made up for it by whipping around and running for all he was worth—and then some.

"Atta, come!" he gasped, and the dog dashed after him.

Nightshade was good at sprinting; he'd had lots of practice outrunning sheriffs, angry housewives, furious farmers, and irate merchants. His sudden burst of speed caught the Beloved off-guard, and he outdistanced them for a bit, but he was already tired from slogging through sand and cutting his hands on boulders. His sprint didn't have any staying power. His strength began to flag. The ruts in the road and the occasional large clumps of dry weeds, grass, and his pork-slick boots didn't help.

The Beloved, meanwhile, had picked up speed. Being dead, they could run all month if they wanted to, while Nightshade figured he was good for just a few more moments. He didn't dare take time to look back, but he didn't need to—he could hear harsh breathing and thudding footfalls, and he knew they were catching up.

Atta was barking furiously, half-running after Nightshade and half-turning around to threaten the Beloved.

Nightshade's breath began coming in painful, ragged gasps. His feet lurched and stumbled over the uneven ground. He was about done for.

One of the Beloved seized the kender's flapping shirttail. Nightshade gave a wrench, trying to free himself, but ended up tumbling head-long into a large patch of weeds. He was ready to fight for his life, when suddenly he was in the middle of what could only be described as an explosion of grasshoppers.

Clouds of the flying, jumping insects whirred into the air. They had been living in the weed patch, and they were furious at being thus rudely disturbed. Grasshoppers were in Nightshade's eyes, up his nose and crawling down his neck and into his pants. He rolled away from the weed patch, swatting, slapping and squirming. Atta was racing about in circles, snapping and biting at the insects. Nightshade frantically brushed several out of his eyes and then saw, to his astonishment, the hoppers had the Beloved under assault.

The two men were literally crawling with insects. Grasshoppers clung to every part of them. The grasshoppers were inside their mouths and swarming around their eyes and clogging up their nostrils. The buzzing, frantic insects crawled through their hair and festooned their arms and covered their legs, and still more grasshoppers were converging on the Beloved, flying up with angry, whirring sounds from the weeds all along the side the road.

The Beloved flailed their arms and did their own hopping as they fought to drive off the insects but, the more they fought, the more the grasshoppers seemed to take offense and attack them in a frenzy.

The grasshoppers that had been annoying Nightshade seemed to realize they were missing out on all the sport, for they buzzed off to join their fellows. Within moments, the Beloved were lost to sight, trapped inside a whirling cloudburst of insects.

"Golly!" said Nightshade in awe, and then he added, speaking to Atta, "Now's our chance! Run for it!"

He had one more little burst of energy left in him, and he put his head down, pumped his feet, and went haring off down the road.

He was running, running, running, not watching where he was going, and Atta was panting along beside him when he ran headlong into something—*blam!*

The kender bounced off and went head over heels to land on his back on the road. Shaking his head groggily, he looked up.

"Golly," said Nightshade again.

"I am sorry, friend," said the monk, and he reached down a solicitous hand to assist Nightshade to his feet. "I should have been watching where I was going."

The monk looked at Nightshade, then the monk looked down the road to where the Beloved were fleeing in the opposite direction, trying to rid themselves of the grasshoppers, which were still attacking them. The monk smiled slightly, and he regarded the kender in concern.

"Are you all right?" he asked. "Did they harm you?"

"N-no, Brother," Nightshade stammered. "It's a lucky thing those hoppers came along. . . ."

The kender had a sudden thought.

The monk was gaunt, slender, and all muscle, as Nightshade had reason to know, for crashing into the monk had been like crashing into the side of a mountain. The monk had iron-gray hair that he wore in a simple braid down the back of his neck. He was dressed in plain robes of a burnished orange color, trimmed with a rose motif around the hem and the sleeves. He had high cheekbones and a strong jaw and dark eyes that were smiling now, but which could probably be very fierce if the monk chose.

Nightshade allowed the monk to lift him to his feet. He let the monk brush the dust off his clothes and pluck an errant and stubborn hopper from his hair. He saw that Atta was hanging back, cringing, not approaching the monk, and then and only then did the kender free his voice, which had gotten stuck in his throat.

"Did Majere send you, Brother? What am I saying? Of course, he sent you, just like he sent those hoppers!" Nightshade grabbed hold of the monk's hand and tugged. "C'mon! I'll take you to Rhys!"

The monk stood immoveable. Nightshade couldn't shift him and ended up nearly yanking himself off his feet.

"I am searching for Mina," said the monk. "Do you know where I can find her?"

"Mina! Who cares about her?" Nightshade cried.

He fixed the monk with a stern look. "You've got this mixed up, Brother. You're not looking for Mina. I never asked Majere about Mina. You're looking for Rhys. Rhys Mason, follower of Majere. Mina works for Chemosh—another god entirely."

"Nevertheless," said the monk, "I am searching for Mina and I must find her quickly, before it is too late."

"Too late for what? Oh, too late for Rhys! That's why we should hurry! C'mon, Brother! Let's go!"

The monk did not move. He cast a frowning glance skyward.

"Yeah, peculiar color, isn't it?" Nightshade craned his head. "I was noticing that myself. Kind of a weird amber glow. I think it must be the Aura Booly-ris or whatever they call it."

The kender grew stern and quite serious. "Now see here, Brother Monk, I'm grateful for the grasshoppers and all, but we don't have time to stand around blathering about the strange color in the night sky! Rhys is in danger. We have to go! Now!"

The monk did not seem to hear. He gazed off into the distance, as though he was trying to find something, and then he shook his head.

"Blind!" he murmured. "I am blind! All of us . . . blind. She is here, but I can't see her. I can't find her."

Nightshade heard the agony in the monk's voice, and his

heart was wrung. He saw something else, too, something about the monk that, like the Beloved, he should have noticed before now. He looked at Atta, cringing and cowering—something the gallant dog never did.

No life light shone from the body of the monk, but unlike the Beloved, the body had an ethereal, insubstantial quality about it, almost as if the monk had been painted on night's canvas. The pieces of the puzzle started to fall together for Nightshade, falling so hard they smacked him a good one to the side of the head.

"Oh, my god!" Nightshade gasped, then, realizing what he'd said, he clapped his hand over his mouth. "I'm sorry, sir!" he mumbled through his fingers. "I didn't mean to take your name in vain. It just slipped out!"

He sank down on his knees and hung his head.

"It's all right about Rhys, Your Godship," the kender said miserably. "I know now why you have to go to Mina. Well, maybe I don't know, but I can guess." He lifted his head to see the monk regarding him strangely. "It's all so sad, isn't it? About her, I mean."

"Yes," said the monk quietly. "So very sad."

Majere knelt down beside Nightshade and rested his hand on his head. He put his other hand on Atta, who lowered her head at the god's gentle touch.

"You have my blessing, both of you, and Rhys Mason has my blessing. He has faith and he has courage, and he has the love of true friends. Go back to him. He needs your help. My duty lies elsewhere this night, but know that I am with you."

Majere stood up and looked toward the castle, its walls bathed in the eerie, lurid glow. He began to walk toward it.

Nightshade leaped to his feet. He felt refreshed, as though he'd slept for a week and eaten fourteen enormous dinners into the bargain. His body hummed with renewed strength and energy. He cast a glance down the ridgeline in the direction of the cave, and his joy slipped.

"Brother God!" Nightshade cried. "I'm sorry to bother you again, after everything you've done for us. Thank you for the hoppers, by the way, and for your blessing. I feel lots better. There's just one more thing."

He waved his hand. "These boulders are difficult to climb over and they're awfully hard, sir," he said meekly, "and sharp."

The monk smiled, and as he smiled, the boulders disappeared and the hillside was awash in lush green grass.

"Wahoo!" Nightshade cried. Waving his arms and shouting, he dashed down the hill. "Rhys, Rhys, hold on! We're coming to save you! Majere blessed us, Rhys! He blessed me, a kender!"

Atta, glad to be finally heading the right direction, skimmed over the ground, passing the whooping kender with ease and soon leaving him far behind.

*R*hys sat in the darkness of the grotto, and as death approached, he thought about life. His life. He thought about fear and about cowardice, about arrogance and pride, and, holding fast to the splinter of wood that had cut his flesh, he knelt to Majere and humbly asked his forgiveness.

Majere asks each of his monks to leave his cloistered life and journey into the world at least once in a lifetime. The undertaking of this journey is voluntary—it is not mandatory. No monk is forced to make it, just as no monk is ever forced to do anything. All vows the monks take are taken out of love and are kept because they are worth the keeping. The god wisely teaches that promises made under duress or from fear of punishment are empty of meaning.

Rhys had chosen not to leave the monastery. He would never have admitted this at the time, but he realized now the reason why. He had thought, in his pride and arrogance, that he had attained spiritual perfection. The world had nothing more to teach him. Majere had nothing more to teach him.

"I knew it all," said Rhys softly to the darkness. "I was happy and content. The path I walked was smooth and easy and went round and round in a circle. I had walked it so long I no longer saw it. I could have walked it blind. I had only to keep going and it would always be there for me.

"I told myself the path circled Majere. In truth, it circled nothing. The center was empty. Unknowing, I walked the edge of a precipice, and when disaster struck and the path shattered beneath my feet, I had nowhere to go. I fell into darkness.

"Even then, Majere tried to save me. He reached out to me, but I rebuffed him. I was afraid. My sunlit, comfortable life had been snatched away from me. I blamed the god, when I should have blamed myself. Perhaps I could not have prevented Lleu from killing my parents if I had been there, but I should have been more understanding of my parents' pain. I should have reached out to them when they came to me for help. Instead, I repulsed them. I resented them for intruding their pain and their fear into my life. I had no feelings for them. Only for myself."

Rhys raised his eyes to the heavens he could not see. "It was only when I lost my faith that I found it. How can such a miracle happen? Because you, my god, never lost faith in me. I walk the darkness unafraid, because I have within me your light—"

A chill, pale radiance illuminated the cave, like the light called corpse-candle—the lambent flame that can sometimes be seen burning above a grave and is believed by the superstitious to be an omen presaging death.

The man materialized in the grotto. He was pale and coldly handsome. He had long dark hair and was sumptuously dressed in black velvet and fine, white linen with lace at his cuffs. He regarded Rhys with eyes that had no end and no beginning.

"I am Chemosh, Lord of Death, and who," the god added, glowering, "are you?"

Rhys rose to his feet, his chains rattling around him, and bowed reverently. He might loathe Chemosh for the evil he brought into the world, yet he was a god and before this god all mankind must one day come to stand.

"I am called Rhys Mason, my lord."

"I don't give a damn what you are called!" Chemosh said perversely. "You are Mina's lover! That's who you are!"

Rhys regarded the god in amazement so profound he could not think of a reply to this astonishing accusation.

Chemosh himself seemed to be having second thoughts. The Lord of Death looked about the bleak grotto, taking in the chains and the greasy remnants of salt pork, the fetid water and the foul stench, for there had been nowhere Rhys could go to relieve himself except in the cave.

"This is not exactly what I would call a love nest," Chemosh remarked. "Nor"——he eyed Rhys with distaste——"do you strike me as a lover."

"I am a monk of Majere, my lord," said Rhys.

"I can see that," said Chemosh, his lip curling as he cast a glance at Rhys's tattered robes that had taken on an orange cast in the eerie light. "The question then becomes——if you are not Mina's lover, what are you to her? She brought you here——a spindly, flea-bitten monk." Chemosh drew closer. "Why?"

"You must ask her, my lord," Rhys said.

He spoke steadily, though that took an effort. Holding fast to the splinter of wood from his staff, Rhys silently asked Majere to give him courage. His spirit might accept the inevitability of death, but his mortal flesh shivered and his stomach clenched.

"Why should you be loyal to her?" Chemosh demanded, irate. "Why is everybody loyal to *her*? I swear by the High God who created us and Chaos who would destroy us that I do not understand!"

His fury blasted the cavern like a hot wind. Sweating, Rhys dug the splinter's sharp point into his palm, using pain to keep himself from collapsing.

"She chains you to a wall and torments you—I see the mark of her anger on your cheek. She has either left you here to starve to death or . . ."

Chemosh paused, regarded Rhys intently. "She plans to come back. To torture you. Why? You have something she wants. That is the reason. What is it, Rhys Mason? It must be of great worth. . . ."

Rhys could have given the explanation, but it went against all his convictions. A man's soul is his own, Majere taught. Its mysteries are for each to reveal or not, as he chooses. Mina had, for whatever reason, chosen to keep her secret. She had not told Chemosh. Though her soul might be black with her crimes, that soul was her own. Her secret was hers, not his, to reveal.

Rhys kept silent. Blood trickled down his palm and between his clenched fingers.

"Your flesh can defy me," Chemosh said, his breath chill as air flowing from the tomb. "But your spirit cannot. The dead cannot lie to me. When your soul stands before me in the Hall of Souls Passing, you will tell me all you know."

Then you will be in for a sad disappointment, my lord, Rhys thought ruefully. For, in truth, I know nothing.

Chemosh drew near, his hand outstretched. "I will kill you swiftly. You will not suffer, as you would have done at Mina's hands."

Rhys gave a brief nod of acknowledgement. His heart beat fast; his mouth was dry. He could no longer speak. He drew in a breath, undoubtedly his last, and braced himself. Closing his eyes, to blot out the terror of the awful god, he commended his spirit to Majere.

He felt the god's blessing flow through him, and with his blessing came an exalted serenity and a bark.

A dog's bark. Right outside the cave. And with Atta's bark came Nightshade's shrill voice.

"Rhys! We're back! Hey, I met your god! He gave me his blessing—"

Rhys's eyes opened. Serenity drained out of him.

Chemosh half-turned, looked toward the grotto's entrance. "What is this? A kender and a dog?"

"My traveling companions," Rhys said. "Let them go, my lord. They are innocents, caught up in this by accident."

Chemosh looked intrigued. "The kender claims he met your god. . . ."

"He's a kender, my lord," Rhys said desperately.

At that unfortunate moment Nightshade shouted, "Hey, Rhys, I've come to deal with that Mina-person!" His voice and his footfalls echoed through the grotto. "Atta, not so fast!"

"Deal with Mina?" Chemosh repeated. "He does not sound so innocent. It seems now I will have two souls to question. . . ."

"Nightshade!" Rhys shouted. "Don't come in here! Run! Take Atta and—"

"Silence, monk," ordered Chemosh, and he clamped his hand over Rhys's mouth.

The chill of death permeated Rhys's limbs. The terrible cold was like shards of ice in his blood stream. Cold, searing pain wracked his body. He groaned and struggled.

The Lord of Death kept fast hold on him, his cruel touch freezing the blood. Rhys sank to his knees.

Atta dashed into the chamber. She saw her master on his knees, obviously in distress and a man bending over him. Atta didn't like this man. There was something fell about him, something that frightened her. The man had no scent, for one thing. Every living thing, every dead thing has an odor, some pleasant, others not so much, but not this man, and that frightened her. The man was, in this, like that loud and obnoxious woman from the sea, and like the monk who had just laid gentle hands on her. None of them had a smell to them, and the dog found that uncanny and terrifying.

Atta was scared. Her simple heart trembled. Instinct urged her to turn tail and run, but this strange man was hurting her master, and that could not be allowed. Her heart swelled in fury, and she leaped to the attack. She did not go for the throat, for the man had his back to her, bending over Rhys. She sought instead to cripple her enemy. Wisdom handed down to her by her ancient ancestor, the wolf, told her how to bring down a larger foe—go for the leg. Break the bone or sever a tendon.

Atta sank her teeth into Chemosh's ankle.

The aspect of a god is formed of the god's essence spun into an image that appears mortal to the minds of men. The aspect is visible to the mortal eye, sensible to the mortal touch. The god's aspect can speak to mortals, hear them and react to them. Since the aspect is made of immortal essence, the aspect feels no pain or pleasurable sensations of the flesh. The god will often pretend to do so, in order to appear more lifelike to mortals. In the case of Chemosh and his love for Mina, the god can even sometimes persuade himself into believing the lie.

Chemosh could not possibly have felt Atta's sharp teeth freezing onto his leg, but he did. In truth, the teeth Chemosh felt were not those of the dog. They were the teeth of Majere's wrath. Thus it was that Huma's dragonlance, blessed by all the gods of good, struck Takhisis's aspect a blow that she felt and forced her to withdraw, spitting and snarling defiance, from the world. The gods have the power to inflict pain upon each other, though they are loath to do so, for each god knows the dire consequences that might result from such action. The gods resort to such drastic measures only when it is clear to them the balance is about to be overthrown, for Chaos lies just beyond, waiting eagerly for war to break out in the heavens. When that happens, the gods will destroy each other and give Chaos his long-sought victory—the end of all things.

A god will rarely attack another god directly but will act only through mortals. The attack is limited in scope and not likely to cause the aspect severe harm—just enough to let the other god know that he or she has transgressed, gone too far, crossed the line.

Majere's anger bit into Chemosh's ankle with Atta's teeth, and the Lord of Death roared in fury. He turned from Rhys, kicked out his leg and flung Atta off him. Lifting his foot over her body, Chemosh was going to show Majere what he thought of him by stomping this mutt to death.

Rhys still held the splinter of the staff in his bloody hand. It was his only weapon and he jabbed it with all his strength into the god's back. Majere's rage drove the splinter deep into the Lord of Death. Chemosh gasped. His kick went wild. Atta leaped to her feet and positioned her body in front of Rhys. Teeth bared, she defiantly faced the god.

At that moment, Nightshade came running into the grotto, his fists clenched.

"Rhys, I'm here—" The kender stopped, stared. "Who are you? Wait! I think I know you! You seem very familiar to me . . . Oh, gods!" Nightshade began to shake all over. "I *do* know you! You're Death!"

"I am *your* death, at least," Chemosh said coldly, and he reached out his hand to throttle the kender.

The ground gave a sudden, violent lurch that knocked Chemosh off his feet. The cavern walls shuddered and cracked. Bits of rock and dirt rained down on them and then, with a small shiver, the earth settled and was quiet.

God and mortals stared at each other. Chemosh was on his hands and knees. Atta crouched on her belly, whimpering.

The Lord of Death picked himself up off the floor. Ignoring the mortals, he stared up into the darkness.

"Which of you shakes the world?" he cried, fists clenched.

"You, Sargonnas? Zeboim? You, Majere?"

If there was an answer, the mortals could not hear it. Rhys was barely conscious, consumed by pain, hardly aware of what was going on. Nightshade had his eyes closed, and he was hoping the next time the ground shook it would open up and suck him down inside. Better that than have Death's cold gaze fall upon him again.

"We will meet in the Abyss, monk," Chemosh promised and disappeared.

"Whoo, boy," Nightshade said, shuddering. "I'm glad he's gone. He could have left us some light, though. It's dark as a goblin's innards in here. Rhys . . ."

The earth shook again.

Nightshade threw himself flat on the ground, one arm clutching Atta and the other arm covering his head.

The cracks in the grotto's walls widened. Rocks and pebbles, clods of dirt, and a few dislodged beetles rained down on top of him. Then there was a horrendous crashing and grinding sound, and Nightshade shut his eyes tight and waited for the end.

Once more, everything was still. The ground ceased its wild gyrations. Nightshade didn't trust it, however, and he kept his eyes shut. Atta started to wriggle and squirm beneath his clutching grasp. He let her go, and she scooted out from underneath him. Then he felt one of the beetles crawling in his hair, and that made him open his eyes. He grabbed hold of the beetle and threw it off.

Atta began to bark sharply. Nightshade wiped the grit out of his eyelids and looked around to find that whether his eyes were open or shut didn't make much difference. It was dark either way.

Atta kept barking.

Nightshade was afraid to stand up for fear he might bash into something, so he crawled on his hands, feeling his way, following the sounds of Atta's frantic yelps.

"Atta?" He reached out his hand and felt her furry body. She was pawing at something and continuing to bark.

Nightshade groped about with his hands and felt lots of sharp rocks and then something warm and soft.

"Rhys!" Nightshade breathed thankfully.

He felt about and found his friend's nose and eyes—the eyes were closed. Rhys's forehead was warm. He was breathing, but he must be unconscious. Nightshade's hand touched Rhys's head, and felt something warm and sticky running down the back of Rhys's neck.

Atta ceased pawing at Rhys and began to lick his cheek.

"I don't think dog slobber's going to do him much good, Atta," said Nightshade, pushing her away. "We have to get him out of here."

He could still smell salt-tinged air, and he hoped this meant the grotto's entrance had not collapsed. Nightshade gripped Rhys by the shoulders, gave him an experimental tug, and was heartened to feel his friend's body slide across the floor. He had been worried that Rhys might have been half-buried in rubble.

Nightshade pulled again, and Rhys came along with him, and the kender was just starting to think they might make it out of here alive when he heard a sound that nearly buried him in despair.

The clank of chains.

Nightshade groaned. He'd forgotten all about the fact that Rhys was chained to the wall.

"Maybe the rock slide dislodged the iron rings," Nightshade said hopefully.

Finding the manacle around Rhys's wrist, Nightshade groped his way along the length of chain back to where it was attached to the iron ring, which was still attached—quite firmly—to the wall.

Nightshade said a bad word and then he remembered. He was blessed by a god!

"Maybe he's given me the strength of ten dragons!" Nightshade said excitedly, and gripped the chain and winced at the pain of his cut hands. Feeling that one with dragon-strength shouldn't be put off by jabbing pain, he dug in his heels and shooed Atta out of the way, then pulled on the chain with all his might.

The chain slid through Nightshade's hands, and the kender sat down on his bottom.

He repeated the bad word. Standing up, he tried again and this time he kept hold of the chain.

The iron ring didn't budge.

Nightshade gave up. Following the chain, he made his way back to where Rhys lay on the ground, and kneeling beside his friend, he smoothed back the blood-gummed hair from the still face. Atta lay down beside him and began, again, to assiduously lick Rhys's cheek.

"We're not leaving, Rhys," Nightshade told him. "Are we, Atta? You see—she says no, we're not. Not this time." He tried to strike a cheerful note. "Maybe the next time the ground shakes, the wall will split right open and knock those iron rings loose!"

Of course, Nightshade said to himself, if the wall does split open the ceiling will crash down on top of us and bury us alive, but I won't mention that.

"I'm here, Rhys." Nightshade took hold of his friend's limp hand and held it tight. "And so's Atta."

The ground began to shake.

_B_eneath the red-tinged water of the Blood Sea, inside the Tower of High Sorcery, Basalt and Caele were hard at work scrubbing and polishing, making ready for an influx of wizards—the twenty or so chosen Black Robes who were going to be leaving their homes on land to join Nuitari.

The Tower of the Blood Sea was now open and ready for business.

Following the meeting between the cousins, Nuitari realized there was no longer any need to keep his Tower secret. He gave the news to Dalamar, Head of the Black Robes, and told the elven archmage to issue an invitation to any Black Robes who wanted to come study in the new Tower.

The invitation included Dalamar, who had respectfully declined, saying it was necessary for the Black Robes to maintain their representation in Wayreth. Privately Dalamar thought that he would just as soon be shut up in a tomb as buried beneath the sea, away from the wind and the trees, blue skies and bright sunlight. He said as much to Jenna.

As Head of the Conclave, she was not at all happy about the

decision made by the gods. She was opposed to separating the Robes again. The same had been done in the days before the King-priest, each Robe claiming its own Tower, with tragic results. Jenna made her opposition known to Lunitari, but the goddess of the Red Moon was so inordinately pleased with having the magnificent Tower of Wayreth all to herself that she would not listen. As for Solinari, his chosen, Coryn the White, was already putting together an expedition of White Robes to go forth to recover the accursed Tower that had formerly been in Palanthas and was now inside the heart of the dark land of the undead, Nightlund.

As for Dalamar, his reservations had nothing to do with the Tower itself, just its location. He considered that a Tower for the Black Robes was long overdue. Only Jenna had serious reservations, and she could not really take time to pursue them as she might have done. The Conclave was in the throes of a bitter argument over how to handle the situation with the Beloved—now that the horrible means of destroying them had become known. The Black Robes were all for recruiting armies of children and sending them forth to do battle. Rumor had it some had done just that.

As the news and the fear spread, any person who had the misfortune to be different from his neighbors or had fallen out with the townspeople, or who was simply in the wrong place at the wrong time might be accused of being a Beloved and either arrested or attacked by mobs. Since wizards tended to be mysterious folk who kept to themselves and were generally feared, they became easy targets. Jenna was now hard at work trying to find a magical spell to put a stop to the Beloved, thus far to no avail. A Tower beneath the sea was the least of her worries, so she dropped the argument.

Nuitari had won and he had Chemosh to thank, which the God of the Dark Moon thought extremely ironic.

Inside the Tower, Basalt was making up beds, while Caele mostly stood around watching Basalt. A large pile of mattresses had been hauled up from the storage room. The apprentice mages had to carry each mattress into each room, wrestle it onto the wooden bed frame, then cover it with linens and a blanket.

The two were working in the chambers where the high-ranking Black Robes would reside—each in his or her own private quarters. The mattresses for these beds were made of goose down, the sheets were fine linen, the blankets softest wool. Rooms for lower ranking wizards were smaller and had mattresses of straw. Apprentice wizards shared rooms and in some cases shared mattresses. Thus far, only high-ranking wizards had been invited by the god. They were due to arrive tomorrow morning.

"You're going to have to help me shift this," Basalt said. He indicated a mattress on the top of the pile that was out of the reach of the dwarf's short arms. "I can't reach it."

Caele heaved the long-suffering sigh of the overworked and took hold of the ends of the mattress. He gave a half-hearted attempt, then he moaned and clutched his back.

"All this bending and lifting. I've torn a muscle."

Basalt glowered at him. "How did you tear a muscle? The heaviest thing you've lifted thus far is a glass of the Master's best wine, and don't think I won't tell him!"

"I was tasting it to see if it had gone bad," said Caele sullenly. "You wouldn't want to serve the archmagi bad wine, now, would you?"

"Just help me lift the damn mattress," growled Basalt.

Caele raised his hands, and before Basalt could stop him, the elf waved his hands and muttered a few words. The mattress floated up off the pile and hung suspended in the air.

"What are you doing? You're not supposed to be using magic for housekeeping chores!" Basalt cried, scandalized. "What if the Master should see you? End that spell!"

"Very well," said Caele, and he withdrew the magic, with the result that the mattress crashed down on top of the dwarf, flattening him.

Caele sniggered. Basalt gave a muffled howl. The dwarf emerged from beneath the mattress with murder in his eye.

"You told me to end the spell." Caele's lip curled. "I was merely obeying orders. You are the Caretaker, after all—"

Caele stopped talking. His eyes widened. "What is that?"

Basalt's eyes were white-rimmed. He shivered at the terrible sound. "I don't know! I've never heard anything like it."

The low rumbling noise, like enormous boulders all being tumbled about, grinding together, came from far, far below their feet. The noise grew louder and louder, coming nearer and nearer. The stack of mattresses began to jiggle. The floor started to shake. Desks and bed frames began to skitter and dance across the floor. The walls quivered.

The shaking entered Basalt's feet and went from there into his bones. His teeth clicked together, and he bit his tongue. Caele staggered into the pile of mattresses and stood braced against them.

The shaking ceased.

Basalt gave a gasping croak and pointed.

The floor, which had been perfectly level, was now pitched at a steep angle. A bed frame came sliding slowly down the hall with a desk right behind it. Caele pushed himself off the mattresses.

"Zeboim!" he snarled. "The sea bitch is back!"

Basalt staggered across the canting floor, walking uphill, and entered one of the rooms. All the furniture was piled up in a heap against the far wall. Basalt ignored the destruction and headed for the crystal window, which provided a spectacular view of the Tower's underwater kingdom. Caele followed close at the dwarf's heels.

Both of them stared out into the water that was thick with red silt churned up from the floor. The silt swirled about the Tower like tides of blood.

"I can't see a thing in this murk," Caele complained.

"Nor can I," said Basalt, frustrated.

The Tower started to shake again. This time the floor canted in the other direction.

Caele and Basalt were run down by a cascade of furniture sliding across the floor. Both ended up slammed against the wall, Basalt trapped by a desk and Caele pinned by a bed frame.

The shaking ceased. Basalt had the strangest feeling that whatever was causing this upheaval was resting, catching its breath.

He shoved aside the bed frame, and ignoring Caele's pleas for help, ran back to the window and looked out.

His nose pressed against the crystal, Basalt could see, amidst the swirling muck and bits of seaweed and frantically darting fish, a coral reef that snaked up from the ocean floor. Basalt had often enjoyed looking at this reef, for it reminded him of the formations of the underground world in which he'd lived for so long and which, on occasion, he still missed.

From this vantage point, he should be gazing directly across at the reef.

Now, instead, he stared down at the reef. It was several hundred feet beneath him. He looked up and saw moonlight and stars. . . .

"Master," Basalt breathed, and then he howled, "Master! Nuitari! Save us!"

The Tower began to shake again.

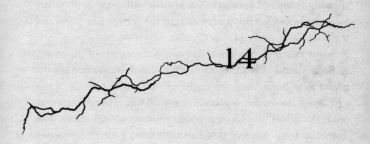

14

Mina stood alone on the battlements of the castle of the Lord of Death. An eerie amber glow lit the sky, the water and the land. She was darkness within its center and none could see her, though they were searching. Gods, mortals, all were searching for the reason the earth trembled.

Mina gazed out upon the water. Her love, her longing, her desire flowed from her and became the water. She willed it to be, and the Blood Sea began to boil and bubble. She willed it to be, and the motion of the water grew erratic. Waves crossed and criss-crossed and were flung back on each other.

Mina thrust her hands into the blood-red water and seized hold of the prize, the object of her lord's desire, the gift that would make him fall in love with her. She shook it loose, then wrenched it from its moorings. Her exertions exhausted her, and she had to stop to rest and recover, then she began again.

The water of the Blood Sea started to slowly swirl around a central point. The Maelstrom—created by the gods to serve forever as warning to mankind in the Fourth Age—returned, moving sluggishly at first, then swirling faster and faster around the vortex that was Mina. Waves crashed against the cliffs, spewing foam and seawater. She felt the salt spray cool on her face. She licked her lips and tasted the salt, bitter, like tears, and the water, sweet, like blood.

Mina raised up her hand, and out of the center of the vortex came an island of black volcanic rock. Seawater poured off the island as it burst from the midst of the maelstrom, the water cascading down shining black crags. Mina placed her prize upon the island, and like a precious jewel on a black salver. The Tower of High Sorcery that had once been beneath the waves now rose above them.

The Tower, with its faceted, crystal walls, caught and held the amber light of Mina's eyes, as the amber of her eyes caught and held the Tower.

The maelstrom ceased to swirl. The sea calmed. Water ran down the black rocks of the newly born island and poured in sheets down the smooth crystal walls of the Tower.

Mina smiled. Then she collapsed.

The amber glow vanished. Only the light of the two moons, silver and red, gleamed in the walls of the Tower, and these godly eyes no longer winked.

They were wide with shock.

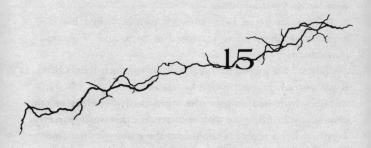

15

Nightshade woke to cold water in his face and a thumping pain in his head. This led him to erroneously conclude that he was a young kender again, back in his bed, being roused by his parents, who had discovered that only a combination of water and a good smack to the cheek would wake the son who spent his nights roaming graveyards.

"It's still dark, Mother!" Nightshade mumbled irritably and rolled over.

His mother barked.

Nightshade found this strange behavior in a mother, even a kender mother, but his head hurt too much for him to think about it. He just wanted to go back to sleep, so he closed his eyes and tried to ignore the cold water seeping into his britches.

His mother nipped him quite painfully on the ear.

"Now, really, Ma!" Nightshade exclaimed, indignant, and he sat up and opened his eyes.

"Mother?" He couldn't see a thing, but he could tell by the feel that he wasn't in bed. He was sitting on a lot of extremely sharp rocks that were poking him in tender places: the rocks were wet and getting wetter.

A bark answered him, a rough tongue licked his face, a paw with sharp nails scratched at him, and Nightshade remembered.

"Rhys!" He gasped and reached out to touch Rhys's hand. Rhys was only lukewarm, and he was also wet.

Nightshade had no idea why a previously bone-dry grotto should now be filling up with seawater, but that was apparently what was happening. He could hear the water gurgling among the rubble that littered the cavern floor. It wasn't very deep yet; thus far it was only a trickle. The water might stick to trickling, but again, it might not. It might decide to start flooding. If the grotto flooded, there was nowhere for them to go. The water would keep getting deeper and deeper. . . .

"Rhys," said Nightshade firmly, and this time he meant it. "We have to get out of here."

He slammed his hand down on the rocks to emphasize his determination and said, "Ouch!" following that up with a "Damn!"

He had slammed his hand down on a splinter of wood that had buried itself in the soft, fleshy part of his palm. He plucked it out and was about to toss it away, when it occurred to him that finding a splinter of wood here in a grotto was an odd thing. Being a kender, Nightshade was naturally curious—even in such a dire situation—and he ran his hand over the splinter, and noticed it was long and smooth and had a sharp point at both ends.

"Ah, I know. It's part of Rhys's staff," said Nightshade sadly, clasping his hand over it. "I'll save it for him. A memento. He'll like that."

Nightshade heaved a sigh and rested his aching head in his arms, wondering how they were ever going to get out of this horrible place. He felt sick and drowsy and once more he was a little kender, only this time his father was trying to show him how to pick a lock.

"You do it by feel and by sound," his father was explaining to him. "You put the lock pick in here, and you wiggle it around until you feel it catch—"

Nightshade jerked his head up so fast that blazing pain burst on the backs of his eyeballs. He didn't notice. Much. He looked down at the splinter in his hand, except he couldn't see it, what with the grotto being so very dark, but he didn't need to be able to see. It was all done by feel and sound.

The only problem was that Nightshade had never successfully picked a lock in his life. In many ways, he had been, as father often lamented, a failure as a kender.

"Not this time," Nightshade vowed, determined. "This time I'll succeed. I have to," he added silently. "I just have to!"

He groped about with his hands until he found one of the manacles clamped around Rhys's bony wrists. The water level was continuing to rise, but Nightshade put that out of his mind.

Atta whimpered softly and licked Rhys's face and flopped down on her belly alongside him. The fact that she splashed was somewhat disconcerting. Nightshade didn't let himself think about that. He had other things to think about, the first being to convince his hand to stop shaking. This took a few moments, then, holding his breath and thrusting out his tongue, which is essential to successful lock picking, he inserted the splinter of wood into the lock on the manacle.

"Please don't break!" he told the splinter, then he remembered the staff had been blessed by the god, so perhaps the splinter was also blessed.

And so, Nightshade remembered suddenly, am I!

"I don't suppose," Nightshade muttered, speaking to the god, "that you ever helped anyone pick a lock before, or that you ever wanted to help anyone pick a lock before, but please, Majere, please help me do this!"

Sweat dripped down Nightshade's nose. He wiggled the splinter around in the lock, trying to find the whatever it was that he was supposed to find that would click and make the lock open. All he knew was that he would feel it, he would trip it, and if he was successful, he would hear it go "snick."

He concentrated, shutting out everything, and suddenly a sweet feeling stole over him—a feeling of joy, a feeling that everything in this world belonged to him, and that if there were no locks, no closed doors, no secrets, this world would be a much better place. He felt the joy of the open road, of never sleeping in the same place twice, of finding a jail that was warm and dry and a jailer as nice as Gerard. He felt the joy of stumbling across interesting things that glittered, smelled good, or were soft or shiny. He felt the joy of full pouches.

The splinter touched what it was supposed to touch, and something went "snick," and that was the most wonderful sound in the universe.

The manacle fell open in Nightshade's hand.

"Father!" he cried excitedly. "Father, did you see that?"

He didn't have time to wait for an answer, which might be long in coming, for his father had long ago gone off to pick locks in some other existence. Crawling over the debris and through the water, keeping fast hold of the splinter, Nightshade found the manacle that was clamped around Rhys's other wrist and he thrust the splinter into the lock and it went "snick" too.

Nightshade took a moment to lift up Rhys's head out of the water. He propped Rhys up on a rock and then fished about until he found Rhys's feet. Nightshade had to dig them out from beneath a pile of rubble, but Atta helped him, and after more expert lock picking, he heard two more immensely satisfying "snicks", and Rhys was free.

An extremely good thing, for by now the water level in the grotto had risen so high that, even with his head propped up, Rhys was in danger of drowning.

Nightshade squatted down beside his friend. "Rhys, if you could wake up now, it would be really helpful, because my head hurts, my legs are all wobbly, and there are a lot of rocks in the way, not to mention the water. I don't think I can carry you out of here, so if you could get up and walk . . ."

Nightshade waited hopefully, but Rhys did not move.

The kender gave another deep sigh then, slipping the precious splinter into a pocket, he reached down and took hold of Rhys's shoulders, intending to drag him across the grotto floor.

He made it about six inches, then his arms gave out and so did his legs. He sat down with a plop in the water and wiped away sweat.

Atta growled.

"I can't do it, Atta," Nightshade mumbled. "I'm sorry. I tried. I really did try—"

Atta wasn't growling at him. Nightshade heard the sounds of feet—a great many feet—sloshing through water. Then there was bright light that hurt his eyes, and six monks of Majere, clad in orange robes and carrying flaming torches, hurried past the kender.

Two of the monks held the torches. Four monks bent down, picked up Rhys gently by his arms and legs, and carried Rhys swiftly out of the grotto. Atta dashed after them.

Nightshade sat alone in the darkness, staring about in dazed wonder.

Torchlight returned. A monk stood over him, looked down on him. "Are you hurt, friend?"

"No," said Nightshade. "Yes. Maybe a little."

The monk placed a cool hand on Nightshade's forehead. The pain disappeared. Strength flowed into his limbs.

"Thank you, Brother," said Nightshade, allowing the monk to help him to his feet. He still felt a little wobbly. "I guess Majere sent you, huh?"

The monk did not reply, but he continued to smile, so Nightshade, knowing Rhys didn't talk much either and assuming maybe this was normal with monks, took the monk's silence for a yes.

As Nightshade and the monk walked toward the entrance, the kender was in deep thought, and just before they left the grotto, Nightshade grabbed hold of the monk's sleeve and gave it a tug.

"I spoke to Majere in what you might call a sharp tone," Nightshade said remorsefully. "I was pretty blunt, and I might have hurt his feelings. Would you tell him I'm sorry?"

"Majere knows that you spoke out of love for your friend," said the monk. "He is not angry. He honors you for your loyalty."

"Does he?" Nightshade flushed with pleasure. Then he felt overcome with guilt. "He helped me pick the lock. He blessed me. I suppose I ought to worship him, but I can't. It just doesn't feel right."

"*What* we believe is not important," said the monk gently. "*That* we believe is."

The monk bowed to Nightshade, who was considerably flustered by this show of respect. He made an awkward bow in turn, bending at the waist, which caused several valuable objects he hadn't remembered he had to tumble out of his shirt pocket. He dropped down to fish about for them in the water, and it was only after he had either retrieved them or admitted they were gone for good, that he realized the monk and the torch had departed.

By this time, though, Nightshade didn't need the light. He was enveloped in the strange amber glow he'd noticed earlier.

He walked out of the grotto, thinking he'd never in his life been so glad to leave anywhere and vowing he would never set foot in another cave so long as he lived. He looked around, hoping to talk to the monk again, for he didn't quite understand that stuff about believing.

There were no monks.

But there was Rhys, sitting on a hillock, trying to calm Atta, who was licking his face and his hands and climbing on top of him, nearly bowling him over with her frantic attentions.

Nightshade gave a glad cry and ran up the hill.

Rhys embraced him and held him fast.

"Thank you, my friend," he said, and his voice was choked.

Nightshade felt a snuffle coming on himself, and he might have let it get the better of him, but at that moment Atta jumped on him and knocked him down, and the snuffle was washed away in dog slobber.

When Nightshade could at last shove the excited dog off him, he saw Rhys stand, staring out to sea, an expression of wonder on his face.

Solinari's silver light shone coldly on an island in the middle of the sea. Lunatari's red light illuminated a tower, black against the stars, pointing, like a dark accusation, toward the heavens.

"Was that there before?" asked Nightshade, scratching his head and pulling off another beetle.

"No," said Rhys.

"Whoa, boy!" exclaimed Nightshade, awed. "I wonder who put it there?"

And, though he didn't know it, he was echoing the gods.

16

The first thing Chemosh saw on entering his palace was Ausric Krell, alive and well and naked as the day he'd come (ass-first) into this world. The formidable death knight sat huddled in a corner of the grand hall, bemoaning his fate and shivering.

On hearing the entrance of the Lord of Death, Krell jumped to his feet and cried in fury, "Look what she did to me, Lord!" His voice rose to a screech. "Look!"

Chemosh looked and wished he hadn't. The sight of the flabby, paunchy, fish-belly pale, hairy middle-aged man's naked body was enough to turn even a god's stomach. He glared at Krell in disgust mingled with anger.

"So Zeboim caught up with you," Chemosh said coldly. "Where is she?"

"Zeboim! It was not Zeboim!" Krell clawed the air with his hands in his rage, as though he were clawing someone's flesh. "Mina did this! Mina!"

"Don't lie to me, slug," said Chemosh, but even as he refuted Krell's claim, the Lord of Death felt a terrible doubt darken his mind. "Where is Mina? Still locked up?"

Krell began to laugh. His face twisted with loathing and fear. "Locked up!" he repeated, mirth gurgling in his throat as though this were the funniest thing in the world.

"The wretch has gone mad," Chemosh muttered, and he left the raving Krell to search for Mina.

The night was lit with an amber glow that blazed through the windows and shone through cracks in the wall and chinks in the masonry. Chemosh found it difficult to see for the blaring light, and as he shielded his immortal eyes against it, his doubt grew.

He was heading for Mina's chambers when the castle shook and walls trembled. A thundering, grinding roar such as he had heard only once before caused him to stand still with astonishment. The last time he'd heard that roar, the world was being born. Mountains were being lifted up, chasms carved through them, and the seas were white with the foam and the glory of creation.

Chemosh tried to see what was happening, but the light was too bright. He ran up the stairs to the battlements and stopped dead in his tracks.

On a new-formed island of black rock stood the Tower of the Blood Sea. The Tower shone with an amber glow, and there was Mina, standing before him with her arms outstretched, and it seemed to his dazzled vision that she held the tower in her hands. Then she sank down onto the stone and lay there unmoving.

Chemosh could only stare.

Zeboim rose from the sea, walked through the ethers and came to stand over Mina.

The three cousins left their celestial homes and came down to look on Mina.

The man-bull, Sargonnas, stepped over the castle wall and planted himself in the courtyard and glared at Chemosh. Kiri-Jolith, armed and accoutered for battle, also appeared; the White Lady, Mishakal, beautiful and strong, by his side.

Habakkuk came, and Branchala with his harp, and the wind touched the strings and made a mournful sound.

Morgion stood in the shadows, regarding them all with loathing yet here regardless, among them. Chislev, Shinare, Sirrion stood together, bound by wonder. Reorx stroked his beard. He opened his mouth to say something, then feeling the weight of the silence, the god of the dwarves snapped his mouth shut again and looked uncomfortable. Hiddukel was grim and nervous, certain this would be bad for business. Zivilyn and Gilean arrived last, the two of them deep in talk that hushed when they saw the other gods.

"One of us is missing," said Gilean, and his tone was dire. "Where is Majere?"

"I am here." Majere walked among them slowly, his gaze going to none of them. He looked only at Mina and there was, on his face, inexpressible sorrow.

"Zivilyn tells me you know something about this."

Majere continued to gaze down at Mina. "I do, God of the Book."

"How long have you known?"

"Many, many eons, God of the Book."

"Why keep this a secret?" Gilean asked.

"It was not mine to reveal," Majere replied. "I gave my solemn oath."

"To whom?" Gilean demanded.

"To one who is no longer among us."

The gods were silent.

"I assume you mean Paladine," Gilean stated. "But there is another who is no longer with us. Does this have something to do with her?"

"Takhisis?" Majere spoke sharply. His voice hardened. "She was responsible for this."

Chemosh spoke. "Her last words, before the High God came

to take her, were these: 'You are making a mistake! What I have done cannot be undone. The curse is among you. Destroy me and you destroy yourselves.' "

"Why didn't you tell us this?" Sargonas roared.

"She was always making threats." Chemosh shrugged. "Why was this any different?"

The other gods had no answer. They stood silent, waiting.

"The fault is mine," Majere said at last. "I acted for the best, or so I believed."

Mina lay cold and still. Chemosh wanted to go to her, but he could not, not with all of them watching him. He said to Majere, "Is she dead?"

"She is not dead, because she cannot die." Majere looked at each of them, each and every one. "You have been blind, but now you see the truth."

"We see, but we do not understand."

"You do," said Majere. He folded his hands and gazed out into the firmaments. "You don't want to."

He did not see the stars. He saw the stars' first light.

"It began at the beginning of time." he said, "And it began in joy." He sighed deeply. "Now, because I did not speak, it could end in bitter sorrow."

"Explain yourself, Majere!" growled Sargonnas. "We have no time for your blathering!"

Majere shifted his gaze from the time's beginning to the present. He looked at his fellows.

"You need no explanation. You can see for yourselves. She is a god. A god who does not know she is a god. She is a god who was deceived by Takhisis into thinking she is human."

"A god of Darkness!" said Sargonas, exultant.

Majere paused. When he spoke, his voice was soft with sorrow. "She was tricked by Takhisis into serving Darkness. She is—or was—a god of Light."

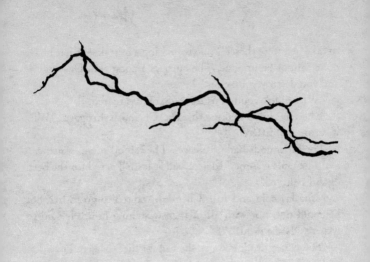

Appendix

The Beloved of Chemosh

of

by Jamie Chambers

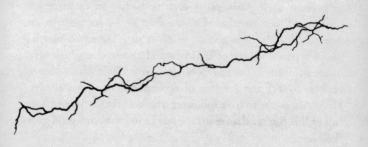

$\mathcal{D}$eath stands as the greatest fear of the mortal races upon Krynn. Maiden and crone, warrior and wizard, sinner and cleric: only the few who have found true peace can look to their soul's passing and not shudder at the passing of death's icy fingertips over warm, living flesh. Chemosh is the god of death and is known by all, either directly by name or simply as a terrifying abstract concept.

Fear of death has won Chemosh many souls and worshippers down through the ages of the world. His clerics wielded dark magic, causing long-dead corpses to tear themselves out from the earth. Wizards loyal for a lifetime to the Conclave and the teachings of Nuitari also came to Chemosh, learning the secrets of lichdom and becoming powerful agents of death. Graverobbers, fearful of offending the Lord of Bones, left offerings for his priests.

The theft of the world by the fallen and slain goddess, Takhisis, forever changed the realms of the gods and their relationship with the mortal world. Some gods struggled over the power vacuum left by their former brethren, becoming determined to occupy the thrones of power. Others were forced to evaluate their goals, plans, and methods—set in place for eons—and look to what place there might be for gods in an Age of Mortals. The god of death is determined to fill the void left by the Queen of Darkness and also to change the very image of death in the minds of the living. Chemosh no longer chooses to seek the devotion of necromancers and embalmers. He would prefer to have followers who are vibrant, young, and full of life. Rather than enjoy the fear of mortals, he would gain their love.

The love of the god of death has spread across Ansalon like a plague.

SEDUCTION

When one of the Beloved of Chemosh enters a community, he is often remembered for a lust for life, not a connection with death. Usually attractive and always confident and charming, the Beloved are the life of the party. They crave flavorful food and strong drink, seek games and rousing conversation. People who stagger home from an evening spent with Chemosh's chosen, their stomachs full and heads buzzing, might more easily imagine they have spent time with a fun-loving gully dwarf than a chosen servant of the Lord of Bones.

Those who go home from such an evening are the lucky ones, however. A Beloved will inevitably choose one special companion for more special attention. Though it could be a man or woman of any age or profession, it is often someone young and attractive, one eager for a liaison with the Beloved.

The encounter goes much as the victim first intends. The Beloved are passionate in intimate company. When desire has built and the victim is most likely to agree to anything, the Beloved makes a request.

The victim must swear his or her soul to Chemosh.

Many times this request is made lightly, as if such an oath carries no consequences. Other times, the requests are solemn and earnest, with claims that Chemosh is not truly the god of death but is actually one of life unending. If a Beloved does not gain his way immediately, it will beg, plead, and even threaten in order to secure the oath of the victim.

Once the words "I pledge myself to Chemosh" are uttered, the Beloved plants a kiss on the victim directly above the heart.

Death then claims the victim, both in the literal and spiritual sense. At first the victim feels panic and pain as his life begins to seep away, but stillness settles upon the body as the spirit is ripped from still-warm flesh. When the victim's eyes open once more, a new Beloved of Chemosh rises, ready to bring new souls to the Lord of Death.

REVELATION

At first the new Beloved believes all of the promises of eternal life and youth have come true. It seems a beautiful, impossible dream, and it is just that—an impossible dream—for instead of eternal life, a Beloved finds unending death.

The lusts and desires that led a Beloved down a path of damnation and servitude continue to plague it in unlife. But wine and spirits neither satisfy thirst nor lead to pleasant, mind-numbing intoxication; no amount of food can cure the Beloved's endless hunger. Though consumed with desire, it can never feel satiated.

The Beloved's memories, both of its former life and its activities after death, eventually fade away like a dream upon waking. Friends, family, and former lovers are all forgotten. Only its endless cravings and the commandments of Chemosh remain.

Eventually, however, the Beloved of Chemosh discover a terrible pain in their existence. Even as other senses dull, they begin to experience a throbbing pressure. Only killing eases the pain. Poisons, swords, suffocation—it makes no difference. All souls go before Chemosh, and the Beloved's suffering is eased for a time.

The only subject known to distract a Beloved from its purpose is the mention of a name: Mina. All other interests and activities cease at the sound of her name. All hope to find her. Though most have never met Mina, all know her name and see her in their minds whenever they close their eyes. Her voice echoes in their ears, bringing with it the commandments of the Lord of Death.

DETECTION

Even those aware of the threat posed by Chemosh's new disciples have trouble seeking them out. Simple spells fail to reveal the wolves among the sheep. Glance among revelers at a village fair, and the Beloved might well be anyone among them. Some keep up the façade of their former lives, so Beloved can even be the acquaintances or loved ones of those who hunt the undead.

Some who look deep into the eyes of a Beloved claim to be able to see the emptiness within, but this is neither certain nor consistent enough in practice to be relied on. Some animals shy away or may even attack at the presence of the undead, but only those who are sensitive or exceptional seem to sense that something is truly wrong.

Physically, the Beloved appear exactly as in life. Though dead, the flesh is still warm to the touch. They breathe, eat, drink, smile, laugh, and weep. The only reliable sign of a Beloved is a mark that can always be found above the heart, a discoloration in the shape of a woman's lips—"Mina's Kiss," they tell those who ask of it, and speak the name with reverence and longing.

Divine magic is the only reliable method of revealing the Beloved, and even this is the province of those whose magic deals with souls or the spirits of the dead. Clerics and mystics who are able to detect the aura of the living, along with the unusual kender who call themselves "nightstalkers," can see that the Beloved possess no soul, no living aura; that they are nothing more than very lively corpses.

DESTRUCTION

After early failed attempts to stop the threat of the Beloved, some feared they could not be destroyed. Indeed, the Beloved give every indication of true immortality. Both arcane and divine spells have little effect on the Beloved of Chemosh and usually rebound on the spellcaster, while rarely making the Beloved so much as flinch. Suffocation, fire, ice, lightning, and holy water might slow the Beloved, but they do little else. Dismemberment merely inconveniences the Beloved, since the undead being is quickly able to pull itself together again.

Though a Beloved is stronger in undeath than in life, it does not gain any special powers beyond its unaging invulnerability. Thus most Beloved have to resort to mundane methods to bring their quota of souls to Chemosh, since very few possessors of true power and ability will swear themselves over to the god of death.

Lately word has spread that the Beloved do indeed have a weakness—one so terrible that few are willing to pay the awful price to end the threat of Chemosh's chosen disciples. The laws of balance and magic on Krynn, set down by the Highgod during the Age of Starbirth, does not allow Chemosh to create immortal servants, so the spell that gives life to the dead can be unraveled . . . by the hand of a child.

If a child strikes a Beloved in anger, its true nature as an ambulatory corpse is revealed, and it will be consumed in an unnatural fire that will not harm anyone but the failed servant of the dark god. Innocence destroys the Beloved, though innocence is in turn destroyed. Children who witness such a terrible sight will very likely be traumatized for life unless the healing powers of other gods can intervene.

FUTURE

The Beloved spread from one town to the next, taking the young and the beautiful, those eager to please or easily swayed by false promises. No one knows how many Beloved are in existence, but it is likely every city has several inside its walls. Though the secrets of their detection and destruction have been revealed, it may be too late to prevent them from fulfilling whatever terrible purpose the god of death has in store.

Beloved of Chemosh

Having given their souls to the Lord of Bones, the Beloved present a convincing mockery of life. Their purpose is to bring more souls to their dark god.

The Beloved appear to most exactly as they did in life and retain much of their original personalities—though people who know them well might notice odd behavior. The Beloved breathe, eat, drink, and otherwise give all indications they are still alive. Someone who gets close and looks deep within a Beloved's eyes might see the truth. Its eyes are flat and empty—devoid of either life or hope. Those with the talent to see living auras or with the power to see and communicate with incorporeal spirits (such as kender nightstalkers) immediately notice something is wrong with the Beloved, for they all lack a living soul.

Beloved speak any languages they knew in life.

Sample Beloved of Chemosh: Cam, Former Vallenwood Guard

Once a Vallenwood Guard, those warriors who protect the stairs leading to the raised walkways in the tree-town of Solace, Cam was seduced into the ranks of the Beloved with promises of pleasure and eternal youth. Still attractive and charming, the Beloved is now consumed with bringing more victims to Chemosh and the woman he has never met, yet he knows her amber eyes and will recognize her commanding voice: Mina.

Cam: Male human fighter 2; CR 5; Medium undead (augmented humanoid); HD 2d12; hp 16; Init +5; Spd 30 ft.; AC 15 (touch 11, flat-footed 14); Atk +6 (1d6+4 short sword) or +6 (1d3+4 unarmed strike); SA Mina's kiss; SQ Beloved of Chemosh weaknesses, fast healing 5, immunity to magic, turn immunity, undead traits; AL NE; SV Fort +3, Ref +1, Will +2; Str 19, Dex 12 Con –, Int 12, Wis 14, Cha 17.

Skills and Feats: Climb +6, Diplomacy +6*, Intimidate +7, Jump +5, Swim +4; Charming, Improved Initiative, Improved Unarmed Strike.

Possessions: Chain shirt, short sword.

Creating a Beloved of Chemosh

"Beloved of Chemosh" is an acquired template that can be added to any humanoid creature (referred to hereafter as the base creature).

A Beloved of Chemosh uses all the base creature's statistics and special abilities except as noted here.

Size and Type: The creature's type changes to undead. (augmented humanoid). Do not recalculate base attack bonus, saves, or skill points. Size is unchanged.

Hit Dice: Increase all current and future Hit Dice to d12s.

Speed: Same as the base creature. If the base creature has a swim or fly speed, the Beloved of Chemosh retains the ability to swim or fly.

Special Attacks: A Beloved of Chemosh retains all the special attacks of the base creature and gains those described below.

Mina's Kiss (Su): A Beloved of Chemosh has the ability to create more of its kind but may do so only with those willing to swear their souls to Chemosh and allow the Beloved to place a kiss on their bare skin directly above the heart. Mina's Kiss requires a full-round action that provokes an attack of opportunity. No saving throw is allowed. Victims appear dead for one minute then rise, acquiring the Beloved of Chemosh template.

Special Qualities: A Beloved of Chemosh retains all the special qualities of the base creature and gains those described below.

Fast Healing (Ex): A Beloved of Chemosh heals 5 points of damage each round, even when it has been reduced to 0 or fewer hit points and will eventually recover even from complete physical destruction. If a limb or body part is severed, it can either re-grow the member in one day, or re-attach it instantly by holding it to the stump. Severed members that are not re-attached will wither into dust after 10 minutes.

Immunity to Magic (Ex): A Beloved of Chemosh is immune to any spell or spell-like ability that allows spell resistance. Those who cast spells against one often report sensing a magical back-lash (though it causes no damage to the caster).

Turn Immunity (Ex): A Beloved of Chemosh cannot be turned. He can be banished with *holy word*, however, just as if he were an evil outsider. (If banished, he is sent to the Abyss.)

Abilities: Increase from the base creature as follows: Str +4, Cha +4. As an undead creature, a Beloved of Chemosh has no Constitution score.

Environment: Any, usually same as base creature.

Organization: Solitary, pair, gang (3–5)

Challenge Rating: Same as the base creature +3.

Alignment: Always evil (any).

Advancement: By character class.

Level Adjustment: Same as the base creature +6.

Beloved Weaknesses

Beloved of Chemosh, for all of their invulnerabilities, are not immortal. Unfortunately, the weakness that the Lord of Bones chose for his new disciples is so terrible that most will be unwilling to exploit it.

Detection: Beloved cannot be detected by normal means. However, their true nature is immediately revealed to clerics or mystics with the Channeling, Necromancy, or Undeath domains and by any character with the Death Sight spell-like ability. Particularly sensitive animals often act skittish or hostile in the presence of a Beloved of Chemosh. A mundane method of revealing a Beloved of Chemosh is to examine the skin directly above his heart, which will reveal a mark in the shape of a woman's lips (the mark of *Mina's Kiss*).

Hand of a Child: A Beloved of Chemosh suffers terrible, permanent damage when attacked by an innocent child. An innocent child must be younger than Adulthood (as defined in the *Player's Handbook*, pg. 109) and one who has never caused the death of any creature with an intelligence score. Any unarmed or armed attack by an innocent child against a Beloved of Chemosh gains the Disruption quality (equivalent to a magical weapon, see the *Dungeon Master's Guide*, pg. 224), requiring the Beloved to succeed on a DC 14 Will save or be destroyed. In addition, the attack causes 1d6 points of bonus damage that cannot be healed through the Beloved's fast healing special quality. An innocent child who witnesses the destruction of a Beloved of Chemosh in this way suffers 1d4 points of temporary Wisdom and Charisma damage and forever loses the ability to harm a Beloved (because they are no longer innocent). All Beloved of Chemosh are aware of their weakness to children and usually avoid direct contact with youngsters.

Beloved of Chemosh Characters

Beloved of Chemosh are always evil and have Chemosh as their patron deity, which causes certain classes to lose some class abilities. In addition, certain classes take additional penalties.

Clerics: Beloved of Chemosh clerics lose their ability to turn undead but gain the ability to rebuke undead.

Sorcerers, Wizards, and Wizards of High Sorcery: Beloved of Chemosh sorcerers and wizards retain their class abilities, but the link between master and familiar is broken, and the familiar shuns its former companion. The character cannot summon another familiar.

THE NEW ADVENTURES

A Practical Guide to Dragons
By Sindri Suncatcher

Sindri Suncatcher—wizard's apprentice—opens up
his personal notebooks to share his knowledge of these
awe-inspiring creatures, from the life cycle of a kind copper
dragon to the best way to counteract a red dragon's fiery
breath. This lavishly illustrated guide showcases the wide
array of fantastic dragons encountered on the world of Krynn.

The perfect companion to the Dragonlance: The New
Adventures series, for both loyal fans and new readers alike.

Sindri Suncatcher is a three-and-a-half foot tall kender,
who enjoys storytelling, collecting magical tokens, and
fighting dragons. He lives in Solamnia and is currently
studying magic under the auspices of the black-robed
wizard Maddoc. You can catch Sindri in the midst of
his latest adventure in *The Wayward Wizard*.

For more information visit **www.mirrorstonebooks.com**

For ages ten and up.

A NEW TRILOGY FROM MARGARET WEIS & TRACY HICKMAN

THE LOST CHRONICLES
Dragons of the Dwarven Depths
Volume One

Tanis, Tasslehoff, Riverwind, and Raistlin
are trapped as refugees in Thorbardin, as the
draconian army closes in on the dwarven
kingdom. To save his homeland, Flint begins a
search for the Hammer of Kharas.

Available July 2006

For more information visit **www.wizards.com**

ELVEN EXILES TRILOGY
PAUL B. THOMPSON AND TONYA C. COOK

The elven people, driven from their age old enclaves in
the green woods, have crossed the Plains of Dust and harsh
mountains into the distant land of Khur. The elves coexist
uneasily with surrounding tribes under the walls of
Khuri-Khan.

Shadowy forces inside Khur and out plot to destroy the elves.
Some are ancient and familiar, others are new and unknown.

And so the battle lines are drawn, and the great game begins.
Survival or death, glory or oblivion — these are the stakes.
Gilthas and Kerianseray bet all on a forgotten map,
faithful friends, and their unshakable faith on the
greatness of the elven race.

SANCTUARY
Volume One

ALLIANCES
Volume Two
August 2006

Volume Three
June 2007

For more information visit **www.wizards.com**